For
my new husband
Ger
— all my prayers are for good health for both
of us to enjoy a long and happy marriage.

Anita Notaro is a TV producer, journalist and director, and has worked for RTE, Ireland's national broadcasting organization. She has also directed the Eurovision Song Contest and the Irish General Election, as well as programmes for the BBC and Channel 4.

THE WWW CLUB

Luckily, you're not literally what you eat, because otherwise Pam would be a hamburger, Ellie a battered sausage, Maggie a jam-filled doughnut and Toni a healthy-sounding, though compact, sushi roll. Together they form The WWW Club. Every woman needs a WWW Club in her life. It's the ideal way to moan about men, sex and cellulite, absorb the nasty details of detoxing — or learn that your latest (killer) accessory has, in fact, just gone out of fashion. All this while scoffing chicken korma and drinking beer without the slightest trace of guilt, fully intending to *definitely* start again tomorrow.

ANITA NOTARO

THE WWW CLUB

Complete and Unabridged

CHARNWOOD
Leicester

First published in Great Britain in 2005 by
Bantam Press, a division of
Transworld Publishers
London

First Charnwood Edition
published 2006
by arrangement with
Transworld Publishers, a division of
The Random House Group Limited
London

British Library CIP Data

Notaro, Anita
  The WWW Club.—Large print ed.—
Charnwood library series
1. Reducing diets—Fiction
2. Female friendship—Fiction
3. Large type books
I. Title
823.9'2 [F]

ISBN 1–84617–427–9

Published by
F. A. Thorpe (Publishing)
Anstey, Leicestershire

Set by Words & Graphics Ltd.
Anstey, Leicestershire
Printed and bound in Great Britain by
T. J. International Ltd., Padstow, Cornwall

This book is printed on acid-free paper

Acknowledgements

Whilst writing this book in 2004, I had some of the happiest and saddest days of my life. In September I smiled all day when Gerry and I finally married, surrounded by family and friends, in glorious Co. Wicklow. The warmth of those memories helped me cope when, five weeks later, my lovely Mam, Teresa, died suddenly. Her loss is immense and my sisters Madeleine, Lorraine and Jean kept me going, as did their families.

I've gained a new family too — my father-in-law, the incomparable Arthur McGuinness — and Donal, Clare, Lara and Gavin.

In October, super-agent Marianne Gunn O'Connor rang to tell me she'd sold the rights to *The WWW Club* to HarperCollins, New York. I was speechless with excitement. So, hello to Claire Wachtel, Kevin Callahan, Sean Griffin and everyone in William Morrow. I'm looking forward to working with you.

Thanks also to Pat Lynch, who is unfailingly cheerful when I ring the office for a moan and also Vicky Satlow, who does Trojan work on my behalf in Europe. No matter what the days bring, I rely heavily on my friends, especially Dearbhla, Ursula, Caroline and Dee. Thanks Frank for years of friendship and the loan of your gorgeous house in Nerja when I need peace and quiet to write. And Dave, who's always around.

I found it impossible to write in December when, four days before Christmas, my friends Liam and Britt lost their gorgeous daughters Jenny and Katherine in a tragic accident. Their strength and courage was extraordinary and that transferred to their friends, me included.

When I needed inspiration for this book it was everywhere. The vivacious Nora McDonell made me decide that Nora was a happy name for a character I grew to love, and Carl Griffith's fascination with painting dinosaurs helped me understand Sam and Jessie, who also feature here. Danielle Gaskin gave me lots of feedback through her Dad Liam, who definitely provided the inspiration for Bill.

I owe a lot to Francesca Liversidge, my editor in Bantam, who does nothing but encourage me. Also thanks to everyone at Transworld — Laura Sherlock, Nicky Jeanes, Angela Duke, and all in sales and marketing, especially Garry Prior, Jonathan King and the rest of the team. Gill and Simon Hess and the gang do a great job this end, and Declan Heeney is still smiling, despite dealing with me for three years now!

I love having Patricia Scanlan in my life and Claudia Carroll feeds me regularly and makes me laugh with her stories.

Finally, Gerry. I'm so glad we found each other.

1

Another day, another diet. It was a sour waking thought on an otherwise marshmallowy-sweet morning. Diets meant only one thing to Eleanora Simpson: pain. And God knows she'd inflicted enough torture on herself in the past ten years to last her a lifetime. She yanked the duvet up around her neck and tried not to think about her latest fad. The phone rang.

'Hello?' None of her friends would dream of ringing her this early on a Saturday. She was the only early-riser she knew. As usual she predicted an emergency.

'Ellie, are you still in bed? You sound sleepy.'

'Oh, hi, Orla.' No need to panic, if there had been any trouble Orla wouldn't have bothered with pleasantries. 'Yep, imagine, still dossing at nine . . . ' she leant over to check . . . 'thirty-seven on a Saturday. Outrageous, isn't it?'

Her older sister's lip curled and her eyes narrowed. Ellie didn't have a video phone, it was just that she'd seen that expression a million times, mostly directed at her. At this stage she could sense it even if she was in another country.

'Well, you should be up. I've just been for a walk out by Sandycove. Dublin looks beautiful, the sea is like glass and there's no pollution evident.' Orla fancied herself as a bit of a poet so she rarely spoke in plain English. 'Maybe you should try some exercise instead of all those faddy diets you're always on.'

'Actually, I was just thinking of a diet.'

'Which one?' In spite of herself Orla was interested.

'Atkins.'

'I've heard it's amazing.'

'Not for me. The first two weeks are cruel. Everything I like is a no-no. Besides, if I never see another greasy fried egg it'll be too soon.'

'Well then, what about the cabbage-soup diet? It delivered amazing results for Joanna next door.'

'Have you actually tried slurping gallons of dirty water several times a day?' She didn't wait for an answer. 'Well, it's disgusting. I tried it six months ago and lost nothing at all the first week. But the curtains in my kitchen still reek of boiled greens. No, I'll pass on a repeat, thank you. Anyway,' she sat up in bed, fully awake, 'I've just heard of an amazing new one called the avocado and Rice Krispies gut-cleansing regime. I'm going to investigate that later today.'

'Well, getting out of bed would be a start.' Orla was back to her normal self. 'I'm just ringing to ask you to please call Mum. She hasn't heard from you in ages and I'm fed up listening to her moaning.'

'Right, will do.'

'I can't do everything, you know.'

'Don't worry, I'll call her this morning.'

'Please do.' Orla's tone was frostier than Mr Whippy's van.

'Bye then.'

'Bye bye. And email me a copy of that avocado thing.'

'Will do. Bye, Orla.' Ellie hid under the duvet then peeped out a minute or two later, just to be sure the coast was clear. When Orla lectured — and she did it all the time — it always felt as though she was right there in the room with you and that feeling had persisted even when she'd gone to Australia for a year. Still, Ellie knew she'd got off lightly this time.

She leapt out of bed, shouting her newest affirmation, as instructed by the latest GMTV guru. 'I feel fantastic and it's . . . fuck, fuck, fuck,' she yelled as she stubbed her toe on the horrible brass bed that her sister had 'given' her when she wanted rid of it. The bed was way too big and didn't suit the room but Ellie never had the courage to refuse Orla. 'I feel fantastic and it's . . . ouch.' She rubbed between her toes. 'It's going to be a good day.' She limped towards the kitchen.

It *was* going to be a good day, she could feel it, even if the feeling was unset-jelly wobbly. Unfortunately for Ellie, there were four types of day — good, shaky, bad and positively nightmare.

Good days always started with hot water and lemon followed by porridge with skimmed milk and a thin slice of brown bread with a scraping of low-fat spread. Recently, those days were rarer than a granny at a Westlife concert. On shaky days the porridge was usually left to congeal after a couple of mouthfuls. Is there anything more unpleasant than the sight of a heap of

3

coagulating, rubbery oats throbbing under its slimy skin? Ellie wondered. It's right up there with walking on runny dog pooh in your flimsiest new sandals, or having to clean out the salad drawer in your fridge after discovering all your healthy options wearing fur coats. Ugh! Shaky days also meant fibre intake was greatly reduced as she abandoned the brown cardboard and tucked into the real thing. Proper toast had to be white and thick, golden in the centre and slightly burnt at the edges. And it absolutely had to be smothered in real butter, preferably cold and hard so the contrast between the soft, warm bread and the smooth, salty butter was maximized.

In a funny way she liked shaky days, even though they invariably meant that she lived on a see-saw. Much better than bad days, or nightmare ones, like yesterday. But she wasn't going there, so she dressed quickly in comfies, and splashed water on her pale face. At least her brown eyes were clear, courtesy of a good night's sleep. She scrunched her dark hair back and headed out to get her fix.

★   ★   ★

'Mornin', Ellie, great day.' Not even Ida Delahunt, the local tragedy queen, was going to put her off today.

'Hi, Ida. Yes it is gorgeous.' Ellie made a run for it.

'Did you hear on the radio about that poor — '

'And best of all it's Saturday, no kids for two whole days.' Ellie kept moving. She'd learnt the only way to avoid hearing bad news was to totally ignore anything Ida started to say.

'Ah now, go on, you love that job of yours. Besides, I saw you the other day minding that little foreign child again. What is he, Russian or something queer like that?' The older woman was momentarily distracted. 'You dote on children.'

'Only when I can hand them back at the end of each day.' Ellie laughed and made her escape, continuing the short trip to the twenty-four-hour shop in her local filling station. She loved working with children but couldn't stand it when parents talked non-stop about theirs as so many did to her, so she avoided a couple of yummy mummies in the store, just to be on the safe side.

With the newspaper safely tucked under her arm she returned home, ate a quick bowl of porridge simply to re-fuel, then made fresh coffee and settled down in her tiny sun-room to savour what her favourite columnist had to say.

Just as she was beginning to think about food again the phone rang.

'Hi, Ellie, it's only me.'

'Hi, Maggie.'

'Well, what did you think?'

'Not as good as usual. I was just thinking that he hasn't written directly about his wife in ages. He also seems a bit more cruel about women in general.'

'I know what you mean, although he's always had a mean streak.' Maggie thought for a second. 'But he's cruel in a gay guy kind of way and they're always horrible but spot on and anyway, that's why we love him so much. And the bit about the nose job was so true. A girl in my office — '

'Which bit was that?' Ellie interrupted. 'My mobile rang twice while I was trying to read it.'

'Hang on, I have it here.' Maggie skimmed through the paragraphs.

'At the school gate the other morning, it struck me that there is just as much competition between mothers as there is in any male-dominated workplace. First up, it seems as if you have to look like a model to drop your kids off, even if you don't get out of the car: You've probably noticed the blond ponytails and baseball-cap-clad thirty-somethings driving their top-of-the-range four-wheel drives around Dublin, but take a good look at the gates of a school next time you're passing and you'll see they've taken the competition to a whole new level — designer jeans, belly tops from BT2 and Orla Kiely handbags are de rigueur. A snow-white dog bounding around in the boot helps too — pure bred, of course.

''I'm so wrecked,' I heard Joanne tell Lucy and Sophie yesterday (not their real names). 'I was at the gym at six, then made cookies for Grace's bring-and-buy day, and I just have to take Rover for a walk before I meet the girls for coffee in the Four Seasons. Tom, of course, flew to New York

this morning so he was no help. And the vacuum is on the blink and my Filipino girl is acting up again. I'm exhausted. Oops, that's my phone, oh no, it's one of the women from the fund-raising committee . . . gotta go, ciao.''

'That sounds just like you.' Ellie laughed.
'No, it's Toni, listen, here comes the nose bit.'

''My God, she looks fantastic, I'm so jealous. And here's me in my rags.' Lucy yanked at her Mariad Whisker pinafore.

'I know,' Sophie replied. 'Still, her husband's fab, he paid for a nose job for her for Christmas and left her a patio heater as a surprise under the tree, boxed up, of course. Me, all I got was a very small package from Cartier and a voucher for that place in Blackrock where I go to get my collagen injections.''

Maggie giggled. 'God, I wonder if that'll be us any day soon?'
'Absolutely. Well, Toni anyway. Is she still meeting us for brunch?'
'Yep, The Unicorn at one. And Toni is not seriously thinking of having anything done to her nose, although she did mention botox twice the other night when we were in Arnotts.' Maggie nibbled at a stale crisp. 'I'm starving.'
'You definitely have a tape worm.' Ellie stretched lazily. 'Anyway, I'd better jump in the shower. See you later.'
'Bye bye.' She was gone.

7

As she lathered herself Ellie thought about her good pal Margaret Owens, or Maggie as they'd christened her years earlier. Their older sisters had been pen pals but because of the age gap and distance between their homes they hadn't really spoken much until they'd met at a party eleven years ago, despite Ellie's family having visited Maggie's gang in the West a couple of times. On that particular night Ellie had been abandoned by her boyfriend and Maggie had simply agreed to go along as a spare because of the free drink she knew would be on offer. After a shy start they'd sat in a corner and drank everything they could lay their hands on, comparing notes on how often they'd tricked their older sisters. Maggie's story about decanting her sister's mega-expensive night cream into another jar then refilling it with Nivea, a dollop of fresh whipped cream and some of her mother's perfume was the best ever.

'But didn't the whipped cream go sour?' Ellie wanted to know as they giggled together in a corner, men forgotten.

'I kept adding another few drops of perfume every couple of days,' Maggie said with a grin. 'She just kept lashing it on her face. Mind you, she did have a rash a few weeks later.'

'I bet your skin was glowing, though?' Ellie asked and they were off again. They'd become firm friends.

At almost thirty Maggie was nearly six years younger than Ellie and worked as a legal secretary in a big Dublin law firm, the kind that have whole walls of glass as part of their offices and receptionists that could wither an entire flower arrangement with one glance. Everyone loved Maggie. Part of her success was that she looked as if you could trust her — and you could. She was a sort of girl-next-door meets Irish colleen crossed with a Riverdance high kicker, with freckles and tumbling auburn curls and green eyes and a cute nose. Quite a combination, or so men seemed to think. Maggie was never short of a date, although they didn't always stick around for long. Men seemed to be slightly in awe of her. One boyfriend had told her on his way out the door that she was just too nice. Ellie made her go to assertiveness classes after that and it had helped — slightly. Maggie was the Audrey Hepburn of the gang, not in looks but because of her kind nature. She wouldn't hurt a fly.

* * *

When Ellie arrived at lunch, the third member of the group was already there and, as usual, she was giving her all to the best-looking man in the room, in this case the only man in the place, a swarthy Spanish waiter who called himself Enrique — not the name chosen by his mother, Ellie suspected. She wanted to warn him he had no chance. What Pamela Fortune wanted she usually got, which was surprising given that she wasn't model-girl material. And at forty she was no spring chicken.

'She sort of looks like a hooker,' Maggie had remarked when they'd first met Pamela at a yoga class nine years ago and Ellie knew immediately what she meant. Pam was voluptuous, size sixteen to be exact. Her clothes were 'out there' and her boobs were only marginally trailing behind. She was a separated mother of two boys and worked on the customer service desk at one of the larger Tesco stores. If Ellie had to sum her up in one word it would be 'bold'. The word shy didn't enter her vocabulary. You either loved her or hated her. Maggie and Ellie adored her, had done since that first ridiculous attempt at the sun salute. She was off men at the moment, had been for ages actually. When her husband left he'd taken all her self-confidence as well as her Bang & Olufsen stereo with him. Since then she'd become even more brash, swore like a fishwife and was still soft as putty inside.

'Hi there, you're late.'

'Sorry.' Ellie flopped down, hot and bothered. She found it hard to get her act together most of the time. 'I came with Maggie and bad and all as I am — '

'Say no more. Where is she?' Pam grinned.

'She's just parking the car.'

'Here's Toni.' Pam waved furiously. 'Great, now we can order wine and I can demolish the bread.'

'Hi, guys.' Antonia Francescone was the most exotic of the four. Born in India where her father still lived, she was a cross between Iman Bowie and Samantha Mumba. Her mother was Italian, which explained where Toni got her style. She used her mother's name. She was beginning to panic because she'd just turned thirty-four and hadn't had a snog for six months, which she put down to the fact that she had the most unglamorous job in the world. She complained about her job as a nurse in a retirement home constantly: 'The youngest man I meet every day is more likely to ask me for a bedpan than for a date.' Toni had been a friend of Pamela's ex-husband and when he'd brought her home to dinner one night Pam decided she'd better become her best mate. Toni was way too attractive for her liking. Surprisingly, they hit it off immediately and even though Pam eventually lost the husband she definitely didn't lose her new good pal. Toni was great in a crisis and had proved herself a loyal friend to Pam. She was an only child and her parents had spoilt her rotten, so that now she sometimes confused generosity with real caring. The others were mad about her, and her slightly bossy manner meant they did lots of things they probably wouldn't have done otherwise, although they teased her about it endlessly.

'Hi, Ellie. Hi, Pammy.'

'Hi, Toni.'

'And hi, Maggie.' Toni smiled as Maggie arrived.

It was their typical little-girl greeting, started when they'd all shortened each other's names years ago to make themselves feel younger.

'And we're off.' Pam was already ordering bottles of the house red and white and plastering some walnut-and-tomato bread with a garlic-and-olive paste.

Lunch was mayhem as always. When they'd no important news to impart about men, talk invariably turned towards dieting.

'How's it going at WeightWatchers?' Toni asked Pam.

'Don't ask. What are you up to?'

'That new low GI thing.' Toni wrinkled her nose.

'Tried it, couldn't figure out what the hell I was actually allowed to eat,' Ellie said with her mouth full. 'The first sentence I read said that scientists created a scale on which to measure the speed at which carbohydrates affect blood glucose. I was so exhausted I had an éclair.' She sighed. 'I've also given up on Atkins.'

'I've just started food combining.' Maggie seemed bright and breezy.

'Tried that too. I couldn't stomach Chicken Korma with salad.' Toni grimaced.

'I've just finished the 'lose ten pounds in three days' idea. I feel sick just thinking about it.' Pam made a face.

'That bad?'

'Bananas on Wednesday, eggs on Thursday and grapefruit yesterday.'

'How much did you lose?' Maggie wanted to know.

'Half a pound.'

'You couldn't. A girl in our office lost nine pounds.'

'I know. I'm hoping it's my period and that it'll all have gone by next week.'

'Even if it has, you've now eaten practically a whole loaf and about a stone of olives.' Ellie laughed. 'Oops, make room, here come the mainers.'

'Look, I'm having skimmed milk in my coffee later, instead of a latte.' Pam was trying to sound keen. 'And a girl has to have a little treat every now and then.'

'Why does slimline milk have to look like dirty bath water, anyway? Very off-putting.'

On and on they went, dissecting everything from quick fat burning to inner hunger signals, until they all agreed they were totally confused and fed up.

'You know what?' Ellie said between mouthfuls of pasta. 'I think we should forget all this for the weekend, then start again with a completely new approach.'

'What kind of approach?' Pam was shovelling food in at the mere mention of the word 'start'.

'I don't know, but between us we've tried everything and no one's found the solution.' Ellie always had been the practical one, great at organizing. A grown-up Girl Guide but hopeless when it came to herself.

'That's because there is no pain-free way to do it. It's all hard slog and sooooooo boring. I've given up. I think for the first time in my life I'm happy being fat.' Pam was smiling.

'You're not fat.'

'Don't lie.'

'Listen, you two, quit arguing.' Toni wanted to know more.

'I propose we pool our knowledge and meet

once a week ourselves. We won't have to pay any money yet we'll still have the support, and come up with a plan that suits us.' Ellie was on a roll.

'Just how is that different to WeightWatchers or Unislim, then, Einstein?'

'No money to spend, as I said. Let's see, no points to convert, diet meals banned — how's that for a start?' Ellie hadn't the faintest idea, really. 'And maybe only weigh ourselves occasionally.'

'I'm in.' Maggie laughed.

'I'm not.' Pam knew she hadn't a hope.

'You're all in and that's the end of it,' Ellie decided. 'So, who's for dessert?' she asked as Enrique cleared their plates.

'I'll have tiramisu.'

'Chocolate squidgy cake with caramel cream.'

'Whiskey and orange sabayon.'

'And I'll have the fruit . . . ' They all looked aghast. ' . . . crumble. Gotcha.' Ellie grinned. 'And cheese as well — runny brie and smelly blue. Now, a toast please.'

'To what?'

'The WWW Club.' Ellie was definitely on something.

'What's that?'

'I dunno, I just came up with it cause I'm sick of everyone banging on about www this and www that. Yesterday on the LUAS two old women were trying to decide what to cook for dinner. 'All we have are eggs, onions, tomatoes and bacon,' one said with a gummy smile. 'I know, let's log on to www. some bloody thing and I bet they'll have loads of recipes that we

14

haven't tried,' said the little grey permed one. My mouth was still open five minutes later. They could barely walk and yet they were surfing. I can't even send an email.'

'That's not cool any more,' Pam tut-tutted.

'I know. Never mind, I'll enrol in a night class just as soon as *Shameless* ends on Channel 4 and I finish the tin of Cadbury's Roses.' Ellie yawned. 'I like the LUAS by the way. Much better than the DART. You really feel like you're beating the traffic.'

'I know, www could stand for 'Wish I Wasn't Wasted'.' Maggie wasn't listening to Ellie rabbiting on. 'Remember our last liquid lunch?'

'Or, how about 'Women Watching Weight'? Toni was getting into it.

'Not bad, we can keep adding Ws as we see fit. How about women watching weight watching wine . . .'

' . . . watching wasabi . . .'

' . . . watching wontons . . .'

'Walnuts.'

'Wyvita, if you're Jonathan Ross.'

'Even if it fitted, do we look like the type who'd be watching cardboard crispbreads?'

'Wonderbras . . .'

'You can't eat a wonderbra.'

'No, but it can help hold in all those wontons.'

'Cheers.' Four glasses almost shattered in their enthusiasm, always easy after plenty of pasta and wine.

'So, what did we all think about CJH this week then?' Pam asked. CJH was the code name for their favourite newspaper columnist, the one

Ellie and Maggie had been discussing earlier. They had code names for everything, it made them feel like a secret club. CJH was easy to remember because they were the initials of a former prime minister who allegedly had an affair with a journalist — and they all fancied having an affair with this particular journalist, even though he was married to an absolute bitch, they'd long since decided. The initials also made up the names of three actors they reckoned he resembled. They'd never seen him, mind you, not even one of those black-and-white photos taken in Junior Infants, the kind favoured by most hacks to show them in the best possible light. The C came from Colin Firth, cause he sometimes appeared dark and brooding and his writing could suddenly switch and be quite black. The J stood for Jude Law. They all just somehow knew he'd be cool in a couldn't care less/forgot to wash my hair/don't know what a skin peel is sort of way. And the H came from Hugh Grant (after some initial protest by Pam, who said he made her want to throw up). But the others persuaded her he would definitely have that 'self-deprecating, ordinary guy who never gets it quite right and is endearing' quality, exactly like Grant was in *Notting Hill* — number 9 on their list of chick flicks to watch with a bottle of wine and a curry when feeling depressed.

Anyway, they reckoned CJH really understood women, and especially their obsession with weight, and his observations were sometimes close to the bone, often really sharp and nearly always hilarious. However, except for the nose job, they all agreed that this week's was not his best work. Roll on next Saturday.

2

The day was not going well for Jack Bryant. He flung down the newspaper and threw out his coffee. He stared at the neglected garden where the local bicycle of a cat, Marcie, was peeing on some sort of exotic plant. He rubbed the back of his neck. The last few days, in particular, had been a struggle. He knew he had to get his life into some sort of order. Mind you, he'd been saying that to himself for well over a year.

He walked back into his study and sat down to work on his latest book. He was getting nowhere fast there too and was avoiding his editor's calls. As he began to tidy up the previous page he heard a high-pitched scream and looked up to see his two daughters running in through the front gate, closely followed by his sister Kate. They'd been swimming, but it seemed that and the exercise hadn't diminished their energy levels one bit. He wished they'd transfer a bit of it his way.

He opened the front door just as his sister had put her key in and they tumbled inside, smelling of soap and chlorine and McDonald's.

'Hi, Dad, we had a great time. I swam twenty times up and down.' Samantha looked all shiny and happy. She was nearly seven going on seventy.

'Are you exaggerating just a teensy, weensy bit,

by any chance?' He bent down and tickled his eldest daughter.

'Hi, Georgia,' he said to Kate's youngest daughter who was behind him.

'Hi, Jack.'

'Did you swim, or were you just helping out with the monsters?'

'No, I swam for ages.' She was a bright twelve year old with twinkling eyes and a cheeky grin.

'I had my arms on.' Someone was determined not to be left out, as usual.

'Did you, Jess? Does that mean that you can take your arms off sometimes?'

'No, silly. I mean my plastic ones.'

'I think you mean arm bands.'

'The pink ones.'

'Them's the very ones. Right, into the kitchen for a glass of milk to build up your bones.'

'We had Coke.'

'You weren't supposed to tell, stupid.' Samantha ran off, followed by Jessica who wanted to do everything the same as her big sister. Georgia followed.

'Sorry.' Kate grimaced at him. 'All the kids were having it and I couldn't leave them out.'

'You know I don't mind. Never did me any harm.'

'I guess it's a hangover from Lorna. She hated them having it.'

'She didn't really, you know — wasn't interested enough. It was the last nanny, what was her name?'

'Victoria.'

'That's the one. She made the rules. Lorna

19

just repeated a few of them ad nauseam because it made her sound like a caring mother.' He moved towards the kitchen and she followed. 'Which, as we all know, is a load of bollocks.'

'Dad, you're not allowed say that word. It's a sin.'

'You weren't supposed to be listening.'

'You have to put ten cents in the Trocaire box.'

'Will do.'

'Put a euro in. You never pay up.'

He grinned at his older sister. 'See what I'm living with? Two conniving, materialistic women.'

'Can we watch *Shrek*?'

'Again?'

They both nodded in unison.

'That is a nice boulder.' He did his Eddie Murphy impression and bent down and grabbed Jess. They loved it when he did the voices and God knows he'd seen that movie so many times he could practically recite it as poetry.

'That's the old one. We're watching *Shrek 2*.'

'Me Darla.' Jess always wanted to be someone else. She lived in a four-year-old fairytale.

'That's not *Shrek*, that's *Nemo*, stupid.' Sam poked the younger girl in the ribs.

'I'm not stupid.' Jess kicked her sister and they were off.

'Any fighting and you won't get to see anything, OK?' Jack put the kettle on as Kate sat at the table watching him.

'Bad day?'

'Bad week.'

'Want to come round for a bite this evening?'

'Any spare friends you could fix me up with?'

20

He was teasing her because she was always hinting.

'Would you want one?' She brightened immediately.

'No.' He was sorry he'd made the joke. 'I think I'll pass on supper, Kate. Not much company, I'm afraid.'

'You don't have to put on an act with us, you know that. Come round and I'll make lasagne and open a bottle of Barolo. I'll even organize Sarah to babysit.' Sarah was her sixteen-year-old money pit.

He gave in because he realized he could do with the company. 'OK, thanks, that'd be great. Sorry for being a bore.'

'It's allowed.' She gave him a hug. 'Sure you're OK?'

He nodded, knowing he was lucky to have her around.

'See you about eight so. Expect Sarah just before. And don't fall for her 'my folks hate me' line. She's a human piggy bank. Five euros an hour and no more.' She blew him a kiss, called her daughter and was gone.

The girls spent the afternoon playing and watching TV and he did manage to get a bit of work done with only a few minor bust-ups to adjudicate over. They were good kids really. He just wished he could see his cup as half full but lately his situation had really been getting him down. He was even beginning to resent the girls sometimes and then guilt almost finished him off.

He left them eating tea — fish fingers and

frozen chips — again. After a quick shower he pulled on faded jeans and the same black, roll-neck sweater. All of his clean shirts needed to be ironed and it took him so long to do each one that he couldn't be arsed tonight. He didn't even bother to comb his hair, simply towelled it dry and ran his fingers through it, annoyed with himself for thinking about Lorna so much today. He'd been feeling way too sorry for himself this week, whereas the fact was that he was actually much better off mentally since she'd left, even if everything else was a mess. Things hadn't been great for a long time, since she'd first become pregnant, really. The second time she was caught she became vicious and he still remembered the look on her face when she'd lashed out and called him a 'fucking nymphomaniac'.

'I think that's a term for a woman.' He hadn't liked her tone of voice much either.

'Yeah, well, you're a bit of a girl's blouse, always were.'

He knew deep down it was over between them, even then, but admitting it was something else. They patched things up because they had to. There was a one-and-a-half-year-old baby and another on the way. He knew he'd been somewhat to blame, he was struggling with his career and he left too much to her and she deeply resented the lack of freedom that having children brought, even though he knew she did care about them.

Things were never really right again and that was even before Jessie was born and way before he discovered she was having an affair with the editor of one of the tabloid newspapers. When he confronted her he was scared by his lack of any feeling whatsoever towards her. Next day when he came in from the office she'd gone. Simply asked Kate to keep an eye on the kids, packed her things (and a few of his), left her keys and a note saying she didn't want anything else and disappeared. It was her PS that nearly finished him off. It simply said, 'Suggest you seek custody of the kids, I'm not the maternal type.' Up until that moment he'd assumed she'd taken them with her. Despite all that had happened, he was gutted.

Being a single parent of two small girls was a nightmare. He'd never really had that much to do with them before Lorna left, they'd always had nannies — three at one stage. One Monday to Friday from nine to five, another for the evenings and a retired nurse all weekend. He couldn't ever remember changing a nappy or feeding the girls. Now he wiped dirty bottoms and mopped up puke and felt he'd completely lost his identity. He worked too much from home, hadn't kissed or touched a woman he wasn't related to in yonks and never went out, except to Burger King or the Saturday matinees.

When Samantha had started school he hoped it would get easier but Jessie was still a baby really and his days managed to be both chaotic and robotic. It was beginning to affect his work now as well. Because he was feeling tired and pissed off more often, wasn't eating properly and probably drinking too much, his output had diminished dramatically and his editor was making more noises lately about taking a trip to Ireland, not a good sign. He decided that some sort of plan was called for, before he was carried off in a white van.

3

'Come on, out with it. You know it's good to talk.' In this sort of mood Kate made Oprah seem shy.

'Only women think that. Men think the person just needs a kick in the arse, which is probably true in my case.'

'You need a ride.' Good old Bill, Kate's long-suffering barrister husband, usually managed to cut to the chase.

'That too, but it's not exactly high on the agenda at the moment.'

'Go on, I'd say your hand's worn out.'

'Bill, that's appalling. Stop it.' Jack could never figure out why his sister still admonished her husband practically every day. It didn't make a scrap of difference, he'd built his reputation on being outrageous.

Now they grinned at each other like naughty schoolboys.

'Ignore him, Jack. He's a thug. Now, tell us what's getting on top of you.' She had on her best school-mistress voice.

'He needs a good spanking, Miss.' Bill recognized the tone and winked at his brother-in-law.

'I'm warning you, Bill Huston . . . '

'I dunno, it just all seems to be one long round of cooking and fetching and homework and ballet and trying to work at night and sleeping with two kids on top of me and . . . God, I sound like a nagging wife.'

'No you don't.'

'Yes you do, Mrs Doubtfire.' Bill was off again.

'I never thought I'd hear myself say this but the house is a tip.'

'What about Mrs O'Sullivan?'

'She's great, I'd be lost without her, but she can only work mornings and by the time she's tidied up after the girls, loaded the dishwasher and put on a wash, she's ready for a cup of tea and a smoke. The other day I found her halfway up the stairs gasping for breath. All I need now is for her to pop her clogs with a toilet brush in her hand.'

'Would you consider another nanny?'

'I don't think I could bear it.'

'Why not? It could be the answer to all your problems.'

'They're all foreigners — and I'm not racist.' He held his hand up because he could see his sister getting ready to deliver a lecture. 'It's the language thing, it's such a bleedin' effort. And they want to talk day and night, to improve their English. And then they sit around all evening watching TV and you have to join them and be polite and watch the soaps. Ugh, I'd rather get married.' He grinned, all three of them knew that he'd insert a burning needle in his eye first.

'Just think of all those buxom Swedes or tight-assed frauleins.' Bill was trying to cheer him up.

'He's been watching too many old Britney Spears videos on MTV.' Kate slapped her husband's face lightly. 'There are Irish nannies, you know, and they don't normally live in, or if they do they go home at weekends.'

'I suppose.' They could see he wasn't convinced. 'I'll think about it, I promise. Now, let's change the subject. Even I'm bored with me.'

They were easy company and he left much later full of wine and stodge but feeling a bit better. Seeing them always restored his faith in relationships. They were complete opposites: Kate was calm and efficient and warm and nosy, Bill a big bluffer who liked to shock, especially some of his stuffy colleagues in the Law Library. He was a gruff man whose unruly exterior hid one of the sharpest brains in the country. Jack was enormously fond of him. He made up his mind to buy them both dinner to say thanks, but knew he'd probably forget until the next time they saved his bacon.

* * *

Sundays were the only days Jack got to spend time mucking about. He usually woke early — it was hard to sleep in with a fist poking you in the ribs on one side and a four year old who managed to spread herself right across a super-king bed on the other. At least the papers were always on his doorstep, courtesy of Tommy, the only newsagent in Ireland still to deliver at six every morning no matter what life threw at him and never, ever, get it wrong. What could be worse than finding the *Observer* on your mat on a rainy Sunday morning if you only ever read the *Star*, or *Ireland's Own* if you were a *VIP* girl? If Tommy delivered pastries Jack would have had sex with him, but the older man would be hard pushed to tell the difference between a croissant and a shrimp, he knew. Still, papers were his main fix.

He tried to read them all, a hang-up from his days as a reporter in the RTE newsroom. Mind you, these mornings he barely skimmed them and if Sam got to any of the tabloids first they were minus most of the pictures. She claimed Holy God told her girls in bikinis were bold and it was a further sign of his depleted energy levels that he hadn't even the strength for a theological argument with a six year old. Usually they went to the park or the cinema — sometimes Eddie Rocket's, cause the girls loved the fries with cheese and the chocolate milkshakes. Occasionally they managed to get to a museum. Both girls loved to paint and to his amazement didn't burst into tears the first time he brought them, out of sheer desperation. Being in some of those other places always made him feel like a separated father, which of course he was. But he didn't get to live the Monday-to-Friday bachelor life he suspected most of the other dads enjoyed, although he cheered up when he saw his own relaxed, happy kids in sharp contrast to the many subdued youngsters and sulky teenagers he constantly encountered. Normally, they ended up round at Kate's house, which is what happened today. Sarah and Georgia entertained the girls as usual and it meant he could relax.

His sister always managed to produce a roast dinner as if by magic and it eased his guilt about proper food and, he always thought, it set the three of them up for the week of takeaways and E-numbers ahead. A bottle or two of good wine which he usually remembered to bring with him helped the adults finish off their day of leisure with a hazy glow.

'I've emailed a couple of agencies to see what kind of Irish girls they have on their books,' Kate announced casually as they all lounged about, half-watching *The Antiques Roadshow*, which his sister loved and both men loathed with a passion normally reserved for erotica.

'What? Kate, I only said I'd think about it.'

'That's as good as signing a legally binding contract as far as our Katie's concerned.' Bill opened one eye. He was dozing in the big squashy leather armchair, his favourite once he could beat Snowy or Percy to it. 'Give in and pray she lets you have someone a bit younger than your last one, what was her name again?'

'Victoria, and she was fine. She *was* young.' Kate tried to remember.

'You're right, she was, but she had a moustache and her backside had a shelf on it.'

'Oh, shut up, you two. Let's just forget it.'

'Ten cent.' Sam always seemed to be lurking somewhere.

'Sorry, darling, I didn't mean it.'

'If you say shut up then you pay up.' Her halo glowed as she held out her hand. 'A feck is fifty.'

'How much is the ball lock word?' Jess was over in doublequick time. 'That's Dad's

29

favourite when he stubs his toe on the side of the bed.' They all stared at her. 'He thinks we're asleep and sometimes he says it and shite together.' Kate looked horrified. It was practically the first full sentence the child had uttered. The two men tried to keep their faces straight.

By eight o'clock they were home and by the time he'd got them organized for bed and sorted Sam's school uniform it was nearly ten. He cracked open a beer, turned on the TV and flopped on to the couch to watch *The Week in Politics*. By ten past he was fast asleep. He woke at two thirty feeling stiff and thirsty, knocked over the almost full beer, cursed and headed for bed, by now wide awake and agitated.

4

'No, we are *not* having wine, it'll just make us all giggly.' Ellie was adamant. 'It's my house and what I say goes.' She looked around. 'OK then, maybe later. How's that?'

'Who's that card from?' Maggie peered at the postcard, nosy as usual.

'You won't believe it, it came this morning.' Ellie handed it to Maggie. 'It's from Des,' she told the other two.

'Des?' Pam's face said it all. 'Des the most boring man in the world from whom you had a very lucky escape?'

'I know . . . Ah, he was OK, really. I should just never have got engaged to him.'

'Thank God you saw sense,' Toni agreed. 'Anyway, what does he say?'

'He's travelling around Australia. Sounds way too adventurous for him.' Maggie looked up. 'He ends with 'wish you were here'.'

The others made various vomit signs and Ellie laughed. 'OK, enough time-wasting, shall we officially declare the WWW Club open for business?' Ellie raised an imaginary toast to the other three.

'Listen, we definitely need something to drink if you want to get me up on those.' Pam was gazing at the weighing scales as one might look on a week-old cottage cheese dessert. Since the idea had first been mooted, Toni had taken control and had emailed them several times over the weekend, a sure sign that it was to become her latest hobby horse.

'Water, that's it. We have to start somewhere, OK?' They all nodded miserably. 'Now, how did everyone do today?' Toni asked, in that 'have you been a good girl' tone she used with the patients. Their mumbled replies were every bit as incoherent.

'For God's sake, come on, you lot, cut me some slack here. We agreed to give this a try. Nothing else has really worked for any of us, so it's this or the gut stapled.'

'OK.'

'Right.'

'Yeah, go on.'

Toni poured four glasses of water. 'Well then, try to sound a bit more enthusiastic. Now, I've been thinking, even if you lot haven't, and I suggest we weigh-in once a week, then make a chart.'

'You mean like a wall chart?' Pam was horrified.

'No, stupid, just for ourselves, to monitor our progress.'

'Couldn't we have a little glass of wine first, just to get us in the mood?'

'No.'

'Sorry.'

'Now, who's first?'

Maggie reluctantly agreed. Even though she was petite, she decided she had ten pounds to lose to get anywhere near the weight she was at her twenty-first. 'I'm nearly thirty, if I keep on going like this I'll be a barrel,' she wailed when the others laughed at the small amount of extra weight she was carrying.

Next up Ellie. She was feeling good today. Her skin was clear and her brown hair was clean and shiny. Dressed in her favourite jeans and a soft, clingy cardigan with a cute little top underneath, she looked young and up for fun. She was of average height and didn't appear to be overweight. 'You're just well built,' her mother told her far too often. She was an M&S size fourteen, sixteen in most other places and eighteen — if she could find any — on a bad day in Zara. The problem was her waist and bottom had thickened very gradually and her face was now 'moon shaped' according to her.

She was greeted with a chorus of 'you don't have two chins' and 'honestly, you don't look like you have a pillow stuffed down the back of your jeans where your bottom is'.

'Trust me, I am miserable. None of my clothes fit me and I've no confidence. Working as a nanny means you're in a kitchen most of the day and I'm always 'testing' the kids' fish fingers and sausages and finishing off the jelly and ice-cream. I need to lose at least a stone and a half.' Everyone knew exactly how she felt.

She jotted down her own details. 'Next.' Toni looked directly at Pam who was trying to blend in with the furniture.

'OK, let's get it over with.' She moved in slow motion and didn't look down. 'Tell me, I can't bear it.'

Ellie was on jotter duty. She looked down and

did a double-take. 'But the other day you said . . . '

'I was lying.'

'OK. Well, you're twelve and a half stone.' Ellie was trying to be matter-of-fact. 'But you're taller than any of us.' She decided she didn't like this game any more.

'Statuesque.' Maggie was adamant.

'Look, stop trying to be nice, I know I'm a sow. Have been for years. But I don't overeat, really. And besides, I'm running around most of the day with the boys. I don't have time to make all this special food.'

'Let's talk about this seriously. First, weigh me.' Toni wanted to get it over with so she elbowed Pam out of the way, much to the older woman's annoyance. She'd been enjoying the attention as well as their sympathy. But Toni was nervous too, she just didn't show it as easily.

Of all of them, she looked the slimmest. She carried her weight so well. Her height helped. 'It's all here, though, look, I've no waist.' She hiked up her blouse and they all prepared to argue with her, but then they saw it was true. She'd put on a good bit around her middle, which she hid cleverly with well-cut clothes. 'Besides, if I were to breathe out . . . ' She did and looked like she was up the duff. 'And I'm wearing those awful knickers made of cement,' she complained, pulling up a stretchy bit of peachy Lycra from her waistband. It did indeed look heavy duty.

'Do we really want to go ahead with this?' Pam was still smarting.

'I'm not sure.'

'Me neither.'

'OK, let's forget it.' Toni was getting fed up with all this wishy-washyness. 'Although I don't think we can afford not to try it, at least.'

'Someone tell us what would we have to do?' Pam was secretly desperate.

'Well, as I said, we'd meet once a week, keep a check on our weight on the chart and basically encourage each other.' Ellie looked around for inspiration.

'That's it?'

Toni decided to have another bash. 'Well, I've given it a lot of thought and I do think it's a good idea but we need lots of incentives and encouragement. For instance, I thought we could each share our best and worst moments of the week.' She beamed.

Maggie looked around. Ellie and Pam were looking like they were in. She didn't like this one bit.

'And the person who hosts it could cook dinner from one of those calorie-controlled cookbooks.' Pam was definitely warming to it. Toni looked like she'd rather eat her own liver at that one.

'Or maybe we could do yoga or something for half an hour at the start?' Ellie suggested, in a vain effort to get them all interested, since it had been her idea. The nodders stopped nodding. 'Well, we will need some exercise,' she added lamely.

'And I suppose we could each give a tip of the week.' Maggie's smile was so false she looked like she was wearing dentures, trying to pretend she hadn't heard the dreaded 'e' word. The others took her seriously and nodded encouragingly. They knew she was always reading those health magazines and digested cookery books in bed with the same fervour that some of her friends gave blow jobs. She had hints on everything.

'OK, let's go for it,' Toni said. 'I'll organize the wall chart.' This was not what the other three expected. They were in it for a bit of fun, a chance to moan and drink wine every couple of weeks. Toni taking control had just turned it into Guantánamo Bay.

'But as soon as I get a date I'm out of here. We're pathetic.' She grinned at them. 'And we need an incentive.' She was racking her brains. 'I know, the first person to lose half a stone gets a date set up by each of the other three.'

'Any single men I know I'm keeping.' Maggie smiled smugly.

'No, that's a great idea. I know loads of men in the supermarket.' Pam was suddenly prepared to consider anything for a date. The others didn't quite like the sound of this, remembering the greasy butcher with blood-red fingernails and grey shiny trousers she'd introduced them to one night in the chipper. He'd even smelt of lamb chops, which had almost put Ellie off her batter sausage.

But Pam was worryingly keen. 'Are we agreed, darlings?'

'Suppose.' Maggie wasn't sure.

'Let's give it a whirl. After all, what have we

got to lose?' Toni thought about the latest old codger who'd just arrived in the home. He wore a rug and once his Pringle sweater was wiped clean he could possibly pass for a date — in a very dark pub, mind you, and only if he left his teeth in.

Ellie didn't want to moan about hen-pecked husbands so she said nothing.

'Now, can we open that bottle before I need it injected into my vein? I'm parched.' Pam made a face.

'Yes, let's.' Ellie gave in.

'But write it down.' Toni was adamant. She produced four diaries, each with a picture of them naked in a sauna stuck to the front. The photo had been taken on one of their many 'healthy' breaks. 'You have to write down everything you eat each day, so that we can look at it next week.' They all stared at the picture. It was not one of their best. Pam laughed the loudest, but secretly she wanted to cry.

5

Next morning Ellie was very determined. She had a smoothie for breakfast — berries with yoghurt, wheatgerm and a little unsweetened apple juice. She felt so good that she even prepared a tuna salad to take with her to work, but then left it on the counter in her usual panic. She was currently working in a crèche, which was not her normal job. She'd always worked with families, but her last one had emigrated to Australia and even though they'd begged her to go with them, and their three boys had cried for a week when she'd said she couldn't, Ellie wasn't sorry. Dublin was her home, where her mum and dad lived, where her friends and her heart were. A week before they left, she'd had a phone call from an old school pal who needed time off to nurse her invalid mother and so Ellie found herself in charge of a very exclusive child-minding facility, supposedly just for a month. She was now into her sixth week and was reluctant to admit it didn't rock her boat. For one thing it was bloody hard work and the days were long and some of the children were miniature Gordon Ramsays. The stressed-out parents were dropping them off in the middle of the night to avoid Dublin traffic and it was seven thirty some evenings before Ellie practically severed an arm shoving the last one out.

Today was proving testing, despite the

optimistic start. Susie, a cute little two year old, started complaining of a headache almost as soon as her mother left. She had a slight temperature and Ellie was concerned enough to phone her mother. Norma Tolan-Vaughan was not impressed and Ellie wasn't good with bullies.

'I can't possibly get there before five. Are you sure she's not acting up? She was fine this morning.'

'Eh, she mentioned that she was sick into her cornflakes?'

'That was only because she put salt on them instead of sugar while the cleaner, who was supposed to be keeping an eye on her, was having phone sex with some scruffy student from Drogheda. Have you taken her temperature?'

'Yes and it's slightly up, although nothing to be alarmed about. But she's crying and asking for you. She might need a trip to the doctor just in case.'

'Just in case what?'

Just in case she has less than twenty-four hours to live, Ellie wanted to say. 'Well, just to be on the safe side.'

'Can't you take her?'

'I'm afraid not, I'm needed here and could only do that in an emergency and —'

'Are you saying my child's life is not important?'

'No, of course not. Look, why don't we monitor her for the next hour or so if you're unavailable and perhaps you could check in with us at lunch — ' Norma was already berating some unfortunate minion in her eyeline and clicked off without so much as a thank-you.

'Charming.' Ellie went in search of Susie.

'Is m . . . m . . . m . . . my mummy coming to get me?'

'Later, darling. Why don't we go lie down for a few minutes.'

'Feel sick.' She wasn't lying. Cue a spurt of cornflakes on Ellie's shirt and a dash of warm milk in her eye. She mopped up, gave the child a drink of water and lay down beside her, thinking about how hungry she was. Once Susie had nodded off she tried in vain to rid her blouse of the hard patch of regurgitated cereal that made her smell like a week-old dish cloth but it was there to stay. Two chocolate biscuits helped.

★ ★ ★

Later she had a call from one of the agencies, wondering if she was interested in taking a job — single parent, two girls. Ellie had had a bad experience once with a single mother, Rachel Mooney, who expected her to look after three kids, two of them babies, keep the house spotless, wash, iron, do the garden and have a home-cooked meal on the table at exactly six thirty. When she complained because her underwear hadn't been ironed properly before being put away, Ellie practically strangled her with her own knicker elastic and left. She later learnt that it was nothing to do with her being a single mother — apparently, Rachel's husband Mike had left because she treated him as badly as she'd treated Ellie. Still, the episode had left

40

her bruised and battered and she wasn't sure she wanted to go down that head-banging route again, but the woman from the agency was smarmier than Bruce Forsyth and she'd agreed to an interview before she knew what had hit her.

Norma whatsit arrived at five to five, complaining loudly and asking why she'd been cut off and how come nobody had kept her informed about her baby's progress. Ellie swallowed two dispirin with a cup of tea and a scone smothered in butter and tried not to smack her. One of the little boys running backwards into a door at twenty miles per hour distracted her just long enough.

★ ★ ★

On her way home Ellie called in to see her friend Olga Blake, even though she could have done without it tonight. Her head was thumping despite the tablets. Still, Olga was the human equivalent of a laxative, and once she started there was no stopping her, so Ellie knew she'd have a bit of a laugh at least. She was a Russian immigrant who'd run away from home to live with, or marry — the story varied depending on the day and who Olga was trying to impress — an American in London. Her family wanted nothing to do with her. The relationship with the American was shorter than the career of a *Big Brother* housemate — as soon as she told him she was pregnant he was already backing out of the room.

'Come in, please,' Olga greeted Ellie, who was laden down with bags. 'I met a very nice policeman today. I tell you all about him.'

Olga's impressions of some of the Irish she met were very funny. She still couldn't understand a lot of the accents, especially the strong Cork or Donegal ones and they'd had many a laugh at the mistakes she had made when dealing with the civil servants in the various government departments. Olga lived on social welfare, in a tiny one-bedroomed council flat near the city centre. She'd called at the door of Ellie's last employer looking for baby clothes and Ellie fell in love with the newborn baby and, with the family's permission, gave lots of stuff away. Olga returned regularly after that and most afternoons Ellie would bring her in and feed her up, always replacing the foodstuff herself. She was great to talk to, full of fun despite her circumstances, and Ellie found her fascinating because she'd taken so many risks in her life. She made Ellie feel like she should do something mad, just for the hell of it.

To her amazement Olga had asked her to be godmother to her baby boy and an unlikely bond was forged. 'You are my only friend in the world,' she told Ellie more than once, which made her feel guilty that she didn't have more time to give to their friendship. It had been a pathetic christening, with just the three of them, and Ellie had taken her out for a slap-up lunch afterwards.

Olga had originally decided to give Dublin a try when she was six months pregnant. She had heard it would be a good place to bring up a baby.

'I vant to find a big strong farmer who would not be mean to me like some of the Russian men,' she'd told Ellie that first day. She'd certainly had enough of Americans and someone had told her that Irish men were lovely. Maggie said she felt sorry for farmers the length of the country. It wasn't that Olga was unattractive, but she had a funny way of pouting and frowning together that made her look like a cross between Cilla and Fiz from *Coronation Street*.

'Face like a bag of hammers,' was Pam's verdict the first time they'd been introduced. Pam summed up everyone she met immediately, and it usually wasn't very complimentary. 'And what unfortunate name did she give that doty little boy?' She could never remember.

'Rudi.'

Pam shook her head. 'Sounds like a labrador.' Next day, though, she put together a sack of old toys for him.

Ellie had quickly become very fond of Olga and she adored Rudi. He had black hair and sallow skin and gobstopper blue eyes that startled everyone who met him. 'At least he got his father's looks.' Olga knew she was no oil painting. 'Only thing he was giving away for free.' Her accent was Boris Yeltsin meets Graham Norton and Maggie had it off to a T.

Ellie brought as much stuff as she could when she visited and was always buying treats for her godchild. Tonight it was some smellies for Olga and a new jumper for Rudi, who looked like he needed a cuddle. His eyes always seemed to follow Ellie everywhere and she longed to take him home with her for a while, although she knew that was impossible. She told herself that Olga did her best.

The Russian woman had just cut up a loaf of fresh, crusty bread and Ellie was starving and couldn't resist. It was so delicious she had a second slice, this time with jam as well as butter. Then Olga poured two vodkas, which surprised Ellie, who wondered how she could afford it.

They chatted happily for an hour or so and Ellie asked to take Rudi out the following Saturday. He needed a bath and some new pyjamas, although perhaps the whiff was more her. It was hard to tell after the milk incident earlier. Still the baby did seem a bit neglected. She had to be careful not to patronize Olga, so she mentioned it casually, suggesting it might give Olga a much-needed break. She readily agreed and Ellie made some mushy Liga with warm milk for the child while Olga was glued to one of the soaps. He ate every scrap and still looked hungry, so she cut him a thick crust of bread to chew on.

6

'So, how's it going?'

'Fine, fine.' Ellie was a bad liar. 'You?'

'Great, yeah. Fruit for breakfast, salad for lunch, drank two litres of water and had an hour's walk just before I rang you.'

'Oh.'

'Ah fuck it, I can't lie.' Maggie folded completely. 'Actually, I did all of the above but then I felt so virtuous that I poured myself a glass of wine when I came in. I'm on my second and it's staving off the hunger pains. Are you sure there're calories in liquid?'

'Certain.' Ellie was tired and suddenly not sure why she was bothering.

'Bad day, huh?'

'Irritating. A lot of the people who use that crèche have so much money that they feel it gives them the right to say anything they like to the rest of us. I had three rows with parents today and ate after each one. Then, I called to see Olga and she was drinking vodka and I had a large one and now I feel like chips.'

'I didn't know she drank.'

'Neither did I.'

'How can she afford it, I thought she hadn't a bean?'

'She hasn't. Rudi seemed hungry too, which worried me a bit.'

'Stop right there, girl. You can't take everyone

45

else's problems on board. Your name is not St Ellie de Paul.'

'Anyway, forget it.' Ellie shook her head as if to clear her thoughts. 'How are the other two doing, d'ya know?'

'Pam's not answering either at home or on the mobile, which makes me think she's got something to hide, otherwise she'd be lording it all over us.' Maggie was laughing. 'Toni's had no temptation, says she can barely serve the food in the nursing home, never mind taste it. Yuck, I don't know how she does that job, there's always a smell in there and the food looks like sick.'

'And it's one of the better private homes, costs a fortune. Imagine what some people must have to put up with.'

'Christ, I'm really glad I rang you. I feel like putting the bottle to my mouth and swallowing a few pills along with it.'

'Sorry, I'm just feeling sorry for myself. Bad day. Olga's situation depressed me a bit, even though she tries to hide it with wisecracks, and I agreed to go for an interview with a single mother on Thursday.'

'You swore that would never happen again.'

'I know. Still, I can't write off all single mothers. She was just a head-wrecker.'

'Mary Poppins wouldn't have lasted a week in that job.'

'You're not wrong there. Anyway, I won't take it but I'm getting out of where I am.'

They chatted on and Ellie had a bath and went to bed, only barely resisting the biscuit barrel.

The texts were flying in Ellie's direction over the next few days:

> R oven bakd chips OK?
> Is whipd crem liter coz of all the air?
> Donuts in Tesco today have huge hols so I bought us all one, can't have many cals
> Mr Munro says vodka only flaverd watr
> Pulld mussel in gym so have 2 eat to keep it warm uderwise will seize up

Ellie kept grinning and sending back a 'hell and damnation' message and she was in good form when she made her way to the hotel on Thursday afternoon for the dreaded interview. They had arranged to meet in a quiet corner of the foyer for an informal chat and Kate Huston had told her she had long blond hair and would be wearing a black suit. Ellie arrived early and was sitting waiting, a habit she'd always had because when she was anxious or stressed she had a slight limp, something she'd been born with. It wasn't a bad one, hardly even a real limp, Pam had said reassuringly.

'Does it qualify you for a handicapped car sticker?' Toni, who hated walking anywhere, enquired hopefully.

Ellie rarely thought about it any more, although she'd been mortified by it as a child, but some people made up their minds about her as soon as they noticed.

She recognized Kate Huston immediately, she

looked exactly like she sounded, calm and friendly.

'Eleanora? Hello, I'm Kate.'

Ellie stood immediately and shook the outstretched hand.

'I hope I'm not late?'

'No, I was early.'

'Coffee?' She summoned a passing waitress.

'Yes, please.' Ellie was starving again and feared for her sanity if she didn't get a caffeine hit immediately.

'Thanks for meeting me. I just wanted to have a preliminary chat with you because the agency sent me a pile of CVs and you were by far the most qualified.'

Ellie decided to plough straight in. 'Actually, Mrs Huston I — '

'Kate, please.'

'Kate. I have a job at the moment and I'm really not sure what I'm going to be doing in the foreseeable future and — '

'Let me explain,' Kate interrupted. 'I'm in an unusual situation here. There are two small children who really need looking after and I'm afraid it's all down to me to ensure they get the best care possible, although my husband says I should leave them to their own devices.'

Wow, you just go right in there and tell me everything. Ellie couldn't believe her ears. The husband, or ex as he was, sounded like a complete bastard. He could be done for neglect.

'How old are they?' was the best she could come up with.

'Six and four, here . . . ' She pulled out the

most adorable photo, they looked cuter than most of the puppies at Crufts. 'They're very good children. Samantha, the eldest, is at school and Jess goes to playschool in the mornings. But they need minding, you know, and I can't manage much.'

'You work long hours?' She looked like she was struggling, although not financially, and as usual Ellie wanted to help.

'No. Actually I don't work at all,' she half apologized.

'Then . . . why don't you mind them? I mean, sorry, it's not for me to pry into your — '

'Oh, no, please, ask me anything you like. It's just that Jack's a bit sensitive about them.'

'Jack?'

'My brother. He thinks he can cope, but I think they're missing out and just between us, he can't really manage, not the way I'd like.'

'Mrs Huston, Kate. Sorry, but you've lost me. If you don't work, why do you need a childminder?'

'For Jack.' She looked as confused as Ellie felt.

'Your brother?' Kate nodded and sipped her coffee.

'How old is he?'

'Forty.' She looked puzzled. 'Is that a consideration?'

'No, of course not.' Get me out of here, Ellie pleaded silently.

'He's a nice man. You'd like him, honestly.' Kate was anxious.

Two kids and a brother who was . . . mentally challenged by the sounds of it. Ellie didn't think so. 'Eh, what sort of handicap does he have, exactly?'

'None that I know of.' They both stared, unsure, each wondering how the hell they could escape. 'Although if you caught him doing his Joey impressions, you'd wonder . . . ' Kate trailed off with a nervous laugh.

'I'm sure he's adorable.' Ellie didn't know what else to say.

'Well, he has his moments but I'm not sure adorable is a word you'd ever associate with him . . . '

Ellie didn't want to hear any more. 'I just don't think I'm qualified.'

'Nonsense.' Kate was decidedly nervous now, but felt she should try once more. 'Honestly, I think you're just what they all need.' It wasn't convincing. She sounded like she'd rather have that nanny from *The Hand That Rocks the Cradle* than let Ellie anywhere near them.

'It's just that I've never dealt with a person with . . . special needs.'

She must be on drugs. Kate decided to humour her while frantically signalling for the bill. 'No, the children are fine. They're normal little girls, honestly, but perhaps we should both . . . '

Jesus, she's in denial. Ellie decided to be patient. 'I'm not worried about the children, I'm talking about your brother.'

'He's fine too, perfectly normal.' Most of the time, she didn't add — wasn't taking any chances.

'Then why does he need a nanny?'

'He doesn't.'

'But you said . . . ' Before Ellie could figure out exactly what to say Kate suddenly copped on and started laughing so hard you'd think she'd been drinking. Heavily.

Ellie joined in, having no idea why. Bit by bit it all came out.

'You advertised for a nanny for a single mother, so I thought . . . '

'No, single parent. My brother, the, eh, mentally handicapped one.' Kate was off again.

'Can we start over, please?'

'Yeah, let's. Christ, I need a drink. Will you join me in a glass of wine?'

Ellie knew it was breaking a cardinal rule.

'Please?'

She glanced at her phone. It was five thirty-nine, no way was she going back to work now. 'OK, then, but I don't normally while I'm working, or being interviewed, you know.'

'Christ, Eleanora, I think we're way past the interview stage.'

Kate signalled the waiter and they started again and chatted happily for the next hour. By the end of it Ellie had agreed to meet Jack with Kate the following afternoon.

7

Once again she was early but this time paranoia simply got the better of her — she knew she wouldn't be able to banish the 'mentally challenged' image until she saw him.

'I just about managed to get him to stop sucking his thumb, but he might dribble a bit,' Kate said with a wink as the two women greeted each other in the same corner of the Westbury Hotel.

'He's on the phone, he'll be here any second.' She sounded nervous suddenly. 'I didn't tell him about our little . . . misunderstanding. Thought it might be best to wait and see how you two get on first.'

'Thank God for that. I'm perfectly capable of creating my own bad impressions without any help from you.' Ellie was scanning the arrivals. A small bald man with a shiny face and a suit to match was heading their way. Pam would have been able to sum him up in one word and Ellie decided it wouldn't have been 'dishy'. He looked kind of crawly, and she was so relieved when he greeted the statuesque blonde with the tits at the next table that she missed the man standing in front of her until Kate spoke and she jumped.

'This is my brother Jack.'

'Hi.' He held out his hand.

'Sorry. Hi. Eh, hello.' He was not what she had expected. Tall, with grey eyes and hair that looked slightly dishevelled, he reminded her of Liam Neeson. It was the slightly crooked smile that did it, she decided later.

'Jack, this is Eleanora Simpson.' Kate looked nervous too. 'I emailed Jack your CV so he's had a chance to look at your qualifications.' She was sure this girl was right for the kids, but her brother might need a bit of convincing.

Ellie thought he looked at her as one would a bunny boiler. Guarded was putting it mildly. But when he spoke he sounded resigned. 'My sister thinks I need a nanny.' Both women nearly started laughing at that and somehow he knew the way this was headed.

'Why don't I leave you two to chat for a while? I've a couple of calls to make.' They had agreed a plan. She would call him after ten minutes and see if he needed rescuing.

'Actually, I probably do need a minder, but the kids are marginally ahead of me on that one and a great deal easier to manage, I suspect.' He smiled as he threw himself down amongst the cushions. 'I'm afraid you'll have to help me out here, I haven't interviewed many nannies. And Kate has this idea that we're right up there with the Osbournes as a family unit.' He ran his fingers through his hair, a gesture guaranteed to make Ellie like him. He looked kind of lost, and even though he was wearing an exquisitely cut jacket and trousers, he didn't look comfortable.

'Mr Bryant, let me — '

'Jack. Otherwise I'd have to call you Miss Simpson and the kids would run a mile. They'd think you were the same age as Madonna. She's their current favourite wrinkly.' Ellie smiled and he liked the way her eyes crinkled. It was a kind face. He was making a huge effort because of Kate, but he had to be honest with her. He threw off his jacket and pushed up the sleeves of his open-necked pale blue shirt.

'I sort of got roped into this, as you've probably guessed by now. The fact is I don't know what I need. I work from home but I haven't been doing nearly enough of it recently and the kids do need a bit of sorting out — you know, clothes, bedrooms, etc. They also need to eat a bit more healthily. In fact, they need to eat anything that doesn't come in a tin-foil container or isn't coated in crispy batter. And the house is . . . in need of some attention, although I do have a lady who comes in for a couple of hours every morning.' He thought he'd better add that in case he frightened her off before he had decided if he wanted her in the first place.

'Well, let me tell you about me. I've always worked with families, at least up until recently.' She explained all. 'I normally devote most of my time to the children,' she finished up, 'although I'm happy to do some housework and of course make sure they eat properly.' He sensed a but and she read his mind instantly, which unnerved him slightly.

'I have, em, worked in a one-parent family only once before and, eh, I'm afraid it all ended rather badly.' What are you doing, idiot? she berated herself. He does not need to know how a helpless, single mother almost ended up feeling

54

her thong tightening around her neck because you nearly lost it.

'Bad, eh?'

'We didn't really work it out properly at the beginning and by the end I was working as hard as one of those women on that house-cleaning programme.'

'The marginally more attractive one with the glasses or the dyed blonde with the bun and the feather duster?' he asked deadpan.

'Well, I was certainly as acerbic as the blonde but my rubber gloves did not have a fur trim.' Ellie grinned.

They were deep in conversation when his phone rang ten minutes later.

'Excuse me.' he glanced down. 'It's Kate. Hi.'

'Have I time for a coffee or have you two drawn daggers yet?'

'No, fine. Take your time.'

'Another fifteen minutes?'

'Sounds about right. See you later.' He clicked off and they continued their chat. Both were feeling more relaxed by the time Kate returned. She joined them and it suddenly became formal again.

'Would you like to meet the girls and inspect the gaff, or do you need time to think about it?' He hadn't expected to hear himself ask that. Ellie liked the casual way he threw in the odd slang word, but Kate gave him one of her looks.

'It is not a gaff.' She didn't want Eleanora to say no.

'I'd really like to see how the girls and I get on,' Ellie replied.

55

Kate beamed at Jack, all forgiven, as they arranged for her to call the following afternoon, which was Saturday. They exchanged numbers and he stood up and shook hands.

'Do you need a lift anywhere?'

'No, no, I'll just stay here for a bit and check my messages.'

'Thanks so much.' Kate gripped her hand tightly and the siblings departed. Ellie saw Jack tweak his sister's hair and laugh down at her and she envied them their easy relationship.

★ ★ ★

'I thought you said you'd rather sauté your own kidneys than work for a single parent again?' Maggie was amused as they sat over their weekly brunch the following day, later than usual because Ellie had taken Rudi on an outing as promised.

'I know, and I haven't made up my mind, really, it's just that he looked like he could do with a break.'

'You're in,' Pamela muttered as she looked at the menu 'God I hate vegetables, they all taste of muck.'

'And you eat much clay every day, do you?' Ellie teased.

'Are we having wine?' Toni asked hopefully.

'No. I can't drink because of this meeting so the rest of you can bloody well suffer too, and leave that bread alone.' Ellie reached for the piece of walnut and raisin that was barely visible under the mound of butter that Pam was

56

shovelling on top. 'You can't use that much fat.' Ellie tried to grab it but Pam got there first and loaded it into her mouth in one go.

'A second on the tongue, a decade on the bum.' Maggie sounded like a smug Carol Vorderman. They all laughed at her.

'Is your face hurting you, cause it's killing me?' Pam teased and stuck her tongue out. She looked like one of the Crankies.

'How's the food thing going for everyone?' Ellie wanted to know.

'I thought we'd agreed not to let it take over our lives.' Pam was getting grumpy.

'Not much chance of that, judging by what you've just shoved in your mouth.' Maggie got a slap for that remark.

'On second thoughts, let's leave this till our Monday meeting, shall we?' Ellie grinned at her friends. 'Otherwise we could be chucked out for throwing bread rolls.'

'I'm so hungry all the time,' Toni wailed. She'd abandoned her role as Hitler's second in command. 'I'm having the sausages and mash, I don't care.' They were in Bang, the latest hot-spot for lunch, and this was one of their specialities.

'I'll have the fish and chips so.' Pamela was delighted.

Ellie and Maggie had marginally more willpower and they settled down for a good natter, although the chat was somewhat subdued without the alcohol.

'How did you get on with Rudi?' Maggie asked Ellie. They were all interested.

57

'I dunno, OK I think. I arrived early to collect him. He was watching TV and Olga was still in bed. There wasn't much food around and he hadn't had any breakfast. Also, that vodka bottle from the other night was empty.' Ellie looked at them. 'Tell me I'm over-reacting,' she pleaded.

'Ellie, you are inventing scenarios in your head again.' Pam smiled. 'You do it all the time.' The others nodded knowingly and Toni rubbed her back in sympathy.

'Don't torture yourself, you're a very good friend and most of the time she's fine, isn't she?'

'Yeah, you're right and it's not like I don't have enough to worry about.' She sighed. 'Anyway, I fed Rudi and gave him a bath and bought him a few bits.'

'What kind of form is Olga in these days?' Maggie wanted to know.

'She seems very quiet this week. Remember when I met her first she was always making me laugh with her stories?' The others nodded. 'She's become a little bit more introverted, I think. Oh, hell, I'm probably just imagining things, like you said.' Ellie ran her hands through her hair. 'It's just that she seems to have given up on her dreams. She doesn't talk about finding an Irish husband any more . . . '

'I'd say men up and down the country are breathing a sigh of relief.' Pam grimaced. 'She's not exactly a good catch, is she?'

'When she's in good form, she's great, and besides, looks aren't everything, she just needs a break, that's all. I suppose in the meantime all I can do is keep offering support.'

58

'What's in it for you?'

'What do you mean?' Ellie was surprised at Maggie's question.

'What are you getting out of the friendship?'

'I like talking to her, she's usually a great listener, and I love Rudi. I feel part of their little family somehow, and besides, she needs a friend. I think she's going through a bad patch at the moment. Things are very tight money wise and she spends a lot of time on her own.'

'I think she's lucky to have you.' Toni wanted to move on. 'So, what did you all think of the column today?'

'I didn't see it.' Ellie hated missing out.

'Here, I brought it with me.' Toni handed it over.

Ellie began to read it and as usual got into it straightaway.

'Which bit are you on?' Maggie wanted to know and Ellie read it aloud.

'Sue, Frances and Terry (that's what I decided they were called) are like any other women friends in the restaurant where I'm having lunch today with my editor. He's late so I'm inventing scenarios for the lives of the other diners when they sit down at the next table. They're fit looking and they have obviously been to a class of some sort, because they drop their designer sports bags and pounce on the menu. At a guess they range in age from late twenties, maybe early thirties to mid-fifties, I decide. They are typical ladies who lunch and don't eat much

either, I'll bet. They order champagne. At first it doesn't seem as if they have much in common except that they are all well groomed, well off and well proportioned. As they talk it appears that the one thing they do have in common, apart from their pecs, is their lovers. Some of the things they talk about would make any red-blooded male nervous about where his wife had been last weekend when she told him she was off to London with the girls for a shopping trip. Some of the snippets I overhear go like this.

''It's all about sex, for me anyway, and I'm absolutely loving the attention. And shopping for underwear has never been more exciting. Mark wouldn't notice if I stripped off in front of him at a board meeting.' (Sue fortyish.)

''I'm not bored with my marriage, this is just a bit of fun. I feel like it's my last chance before I get my bus pass.' (Frances, anywhere between fifty and sixty.)

''I met him on the Internet. He's horny. I haven't had a relationship with my husband since our last child was born. He makes me feel special, but I wouldn't want it to go any further. I mean, I'd shag him senseless, but I wouldn't want to go shopping in Homebase with him.' (Terry, the youngest-looking of the three.)

'So, husbands everywhere, as you tuck into your cereal and prepare to watch Sky Sports, think about how well you really know your wives.'

'And on it goes. Everyone is doing it, apparently.' Maggie laughed.

'Oh for a husband to worry about me in the first place.' Toni smiled and they were off into their fantasy world again and even without the wine it was fairly raunchy.

★ ★ ★

An hour and a half later Ellie drove to Jack's house with the top of her jeans cutting into her waist and her Lycra T-shirt almost preventing her from breathing. The 'gaff' was in Howth, a white, flat-roofed building with fantastic views and a sweeping driveway. It made her nervous.

8

The girls were very excited and that simply added to Jack's unease. He had a funny feeling about this, as if he was being steamrollered down a path he wasn't sure he wanted to take. Despite all his moaning, he liked having the girls to himself. They were an odd little unit but somehow it worked. He dreaded any intrusion, fearing it might highlight his inadequacies.

'Hi.' He was relieved to see that she looked exactly the way he felt.

'Hello. Am I too early? The traffic was light . . . '

'No, no, come in. The girls have been watching for you for hours and suddenly they seem to have . . . vanished, or . . . maybe not.' He spotted a shoe poking out from the living-room door. He was stepping backwards as he spoke, extending an arm in the direction of the scuffed toe.

'Come on, girls, don't go all shy on me now.' A body attached itself to the outstretched hand and a smaller version of the same stuck its head through his legs.

'Let's go to the kitchen and grab a coffee.' Two small bodies sprang into action.

'I'll get the biscuits.'

'Me too.'

He led the way to a long narrow kitchen with huge windows and great light. It was a mess.

'Tea or coffee?'

'Coffee, please.'

'Coming up. Girls, say hello to Eleanora.' It was her first good look at them. Samantha was a beauty queen in the making, long wavy blond hair, a button nose and smooth olive skin. Jessie was all tumbly curls and puppy fat. She looked mischievous, like one of those children you sometimes see in kitten commercials.

Ellie decided she'd better put the record straight. The full version of her name made her sound way too efficient. 'My friends call me — '

'Hi, Nora.' Jessie made the first tentative move.

'Nora sounds old.' Samantha was less willing.

'Actually, my friends call me Ellie.' She crouched down so they could get a good look.

'I'm going to call you Nora.'

'Me too, just in case you really are an old witch.'

'Sam, stop it.' Jack was alarmed, she was normally so placid.

'That's OK.' Ellie glanced up at him, not at all offended. 'Actually, I am old, but I'm definitely not a witch. I don't have any magic powers.'

'Haven't you got a broomstick?' Jessie again, eyes wide, always ready for the big story.

'Just a mop.' Ellie apologized. 'But I do have a witch's hat that one of the children from the crèche made for me at Halloween.'

'I'm a fairy,' was Jessie's current favourite phrase. In the last few days she'd twirled everywhere, leaving a trail of imaginary gold-dust in her wake. She looked high on life. 'Nora, would you like one of my animal biscuits?'

'No thanks, I've just had lunch. I'm bursting.' Ellie smiled at the two girls.

'Do you need to do a wee wee?' Jessie was all concern.

'Jessie, that's enough. Have some milk.' Jack poured the coffee and the adults sat down.

'Can you cook?' Sam demanded in a precocious voice. Jack looked like he was going to intervene again.

'A little bit. Can you?' Ellie's eyes told him to let them be.

'Only French toast.'

'Well, I can make great butterfly buns, with jam and cream, so maybe we could teach each other?' Sam nodded and the two girls sat up and watched her.

'Are you going to slap us?' Jessie cut to the chase.

'No, but I might tickle you to death.'

'I don't need a nanny.' Sam was watching her intently.

'I'm sure you don't. That's why I came here, to see if you needed me at all. You're both so grown up — '

'Will you help me clean my room?' Jessie sounded like she had a list of questions.

'Sure.'

'Will you wash and iron all my clothes?' Sam was reminding her of her position. Amazing how devious a six year old could be when her territory was being invaded.

'Are they all dirty, or do you only have a few?'

'I have lots, dresses and tops and jeans and T-shirts.'

64

'And where do you keep them all?'

'In my wardrobe.'

'You have your own wardrobe?'

'And my own room.'

'You must be a very important member of this family so.'

'Me too.'

Ellie smiled at the little girl. 'I'll bet you are.'

'Want to see my room?' It was said in a couldn't-care-less voice but Ellie knew it was a slight thaw.

'Yes, please, if it's OK with your dad?'

'Be my guest.' Jack was watching the psychology of the whole thing, fascinated.

'C'mon, Nora, I'll show you my Nemo poster.' Jessie's fat little legs led the way.

★　★　★

By the time they returned twenty minutes later Ellie knew it was going to be OK and even Jack sensed the lightness.

Jessie was skipping and Sam was admitting to her current addiction, *Harry Potter*. She had all the gear courtesy of her cousin Georgia.

'I know, it is definitely a bit scary, I hate the bats, too,' Ellie was agreeing earnestly.

'OK, girls, enough. Go watch TV. I need to talk to Nora.' It slipped out, but he was secretly relieved that the girls had shortened her unfortunate name. Eleanora sounded vaguely horsey. What had she said her friends called her? He couldn't remember.

'Well?' He raised an eyebrow. 'Too much?'

'Not at all. Fairly typical, I'd say. Jessie's a dote and Sam is protecting her turf, but she's great too.'

'It hasn't been easy, but they're good kids. So, what are your thoughts now that you've had time to think?'

'I think I'd like to give it a try, provided you're happy. I'm worried that this might be all down to sister knowing best.'

He shrugged. 'I think we do need someone, but what if it doesn't work out?'

'Well, we could both agree to give it a month's trial on condition that if it's not working for either one of us we call it quits.'

'But aren't you giving up a job?' He was taken aback by her easy attitude.

'I want out, to be honest. Crèches aren't for me, I've discovered. The kids are fine but the parents need a good spanking.' She grimaced. 'We do need to work out my duties, though. This is a big house.'

'As far as I'm concerned if you can look after the kids and feed them properly and keep their clothes sorted, I'm happy. As I think I mentioned, Mrs O'Sullivan comes in for a few hours every morning. She does the bathrooms and the hoovering and tidies the kitchen.' They both glanced around, or at least he did. Her eyes merely darted.

'It's usually a bit better than this. She was off yesterday and it sort of piled up.'

'I don't mind helping around the house as well. But I should warn you that I'm not a great cook. I'll make sure the children have fresh food

66

every day and I can shop in the mornings and I'm happy to leave you a plate of whatever I'm making but it won't be gourmet food. Not by a long shot.'

'I don't expect you to cook for me.' He seemed surprised that she would even think he might.

They chatted on about hours and rates and both seemed relaxed as she prepared to go. The girls appeared and Jack guessed they'd been keeping an ear cocked.

'So, are you coming to work for us?' Samantha asked.

Jack and Ellie glanced at each other.

'Yes and I want you two to promise — '

'But only if you give your approval.' Ellie knelt down again and looked up at Sam.

'What's approval?'

'Only if you say yes as well as me.' Jack was quick to join in.

'After all, we're a family, we make decisions together.'

'Yes. I say yeeees.' Jessie hopped about on one foot and held her other leg behind her, clutching her shoe. 'When can we do the butterflies?'

'Soon,' Ellie promised. She glanced at the older child. 'But Samantha hasn't said yes yet.'

'It's OK by me.' Sam hesitated for just a second. 'But I'd like you not to move things around in my room unless I say so.'

'Sure, I won't even go in there if you don't want me to. We can have a basket outside your door and you can leave your washing out and I can leave your clean things back on top of it.

Would that be OK to start, and we can see how things go?'

The child nodded and Jack looked sorry for his daughter. She was a little mother and she was way too young.

'She's weird.' Jessie made a face. 'You can come into my room any time, even when I'm at playschool.'

They walked towards the door and Ellie promised to see them bright and early on Monday week.

'Bye, Nora.' Jessie was all waves and puckered lips.

'Bye, Jessie.' Ellie returned the kiss via warm air on her palm. With Samantha she was more formal. 'I'm looking forward to you showing me everything in the house, so that I don't annoy you all and break the ornaments. By the way, I should have asked you, do you like to be called Sam or Samantha?'

'Sam is fine. Dad only ever calls me Samantha when he's yelling at us.'

Ellie shot him a 'bold boy' look and he ran his fingers through his hair. It was an oddly familiar gesture, even though she barely knew him.

'God, I don't know if I can cope with three women.' He laughed but she sensed he was serious.

'Don't worry, Dad, just do as we tell you and you'll be fine,' Samantha looked earnest.

'Exactly what I was thinking, Sam, but I wasn't going to say it. I don't want to get fired before I start.' Ellie smiled and left them and felt she was making the right decision.

She had a text message. It was from Toni, who used predictive text and whose messages were always like letters. All that was missing was the Dear Ellie.

> In Merrion Hotel. They ran out of water. Reluctantly switched to G & T cause it's the same colour! How did you get on? Come in and tell all.

Forty minutes later she joined her friends in their luxurious surroundings opposite Government Buildings. The place was full of yummy mummies and political types.

'What are you doing in here?' Ellie said as she collapsed in beside them. 'It's not one of our usual haunts.'

'It's comfortable and we're getting old,' Pam said, stretching out her legs.

'Speak for yourself, darling.' Toni was having none of it. 'It's just that, since the Shelbourne closed, we're lost. It always felt just right for afternoon drinkies.'

'And you could stroll around the Green first and pretend you'd had some exercise.' Maggie was the realistic one.

'Well, I'll have a large version of whatever you're having.' Ellie was suddenly gasping.

Pam was relieved that she wasn't going to lecture them, so she sprang up with alacrity. 'Coming up, ma'am.'

'Well, do tell all.' Toni wanted the details.

'Don't start without me.' Pam warned, so they made small talk for a moment but she was back in a jif. 'I forgot it's all waiter service here.' She made a face. 'Bit posh for me, I think. They called me madam.'

'Well, let's hope they hurry up. Anyway, I start on Monday week.' Ellie waited for their reaction, there was no point in delaying.

'Ha, I knew it.'

'Good for you.'

'Well done, but are you sure?'

'Yes. No. Well, kind of. I want out of the other place and the kids are great and it's a fantastic house, although Howth is a fair journey. Still, I can go over the toll bridge. He's a bit grim, but then he smiles and I sort of like him. Also, his sister is nice and I feel I'll be able to talk to her if I have any problems. Anyway, I think he deserves a break.'

'Well, he's got one if you've agreed to work for him. Until he samples your cooking, that is.' Pam elbowed her friend. They'd all had their share of Ellie's attempts to be adventurous in the kitchen. 'Remember the famous Indian food night. It was after midnight by the time we sat down. We were all plastered.'

'Stop it. Poor Ellie really tried that night.' Maggie knew what they were like.

'She nearly poisoned us.' Pam was enjoying herself. 'Ugh, I can still taste that chicken.'

'It wasn't my fault the chicken was a bit off. I couldn't smell it because of all the spices.'

'It wasn't a bit off, it was mingin'.' Toni gave her an apologetic look as she wrinkled her nose.

70

'I couldn't face poultry of any description for six months.'

'And then there was your attempt at Peking Duck, remember?' Drink had loosened Pam's tongue. 'It was charred, and when you sliced it a litre of fat spurted out.'

'And all that soy sauce made it way too salty.' Maggie wasn't about to be left out of the slagging completely.

'Well, he said he doesn't expect me to cook for him at all.' Ellie made a face. 'So a trip to A & E won't be on his agenda.'

'Pity the kids, though. They'll get to know the Crumlin area quite well, I'd say.' Pam was referring to Dublin's major children's hospital, well known to parents the length of the country.

'Very funny. I can cook perfectly well and you all know it. I just get carried away every now and then. Now, can we please change the subject?'

'So, what's he really like?'

'OK. A bit odd, as I said. Aloof. Preoccupied, sort of.'

'Attractive?'

'No, well maybe . . . no, not really. Tall, dark, dishevelled. Broody eyes. Needs looking after.'

'No better woman, I'd say.' Pam was bruising Ellie's ribs again and it was beginning to irritate her.

'Sounds a bit like Gabriel Byrne from that description.'

'Yeah, maybe. But he's taller. He does have that intense look, though.' Ellie couldn't remember who he'd reminded her of on that first day. 'The kids have christened me Nora, despite my protestations.' That set off a chorus of name jokes. They all knew Ellie hated her name and thought it was a riot that she now had another nickname to add to the list.

'Well, you certainly don't live up to your quaint, old-fashioned name, that's for sure,' Maggie teased. 'Would you like a sweet sherry, Nora?' she enquired and they spent the next ten minutes telling her how she should dress and behave to suit her new image. None of it was flattering.

9

The first real meeting — the last one had only been a dry run — of the WWW Club was not off to a good start. Ellie arrived at Toni's stylish apartment in the IFSC — the ultra cool financial services building in the centre of Dublin — early and crotchety. 'Don't talk to me. I've just had a run-in with a mother because I scolded her darling son who peed into another child's rice pudding.'

'Ah sure God love him, babies do that. All this macho stuff about getting their willies out and admiring their aim starts in nappies, you know.' Toni had had a flirtation with a rather attractive doctor in the lift that evening so she was feeling generous.

'He's nearly five.'

'Ah, right.'

'And while I was arguing with the mother the other child started to eat the pudding and her father came in and threw a wobbly and while I was dealing with the two of them the child with the rice thing emptied it into a cot on top of one of the sleeping babies.'

'You need a cup of tea, so . . . ' Toni was sympathetic. She'd had problems of her own with patients and food that day and hers were definitely old enough to know better. Still, even crotchety geriatrics were better than children most days, she consoled herself. She went to put the kettle on.

'I'd love a place like this, Toni.' Ellie always liked coming here. 'You've got so much light, and the rooms are huge.'

'Well, I couldn't afford it without the allowance from my father, you know that.'

'You deserve it. After all, you never really had a base when you were a child.'

'That's true, I suppose . . . ' The buzzer went and she trailed off as she saw Pam's face pressed against the video screen. Laughing, she went to let her in.

'I don't care . . . I need a drink.' Pam fell in, clutching wildly at a bottle in a brown-paper bag like a wino, and brandishing her umbrella at Toni.

'Don't be a baby,' Toni scolded playfully as she headed for the kitchen again. 'Poor Ellie's been peed on and had rice pudding thrown at her,' she called over her shoulder.

'Not quite,' Ellie whispered to Pam. They both knew Toni liked to embroider stories. 'But it definitely wasn't pleasant.'

'A tall glass of organic carrot juice will revive you. We're being good.' Toni reappeared and commandeered the offending bottle. 'Anyway, it's Chardonnay — with a screw top. Where's your sense of style?' she teased her friend.

'It was the only cold bottle and besides, who are you to complain?' Pam practically spat at the lurid orange glass. 'Your mother drank it from a teat, as far as I can recall.' It was said with a smile, but Ellie sensed a row and rowed in to calm things down.

'Actually, I could do with one myself. It's our

first week and we've all been good, so let's reward ourselves.' Toni was still smarting, so Ellie whipped off the cap and poured a glass each.

'No, I'm sticking to peppermint tea.' Toni was definitely in a snot and Pam stuck her tongue out behind her back. The buzzer went again.

'That was a bit mean,' Ellie admonished Pam. 'You know she's sensitive about her mother.'

'I know, I don't know what's got into me today. I'm like a bag of cats.'

Maggie appeared like a ray of sunshine. 'Evening, campers,' she said with a grin, hair and make-up immaculate. 'I brought us a treat in case we've lost loads.' She produced another bottle and a couple of cellophane bags of Bombay mix. 'They're very low in calories, I checked,' she said to no one in particular as Pam pounced on them. 'My arse, they're mostly nuts, but I adore them.' She had ripped open one of the bags and was shovelling a handful into her mouth as Toni produced a couple of delicate little Chinese bowls.

'Oh, you've already started.' Maggie glanced at the wine glasses. 'Well, I'll have a glass of my very snazzy Sauvignon Blanc, so.' She eyed the Chardonnay warily. 'Much more classy, I think.'

'Bullshit, you should have bought a Riesling if you're trying to appear sophisticated.' Ellie stuck out her tongue playfully at Maggie. She didn't want Pam upset any further. Obviously the other two were coping better.

'Sorry, Toni, I didn't mean what I said earlier.' Pam was feeling guilty.

'No worries, you were spot-on about my mum.' Toni shrugged. 'But Chardonnay's still for chavs.' She got in a last dig. 'Right. Weigh-in before we do anything, that way we have until next week to burn off this little lot.' She decided to take control, sensing that no one else was about to. 'Then, a spot of floor exercises, followed by our best and worst moments of the week. Later I've two tips to share and then I'm cooking Potassium Broth. How does that sound?'

'Right up there with having dinner in the Simon soup kitchen if I'm honest, not that I'm knocking it.' Pam had been a volunteer for ages and was a veteran of their soup-run for homeless people along the east coast as far as Wicklow. She swallowed her wine and got up quickly, before her courage deserted her. 'OK, I'll go first, I think I've had a good week, mostly. I'm on the four-week 'bikini fit and flat' plan and it seems to be working.'

'I thought we said no more mad diets?' Toni sniffed.

'Are you intending to wear a bikini?' Ellie asked what everyone else was thinking. Pam was sexy, voluptuous, gorgeous, but picturing her in a bikini was similar to imagining Roseanne in a lacy thong: it required a slight stretch of the imagination.

'Yep, I'm determined to do it this year. It helps release your inner child, according to the book.'

'But you never wore a cossie as a child, you were always covering up in your knickers and a T-shirt. You told us.' Maggie was puzzled.

'No, idiot, it's not to be taken literally. It's the whole freedom thing. Children don't care how they look, they're completely unselfconscious.'

'Right.' Toni was intrigued. 'Hop up and inspire the rest of us.'

She did and Toni looked puzzled. She consulted her notes and squinted at the scales again. 'Eh, you won't be releasing your inner child just yet, I'm afraid, because at the moment it's a teenager. You're 12 stone 11, up 4 pounds. Sorry. Who's next?'

There was silence. Pam, for once, said nothing, merely scuttled down off the scales, mortified. Ellie and Maggie nearly lost a foot each trying to get on to the wretched thing to cover her embarrassment. Ellie just about made it ahead of her friend, yelling as Maggie stood on her toe.

'Never mind, Pam. I don't think I'll be much better.' She felt guilty. It was one of those peculiarly girly lies intended to comfort. Actually, she was secretly quite pleased with herself.

Again Toni looked puzzled for a second, then shrugged. She was getting used to this. 'You're up 3 pounds.'

'But I can't be, I mean, that makes me . . . ' She trailed off, not wanting to tell.

'Eleven stone, exactly.' Toni grinned.

'Bitch,' Pam mumbled, still smarting. Ellie was too confused to be upset.

Maggie was beginning to feel uneasy. 'I still have my period,' she announced proudly, like a two year old who'd just done her first wee in a potty.

'So, how much do tampons weigh, then?' Ellie tried to laugh it off. 'Anyway, that period's lasted for weeks. I think you're fibbing.'

'I am not, you cow . . . Just you wait.'

'9 stone 7 pounds.' Toni sounded almost disappointed. 'Same as last week.'

'Oh.' Maggie would have been upset had she not heard the other disastrous results. Now all she felt was guilt, as if she'd let the side down. 'I took a laxative this morning,' she whispered to a still smouldering Pam. 'Spent the whole afternoon on the loo.' But Pam hardly heard her, she was leaping into action. 'OK, your turn, St Antonia.' She wore a saccharine smile, showing enough teeth to make Esther Rantzen seem gummy. 'Hop up.'

Toni was feeling confident. 'I only had an OK week, although this skirt is definitely looser at the waist,' she said conspiratorially, looking at Pam with a wide-eyed 'didn't I do well' gaze.

'Well, the fat's dropped to your bum so, I'd say, because you're up 2 pounds.' Toni stared at the scales and turned beetroot. After all her lecturing. Pam sat down with a flourish, threw her head back and shoved a handful of nuts into her mouth triumphantly. Half of them fell down her front and she knew she'd be squirming about uncomfortably for the rest of the night picking them out, although it did at least mean she'd have a secret supply.

Maggie refilled the glasses hastily.

'So, what went wrong?' Ellie ploughed straight in, as usual.

No one answered for a second. 'Fucking life, I

suppose,' Pam admitted reluctantly. 'Listen, my husband spent years trying to convince me to shed a few pounds. We split up. So what chance do you lot have, then?'

'We'll get there, it's OK.' They'd heard all her doubts before. That Stephen had a lot to answer for, Maggie hoped he was leading a miserable life in abject poverty, but she doubted it. 'So, tell us more about the 'bikini fit and flat' plan? What do you have to do?' she asked hopefully.

'Not much to gain four pounds, I'd say.' Toni was still smarting from Pam's put-down.

'Very funny. Well, it is a four-week approach so I've started cutting down my portions, not drinking alcohol, except occasionally.' She gestured guiltily towards the glass in her hand. 'I'm also doing some body brushing, detoxing, skin peeling and some gentle exercise — an hour or so a day — oh, and drinking two litres of water and eating five portions of fruit and veg.'

'That all? Sure that's hardly any different to my normal day.' Ellie grinned uncomfortably, unable to believe her ears.

'And that's only week one?' Toni was horrified.

'Anyone else got any better ideas?'

'I'm going to try the 'Say Yes to S and No to O' routine, it's subtitled 'bottle your fat and fling it behind you'.' That got their attention, Toni was pleased to see.

'What's that? I haven't heard of it.'

'You can eat a list of things beginning with S . . .'

'Such as?'

'Em, let me see . . .'

79

'Sugar?' Ellie looked hopeful.

'No, it's quite complicated, if there's a U or a W after the S then they're banned, as far I can make out. But, em, soya's allowed, that's definitely OK and — '

'Oh yummy.'

'And spaghetti, although only wholewheat, I think.'

'Mmmm, my favourite.'

'Oh and Solpadeine's in there, I think, 'cause you get awful headaches.'

'And the Os?'

'Oh yes, they're quite easy, you can't have okra or, let's see, oh yeah, oxtail and . . . oh, oregano is out too.' Toni was warming to her theme.

'Shame, I particularly like an oxtail and okra pizza with lots of oregano. Still, wholewheat spaghetti with soy sauce and a sprinkling of Solpadeine sounds so yummy that I think it should be next week's dinner.' Ellie needed a large helping of Ss herself, the sweet, banned kind.

'Now, now, don't be nasty, Ellie. It worked really well for Russell Crowe, according to some magazine I read.'

'OK, babe, why don't you try it and tell us next week? No, even better, prove it to us next week.' Maggie had had enough. She opened the second bottle of wine and the third packet of Bombay mix. 'Look, we all know why this isn't working.'

'Why?' Three pairs of eyes innocently asked.

'Because we're eating too much, drinking too much and not getting up off our arses. What about meeting in the morning for a jog at six thirty, followed by a quick smoothie in that juice bar in Ranelagh? Then home for showers and we'll be feeling so virtuous, so ahead of the posse, that we will not, I repeat not, over-indulge for the rest of the day.'

'OK, you're right, let's just take it a day at a time.'

'One day at a time, Sweet Jesus . . . ' Pam did her best Daniel O'Donnell impersonation, dropped to her knees and folded her hands in prayer. They all corpsed.

'I'll agree on one condition,' Ellie was adamant.

'What?'

'That we abandon today — it was sooooo not pleasant — and order in Indian.' The smiles told her that no one was going to argue.

'Order through that crowd Restaurant Express, that way we can top up on wine or beer with our order. They deliver from the Chilli Club, don't they? Or there's that lovely Chinese in town, what's it called?' They were happy again, for the moment.

10

The week wasn't going well for Pam. Tuesday had been another disaster. Jogging had never been her forte, and jogging with a hangover and a belly full of lamb chilli masala was tantamount to tying your arteries together and wondering why you suddenly got chest pains.

The girls had been kind, but she knew she was the most unfit of the group and her boobs were bobbing up and down so hard under her lacy bra that they practically dislodged her double chin — the only positive — and the tops of her legs rubbed together for most of the ten miles she imagined they'd covered. They were red raw by the time she'd managed to yank away her leggings, which had stuck firmly to the chaffed mess that was her thighs.

She struggled to behave till about three o'clock, then she wolfed down a packet of Tayto salt-and-vinegar crisps and a Twix and felt horribly guilty for the rest of the afternoon.

Working on the customer service desk in Tesco should have been pleasant, and it would have been if it wasn't for the customer bit.

Pam did her best. The men were OK — mostly, they all flirted outrageously with her and the old codgers were the worst. Guys were pretty straightforward on the whole although the barrister types in their starched white shirts and pinstriped suits never said please or thank you.

The haughty women were the ones she hated most. They were easily identifiable — too tanned, sporting masses of platinum and diamond jewellery — and talked in loud voices on their credit-card-slim, silver phones, which they pulled from their Louis Vuittons as soon as they got within spitting distance of a member of staff.

'Darling, coffee in the Berkeley in an hour? OK, no worries. Yes, their facials are divine. Will I see you in Rolys then for a quick bite?' Pause, followed by a throwaway 'I need to get a refund on that,' delivered to the cigarettes behind Pam's head. Resume conversation. 'Mmm, me too, I had the most gorgeous swordfish there the other day, with wild rocket and parmesan shavings and a glass of Moët.'

'Do you have a receipt for this, madam?' Pam always tried to smile, even though sometimes she detested them all. The answer was at best a shake of the head, more often a shrug of the shoulders and a cursory check with Louis V. Usually they simply waved her away and continued the darling ritual. It drove her insane.

Then there were the liars. They usually wanted to change something that was 90 per cent eaten — smoked ham or pate or cheese. 'I'd like to return this, it's rancid.'

'Do you have a receipt?'

'No. Why would I keep a receipt? I don't expect to have to return something. But this is clearly off. Have you smelt it?'

No and I don't intend to, either. 'When did you buy it, madam?'

83

'Yesterday, I think, or the day before.'

'It's just that the use-by date is three weeks ago.'

Very slight pause. 'Oh, on the bag, you mean? That's not the original one. I just threw it into the nearest thing I had.'

'And how much did you pay for it, madam?'

'About twelve euros 43, as far as I remember, I don't really know.'

'That's rather a lot to pay for cooked ham.'

'Yes, well my children love it and now one of them probably has food poisoning and here you are querying the price, it's outrageous.' Pam knew there was no point in calling one of the managers, they always caved in. She would simply guide them to the deli counter and ask the young Croatian or Indian boy for thirteen euros' worth of ham. She would then hand the huge mound to the brazen hussies in exchange for their half slice of decaying pig and smile sweetly. Most of the time they had the grace to blush.

★ ★ ★

Thursday was one of those days when she wanted to crawl into a hole and howl and yet she was forced to spend an extra hour in the torture chamber because it was weekly shop night and her two sons would be hovering like vultures, awaiting her appearance. They got whatever they wanted for dinner on Thursdays, as long as it came from the hot food counter at the store.

'Hi, I'm home. Could someone help me

unload the groceries, please?' Paul, the ten-year-old monster appeared immediately. 'What's for dinner?' He loved Thursdays because they always got plenty of goodies. Then there was the weekend coming, which meant takeaways or meals out. Monday to about Wednesday was the part of the week he hated most because his mum was always on a diet, or a tight budget, and was usually forcing them to eat rabbit food of some description, or the gloopy, runny mess she called shepherd's pie. That was really gross.

'Dinner tonight is pizza, darling. I got you pepperoni with extra cheese, as per your detailed instructions this morning. Remember?'

'Oh yeah. Cool.'

'Where's Andrew?'

'On the phone.' Pam tried not to think of the amount of time her eldest spent calling his mates, mostly ringing mobile numbers despite her banning them. Otherwise he was on the Internet, another forbidden means of communication unless she was present. His only other interests were renting computer games or DVDs and texting the entire universe.

'Andrew, I need help, please.' No response.

'Dinner's here, BBQ chicken and spicy wedges with chilli sauce,' she yelled. He was thumping the boards in a flash.

As usual they carried in one bag each then emptied the contents on to the kitchen table for inspection. She normally managed to hide the bag containing dinner, the only way they could be persuaded back outside to the car without the aid of a cattle prod. By the time she finally came inside, dumped her jacket and kicked off her shoes they had both taken up residence in front of the soccer, dinner already well underway on their laps and most of her bags vandalized.

Pam surveyed the contents of her shop in dismay. Spread out in front of her, it was a ready-made discussion on one of those 'you are what you eat' reality TV shows. There were too many biscuits, fizzy drinks, fish fingers and chicken kievs and not enough fruit and vegetables, and certainly no healthy brown options anywhere. She picked up her portion of chicken wings, added salt and ketchup, poured a glass of coke and flopped. She sighed heavily.

'Are you OK, Mum?' Paul looked anxious.

'Just tired.'

'I'll help you put things away later, then.'

'Thanks, love. And you.' She prodded Andrew's foot with her own. 'It's your turn to do the dishes, OK?'

'I did them last night.'

'No, I did them last night. No arguing.'

He said nothing. 'Andrew?' It was a warning.

'What?'

'Take that sulky look off your face.'

He sighed and shifted in his seat, and she was too tired to argue. They weren't bad kids really, just lazy, and a bit spoilt.

★ ★ ★

Maggie was really trying and it was killing her. On Tuesday after the jog she *was* feeling very virtuous, just as she had predicted, so her

86

morning coffee-break was a glass of water and an apple, instead of cappuccino and a blueberry muffin. She felt positively saintly. She dithered a bit at one o'clock but finally ditched her chicken tikka garlic baguette in favour of a brown salad sandwich with Low Low and her halo gleamed brightly as she walked down Nassau Street towards her lunchtime Pilates class. By the end of the day she was the talk of the office, although her beatification suffered a setback on Wednesday evening after two Bacardi Breezers in the company of the cute guy from Mergers and Acquisitions who was leaving work.

On Thursday she had lunch with Toni, who was also doing well, according to herself.

'I went for another jog last night, then felt so good that I called in to the gym and did a bums 'n' tums class. After that I was so bushed that I skipped dinner and went to bed with some hot milk, slimline of course.' She beamed at a startled Maggie as they sat at the counter in Aya nibbling bits of seaweed.

'Good grief, that makes the low-fat organic natural yoghurt I had for breakfast sound positively over-indulgent.' Maggie was only half joking.

'Be careful of too much dairy.' Toni popped a nori something-or-other into her mouth. 'And try to exercise at least three times a week if you can.' Toni was smiling kindly but it all sounded just a bit too virtuous.

'What are you on?'

'Nothing, just all geared up.' She grinned at

her friend. 'And you know what I'm like in determined mode.'

'It's the weekend I'm dreading,' Maggie moaned. 'The girls from work are all going out for an Indian tomorrow night and my mum's invited me for Sunday lunch. Maybe I'll skip brunch with you lot on Saturday, otherwise I'll definitely be up on Monday.'

'I think it's off anyway.' Toni was hoovering up a green salad. 'Pam has something on with the boys and I'm working all weekend. I need the overtime.' She made a face. 'Although I'm definitely looking for another job. I've had enough of old people, they're so aggressive sometimes and they moan constantly.'

'You're always saying that, yet you never do anything about it. Must be all those doctors who keep asking you out.'

'I wish. Even the visitors are mostly retired relatives.' Toni brushed an imagined speck off her immaculate suit. 'People our age are too busy to visit nursing homes. I haven't had a date in yonks. And most of my colleagues are married and they all envy me, imagining me whirring round town in totally impractical shoes, buying lilies and fig candles.' She sighed. 'Single women are supposedly ruling the world. *Sex and the City* has a lot to answer for.'

'I know. Flowers and candles only come out when visitors arrive, along with home-made organic pesto and drizzled lemon cake. Other-wise it's Waitrose Chow Mein and one of those instant fire-log things in front of *Property Ladder*, although,' she paused for effect, 'I do have a date lined up for next week.'

'Who?' Toni was delighted with this juicy bit of gossip.

'His name's Doug and I met him at the office thingy the other night. He's away until the weekend but said he'd ring me Monday.'

'Lawyer?'

'Accountant. Friend of one of the guys from upstairs. Cute though — at least I hope he is, those alcopops would make Johnny Vegas look appealing.' She grinned. 'And that's Johnny after fourteen pints and a kebab.'

'Well, I can't wait for the blow-by-blow account of the night.' Toni smiled at her friend. 'You deserve to find a really nice guy.'

'Thanks.' Maggie was touched. She knew that underneath Toni's couldn't-care-less exterior, she was as insecure as the rest of them. 'So, anything lined up even for Saturday night yourself?'

'Nope. All I've got to look forward to is tapioca pudding and bedpans for the weekend.' She sighed. 'I've decided singledom is overrated.'

11

Jack's editor had finally nailed him and made the long-overdue visit to Dublin. They were having dinner in the King Sitric, a local restaurant renowned for its spanking fresh seafood. They'd downed two G & Ts while they scanned the menu and were now happily tucking in to a bottle of Marques de Riscal Gran Reserva and Jack, at least, was feeling no pain.

'So, when are you going to bring up my deadline?' He decided to get it over with.

'Which one?' Robert Sorohan enquired mildly. He was a gentle giant of a man with red hair and a beard and a figure that showed he loved his grub.

'Ouch. You sure know how to hit where it hurts.' They were both smiling. 'I suppose I have been a bit off form lately.'

'It's when you don't return my calls or emails that I get slight chest pains.' The older man leant back and sampled the plummy red wine.

'So that's why you hot footed it over from London?'

'Well, you're one of our top authors. I thought maybe you were unhappy about something. Besides, if you've time tomorrow I'd like to talk to you about some more promotion for the paperback in January. Fancy a few days in the big smoke?'

'Christ, the Americans are looking for me to

go to New York as well.' Jack knew he'd have to get his act together. He'd been avoiding travelling as much as he could because of the kids.

'How's it going over there? Are they treating you well?'

'Yeah, they don't really hassle me much.' He grinned. 'Not like you.' The older man smiled and said nothing.

'Still hanging in the bestseller list, too, it's been months.' Jack ruffled his hair. 'My agent's had an offer from one of the studios. They want to buy the film rights. I was supposed to talk to him this week.' He sighed. 'I'm just not on top of things at the moment, Bob.'

'That bad, eh?'

'No, I shouldn't be complaining. It's what I've always wanted. Remember when I started off and I was freelancing for all the papers? I never imagined even half of this.' He stretched his arms behind his head and rubbed his neck. 'Success in the States, movie deals, publicity tours, publishing houses fighting to sign me, it's great. It's just that, on the home front, things have been tough. The kids are very demanding and the house closes in on me sometimes. I miss adult company. Sometimes I don't talk to anyone except the kids for days.'

'You need a holiday.'

'I need a hooker.'

'There are places where you can have both. Hop on a plane. You'd be in Amsterdam in just over an hour.'

'You know, in my younger days, the gag with

the lads on the rugby team was that I'd get up on the crack of dawn, but the truth is I've never really gotten off on one-night stands. It's the intimacy I miss. I like the laughs as much as the lust. Well, almost.' He'd forgotten how much he enjoyed the older man's company and it was ages since they'd talked properly.

'Jack, you're a good-looking guy and a major success story, you have it all, kid.' He took a cigar from his pocket and Jack shook his head at it. 'Damn this smoking ban anyway, it's uncivilized.' He was rarely grumpy and Jack laughed.

'It'll do you good. You smoke too much but if you really insist on shortening both our lives we can have coffee and brandy back at my place and you can indulge your filthy habit. Now, take that scowl off your face and tell me more about how wonderful I am.' Jack looked relaxed for the first time all evening.

'I mean it, you need to get out more, meet some young things, model types.' He waved his arms about. 'Look around you, there are plenty of women here who'd give their right arm to be sitting in my chair this evening.'

'And they're all wearing milk-bottle glasses or carrying white sticks.' Jack swallowed his drink. 'No, Bob, I've been out of the loop too long. And besides, I'm not going down that road again. Too complicated. I've got enough women in my life to keep me happy.'

'What about when they grow up and leave?'

'Jesus, gimme a break, they're barely walking.'

'It passes fast, let me tell you.'

'Where are your three now?'

'Jean is in Barbados, working for the same bank. Showing no signs of settling down. Paul is getting married to a vet from Sweden and Irene is in college in Edinburgh.'

'And how's Jo?'

'Still beating me up about my weight.' Jack knew Bob's wife well. 'You should come over for a weekend, we bought a holiday home in Padstow. Great restaurants. I'll introduce you to some lovely fillies.'

'What are you like?' Jack topped up their glasses. 'Seriously though, I know I need to knuckle down and finish the book. I have a girl starting next Monday. That should help a lot.'

'I'm not hassling you, son. You're one of our biggest earners. I know you'll deliver.'

'Eventually.' Jack laughed. 'Thanks, Bob. I know I've been a pain in the ass lately.'

'So, who's the girl?'

'A nanny, chosen by Kate.' The Englishman laughed knowingly. 'Bill thinks I'm lucky she's under fifty and weighs less than twenty stone.'

'What's she like?'

'I can't really remember. Seems nice enough. Kids liked her, so I'm willing to give it a shot. Otherwise Kate has a Scottish widow in tweeds and a riding crop standing by. Bill reckons it's going to get much worse if I don't give in.' Both men laughed, knowing it was true.

* * *

Telling her friend she was leaving had given Ellie a fresh perspective on life. She even managed to smile at the smug marrieds. Her new regime was going well, too. She had exercised most days, although admittedly she was cheating at sit-ups, but her days of snacking on Pringles were over. She'd managed to have four portions of fruit and veg each day, and was feeling very virtuous until one of her colleagues had casually mentioned that she didn't think two slices of carrot cake with cream-cheese icing strictly constituted two veggie portions. Still, she was drinking plenty of water and munching her way through diet this and low-fat that, so she felt cleansed and consequently much thinner overall.

The second WWW Club meeting was held later in the week and christened the weird wacky women night, because they were all feeling a bit giddy, thanks largely to the magnum of champagne Ellie had been given by one of the fathers as a thank-you for not calling the police when his ten-year-old darling — one of the after-school kids — had locked a younger boy in the boot of a car while its owner was changing a puncture. Luckily, it had been nothing to do with her, really. Both children had been collected and one father offered a hand to the mechanically challenged mother while their offspring amused themselves near by. Unfortunately their game of cops and robbers meant the younger of the two found himself gagged with his mother's cashmere sweater and dumped into the open boot and almost buried alive under golf clubs and a couple of cases of Château Margaux. The resulting hunt left everyone in a sweat until Ellie, just about to seek uniformed help, overheard the perpetrator on his mobile to his brother, informing him that he was owed ten euro for 'mission accomplished'.

As usual they had a great laugh at Ellie's expense, then tucked into the Moët and almost forgot the dreaded weigh-in until Toni called 'time please, ladies' in that voice she usually reserved for her more lecherous male geriatrics.

Overall, they decided that things were on the up. Pam had lost a pound and was delirious. Ellie had stayed the same and was a bit puzzled but her brain was fuzzy from fizz. Maggie was up one but giggled in spite of it and Toni had lost two pounds so she relented and let them off the lentil and split pea purée on rice cakes originally planned for dinner. In a flash, Ellie had ordered fish and chips and they made a Girl Guide pact to do better next week.

12

Ellie was nervous as she pulled into the driveway to start her new job the following Monday morning. Her initial concern was wondering if she should have worn a uniform. Some people preferred to have their domestics, nannies, housekeepers, au pairs, grannies — she'd been called everything — all in white, like a proper nurse. But those kind of things made Ellie itch, so she dressed simply in a plain navy skirt and white blouse. The outfit made Julie Andrews leaving the convent in *The Sound of Music* look like a sex siren.

She knocked gently and waited. By the sound of things all hell was breaking loose inside. When the door opened a very large dog threw himself at her and Ellie screamed and fell over. The beast had been strangely absent on her last visit, a clever move organized by Kate, she imagined.

A pair of glassy eyes looked down at her as she struggled to escape a pink slimy tongue, but not before an elasticated spit had given way and got her in the eye. Her carefully coiffed bun had come undone and there were paw marks on her blouse.

'Rashers, come here. I'm so sorry about this . . . ' Jack Bryant grabbed the monster's collar with one hand and sort of yanked her to her feet with the other. Ellie felt winded.

'I, eh, didn't realize you had a . . . pet.' She

eyed the gorilla-like face warily. In turn the dog warned her with a sullen look that he was higher in the family ranking than she could ever hope to be.

'Is it a problem? He stays outside most of the time, in fact — '

'He sleeps on my bed sometimes.' Jessie put paid to that particular lie instantly.

'Jess, go upstairs and finish getting dressed.' He spoke sharply to the little girl, who was wearing a very fetching pink bikini top and nothing else. Instantly her bottom lip trembled.

'Shall I help?' Ellie offered, and the child nodded, trying to decide whether to cry like a baby or behave like she thought a big girl should. The baby won out and a big tear ran down her face.

'I'm sorry, honey, I shouldn't have spoken to you like that.' Jack ruffled her hair and bent down to kiss her head.

'You've been like a bear all weekend and it's not fair.' Sam appeared and gave him a knowing look. Ellie decided she didn't want to be part of whatever was going on here. She held out her hand to the younger child, dropped her handbag and straightened her blouse and they headed off upstairs, leaving the other two to talk.

'So, what are you wearing today?' Ellie asked. 'Do they have a uniform in playschool?'

'No, silly.' Jessie was smiling. 'Only in big school. 'Cept when we're making paint, then we have to wear a apron.' She was pulling on her worn-out Barbie T-shirt and the matching bikini bottom and had upended most of her drawer looking for her favourite blue jeans.

'Are you going swimming today?'

'No.'

'Then why are you wearing your bikini, darling?'

'Cause . . . cause, just in case.'

'Do you like to swim?'

'Yep.' The tears were forgotten. 'Only we don't get to go much, only when Aunty Kate has time to bring us and she's very busy all the day long. But I still wear it cause that way someone might bring me.'

'Well, let me talk to Dad and see what we can do, OK? But I'm not promising anything.' Jessie had one foot in the jeans and almost fell over as she tried to clap her hands and pull on her trousers at the same time.

'Have you brushed your teeth?'

The answer was a display of crooked pearly whites.

'Let me see, open wide, yes they look spotless. OK, can you comb your hair or would you like me to do it?'

'Can you do a Barbie ponytail?'

'I think I could manage.'

'Great. Dad always gets the scrunchy mixed up with my hair and then it hurts when he pulls.'

'Well, you get me your favourite one and some slides and I'll be down in the kitchen, OK?'

'OK.' Jessie ambled away, happy now.

'Sorry about that. Not a great start, eh?' Jack was leaning against the counter top sipping a mug of coffee and looking pensive when Ellie arrived in the kitchen.

'She's fine. Not a bother.' Ellie rightly sensed that he was very unsure about her and didn't want to make him feel any more uncomfortable.

'How about you?' She wasn't sure what he meant and her eyebrows formed a question. He gestured towards the table. 'Rashers hasn't put you off?' Ellie looked warily and saw the dog properly for the first time. It had the ugliest, wrinkliest, saddest face she'd ever seen on an animal and she burst out laughing.

'How on earth did he get a name like Rashers?' She shook her head and looked at him again in amazement.

'The girls thought he looked like a pig, and they adore *Babe*. So, pig . . . bacon . . . rashers . . . yeah?'

'He's not a dog or even a pig, he's a donkey.'

Jack handed her a coffee and sat down, reaching out to stroke the bit that protruded upwards from the hammered-out face that had glued itself to the floor as if asking for forgiveness. 'Actually, I usually tell people he's called after that character in *Strumpet City*, sounds much more intelligent. But in your case I reckon there's no point in lying about anything. The girls have a nasty habit of telling it like it is.'

'Couldn't you have called him Fido or Rufus, even?'

'Believe me, I tried. The girls wanted Pig or Babe or Rashers and I wanted Rover or Lassie or something equally macho and for a while he answered to anything, which saved face for me in the park. Eventually, he decided he liked Rashers more, probably because I regularly forgot to feed him whereas the girls had to be handcuffed to stop them giving him beggin' strips — the latest dog treat — bacon-flavoured of course.' He grinned at her. 'I even offered to compromise but they didn't like Tyson either.'

'Tyson?'

''Cause he's a boxer?'

Ellie nodded. 'Can't say I blame them. That's a terrible pun and besides, I'd say there are a million Tysons out there, and I bet each owner thinks they're so original.'

'So you like Rashers?'

'Can't say I do, no. Wasn't there any alternative?'

'Oh yes, there were others up for consideration, but just try shouting 'come 'ere, P. Diddy' in the park of a morning and see where it gets you.'

Ellie spluttered her coffee at the image he conjured up. 'They can't be into pop stars yet, surely.'

'No, but Sarah, Kate's teenage daughter is, so they know all the names. I don't think they even know what a pop star is, but they're learning fast, that's all I know. Every day there's something new at school. It's exhausting trying to keep up.'

They chatted on and it helped break the ice until Jessie arrived with her 'hair box'.

Jack pretended to be engrossed in the newspaper as Ellie expertly created a miniature horse's mane and kept it all in place with the sparkliest clips in the box, but he kept an eye on the two of them and felt happy and sad and jealous at the same time. He realized all they'd missed since their mummy had left. And whatever faults she had, Lorna always made sure the children had the best of everything. They'd always had matching this and designer that. Now he only remembered they needed new things when Kate told him.

* * *

The girls were ready for school just in time and came to kiss their father. 'Will you be here when I get back? It's merely to run through a few things, just so I know your routine and what you expect . . . ' Ellie trailed off.

'Yeah, sure, I'm just going to jump in the shower.' Ellie nodded and they turned to go. 'Have you got your lunch box, Sam?'

'No, there was nothing in the fridge,' the child replied matter-of-factly and Ellie was immediately sorry she'd asked. Jack's face displayed a guilty look and it manifested itself as anger.

'That is not true, young lady, and you know it. There's ham and cheese and — '

'They're all past the sell-by date.' She was a budding nutritionist suddenly. 'And the cheese is green and the whole fridge smells and I'm not eating anything out of it.'

Ellie jumped in once again. This was going to be tougher than she thought.

'We can pick up something on the way for today.' She nodded encouragingly at them all. 'And you, young lady, can help me clean out the fridge later, so you'll have no excuse tomorrow.'

She smiled and herded the two girls outside as fast as she could.

'Oh Nora, I almost forgot, I'll get you covered to drive my car from today. I think I have all the details I need on your CV.' He scratched his head as if wondering where the hell that was.

'Why don't you just jot down the name of the insurance company and your policy number on a yellow stickie and I'll look after it as soon as I get a minute,' Ellie offered, but realized that offering was probably making him feel even more useless.

'No, it's fine, I'll do it,' he said brusquely, confirming her suspicion. She could have kicked herself. This was going to be like walking on eggshells. She had to remind herself that this family's mental health wasn't her responsibility. Clearly, there was a lot going on under the surface for the three of them. All she had to do was keep out of it.

13

When Ellie returned Jack was smiling. 'The insurance company assumed that Nora Simpson was my grandmother,' he told her when they met in the hall. He had showered and changed and smelt of lemon oil. 'You were nearly having to produce a doctor's certificate of mental competency, the way they were talking.'

'I can imagine. I really hate my name, you know,' she said without any preamble. 'And the medical cert might have been difficult. You see, every time I get a twinge I'm convinced that I've six months at most to live and I turn up at the surgery and try to persuade my doctor to break it to me gently, so he's highly suspicious of me.' Jack was amazed at some of the things she came out with, especially as they barely knew each other at all. She was the polar opposite to Lorna. It was going to take some getting used to.

'Last time, a pain in my gums was cancer of the mouth, as far as I was concerned.'

'What did he say?' Jack was trying not to look like he was a bit freaked by all this.

'I'd swallowed a filling in my sleep, apparently. He sent me to the dentist. But I then became convinced that the filling would perforate my bowel, I spent weeks watching my . . . actually, you don't really need to know this about me.'

'On the contrary, it's fascinating.'

'Oh believe me, I could bore you for hours.

The time before that my big toe hurt. I immediately thought of gout and hot footed it down to the doc for the second time in a week, if you'll pardon the pun.'

'What is gout, exactly?'

'No idea, but I'm almost sure I had at least a threat of it.'

'Anything else I should know about?'

'Lots, but you'll begin to recognize the signs soon enough, when you see me with my head stuck in the *Good Health Guide* or on my favourite website, which is www.ten-fatal-diseases-and-how-to-avoid-them.com or something similar.'

'Fascinating. I trust you won't pass on your, eh, slight neurosis to the children.'

'Oh no, don't worry, I've absolutely no sympathy for anyone else who's ill. Broken fingers, legs hanging off, they all get told to offer it up for the holy souls in purgatory. That's what my mother used to tell us.'

He was beginning to wonder what exactly he'd let himself in for here but decided to get his sister to do any further investigating. Luckily, the arrival of Mrs O'Sullivan forced them to change the subject.

More coffee followed and Jack hoped he wasn't going to be nabbed by one of them every time he put his head outside his study door. They were making lists at the kitchen table. What was it about women and lists? he wondered.

'So, Jack, if I look after the girls' rooms and clothes, do the shopping and organize something to eat for them, then I can help around the house if I've any spare time? Would that be OK?' Ellie asked him as he tried to sneak past.

'Yes, fine.' He looked distracted. 'Oh and, I should have mentioned, my study doesn't need any tidying. In fact, I'd sort of prefer it if you didn't go in there at all, if that's OK?'

'Sure, no problem.' She gave him a strange look.

'Thank you.' He wasn't going to explain any further.

'The Filipino we had for a while tidied his desk once and he was like a bear for a week.' Mrs O'Sullivan filled Ellie in as soon as Jack departed, coffee cup in hand.

'Just as well you told me. It's the sort of thing I do all the time.' The older woman looked puzzled. 'You know, convince myself that the other person is only trying to be nice — not giving me too much to do at the start. So then, I'd probably clean his office as a surprise some day.' She smiled and Mrs O'Sullivan decided she's better keep an eye on this one or there could be trouble ahead.

'No, definitely not. Trust me. I once tried to hoover and he nearly had a fit. Nobody else is allowed inside the door. It's the artistic thing, I think.' She sounded far more knowledgeable than she looked.

'What sort of books does he write?'

'Crime, the serious end, I think. My sister-in-law said there was a big article on him in The Times recently. He's very big in America, I believe. Been on the bestsellers list there five or six times. I keep hoping he'll give me one to read, I love blood and guts.'

Ellie was off in her own little world for the rest of the morning as she washed and ironed the girls' clothes, imagining herself featuring in one of Jack's stories, a sort of modern-day Cagney or Lacey.

* * *

In the afternoon, as soon as she and Jess had collected Sam from school, they all hit the supermarket. She was a sucker for letting them have what they wanted and was nervous about presenting Jack with the bill, so she made her only foolproof recipe for dinner — roast chicken with all the trimmings. It looked great, even if the roast potatoes were a little bit black around the edges and her minted peas gave new meaning to the term mushy.

'I've, eh, left you a plate in the oven. You were on the phone for a long time when I was feeding the girls and I didn't want to disturb you. I just wasn't sure if you like to eat with them or not?'

'Never disturb him when he's on the phone. He talks for hours and gets really cross if we ask him anything in the middle of one of his chats.' Samantha sounded like his boss. 'And he never eats with us, anyway, we always have ours in front of the TV.'

'That's not true.' Jack looked at her apologetically. 'I try to sit down with them but sometimes my publisher calls from the States, different time zones and all that, you know how it is . . . ' God he hoped he wasn't going to have to constantly explain himself, or worse still keep apologizing. He'd have to have a word with Sam later.

'I . . . eh, spent a fair bit in the supermarket.' It was her turn to look mortified as she handed him a receipt as long as the average toilet roll.

'That's fine, thank you.' He didn't even glance at it. 'How much do I owe you?' He was searching for his wallet.

'Em, two hundred and forty-two euros and sixty cents.'

His eyes widened. 'We needed a lot of basic cleaning products and I did get all the stuff for the girls' lunches for the week and . . . ' Ellie was pink and waffling.

'I expect I could have brought them to the Four Seasons every day for that kind of money.'

'What's the Four Seasons?' Jess always had a question.

'It's a well-known five-star hotel, darling,' her father told her, but he was smiling so Ellie guessed he wasn't too upset.

'We got new toothbrushes, and I got a Peter Rabbit bubble bath,' Jessie told him happily.

'And I got my first face cream.' Samantha was equally jubilant.

'Are you planning to wear make-up any day soon?' Jack was beginning to wonder if he should limit Ellie's little shopping expeditions, in order to avoid bankruptcy.

'I allowed them one treat each, cause it was our first time.' Ellie read his mind. 'Don't worry, I'm quite careful, usually.'

He didn't like the sound of that usually, for

some reason, but he was too tired to care tonight.

'I'll have cash for you first thing in the morning, if that's OK.' He was rifling through his wallet but a solitary ten-euro note seemed to be the extent of his bounty.

'Oh, no problem at all, Mr Bry . . . Jack. If it's OK with you I'll be off now. I've got a girls' club meeting . . . ' She was embarrassed. She hadn't meant to say anything.

'Like the Brownies?' Jessie was all ears.

'Sort of.' Ellie was backing out the door. 'See you all tomorrow, goodnight.'

'Night night, God bless was what my mum always said.' It was the first time Sam had mentioned her mother in ages and it gave Jack a bit of a jolt. Sam made it sound like Lorna was dead.

'G'nite, Nora.' Jess blew her a kiss and Ellie escaped.

★ ★ ★

'So, how was the first day?' was all Jack was interested in as soon as she'd gone.

'OK. She bought us new lunch boxes.' Sam was reserving judgement.

'I love Nora.' Jess wasn't.

14

The meeting that night was a short one because it was only a few days since their last weigh-in and besides, everyone was wrecked. They got the scales bit over with quickly and with the exception of Pam, who stayed the same and was greatly relieved because she'd had two pastries at lunchtime, the others had lost between half a pound — Maggie — and one and a half pounds — Toni. Pam was finding it hard to resist the goodies in the reduced section of the chiller cabinet in the supermarket every day. Today it had been those gorgeous frozen éclairs and she'd bought three boxes simply because they were a steal at 99 cents. The problem was they couldn't be re-frozen so she had until tomorrow to eat or bin twelve of them. Still, the boys had been demolishing them in front of the TV as she left.

Ellie had lost a pound and was delighted. She regaled them with stories of her first day in the new job, while they tucked into a delicious beef stir-fry with masses of vegetables courtesy of Maggie. No one looked too closely at the label on the jar of Ken Hom black bean sauce that had been tipped in at the last minute. There couldn't be many calories in beans and garlic, and besides they were all far too busy feeling virtuous as they sipped Evian and planned to go to a spin class later in the week, which might give them a boost before another dreaded weekend on a diet. Toni handed out leaflets as they left entitled 'What your Pooh Says About You' — a fascinating, according to her, study of thirty faeces in terms of colour, texture and stickiness. In spite of herself Ellie was glued to it as she sipped her herbal tea in bed later.

Apparently, yellow pooh said bad things about your liver, and sticky, mucousy ones weren't great either. They were meant to be nice and solid and chocolatey. Ellie vowed to check hers next time but she had them so rarely compared with most people that she knew she'd forget. A yellow sticky on the bathroom door reminded her to 'test the turd' but it didn't last long so she pinned the pooh article to the wall behind the loo and vowed to eat more fibre, having learnt that a really healthy person empties their bowels three times a day. Once a week was her norm.

⋆ ⋆ ⋆

Next day in the Bryant household was definitely easier. Ellie had a key, for one thing, so she didn't have to make an entrance. The girls were up and dressed and Jack was apparently in the shower. Ellie put on the kettle and helped them with cereal and brown toast and was making lunches when he arrived in the kitchen, wearing only an old pair of sweat pants and towelling his hair.

'Oh, sorry, I . . . didn't hear you arrive, I was just going to get dressed, I — '

'Daddy, you're very fat today,' Jess told him and it lessened the awkwardness.

'Thank you, darling, I needed to hear that. Please be every bit as kind to Nora.' He smiled at them, noticing she was trying to keep a straight face. Jessie ran over to poke him in the ribs.

'Your tummy is all wobbly.' Ellie kept her back to him and buttered bread furiously.

'What happened to that gym you used to visit?' Sam asked.

'They expelled me.'

'What's spelled?'

'They threw me out.'

'Why?'

'Cause I was too fat.'

'I love you really, Dad, you're cuddly.' Jess gave him a hug. 'So are you, Nora.'

'Thanks, I think.' Ellie patted the little girl's head. 'Although I'd rather be called something like slim or . . . trim . . . or curvy even.'

'You are curvy, you've got a big curve around your waist,' Sam told her and Ellie wasn't sure it was meant kindly.

'I'm off to put a shirt on before anyone starts to admire my bulging muscles,' Jack said as he made a hasty retreat.

When Ellie came back from school he was in the kitchen polishing off a bowl of muesli.

'I hope the girls won't frighten you off. Kids can be cruel, sometimes.' He was looking at her warily. But Ellie was completely laid back.

'There's virtually nothing I haven't heard already. One boy in the crèche told me recently he liked my bottom because it shook when I laughed, like it was laughing too.' Ellie made herself a cup of coffee. 'Speaking of bottoms, I read a fascinating article last night on . . . ' Ellie suddenly remembered who she was talking to. 'Actually, I won't go there, it's not a breakfast-time chat.'

'Please do.'

'No really I — '

'Go on, you can't start something like that then back off.'

'No honestly, it was nothing really, just, eh, pointing out that your, eh, number two says a lot about your health.'

'Your number two?' He was trying not to laugh.

'It's this job,' Ellie apologized. 'I constantly talk like a child. I told my father to stop watching the moo cows and let the nee naw pass last week when we were out in the car together.'

'Well, why don't you have that coffee in a plastic beaker and open a packet of choccy bikkies and explain what my . . . number two should look like?'

'Well, it should be a nice rich brown, solid and not too sticky.'

'Sounds like a chocolate mini roll.'

'Exactly.'

'And what are we comparing it to then?'

'Oh, I haven't got that far yet, but apparently some are quite yellow and runny and have a sticky, mucous-like substance.' Ellie was delighted to have someone to share her knowledge with. It was just like talking to a woman sometimes, when he let his guard down. She liked him.

'And how exactly do you check this out? Do you box it and take it to the pooh emporium?'

'No . . . actually, I'm not sure, but some places do request a sample if you go for a colonic, according to my friend Pam, who knows these things.'

'You've been for one?'

'No, but the girls in the . . . gang are . . . discussing it.'

'And do you know what's involved?'

'Well, apparently they put a tube up your . . . '

'Botty B?' It was Jess's favourite phrase at the moment.

'Ha ha. I was going to say back passage, actually. Then you feel a whoosh and, eh, it all comes out.'

'It just pours out? Ugh.' He sounded horrified.

'Through the tube, idiot. And the tube is partly clear . . . and they examine the . . . floaty bits.'

'Why?'

'To see what's stuck to the inside of your colon, I imagine. Lumps mean you're not chewing your food properly. You have to chew until it's liquid, apparently. Except for sweetcorn, which doesn't break down.' Ellie was feeling quite well-read.

'Sounds gross. Why would anyone want to have liquid fillet steak running round their mouth at dinner?' he wondered.

'Or liquid chips, all greasy,' Ellie marvelled.

The arrival of Mrs O'Sullivan put an end to their chat. Neither felt she'd appreciate the finer points of digesting and excreting food.

Ellie had a very productive morning, she tackled the girls' rooms with gusto. The older

113

woman tidied downstairs and scrubbed the bathrooms and looked quite flushed by the time she left a few hours later.

Ellie made herself a salad sandwich on brown bread, then made one for Jack as well. He hadn't appeared all morning so she assumed he must be ravenous. She knocked on the door of his study with a tray just before she went to collect Jessie.

'Yes?' He sounded distracted and she poked her head around the door.

'I thought you might like a sandwich, it's lunchtime and I was making one for — '

'Thank you.' He hopped up immediately and came to meet her. 'But really you shouldn't have, I don't expect you to.'

'No trouble.' She handed over the tray and looked around. It might as well have been midnight, the heavy curtains were closed and he was working by the light of a lamp, his desk covered with papers. The room smelt vaguely musty. It was a large room, with a great big period fireplace and high ceilings and as far as she could remember it faced the garden. She wondered how he could work like this.

He put the tray down on a side table and picked up the sandwich. 'What's this?'

'Salad.'

'This is salad?' He pulled out a beansprout and looked at it doubtfully.

'Well, I added bits and pieces, peppers, radishes, celery.'

'Any ham?'

'No, I was being extra healthy.'

'I see.' He closed the lid on the offering and

took a gulp of coffee. 'Well, thank you, Nora, I appreciate it, but, really, I'd actually rather not be disturbed when I'm in here working.'

'Fine.' That put her firmly in her place. 'I was thinking of taking the girls swimming this afternoon, if that's OK?'

'That'd be great. They love it. Thank you very much.'

She nodded, harmony restored. 'Would you like me to pull the curtains and let some — '

'No.' There was no negotiating that one. Damn, she hadn't meant to sound like a nosy mother.

'Sorry.' She headed for the door.

'Oh, and Nora . . . '

'Yes?'

'Don't forget to turn those beansprouts into dirty water in your mouth.' He was chewing a bite of bread ferociously and contorting his face and she laughed in spite of herself.

15

Maggie had a date on Thursday night with Doug the accountant, so she existed on soup and fruit on Tuesday and Wednesday and drank lashings of water. He was now known as Da — Doug, Accountant — it was always the same with the girls. They loved their codes. She'd seen him twice and she liked him. He was quite good-looking and had a lovely smile. And it felt nice to have a boyfriend.

She arrived home from work early, determined to go the whole hog tonight. She'd had a leg and bikini wax at lunchtime and it made her feel all sexy, or at least it would once the swelling had died down, and she'd bought herself a new lacy black thong. A bath overflowing with smellies was on the cards first, though. She needed it badly, she was absolutely exhausted — lack of energy from too little food, she suspected. She soaked for ages and then, afraid her hair would frizz, she got out and settled for masses of body butter and cucumber slices over her eyes while she lay with her feet up for ten minutes. The only problem was she promptly fell asleep and woke with fifteen minutes to go and a raging headache.

'Fuck, fuck, fuck, why do these things always happen to me?' she asked herself aloud. She couldn't find her new thong and had to make do with the cheaper black one she only ever wore to the gym, and her eye make-up was a bit shiny because of all the cucumber juice, but she struggled on regardless and was fixing her shoes when he rang the bell.

'Coming,' she shouted and dashed out. She wasn't quite ready for him to see the tiny house she shared with her sister, and anyway, as long as Karen was around, she wasn't risking bringing anyone back.

'Hi.'

'Hello there. All set?' He was standing by the door of his nice shiny black car. It wasn't a frivolous car, more a solid, family model, and she liked that. She also liked the way he held open the door and settled her in.

'How's your week been?'

'Fine, I've been out with clients doing their books all week. Nice to get away from the office. How about you?'

'Same boring old office for me, I'm afraid.' But she smiled as she said it. Really she liked her job, her boss was the youngest partner in the firm and he was decent to work for. Doug was taking her to a new vegetarian restaurant and she hoped it wouldn't be all brown rice and pulses because she was absolutely starving, so hungry she'd eat a horse and the jockey riding it.

She wondered later, as she gazed at the menu and wanted sweet-and-sour chicken balls instead of tofu burgers, if she hadn't been too compliant. That was one of her problems. She so badly wanted everyone to like her that she'd agree to almost anything, especially when it came to

117

impressing new boyfriends. Vegetarian restaurants weren't really her thing, but one of Doug's colleagues had urged him to go.

'They have a fab Mexican bean and vegetable soup.' He was looking all shiny and happy and she felt her stomach heave. It was going to be a good night, although she drew the line at another spoonful of soup.

'Nope, I'm going for the vegetable tacos with stilton,' she announced and he looked put out but quickly hid it.

'Is that OK with you?'

'Yes, I'd just thought we might share that as a main course but never mind, you have whatever takes your fancy.'

'Sure?'

'Certain.'

'I'm just so hungry and I had soup for lunch.' She smiled at him. 'I'd murder some wine, though. What'll we have?'

'Not for me, thanks, I'm training early in the morning.' Maggie knew he took his rowing very seriously. 'But you go ahead. Shall I order you a glass?' She wanted at least half a bottle but she opted for a glass of the house red and hoped it was a decent one. They had a great laugh and he complimented her on how well she looked and she smiled brightly at him, even though the cheap satin of her thong was beginning to rub and it was riding up her bum and cutting into her a bit. Still, she felt very girly in a thong, always did.

The food was delicious, although Maggie was slightly disappointed when he turned down dessert too, so she had another glass of wine with her coffee and decided it was good for her waistline.

He dropped her home at eleven and kissed her tenderly — their first real kiss, the others had only been pecks. She liked kissing him, so she wound her arms round his neck and he pulled her closer. Eventually he broke off and smiled at her.

'You're lovely.'

'So are you.'

'Are you free at all this weekend?' She liked the slightly formal way he asked.

'Sure, why?'

'I wondered if you'd like to come with me to my parents' house on Sunday afternoon? They're having a barbecue — just a small crowd — and my two brothers will be there with their wives.' She knew Doug was the baby of the family and instantly wondered if they'd like her.

'Yes, I'd love to come. Where do they live?'

'Clontarf. I could collect you about three.'

'Will I bring anything?'

'I dunno, maybe a cake or something.'

'A cake, eh, sure, I could probably . . . ' she was about to say 'buy a nice chocolate roulade or something' when he mentioned that 'mother loves home baking'.

This was slightly frightening but thankfully she knew Toni was a great cook and Pam was an expert at jazzing up the Tesco 'Finest' range and passing it off as her own.

They kissed again, this time even more passionately, and her lips were tingling when she waved him off. Shame about that bloody thong, it was strangling her.

★ ★ ★

Toni was working all hours and her nerves were frazzled. It was physically demanding and her mouth hurt from smiling all the time, especially when visitors were around. Hers was a very exclusive nursing home and all the 'children' were very anxious to ensure that their mums and dads had every convenience imaginable, although they rarely stayed long enough to find out.

'Mummy was asking if you're going to serve carrots again for lunch tomorrow, it's just that they give her heartburn. I was just wondering if she could have a little asparagus instead, perhaps?'

Toni could just see the chef's face. 'I'll certainly ask, although it is out of season at the moment.' She smiled brightly at the velvet hairband sitting on top of a pale pink twinset and pearls. All these women looked the same.

'But I saw some in Superquinn yesterday and she loves it with a little hollandaise sauce.'

'We do try only to eat foods in season and which are locally grown,' and that asparagus you saw was local only in Zimbabwe, she didn't add. 'And organic, of course, where possible.' It was the standard answer and one they found very difficult to argue with.

'Yes of course. I understand.'

'Perhaps you could cook it for your mum as a

special treat next time you take her home for Sunday lunch?' Toni was all smiles, knowing that this particular family never did more than pop in once every three weeks for five minutes to throw their weight around.

'Oh, I'd love that, darling.' The mother was beaming. 'Besides I don't want to bother the chef, he's Chinese and he carries a cleaver.' She winked at Toni.

'Well, let's see how we go, shall we?' End of conversation.

Toni was becoming an expert at it but by Friday she was about to kill someone, although she did her best with the Rolex-watch type who stopped her just as she was about to finish her shift.

'Excuse me, miss?'

'Yes, can I help you?' She pretended she'd never seen him before but she knew him well, had spotted him driving a brand-new Jag at high speed through the car park on one of his occasional visits last week. He'd almost knocked down poor Miss Thompson, who was bent over smelling the last of the sweet peas. She knew he fancied her, he'd been finding more and more excuses to corner her over the last few weeks.

'I'm afraid my father is anxious about his new Pringle sweater. He sent it to the laundry last week and it hasn't come back.'

'Well, I'll certainly check and see where it's got to.'

'I'm afraid he's quite upset. It's the second time this has happened recently. The last one was cashmere and they're very expensive.' He grinned at her. 'And he keeps giving me a tenner to go out and buy him another one. If you could rescue this one it might be cheaper to shower you with diamonds.' He winked. 'And I'll be forever in your debt.'

Toni bit her lip. He could be very charming when he wanted to be. She'd seen him with one of the juniors the other day. It was the wealth-and-power thing, she decided now. He was an Irish version of Donald Trump, she just knew it. 'Actually I'm just about to go off duty but I'll have one of the assistants go through the laundry room first thing in the — '

'Couldn't you just do a quick check now? He's worked himself up into quite a state and I'm not happy leaving him like that.' He smiled at her, knowing he'd get his own way in the end.

Toni could smell the alcohol, although it was barely six thirty in the evening. She was too tired to argue. 'Fine. If you'll wait in your father's room I'll — '

'Can't I come with you? I've got an appointment in half an hour.'

In the pub, I'll bet, Toni thought. 'I'm afraid our insurance doesn't cover visitors in the cleaning areas.' Another standard answer. 'I'll be as quick as I can.' She smiled coldly, leaving him with no choice.

She made herself a cup of strong coffee just to annoy him, even though her shift was over and it was probably inconveniencing her more than him. She checked the news headlines and sauntered towards the laundry room. It was hot and stuffy and she was not a bit happy. The blasted Pringle or whatever was nowhere to be found.

'I'm afraid I can't easily locate it, I'm sorry.' Toni popped her head round the corner of the room. 'I will leave a note for Anna, who knows all about these things, and she'll drop in to see you in the morning.' She smiled sweetly at the old man and ignored the younger one pacing the small corridor.

'That's OK, my dear. I'm not really sure whether I gave it in for cleaning anyway.'

'Have you checked your closet?'

'My son has.'

'It's just we've no record of it, as far as I can see, which is unusual.' Toni felt a migraine coming on. 'What colour did you say it was again, Mr Thornton?' She was rummaging in his closet.

'Dark grey.'

'Would this be it, by any chance?'

'By George, it would. Gordon, I thought you said you checked?'

'I did, but you told me it was fawn.'

'No, I threw that one out years ago.'

'Sorry.' His smile was angelic.

'Please forgive my son, he's just so busy . . . '

'No problem at all.' She was out of here.

'Thank you very much, I'm so sorry to have taken up your time, it's just, he was getting agitated and I'm never sure . . . what to do.' Add helpless little boy where women are concerned to that list, Toni thought. He was so smooth she felt like throwing up all over his Armani suit. Although secretly she liked the attention.

'Pleasure.' She shot him a 'don't try that with me again' look and made her exit. He followed her.

'I was wondering, eh, Toni,' he read her name badge, pointedly. It was pathetic, he'd known her name for weeks. 'You mentioned you were off duty and I'm just meeting a couple of people in the Berkeley Court. Would you like to join us, by any chance?'

'I'm sorry, I have another appointment.'

'Some other time, then?'

'Maybe.'

She smiled sweetly and sashayed off down the corridor, treating him to a good old bum swagger.

'Give me your number and I'll call you to arrange,' he called after her.

'I have yours on your father's chart. Why don't I call you?'

'Eh, better take my mobile, I'm not often home.' He looked like he'd played this game many times.

'Don't worry, I'll leave a message with your wife.'

16

Pam was working late on Friday night, something she normally detested. But tonight was OK, the desk had been quiet all day and she was off for the next three days. Bliss. Their particular branch was now open twenty-four hours and Pam lived in fear of being asked to work nights. According to Vera — their cleaning lady who knew everything and should have retired ten years ago except she claimed she was still only sixty — the place was full of drunks and weirdos. 'Who else would go shopping for toilet cleaner when they could be tucked up in bed drinking hot chocolate and listening to Val Joyce on *Late Date*?' she asked no one in particular as she mopped the loo floor.

'Insomniacs?' Irene from toiletries suggested.

'They're very strange too, don't you think, love?' Vera mopped Irene out of the way. No one could think of an answer to that, really.

Anyway, Pam refused to worry about anything tonight as she sat enjoying her last coffee break of the day with a couple of the other girls. They were telling Pam how great she was looking. Every one of them received daily updates with a blow-by-blow account of the WWW Club.

'You know, in a way I think it was turning forty that did it,' Pam told them. 'For a while, I felt really old, started buying big jumpers, the sort that make you feel special simply because they cost a fortune and then have to be treated like purebred sheep. You know the kind — the ones that have to be hand washed in soap flakes, wrapped in cotton wool and dried flat away from direct sunlight then reshaped while damp and ironed on the reverse.' They all nodded, although none of them had a clue what she was on about. 'Then, I couldn't decide what to do with my hair, was it too long, too curly, too coloured? I mean, there's a very thin hair line between funky and Cher.' The others all sympathized. This they knew about.

'Well, we should all take a leaf out of Dot's book,' Marjorie, a glamorous, if slightly too denim clad, fifty-something told them.

'What's she done now?'

'She's left her husband and handed in her notice.' Marjorie was delighted that she had the goss first.

'No!'

'Yep, apparently she's bought herself a two-carat diamond ring and is studying to teach Pilates. She looks amazing. Did you see her this morning, wearing no bra and a mini-skirt?'

'But she's forty-three.' Eileen from the deli counter was horrified. 'It takes me all my time to keep my boobs from looking like an extension of my waist and that's only with the help of a gel-filled bra.'

'And you all know how long it takes to recover from a night on the town, never mind an exercise class.' Pat from bleaches and polishes was on a roll.

'Well, apparently she's having an affair with

Mr Ahern from wines and spirits.' Marjorie delivered the final bit of juice.

'I don't believe you, he's barely thirty!'

'So what? More power to her.' Pam was thrilled. 'What exactly are we saving ourselves for, girls? I still regret the fact that I turned down Dave the fishmonger at the office bash last year.'

'Ugh, he smells of smoked cod.'

'I could have pegged my nose, he has a great body, works out every second day and is a kick boxer.'

'All I know is it's getting harder. I'm now opting for the dearest moisturizer in the chemist and I've been buying all those good one-piece underwear things in the sale in Arnotts recently.'

They all agreed you needed all the help you could get once you hit the big 4-0 and were still moaning as they prepared to finish their shift. Pam decided to give that exercise class another go and was feeling really quite pleased with herself as she paid for some salady things and headed home at ten.

'Dad called.' Andrew barely looked up as she put away the few healthy bits in the fridge.

'Oh?' She was immediately on the alert.

'He wants you to call him.'

'Why?'

'Dunno.' He'd already lost interest.

★ ★ ★

Pam changed into her comfy dressing gown, made a cup of tea and wondered whether to put it off till the following day. Talking to her ex-husband rarely cheered her up. Stephen Fortune only asked to speak to her when he wanted something. After they'd separated five year ago he'd moved to New York where he had a trendy apartment and an even trendier girl-friend. Ronnie or Minnie or something. Pam called her Winnie, actually, Winnie the Whinger, because any time she answered the phone she sort of whined like an animal in pain. She also talked through her nose.

After a long drawn-out few months all those years ago they'd reached a compromise about the boys, greatly helped by the fact that he'd moved abroad. He paid regular maintenance, although not a huge sum, and visited twice a year. He called every couple of weeks and she rarely spoke to him but she knew he kept in touch with the boys by email. She supposed it worked, although she was still bitter that he'd opted to get out of the home suddenly because he felt 'restless and hemmed in', leaving her with two boys — one just about to start school — and a hefty mortgage. Mind you, when she found out he'd had two affairs under her nose she almost kicked him as far as America. Her confidence had never really recovered, especially as one of his affairs had been with a so-called friend. Still, at least she didn't have anyone breathing down her neck to lose weight any more, although come to think of it, Toni was doing a good job of it with all of them these days.

Checking the time in New York, she dialled quickly, determined not to let him spoil her precious weekend.

'Hi, it's me. You were looking for me?' They had never been into small talk.

'Yeah, hi. How are you?'

'Fine. Tired. Just in from a long day.' He got the message.

'I was just wondering if the boys could spend Christmas with me this year?'

'What?'

'Well, they've never been over and I have a long break and they have two and a half weeks off school.' So they'd already discussed it.

'You've talked to them about this? Without checking with me first?' She could feel her voice straining.

'Calm down.' She hated it when he said that, he'd been doing it since the day they married. 'I only asked them about their time off, nothing else.'

'They've always spent Christmas with me.' End of story.

'I know that, it's just that I miss them and I realize they're growing up fast and I . . . I want to be part of their lives.'

'What you mean is, they're easier, less hassle, more civilized.' She didn't like her voice. 'You can show them off now.'

'Why the hell do you always have to start a row?'

'They're not going.'

'I think you should at least discuss it and see what they think.'

She knew she had no choice. If she didn't he would.

'I'll think about it.'

129

He took a deep breath. 'Thank you.' Rhonda had warned him to stay cool. 'It'd be a great experience for them.'

'I'll call you next week. No, on second thoughts you call me in a couple of days. I'm fed up with huge phone bills.'

'Fine.'

'Bye.'

'Thanks. Bye.'

Pam felt tension grip the back of her neck and wandered slowly upstairs to run a hot bath. She'd always known he'd want them sometime.

17

'Anyone seen the column today? My local shop was sold out of papers.' Ellie made a face. 'I hate it when I miss my little breakfast treat on Saturdays.'

'Wasn't in today. It was someone else writing about reindeer meat. At the bottom it said he was 'away'. God, I hate brown toast. It's like nibbling on the sole of a shoe.' Pam was not in a good mood.

'What's up?' Toni was tucking into fresh fruit with low-fat organic crème fraîche. They were having a healthy brunch instead of lunch, on their way to a 'toning without moaning' class.

'Stephen wants the boys to go to New York for Christmas.'

'Wow, great for them.' Maggie, usually so tactful, took one look at her friend's face and backtracked. 'I mean, it would be educational, I suppose, although it never did anything for me at that time of year. All those crowds and slushy pavements.'

'How do you feel?' Ellie asked warily.

'Pissed off, to be honest. Suddenly they're becoming civilized and he wants to show them off.' She was getting into her stride, they could feel it. 'He's hardly seen them over the last five years. Where was he when Paul had chickenpox and Andrew was wearing braces and being bullied at school? Between the legs of the fucking

131

whining hyena, that's where.' It was classic Pam fighting talk.

They all laughed nervously.

'Speaking of loud-mouthed, over-dressed types with new money and fat cigars . . . ' Toni intervened when no one said anything else.

'Stephen is not loud-mouthed and he doesn't smoke,' Pam had no idea why she was defending him.

'No, I was talking about Gordon Thornton. Actually, I'm being unfair, he's not that loud and his clothes are impeccable, but he's definitely new money. Anyway, he tried it on again last night. This time he even took the trouble to read my name off my badge.' Toni decided it might be a good time to change the subject. Besides she got bored with Pam's troubles sometimes.

'G & T? Again? Do tell.' Maggie used their code name, they knew all about fabulously rich Gordon the gregarious.

'Actually, I'm beginning to secretly admire him. He's got balls, I'll say that for him. Didn't even flinch when I said I'd call him at home.'

'I'd say his wife is too doped up on pills and gin to even realize what he's up to.' Ellie had a thing about him and he'd been giving Toni the eye for months now. They both seemed to enjoy the sparring.

'How can you possibly make an assumption like that about his wife?' Pam was astonished. 'You've barely heard of him, let alone her.'

'I know, you're right, I'm just being a bitch.' Ellie felt guilty. 'I just don't like the sound of him.' She turned to Toni. 'And you, madam, are enjoying this game far too much for my liking.' She gave her friend what she hoped was a disapproving-mother look.

'You know something, I haven't had a date for months and I could maybe put up with him if he was dynamite in bed and bought me fabulously expensive presents.' Toni had a glint in her eye.

'You wouldn't!' Maggie wasn't sure whether she was horrified or jealous.

'Why not? I know he's not 'the one' but I'm getting pretty fed up waiting around.'

'But it'd be like getting paid for sex.' Ellie didn't like the image it conjured up. Besides, she still felt sure Gordon was fat and slimy and lecherous.

'Listen, is there anyone here who hasn't had sex for no reason at some point in their lives and regretted it afterwards?'

'Nope.' Pam was first to admit.

'But at least there was some connection at the time . . . ' Ellie didn't want to believe otherwise.

'A bottle or two of wine was the only connection, I'd say, so don't go all self-righteous, Ellie. Anyway, I like him, he's funny, charming and rich and at the moment I'm only talking about dinner.'

'And married,' Maggie added.

'Well, I'm only in this for the short term, if I'm in it at all. His wife is not losing anything because of me. And remember, I'm not the one doing the chasing.'

'Just don't get hurt.' Ellie knew her friend really wanted a relationship.

'I won't. Anyway, I'm bored with him. What

about your great romance with Da, Maggie, how's that going?'

'Good, I'm going to meet his parents tomorrow afternoon. Speaking of which, fuck, I need a cake that looks as if I made it myself. Apparently, Mummy loves homemade buns.'

'Buy an apple tart and I'll disfigure it for you — we can dredge it with too much icing sugar and burn a few apple bits and stick them to the sides.' Pam had abandoned the toast and was eating a croissant. 'But, more importantly, what's he like?'

'Really nice, actually. A bit old-fashioned in a good sort of way. Very kind, good sense of — '

'I meant in bed.'

'Mind your own business.'

'So you haven't done it?'

'No, and that's what I like. He's taking it easy and it suits me.'

'Are you sure he's not gay? He doesn't want sex with you and he loves his mammy, that sounds familiar.'

'Don't be ridiculous. We've had some great snogs.'

'Has he put his hand up your jumper even?'

'What's all this about, you shower of bitches? Get off my case. I told you, he's a gentleman and I'm enjoying it.'

'Good for you. I wouldn't mind a nice reliable guy myself for a change.' Ellie sounded wistful. 'I'm fed up spending Saturday nights on the couch watching *The American President* or something similar.'

'Ugh, isn't that Michael Douglas? What a jerk.'

'Yes, but Annette Bening is great. Imagine having a date with the President of the United States, and she's so down-to-earth and not at all, you know, sexy or especially attractive.'

'She's a dog,' Pam said with her mouth full.

'If she's a dog, then the rest of us are alligators. I think she's quite pretty,' Maggie said. 'Mind you, the movie sucks.'

That started a huge discussion about dates and their lack of anything vaguely resembling one and Toni reminded them yet again that whoever lost half a stone first got three blind dates, which cheered them all up except Pam, who knew she'd no hope of getting there.

The exercise class was horrific. It was full of high-bottomed thirty-somethings in designer gear wearing no make-up and glowing. The girls felt like spitting. The instructor was a cute guy, though, and they all cheered up until he took off his track-suit jacket and opened his mouth. They couldn't decide which was worse, his 'I love Mum' tattoo or his accent. His gold identity bracelet and signet ring didn't help, either. 'Right, yis are all very welcome.' That was the only Dublin bit they heard, and it was very Dublin. 'Yo, y'all, let's tone those tums and get with the groove.' He put on sunglasses and hit a button and 50 Cent blasted out at 1,000 decibels. 'I said shake it, sisters.' He did what appeared to be an updated version of Michael Jackson's Moonwalk and clapped his hands. 'Can you hear me, Dublin?' He pretended he had a mic in his hand. 'I said, can you heaaaaaaar me?'

Ellie looked around. There were about ten other people in the room and they were all going along with this.

'Kick it out, two three four. Slap your thigh, two three four. Come on, y'all at the back, shake your booty, I said shake it, baby.' They were mortified, but they shook it.

Fifty minutes later he reverted to type. 'Deadly buzz. See yis all again. Tanx.' He blew a bubble with his grey gum. Pam almost fell over in her haste to get to the changing room. The girl on her left had barely broken a sweat.

Once they'd recovered they were laughing so much that they just had to go for more coffee and bitch about it all, as usual.

★   ★   ★

Ellie chilled out on Sunday, although calling in to see her mum and dad couldn't be termed relaxing. Toni phoned her on her mobile just as she was leaving.

'Where are you? I was going to drop round. I got a present of some moisturizer that I thought you might like.'

'Another dead housemate?' Ellie was referring to the nursing home.

'Yeah. I must look as if I have really bad skin. The families keep giving me anti-aging creams as thank-you presents. This one's Clarins and I know you use it.'

'Great, thanks.' Toni was always sharing. 'Only I've just left my folks and I'm on my way to see Olga.'

'Oh, how did that go?' Toni had often wondered how kind, scatty Ellie had survived growing up in a house full of misery gutses.

'Well, Dad's in great form, which is something. Mum is fighting with everybody — the ESB because she says her electric meter is a fire hazard, Bord Gáis because she's convinced they're robbing her with charges on her gas fire, and she has about ten other items on her hit list. Sadly for me, she insists on telling me about them in great detail each time I phone or visit. After about an hour Orla called, so I made my excuses. They were having a good moan together over a cup of tea and planning revenge on some poor unfortunate gas fitter as I left.'

'You're one lucky girl, Ellie.'

'How d'ya mean?'

'You could so easily have ended up like the rest of your family.' They both laughed.

'Well, Claire's not so bad. Mind you, she escaped early and went to London so I never really got to know her. And growing up she was always into her music, so I remember going off by myself all the time to play with my dolls, anything to escape Mum and Orla's constant nagging. It's no wonder I blurt out everything I'm thinking these days. I spent years with no one to talk to, or at least no one to answer me back.'

'Well, when I see how you could have turned out, I'm very glad. No offence,' Toni added quickly, not wanting to upset Ellie.

'None taken. Well, it should be easier in Olga's

house, at least. Don't suppose you'd like to join me?'

'Yeah, OK, although I can only stay an hour or so.'

'Suits me. I'll swing by and pick you up and I can collect the Clarins.'

★　★　★

Olga was delighted to see them and Toni brought a cuddly toy for Rudi.

'Antonia, so nice. Come in, come in.' She was in good form. Toni always cheered her up. Olga told Ellie once that she'd never met anyone so exotic.

'Olga, I hope you don't mind, but I brought you some things I picked up in a sale recently. They were all wrong for one reason or another and generally you can't return the reduced stuff.' The Russian woman seemed really pleased and tried everything on. Rudi played away happily and the gas fire was lighting and they ordered in Chinese — Ellie's treat. Toni only had a starter and a vegetarian one at that, and left shortly afterwards to get a taxi into town.

'I like your friends. They make me smile,' said Olga.

'Yes, they're great. You should come out with us for brunch some Saturday.' No matter how many times Ellie suggested it Olga always made an excuse and she was never sure if it was only the money aspect — Ellie had told her often enough that they normally went to little cafés that served snacks as well as full meals. Olga just

138

didn't seem to want to make the effort.

'Are you OK? You seem a bit . . . off form lately?'

'Yes, I'm just tired. Once I am feeling stronger I will come, I promise.' It was always the same comment lately, although Olga looked as strong as a horse.

'Are you still feeling down generally? Although, you do seem in great form today?' Ellie asked.

'Physically I am fine; mentally I am fragile.'

'Well, getting out might help. And don't forget I'm around to babysit, if you fancy a night out with other people.'

Olga hugged her. 'You are a true friend.' It wasn't the first time she'd said it and it always made Ellie feel guilty that she wasn't doing more.

★ ★ ★

Ellie was in bed by ten with only a cup of cocoa for company and felt rested and bright on Monday morning, although she couldn't help feeling her weekends were lacking in excitement. Maybe there was something in Toni's philosophy after all. She could do with a bit of the buzz that a new relationship brought herself, although even as she thought about it Ellie realized she didn't have the balls for an affair.

18

Jack was whistling in the kitchen and the hound was nowhere to be seen, a good start to the week. The girls jumped up when they saw Ellie. Jessie hugged her and Sam wanted to show her the new dress her Aunty Kate had bought her.

'Wow, it's so pretty. Will you try it on for me after school?' Sam nodded shyly, loving and hating the attention.

'Cup of coffee?' Jack asked, pouring one without waiting for her answer.

'Thanks, just a half. I'm trying to cut back on my caffeine intake.'

'Listen, next week there'll be a survey saying it's good for you and water is bad. Just enjoy life, that's my philosophy.'

'So I see.' She eyed the empty wine bottles lined up beside the waste bin.

'Oh yeah, Kate and Bill came round for Sunday lunch. It sort of went on a bit. I actually cooked a roast, can you believe it? I must get to the bottle bank later, though.'

'Want me to do it? We pass one on the way to Sam's school.'

'Sure, great. There are rather a lot, mind you. There's a crateful on the patio.'

'I'm a big girl. Besides, with my friends I have to hire a dumper to get to the bottle bank.' She grinned and he smiled back.

'Thanks.'

Later that morning, Ellie had an hour to spare so she decided to hoover and polish his bedroom to give Mrs O'Sullivan a hand. It was the same as his study, heavy curtains pulled, books and newspapers everywhere and it had an airless, stuffy sort of smell, though it was not unpleasant. She'd sniffed far worse at the gym. She threw open the huge window and changed the bed, then tidied away his clothes and emptied the overflowing laundry basket. It felt a bid odd to be going through his clothes, though, so she merely gave the room a quick vacuum and polish and left it to air.

In the afternoon she took the girls to the park and they played tennis and bought ice-cream, even though it was quite a chilly late-autumn day. As they fell in the door later, laughing and teasing, Jack was coming down the stairs with a face that would turn milk sour.

'Hi, Dad. We had a great day. I beat Nora at tennis.' Sam didn't notice anything was wrong.

'I had a nana ice-cream.' Jess was determined not to be outdone.

'I bet you get a pain in your tummy later.' He tickled her and she screamed and curled up in a ball on the floor.

Ellie headed for the kitchen and the mutt eyed her suspiciously. He doesn't like me, she thought. 'It's mutual,' she hissed as she passed and then felt guilty and decided to try and bribe him with a few treats when no one was watching later.

The girls headed upstairs to change and Ellie started their dinner, knowing they'd be ravenous from all the fresh air.

Jack followed her into the kitchen. 'Is something wrong?' she blurted out as soon as Sam and Jess had gone, knowing something bloody well was.

'You were in my bedroom.' He might as well have said 'you nicked my granny's antique jewellery'. The air of gravity was about the same. Damn, he'd got her again, she should have checked. It was just that most women were so grateful if you did anything you hadn't been asked to do. She was learning that men were different.

'Don't worry, I avoided the porn mags.' It was the wrong thing to say but she desperately wanted to get back to the easiness of this morning. He looked taken aback, then looked as if he might see the funny side but just as quickly changed his mind.

'I don't like anyone going near my personal space.'

'I just thought it neede — '

'You should have checked with me first.'

'Look, we have to lay down some ground rules here. I feel like I'm walking on eggshells. You said not to go near your study but you never said anything about your bedroom.'

'I wasn't expecting you to clean my room. Mrs O'Sullivan normally does that kind of thing.' He clearly wasn't happy.

'I was only trying to help out.' Ellie felt frustrated. 'Mrs O's been feeling tired lately.'

He ignored that. 'I don't like people prying. I'm a very private person.'

'Well, I apologize but I wasn't to know. Besides, all I did was change the bed and clear out the laundry basket.'

'I'm quite capable of looking after myself. I told you that at the start. I've been doing it for a long time. Even my wife never had to wash my boxers.'

'That bad, eh?' It was her second mistake. His eyes narrowed and she didn't like the look he gave her. She could feel her face warming up nicely.

'Please don't go near my bedroom or my study without my permission.' It was icy cold.

'Fine, I understand. Sorry again.' They both turned away at exactly the same moment and he slammed the door just as she banged a pot.

The atmosphere was still as frigid an hour later when Kate dropped by unexpectedly.

'Hi, Eleanora, nice to see you again. How are you settling in? Are they driving you nuts?'

'No, it's fine.' Ellie was genuinely glad to see the other woman. 'Can I get you a coffee?'

'Love one, thanks. So, girls, what did you have for dinner?'

'Fish.' Sam made a face.

'I hate fish but Nora does it and it's lovely,' Jess told her. 'And we were allowed waffles, my favourite.' She finished her milk and tottered off in an old pair of high heels she'd found, after bringing her plate over to the sink to Ellie.

'Thanks, hon.' Sam followed. 'Do you two want to watch a video?' Ellie asked the older child.

'No. I'm drawing a picture of schoolgirls for

Dad. He likes short skirts.'

'And when did he tell you this?' Kate was smiling.

'He didn't. It's a surprise. Georgia and me heard him talking to the . . . Nora, what do you call the man from England with the red hair?'

'His editor?' Ellie had no idea.

'Yep. He said girls in short skirts do it for him every time. Georgia said that means he likes them.' She wandered off, crayons in hand.

Both women were still smiling seconds later when Jack came into the kitchen.

'Oh, hi, sis. Didn't hear you come in. What's up?' Kate sensed the atmosphere immediately, Ellie positively bristled when she heard his voice.

'Nothing. Just passing and wanted to say hello to Eleanora. Make sure you weren't working her too hard.'

'Not a chance, although she might be doing that all by herself.' It was an obvious reference to his bedroom. Well, he could rot in it from now on.

'We're both still getting used to each other, working out a routine. I expect it will take a while.' Ellie's smile could have curdled the milk, but she was not going to slag him, no matter how fed up she was with his moods today.

'Well, I've never seen the kids so relaxed and I've never, ever known them to eat fish, so well done you.' She winked at the younger woman.

'Thanks.' She turned to Jack and smiled sweetly. 'It's fish pie. I've left you a portion ready to be heated up.'

'Thanks. I'll probably work late tonight anyway.'

144

'Got a lot on?' Kate was still wondering what had happened between them.

'Yeah, my editor's being a right pain this week — emails flying.' He looked tired and stressed. 'Actually, that's not fair, it's my fault. Having missed my deadline I'm now taking almost as much time again with the edit. I'd be tearing my hair out if I was dealing with me.'

'Is that the editor who likes chatting to you about girls in short skirts?'

'What?' He looked bemused. Kate explained and he smiled. 'Oh that, just typical male fantasy, I'm afraid.' He made an excuse and left.

'So what's up?'

'Nothing at all.'

'He's obviously said something to upset you.'

'No, really.' Ellie was not about to bad-mouth him, no matter how much she wanted to burst into tears at that moment. Must be PMT. 'As I said, we're just getting used to each other. It must be difficult having a stranger come and go every day.'

'Look, Eleanora, I . . . '

'Please, call me Ellie.'

'Ellie, I know my brother. He's very private and he can be a bit brutal with words sometimes, but I promise you he's a good man and — '

'Please, Kate.' Ellie didn't want to hear this. 'It's fine, really. Just one of those days. By tomorrow it'll all be back to normal.'

'I'd be happy to talk to him if he's upset you.' Ellie shook her head fiercely. 'It's all to do with Lorna, I'm afraid. She rode roughshod over

145

everyone, including him, and now he's become a bit paranoid.'

'Listen, I'd really rather just forget it, if that's OK. Talking about it is just turning it into something major, and it's not, honestly. I just overstepped the mark earlier, that's all. I'm still learning.' She smiled weakly. 'More coffee?'

'No thanks, I'd better be off. Monsters to feed. Promise you'll call me if things get on top of you?'

'Sure.'

'OK then. Talk soon. Bye.' On her way out she put her head round the study door but stayed where she was, anxious not to disturb him. 'I'm off.'

'OK. Everything all right?'

'You tell me.'

He sighed. Women, they always ganged up on him. 'What's she been saying?' he asked reluctantly.

'Absolutely nothing. And I really tried, you know me.' She took a step into the room and closed the door. 'Look, Jack, she's exactly what you need. The kids love her, they've been to the park, played tennis, had fish for dinner, for God's sake.' She sounded slightly exasperated. 'Also, she seems like a really nice, ordinary girl. What more can you ask for? Your dinner is made and the kitchen is spotless.'

'Look, I don't care about the goddamn kitchen and I care even less about having food prepared for me.' He made an effort to tone down his voice. 'A bit of privacy would be very nice, though,' he mumbled.

'So that's it. I knew it. What did she do?'

'Nothing, forget it.'

'OK.' She sighed. 'Please, Jack, give her a chance. Talk to her, tell her what's acceptable and what's not.'

He said nothing so she made her exit. 'You can be a bit odd about things sometimes, you know.' He didn't answer and his face looked set again.

'Bye then.'

'Bye.'

When he returned to the kitchen all ready to call a truce Ellie was ready to leave for the evening. Her goodnight was curt. Jack looked around. Kate was right. The kids were shiny happy people and the place was spotless. There was even a loaf of brown bread cooling on a wire rack. He nooked the pie and reluctantly admitted it was delicious. Damn, he was going to have to grovel in the morning.

★   ★   ★

Ellie bought herself two jam doughnuts in Superquinn on the way home, and ate them in the car. How could a day that had started so well end up so miserable? She hated tension and as usual she'd stuck her two big feet right in to lighten things. She couldn't believe she'd made that stupid joke about porn mags. Or boxers. She groaned

Well, she'd just have to tread more carefully where he was concerned. She'd dump all his clean clothes in a laundry basket first thing in the morning and leave it outside his door. She

147

just realized she'd forgotten to close the windows in his room. Now he'd have something else to moan about.

She couldn't get a parking space when she arrived home, which rounded off a horrible afternoon. At least she'd also bought a Waitrose Chicken Chow Mein and a 'mini trifle with glacé cherries and real dairy cream'. Fuck the club, she wasn't going.

19

'Where's Ellie?'

'Not feeling well, apparently. She left a message about an hour ago.'

'Great.' Pam cheered up instantly. 'Not that she's sick, no, that's not good, but look, let's put this off till later in the week.' As usual, she was looking for an escape.

'No way. I've made us a chicken Caesar salad without the anchovies or parmesan or dressing.'

'Any chicken?' Maggie asked hopefully.

Toni laughed at the dripping sarcasm. 'Of course, but it's boiled instead of fried or roasted. All that oil. Yuck. And I've added beansprouts, pumpkin seeds and some polenta.' She glanced around, hoping for some brownie points.

'Well, forgive me for asking because the last dinner I prepared from scratch was in 1987, but in what way does this resemble a Caesar salad exactly?' Pam raised her eyebrows.

'Look, you wouldn't know an anchovy from a smoked cod in batter, so shut up until you've tasted it.' Toni swiped at Pam with a tea towel.

Maggie decided it just might get nasty. Toni was trying but Pam was obviously hungry and not in the mood for rabbit food. 'Listen, I have a proposal. Let's leave the weigh-in until next week so that we're all still together on this, OK?' Pam breathed a sigh of relief and Toni opened her mouth to protest, so she rushed right on. 'It's raining and miserable out there so I can't really see us going for a jog. Besides, there's a double episode of *Corrie* on, so how about we enjoy our, eh, dinner and that way we won't have ruined the day and we'll feel very healthy for tomorrow.'

'Are we allowed a glass of wine?' Pam asked hopefully.

'No way. Water or green tea.' Toni was adamant. 'Oh, go on then. And there's some focaccia bread in the kitchen if anyone fancies a slice.' They did.

★   ★   ★

Ellie felt tired and bloated the next morning. She'd polished off the Chinese, which was supposed to be for two — like everything else in the world — scoffed the trifle plus a Mars bar that was in the fridge, and opened a packet of Tayto crisps for the second *Corrie*. When she was getting ready for bed she felt all shivery, sure sign of a cold coming on, so she made herself a Lemsip and, in a fit of pique — or madness — added a generous splash of whiskey to help her sleep. It was definitely not recommended by the manufacturers and she climbed under the covers feeling like the world was against her. Everything must have congealed nicely during the night because she hardly slept a wink and woke with foul, oniony breath from the crisps and a headache from the alcohol. The occasional belch of chow mein and Lemsip on the way to work didn't help.

She arrived determined not to let them see she

was still upset, so she breezed in calling good morning in the vague direction of his study and went in search of the girls.

'Hi, Nora.' They were both still in their night clothes in front of the TV, eating bowls of cereal. 'Want to watch *SpongeBob, SquarePants*?'

Jess made room for her.

'Hello there. What's up? You'll be late for school. How come you aren't dressed?'

'Dad's still in bed so we had no one to shout at us,' Sam explained.

'OK, well I'm here so hop it, now.'

'I want to watch this.' Jess kicked her legs against the sofa.

'Not now, Jess. You'll be late.'

'Don't care, you can't make me.' Not a good start.

'Oh yes I can.' She reached over and turned off the TV. 'Now, upstairs both of you and get washed and dressed.'

'You're not our mother.' Sam's eyes were angry.

Not today, Sam please, Ellie's eyes pleaded. 'No and I'm not trying to be, but I am responsible for getting you two to school, so — '

'What's going on? Why all the shouting?' Jack appeared in his dressing gown.

Great, Ellie thought. Just what I need. 'Nothing,' she replied brightly. 'We were just getting organized.' She scooped Jess up and began to tickle her and Sam followed reluctantly.

She stayed upstairs long enough to give him time to have a coffee and when she eventually had to go back down he was in the sitting room, with a bowl of Rice Krispies, watching some rubbish on TV. With his hair tossed he looked just like Jess. Same lost look.

She made ham and cheese sandwiches using last night's brown bread, added fruit and yoghurt and headed out the door with the girls in record time, after they'd trooped back in to kiss him goodbye.

'How come you can watch sport and we're not allowed the toons?' Jess demanded.

'And you get to have Krispies and put sugar on and we have to have Shreddies,' Sam added.

'Only on school days. Saturdays and Sundays you can have what you like. It's what your dad and I agreed.' Ellie made a 'we're in this together' face at him. 'OK, time to go, here is your lunch, Sam. And there just might be a treat after school if you're good.' She didn't want Jack to think she was running a boot camp.

*　*　*

By the time she got back, having been to the shops, he was ensconced in his study and Mrs O'Sullivan was hard at work. Ellie was sorting the washing when she noticed a lot of pale-pink clothes. Funny, she was sure that it was the white wash she'd left drying last night. Her heartbeat quickened when she pulled out one of Jessie's red pyjama bottoms.

'Oh no.' Her shoulders sagged.

'What's wrong?' Mrs O'Sullivan appeared behind her and made her jump.

'I put this in with the whites by mistake.' She

held up the offending article. 'What am I going to do?'

'Just put everything back as normal. No one will notice.' Mrs O'Sullivan had done this before, it seemed.

'I can't. Look, this is meant to be a white shirt. It's practically rose pink.

'He never wears shirts, normally.'

'Well, he wears boxers. And these are not cheap.' Ellie examined a pair of baby-pink Calvin Kleins. 'And they're ruined.'

'Tell you what, I'll run down to the shop. They sell something in a box to deal with colours running. I've seen it.' The cleaner was putting on her coat, glad of a chance to escape and have a fag.

'No, really, I'll get — '

'Back in a jif. Don't fret yourself now, that's a good girl.' She was gone.

Ellie was still wondering what to do when Jack appeared. She flung the clothes back into the wash basket.

'Coffee?' he asked casually.

'No thanks.' She was worried. Whether he wore them or not, those shirts were expensive. 'Eh, I've just finished one.'

'Nora, I'm sorry about yesterday. I shouldn't have lost my temper like that.'

No you shouldn't, was what she would have said if she hadn't just ruined all the clothes he had told her not to touch in the first place.

'Forget it, I shouldn't have . . . done . . . that.' It sounded like she'd mugged an old lady.

'I am a bit strange, I know that. People looking

153

after me has always made me uneasy and, in the last few years,' he scratched his head, 'I guess I've grown used to my own space and . . . '

'You don't have to explain. It's my fault, I'm useless sometimes and I do stupid things and . . . ' Her weepy PMT voice took over again.

'Stop it.' He'd no idea where all this was coming from, couldn't she see he was apologizing? He came closer. 'You are not useless, you're great with the girls and . . . I hate to admit it but I slept really well in a clean bed with the window open.' He grinned sheepishly. 'And thank you for the fish pie, it was delicious. That sauce, whatever it was, was very tasty.'

'There was a packet in there somewhere,' she felt bound to admit.

'Well, I certainly couldn't tell. And the brown bread cooling was very impressive too.'

'Odlums instant mix. I'm addicted to that woman on *Ireland AM* on TV3 in the mornings who bakes bread and scones and flapjacks and corn fritters in seconds.' She was waffling.

'Well, we all look forward to being your guinea pigs, only, please, don't feel you have to look after me.' He shrugged his shoulders. 'It makes me uncomfortable.'

'And I always want to play Mammy, which doesn't help.'

'Well, we're both learning. It'll take time, I guess.'

'Here we are, one dose of this and he'll never notice a — ' Mrs O'Sullivan burst in, saw Jack and kept going. 'I'll just sort out the ironing.' She disappeared into the utility room, leaving Ellie no option but to confess.

'I'm afraid I had a bit of an accident with the white wash.' She screwed up her face as if in pain, which she was. 'Left this in by mistake.' She held up the culprit. 'But we're working on it.'

'Thank God that's all it is. Mrs O made it sound like you were about to force feed me a laxative or something.' He reached into the laundry basket and pulled out a rose-pink shirt and held it up to his face. 'What do you think?'

'Not your colour, I suspect.'

'Don't worry, I hardly ever wear shirts and I need to restock anyway.'

'You have a few pairs of pink boxers too, I'm afraid.' She thought she may as well get it over with.

He'd picked up his coffee and took a sip, added more milk and headed for the door. 'Nobody's seen my boxers for a long time, so I wouldn't worry if I were you.'

'Well, you never know when you might . . . ' She was about to say 'get lucky' but decided against it. 'Have an accident,' she offered lamely instead.

'On the potty?' He was teasing her again.

'I'll pick up some new ones, at my expense, of course . . . if that's OK . . . ' She was waffling again.

'Nora,' he turned to look at her, 'the last thing I need is for you to go shopping for my underwear. Remember, I'm paranoid.' They both smiled grimly and he disappeared.

'Want me to iron your shirts for you, or should

I just . . . mind my own business?' Her voice trailed off.

He reappeared and seemed about to say no but changed his mind. 'Actually, that would be great, thanks. You can just leave them here and I'll put them away later. And Nora . . . ' He gave her a Princess Diana coy look, or else he thought he was wearing glasses on the tip of his nose. 'Thanks.'

'Pleasure.' She beamed and it was all over.

20

Maggie was feeling good about herself. She'd had her hair cut short on the spur of the moment and everybody in the office said it made her face look thinner. Everybody except Rosemary Quinlan, the office manager, who had her own peculiar way of paying compliments.

'Ooh, it looks lovely.' Her breathy voice made Marilyn Monroe appear butch. 'It sort of hides your strong jaw and makes your chin look more pointy.'

Maggie's friend Eilis was passing and overheard the nasty remark. 'Well, nothing could disguise your droopy tits, babe, so I wouldn't bother trying. Just let your hair grow very long.' She smiled sweetly at the older woman. Maggie wanted to duck to avoid the verbal mud-slinging she knew would follow. 'You're a ride, Mags, don't mind the cow,' Eilis added, grinning at her friend and ignoring the gasp from Rosemary.

'How dare you, you . . . ?'

'Trollop? That's what you called me in the canteen the other day, isn't it? Well, at least I'm getting it. I'd say you'd ride anything with a pulse. Shame George Devlin said the other night he'd rather fuck a corpse than wake up to your bad breath.'

Rosemary's mouth opened, but nothing came out. Maggie swallowed hard. She knew exactly what Eilis was capable of coming out with

— and frequently did — but this had taken things to a new and potentially disastrous level. The aggro that had previously existed between the office manager and Eilis, who was a very junior secretary, had been a love affair compared to this. She dragged Eilis into the ladies.

'What are you doing, antagonizing her like that?' Maggie whispered in case someone was lurking. 'She could make your life hell, she has before.'

'Not any more. Mr Pearson has just asked me to be his secretary when Molly retires at the end of the month.' She grinned broadly. 'Which means I'll have absolutely nothing more to do with the head-wrecker. Imagine.' She did a little dance. 'I'll be a proper legal secretary, just like you, instead of a glorified typist with that cow for a boss.'

'That is brilliant.' Maggie hugged her friend. 'But Jesus, Eilis, you went a bit over the top this time.' She couldn't help smiling. 'You usually make some effort to control that razor tongue of yours.' They were sniggering again and Maggie glanced towards the cubicles. 'But that bit about the corpse . . . ' She wrinkled her nose. 'Yuk. She could have you up before a . . . tribunal or something.'

'I'll deny it.' Eilis shrugged, she was too happy to let that fat bitch bother her today.

Maggie bit her bottom lip at the memory of the other woman's face. It was difficult to have any real sympathy for Rosemary Quinlan. As bosses went, Maggie would have preferred to work for Judge Judy. Thank God she's never had any real dealings with her — Rosemary only got to bully the juniors in the general office.

'Anyway, she'd be afraid to repeat it.' Eilis sniffed. 'So, what do you think? Isn't it great news? It'll mean a good salary increase too.'

Maggie was thrilled. She knew that Eilis, who was from County Sligo, constantly struggled to pay for a flat and send money home. 'I'm so happy for you. Listen.' She kept thinking they were being overheard: toilets were notorious places for picking up things you weren't meant to hear. She glanced under the loo doors to make doubly sure the place was empty. 'Did George really say that about her?'

'What planet are you on? As George very eloquently told everyone in the pub the other night, he'd screw anything with a hole and a heartbeat. I only said it because we all know she's got the hots for him.'

'You can talk about being eloquent!' Maggie gave her friend a dig in the ribs. But Eilis had a grin the size of a banana.

'God, I've waited a while to leave that blabbermouth speechless. Listen, tell me quickly, how did Sunday go with Dougie boy? I've hardly seen you since.'

'Great, I'm seeing him tonight for a drink. His family were nice to me, very respectable, not like my gang, half of whom were sitting on my doorstep waiting for a bed when I arrived home at ten.'

'And were you hoping that someone other than your mother would be sharing your bed that night?' Eilis knew they hadn't done it yet and her eyes were teasing. Maggie was the only friend she had who still 'saved herself' a bit. Everyone else was gagging for it.

'Stop it, would ye?' She slapped her friend on the wrist but from the way she turned pink Eilis knew it was true. 'My mother drove all the way from Galway to visit a neighbour in hospital and expected a bed for the night without even asking. Said she forgot her mobile so couldn't ring me on the way. My two brothers were with her so I ended up making them all a big fry-up and of course I had a couple of sausages myself.' She patted her tummy. 'Not good. Anyway, poor Doug couldn't believe their appetite — or their manners either, I'd say — but he's too polite. They had bread on the table, butter still in its wrapper, mugs out and the tomato ketchup bottle turned upside down ready for action before I'd got the pan hot. He made an effort for about fifteen minutes then legged it.'

'Still, at least you got an early night, ready for tonight.' Eilis leered.

'No, you know me. Too soft. Of course Queen Karen arrived home and headed straight for bed, claiming a migraine and leaving me to do all the dishes. Then Mum got stuck into a bottle of gin she'd brought me 'as a present'. I ended up chatting with her till two.'

One of their colleagues came in at that point so it was back to work fast. News of Eilis's encounter with the office manager was hot gossip for the rest of the day in Arthur Bowles and Co.

That evening Maggie was ready bang on time. Doug seemed a bit taken aback at her new hairstyle. 'It's lovely, darling.' He twirled her around. She felt a bit young to be called darling but liked the way he said it. 'Though I loved your long hair too.'

'I know, but I wanted a change. Cost a fortune so you'd better admire it all evening.'

'How much?' he asked casually as he started the car.

'Hundred and fifty.'

'What? That's outrageous. Mick the barber charges me eleven euros and does whatever I want.'

'Since when did you start having colour and highlights and a 'follicle-rejuvenating and tone-enhancing masque'?' she teased him.

'Oh, at least once a month,' he joked back and he told her again how much he liked it but he referred to the price several times during the evening. It made Maggie slightly uneasy, after all it wasn't as if she'd spent his money.

They went to the Wishing Well in Blackrock and he had two bottles of beer and a Ballygowan because he was driving. Maggie had three quarters of a bottle of wine and felt giddy as they prepared to leave.

'Oh, I've left my wallet in the car.' He patted his trouser pockets. 'I'll just run out and get it.' He picked up the bill and stood up.

'Don't bother, I've got money here.'

'Sure?'

'Positive.' She grabbed the bill playfully and leant up to kiss him impulsively. 'You can get the next treat.'

'Oh dear, you'll probably choose the most expensive place in town,' he teased her as they left.

'Definitely and I'm having a starter and a dessert.'

'Well, you'd better start saving, so. Instead of wasting all your money on that head of yours.' He yanked her hair and kissed her. Maggie dug him in the ribs, but it rankled.

★ ★ ★

'Oh no, sis is home.' She was slightly disappointed as they pulled up at her house.

'Are the family still with you?'

'I hope not, they've eaten me out of house and home already. Breakfast yesterday was juice, fresh fruit, cereal, at least a dozen scrambled eggs and a sliced pan of toast with a half-pound of butter and a jar of marmalade.' She laughed. 'Luckily, they ordered in Chinese last night or I was going to have to shop on the way home.'

'I hope you didn't pay for it?'

'No, Mum did.' She gave him a funny look. 'But sure, what does it matter? They're my family.' She smiled questioningly.

'You're too generous. If it had been mine I'd have booked them a B. & B. for the night.' He fingered her hair and pulled her close and put an end to the conversation. They had a very satisfying snog, as good as it gets in a car on a busy street in Dublin, anyway. But his remarks about money took a bit of the hazy glow away for Maggie.

'I was thinking . . . ' He smiled shyly as she picked up her bag and prepared to leave twenty minutes later. 'Would you . . . like to stay over, at my place, that is, on Friday night? I could cook you dinner and you'd be able to relax after all the trauma of your family and everything.' He looked embarrassed and her earlier worries disappeared. She loved him for it. 'That would be really nice. I'll bring my flannel PJs,' she teased and he blushed.

'I look forward to seeing them, I think.' He grinned and she reached over and kissed him again. She knew it was all going to be OK.

'I'll bring the wine,' she told him as she closed the door.

'Great. I'll pick you up early, about seven thirty.'

'Why don't I drive over, if you're cooking?'

'OK, yeah. I'll ring you during the week and give you directions.'

'Great. I'm looking forward to it.'

'Me too. Oh, and I picked up that lock you want for the bathroom window. I could put it on on Sunday if you like.'

'You are so thoughtful, I only mentioned it in passing.' He was always doing little things like that and she loved being looked after.

'Nite.'

'Nite nite.' She was smiling as she let herself in and wondered what the girls would think when she told them on Saturday.

Olga Blake had called Ellie twice, which was unusual. On the second occasion she asked her to babysit while she went to the doctor.

'Is everything OK?' Ellie didn't want to pry, but her friend looked as if she'd been crying when Ellie called round after work.

'Yes. I am tired all the time, so I go to the doctor.' She had her coat on, as if she'd been waiting.

'OK, well, take your time. I brought us some Marks and Spencer takeaway for later. Has Rudi been fed?'

Olga looked as if she wasn't sure. 'He'll be fine. I must go, the surgery ends soon.'

Ellie gave Rudi a good wash and aired his pyjamas, then she played with him for ages. He was such a gorgeous little boy, growing and changing every day. Even though he was still a baby really he was interested in everything around him. Despite what Olga had said, Ellie made him a bottle and he gulped it down. An hour and a half later she heard Olga's key in the lock.

'How did it go?' Ellie had tidied up and laid the table. She'd even found some old candles and thought the nice setting, even in these grim surroundings, might cheer up her friend.

'Fine. He thinks I am depressed. He gave me some tablets.'

'Aren't you on some form of anti-depressants already?'

'Yes, but they are for the night, to help me sleep.'

'Oh, sleeping tablets.' Ellie was confused.

'Yes.' Olga shrugged. 'These are to pick me up in the morning. Mornings are not good, mostly.'

'Sit down, dinner is ready.' Olga's eyes had a vacant look and Ellie wanted to throw her arms around her friend.

'I brought us a bottle of red wine.'

'Oh Olga, you shouldn't have. I purposely didn't bring some because of my diet.' Ellie made a face. But Olga was already opening the bottle and pouring them each a large glass. She swallowed a tablet with hers.

'Are you sure you should be . . . ?' Her voice trailed off. She sounded like her own mother.

'Don't worry, my friend. It's OK. A little wine won't hurt. Cheers.' She raised her glass. 'And thank you, my dear, sweet Ellie. You are my very good friend and I love you.'

'Then tell me what's wrong. What's really bothering you?'

'Nothing. I feel a bit trapped here lately. But it will pass.'

'Is it the baby?'

'The baby, the flat, no job, no money, everything.'

'What about that rich farmer? You'll have to get out more if you want to find him.' Ellie smiled gently.

Olga did one of her accents as she told Ellie about a dating programme she'd watched earlier and soon she seemed back to her old self. Ellie relaxed a little and decided she'd try to call in more often.

Toni was sticking reasonably well to the healthy eating plan and a couple of her friends at work had said how well she looked. A couple of days after the incident with Gordon Thornton a huge bunch of lilies arrived at the nursing home addressed to Toni Nightingale. She was puzzled for a second as she ripped open the card and then not surprised at all after she'd read the message.

Thanks for saving me a fortune in Pringle sweaters. Any chance you'd stop looking down your nose at me long enough to have a drink?'

He hadn't signed it. Arrogant bastard, she thought, but she approved. And those flowers had cost more than a new sweater, which pleased her.

He rang the next day but she pretended to be busy and asked if she could call him back. He said he'd call again later for a chat. He did call but she didn't chat. She let him ring twice more before she spoke to him.

'Jesus, who are you, Mary McAleese or something? It's like trying to get an appointment with royalty.' But he was laughing, she could tell from his voice.

'I'm a busy girl.'

'And an extremely attractive one, may I say. Sorry if I was a bit off form the other night. My Chablis premier cru was getting warm.'

'Lucky you. My bedpans were getting full.'

'I thought you were just about to go off duty? Or were you lying to me, Nurse?'

'Actually I was off duty already when you nabbed me.'

'How was your weekend?'

'Fine, relaxing. A few very late nights,' she lied. She didn't ask him about his, or acknowledge the bouquet. It was all part of the game.

'I wondered if you'd like to come sailing with me on Saturday. The forecast is good for this time of year. You could stretch out on deck and guzzle a glass of Krug.'

'I'm afraid I don't stretch out anywhere with married men, and I've guzzled many things in my life but Krug is not one of them. It needs to be savoured.' She liked his dirty chuckle.

'Well, I'll be in on Friday to see Dad. At least let me buy you a bite of supper at the Tea Rooms to say thank you properly. And I promise you won't have to lie down once. Just sit there nicely and sip Dom P.'

'I'm on until nine.'

'I'll come in late.'

'I don't drink and drive.'

'My driver will take you home and drop you wherever you want to go next morning.'

He was persistent, she had to hand it to him. 'Let me think about it.'

'I'll be in about eight and I'll wait in the car for you.'

He hung up at the same time as she did, but she guessed he marginally beat her to it, which was unfortunate. She thought about it on and off all day. He was wealthy and powerful and that gave him a very sexy aura. She liked his sense of humour as well. And she supposed he wasn't bad-looking — which helped. He could be a bit over the top sometimes with his Dom P this and Bolly that, but she was attracted, and she'd known this was coming for ages. That evening she phoned Ellie for a chat, not intending to say anything.

'How are you?' she asked in the 'you poor thing' voice she used often during the day. 'You weren't well and the club missed you.'

'I'm fine, great.'

'What was wrong?'

'Nothing, just a shit day and I couldn't be arsed, to tell you the truth. Also I did have a bit of a cold coming on,' she thought she'd better add, in case Toni didn't like the sound of the couldn't-be-arsed bit. 'How did it go, anyway? I've been so busy that I haven't spoken to anyone.'

'The usual. How's the job going, by the way?'

'Actually, very good. I'm settling in. He doesn't really bother me and the kids are easy.'

'What's he like?'

'Fine, mostly. A bit intense, as I think I told you.'

'I mean to look at. Any chance of a bit of nookie there?'

'For you or for me?' Ellie laughed out loud at the idea.

'Me, of course.'

'God, no.' She assumed he'd be too uptight to

168

unwind long enough to have sex. 'He doesn't seem interested and, besides, he's married.' Ellie wasn't sure why she said it. He wasn't really.

'Speaking of which . . . G & T sent me flowers and wants me to have dinner with him on Friday.'

'And will you?'

'Probably.'

'Be careful. I already told you I don't want you getting hurt. You could be biting off more than you can chew.'

'Darling, at best I'll get sex, presents, maybe even a car, but I don't do pain. I see enough of it all day.'

'Toni, we've talked about this before. Presents are great but they're not what it's about, you know? 'Can't buy me love' and all that stuff.'

'I was joking about the car. I do have some principles, darling.' Toni sighed. 'Actually, I'd do it for the excitement. He's fun. I feel important when he's around. He could take me places . . . '

'Not many when there's a wife on the scene.'

'He's already invited me onto his yacht and to practically every good restaurant in the city. I'd say they lead fairly separate lives.' Toni wasn't sure who she was trying to convince.

'Well, keep me posted.'

'OK, hon. Talk soon, ciao.' She mouthed a kiss down the phone and Ellie laughed as she hung up. She didn't have to worry about Toni, it was the man in question she felt sorry for, although on second thoughts maybe not in his case. She had a weird feeling about G & T. And no matter how much Toni pretended, Ellie knew her friend was as vulnerable as the rest of them.

21

'But, Mum, it'd be so cool.' Paul was starting to look like a younger version of his father. It was the way his blond hair fell across his face. His bright blue eyes were pleading and he pushed away his hair petulantly.

'I said I'd think about it.'

'You just don't want us to have any fun.' Andrew had no such problems with his hair. He'd recently discovered gel and it was costing her a fortune. He was the image of Pam, chubby faced with an almost permanent grin.

'Look,' Pam gave her two offspring a look that had withered half the shopping elite of Dublin 4, 'just leave it, OK?'

Ten-year-old Paul started to say something else but his older, wiser brother pulled his jumper. 'C'mon, let's go outside and kick a ball around.'

Pam was furious. It was just like her ex. When she hadn't come back to him immediately with the response he wanted, Stephen had 'casually' mentioned what might be on the cards in an email to the boys. After he'd promised her he wouldn't.

She wanted to spit.

The real problem was that she hadn't figured it out for herself yet. She'd tried to talk to her mother about it the previous night, but she'd pooh-poohed Pam's reservations and insisted it would be great for the boys. It was her parting words that had stung the most. 'You can't hang on to them for ever, Pamela,' she'd said in her best Mother Superior tone, or maybe it just sounded like that to Pam's embattled ears. It wasn't like her mother to be so judgemental. 'Don't become a clinging vine or they won't be able to wait to get away from you once they're older,' she'd warned, moving herself into second place on Pam's want-to-kill list.

She'd rung Ellie as soon as she put the phone down.

'Is it normal to hope your mother meets her death by stoning, or something even more violent?' she had asked sarcastically, without as much as a greeting.

'That bad?'

'As soon as I told her about Stephen's call, she lit on me, called me a creeping ivy or something.'

'A clinging vine, perhaps?'

'She's a bitch.'

'Listen, your mother's fine, she probably just couldn't help offering advice. It goes with the territory.'

'Fine compared to whom, exactly?'

'Mine?' Ellie had ventured.

'OK, point taken.'

'Have you thought any more about it?'

'What do you think? It's keeping me bolt upright in bed. I'm a basket case.'

'You'll do the right thing, I know it.'

'What would you do, Ellie?'

She thought for a moment. 'Probably let them

go and cry myself to sleep for a week after they'd gone.'

'I don't think I can do it. It's too long and it's too far and they're too young and it's Christmas. Call me a selfish pig but that's the way I feel.'

'Look, just live with it for a while longer, but try not to let it take over your life. And at least they don't know anything about it yet, that's a relief.'

Of course, all that had changed by the following evening and they'd been pestering her ever since. There was simply no other topic of conversation and twelve-year-old Andrew, at least, was behaving exactly like his father. It was doing her head in.

⋆   ⋆   ⋆

When she called them in for tea an hour or so later, they'd obviously decided to try a different tack.

'Thanks, Mum, that's great.' Andrew tucked into bacon and cabbage as if it were a Big Mac with double cheese.

Paul was less effusive, or maybe wasn't quite as much of a hypocrite. She gave him the benefit of the doubt until he announced, 'I'll do the dishes.' Washing pots was right up there with drilling your tooth without an injection as far as her youngest son was concerned. Still, she let them pamper her and took the cup of tea and chocolate biscuit with as gracious a smile as she could muster, given that she was about to assassinate somebody.

Their new plan lasted about an hour, and then they started again.

'Please, Mum, I'll do anything. I'll work all next summer, I'll keep my room tidy, I'll even do Gran's shopping every week.'

'And I'll . . . I'll rinse the bath after me and . . . and . . . I'll clean the skid marks off the toilet.' Paul beamed, knowing if anything could change her mind, that would. It was the job she hated most in the whole world.

'It's right up there with wiping someone's bum,' she'd yelled at them only last week in a temper, 'and I wiped both of yours for long enough. I do not intend to continue.' She'd almost laughed at the look of disgust on their faces. They were mannerly boys, even if they were a handful, and she knew she shocked them sometimes with her outbursts. The manners came from their father, he was always perfectly polite — irritatingly so. Shame he hadn't stuck around long enough to teach them how to do a bit of housework, or pick up after themselves.

Now she looked at their two faces, Paul's angelic one and Andrew's silently pleading one and knew she'd lost this fight.

'If — and it's a big if — I do let you go, you'll be doing a lot more than that.' Most of the sentence was lost in their whoops of joy.

'I'm not promising,' she cautioned, but Paul ran towards his room and she'd be willing to bet he was already packing.

Andrew gave her a hug. 'Thanks, Mum. I love you.'

'I haven't said yes yet.'

'But you will, I know that face.' He grinned cheekily. 'Can I ring Dad?'

'No you cannot.' She saw his face. 'Andrew, one word to anyone and it's off, OK? I want to work out the details myself and then I'll talk to your father. After that you can speak to him about it. Now, go tell your brother the same. Not a whisper, not even by email, or you're spending Christmas in Shannon with Aunty Phyllis.' Threatening them with her mother's very mean sister was akin to promising them a weekend without computer games — unbearable — so she reckoned she was safe enough, for now.

* * *

Ellie was enjoying the rest of the week after the earlier trauma. Jack seemed finally to relax a bit with her and the kids were a joy. They went swimming twice, played tennis and rounders in the autumn sunshine and baked buns for Sam's friend's birthday party. They were icing them and Jess was covered in coloured bits when Kate dropped by again on Thursday, just as Jack put his head into the kitchen to grab a coffee.

'What's going on here? It looks like fun. Is it a party, and if so, why wasn't I invited?' he asked.

'I made this.' Jess held up a bun that looked good but weighed a ton.

'Mmm, I'd love some of that.' Kate went to grab a bite and the child squealed and hid under the table.

'Try one of mine,' Sam offered, 'but wait until we put the cocunut and jam on top.'

174

Jack made the three of them a cup of coffee and was just about to retreat to his study when Kate stopped him.

'Fancy a BBQ at my place tomorrow evening?'

Jack looked puzzled. 'It's Bill's birthday and I thought we'd open a bottle of bubbly and eat early, before we freeze.' Kate smiled.

'Is it not a bit late in the year to be outdoors?'

'Bill has this tradition.' She gave Ellie a look that said he was mad but she loved him enough to indulge him. 'He claims that if he can eat out on his birthday without his fingers going numb he's still young. So last year we all wore hats and gloves and layers and fought like cats and dogs to be sitting closest to the patio heater. How pathetic is that?'

Ellie looked a bit bewildered. It did sound odd. 'You'll understand once you've met him.' Jack smiled at her.

'Sorry, Kate, I completely forgot. Be an angel and buy him something nice from me, will you?' Jack turned to the kids. 'What do you think, girls?'

'Can I have some of the bubbly stuff?'

'Not unless you mean Coke?'

'OK.' Jess always gave in far too quickly. Kate sensed the lightness in the atmosphere and was pleased.

'Speaking of meeting him, will you join us, Nora?' she asked quickly.

'Oh no, I couldn't. But thanks for asking.'

'Why? My husband is dying to meet *you*. He thinks you have plaits and yodel. Please come, it'll be early, about six, so you can eat with us and leave if you're going out later.'

Ellie hesitated, uncomfortable, sure they'd rather be on their own, as a family.

'Please come, Nora, I want to show you Percy.'

'Sounds like you've no choice,' Jack added.

'OK, if you're sure, I wouldn't want to intrude.'

'Nonsense, you're part of the family.' Kate desperately wanted to include her, so that she'd become close to them and stay on as a nanny. The girl was remarkable — pleasant and efficient and warm and the house was finally beginning to feel like a home.

'OK, well, we'll bake a cake for your husband. How about that? Do you want to be my assistants?' she asked the two cream- and jam-covered faces next to her.

The girls whooped with delight and pulled open the larder door to get flour and sugar and anything else that had a picture of a cake on the packet. Ellie had no idea how to bake a cake, the buns had been courtesy of Betty Crocker. 'If I can find a recipe, that is.' She laughed nervously and went to wash her hands and ring Pam.

★   ★   ★

Next day the girls were in a state of high anxiety. The cake, although lopsided and a bit thinner than she expected considering it contained enough eggs to make an omelette for a family of ten, had been left to cool overnight and was now being iced, with the help of a million e numbers in the little bottles of colouring they'd found in the cupboard. Sam had wanted to do the writing on top and had started with a very passable happy, but then forgot about birthday and just put Bill. She was deeply disappointed when she discovered her mistake and time was not on their side.

'I'll tell you what, let's just put a question mark after Bill and see if he's not delighted with it.' Ellie did the appropriate squiggle.

'What's a mark?'

'We're asking Bill if he's happy, see?'

'Of course he is, it's his birthday, silly.'

'Yes, but this is asking if he's happy with the cake.' It was a tenuous link but she needed to get them ready. It was already ten past five.

While they were dressing Ellie changed into jeans and a warm, funky sweater by one of her favourite Irish designers. It had been a massive purchase for her but it was soft and feminine and girly and she loved it to bits. She put on a bit of foundation, blusher and lippy and unpinned her hair. She heard the shower going and Jack emerged twenty minutes later in clean black jeans and a fine-knit black roll-neck sweater. His hair was still damp and he was wearing small, square, black-rimmed glasses. He looked different, younger, a bit preppy. She liked it.

'Daddy, you're wearing your glasses, you look like 007,' Sam announced dramatically. She'd watched the latest Bond movie with her older cousins the previous weekend.

'I'm going to assume that's Pierce Brosnan and not Sean Connery.'

'Who?'

177

'Never mind, I'm only wearing my glasses cause my eyes are a bit tired today, that's all.'

'Are you sick?'

'Only of answering your questions.' He picked Jessie up and swung her round. 'Let's go torment Percy.'

'Dad, you're cruel,' Jess admonished.

'Dad hates Percy,' Samantha told Ellie.

'I meant to ask yesterday, who is Percy?'

'The fattest, whingiest, scruffiest, most ill-tempered cat you're ever likely to meet.' Jack made a face. 'They once brought him to an audition for a cat food commercial but all the kids auditioning had convulsions when they saw him.'

'I love Percy. And Snowy.'

'The mongrel.' Jack mouthed to Ellie. He tousled Jessie's hair and she ducked. 'I know you do, darling, we nearly had to adopt him but thankfully Sarah grew out of her allergy. Let's go, dinner's at six thirty and Kate warned us not to be late for the fizz.'

22

There were fairy lights flickering and candles winking and two patio heaters going full blast when they arrived. The girls were delighted and presented their cake as if it were the crown jewels.

'Hello hello, what's this? A cake, good grief, I wouldn't have put any of you three down as cooks, the only thing your father ever made for dinner is a phone call.'

'Nora really made it, but I mixed it all up.' Jess was hopping about on one foot and almost toppled over in her eagerness.

'Well done, my sweet.' He planted a big kiss on her head. 'And what's this — Happy Bill? Of course I'm happy, it's my birthday and I can still feel my fingers.'

'I left out birthday.' Samantha turned beetroot.

'What? I never noticed.' He got down on one knee and whispered to the child. 'You see, nobody ever asks me how I'm feeling round here. They all ignore me, mostly. So, I want you to promise me you'll always put that on my birthday cake, every year, until I'm so old I have to stay in bed. Then, it won't matter how I'm feeling really, I'll be gaga.'

Sam had never heard of gaga but she was delighted and nodded enthusiastically.

'And you must be . . . .' He held out his hand.

'Actually, I'm not sure what to call you. Katie calls you Eleanora, the kids call you Nora and someone told me you call yourself Ellie.' He held out his hand to grasp her outstretched one and planted a big smacker on her cheek at the same time. 'I always thought you were called Heidi for some odd reason.'

'Ellie or Nora will do nicely.' She beamed at him, he was so friendly, it was impossible not to respond. Besides, he looked like Father Christmas.

'Thank God, I'm afraid Eleanora makes you sound like you're partial to the odd sugar lump as a bribe.'

'Bill, I warned you.' His wife was in like a shot. 'Open the champagne and give Nora a glass before she makes a quick exit.'

He did and soon they were all clinking and toasting and slagging, even the kids were allowed a tiny drop and Jess was giggling cause the bubbles ran up her nose. The two men went off to crank up the barbie, clutching cold beers and talking about sheds in a rather worrying way.

'Don't mind us,' Bill told Ellie. 'A shed is to a man what a handbag is to a woman, without the dartboard and homemade beer, of course. Wouldn't fit,' he explained. His logic left her trying to figure it out, fatal as far as dealing with Bill was concerned.

⋆ ⋆ ⋆

'So, how's it going? I must say she's not half as bad as I expected.' He glanced over at her again as if to make sure. 'Quite pretty, actually, and not a stick insect, which I like.'

Jack watched as Ellie put an extra fleece on Jess and bent down to zip her up. 'No, she's fine.' He realized that she'd changed her clothes and let her hair down. 'The kids adore her and I'm managing to get some work done, which is keeping my publishers very happy. All in all I'd say it was a good move, although never admit that to your wife.' He winked conspiratorially.

'Listen, you don't need to warn me.' Bill grinned. 'I've learnt over the years. Anyway, you should see the pile of photos attached to the CVs on her desk. One of them makes Ann Widdecombe look like the Rose of Tralee. I'd say you've done very well out of this.'

'Actually, tonight is the best I've seen her looking. She normally wears a sort of uniform, at least I think that's what it is. Makes her seem a bit strict, you know, like Anne Robinson.' He grinned at his brother-in-law. 'Still, the house is clean and she's a passable cook, although her chicken casserole tasted faintly of fish the other night.' He tried to think of something negative to say about her, because it seemed to be expected, a sort of man-to-man thing. 'She cleaned my bedroom, though, which drove me nuts at the time. Am I odd, do you think? I really hate people invading my space.'

Bill understood perfectly. 'Just thank your lucky stars you don't live here. I was sitting on the loo the other night reading the *FT* when Sarah casually walked past me to get her hair brush. She was talking to her friend Lizzie on her mobile and didn't even excuse herself. Now, there must be five bathrooms in this house but unless you bolt yourself in you can expect company at any moment. They're worse than prison officers.' He shook his head. 'Very disconcerting, I must say. They take after my wife, nothing is sacred, as you well know.'

'Well, I don't know where they got me in our family, so. Although, now you mention it,' he thought back, 'Katie was always popping her head round the door when I was in the shower. She usually claimed to be playing detectives and looking for clues.' He smiled at the memory. 'Eventually, once I turned ten, I barricaded myself in with my comics. Maybe that's where I get my paranoia from. Nothing was sacred then either.'

'Confiscated a few harmless magazines from me the other evening — very annoying.' Bill shook his head. 'Last week she was going through my pockets.'

'Still looking for clues?' Jack laughed as Bill scratched his head.

'Claimed her new French knickers were missing, I ask you! Just because she caught me wearing her tights a few years ago.' He winked at Jack. 'Yesterday, she was looking for her earrings in my briefcase. Why she couldn't have just asked me, I'll never know. Way too obvious for Kate though, she likes interfering, it's what keeps her young.'

'What are you two grumbling about now?' his wife asked as she and Ellie carried plates out to a buffet table. 'And are the steaks nearly ready?'

182

'Nothing, darling, Jack was just saying what an adorable child you were, a miniature Miss Marple. We're just agreeing it's one of the things we most like about you.' Both men grinned innocently.

'You look nice tonight.' Kate stroked her brother's cheek lightly as they headed back indoors. 'Those glasses suit you, she called over her shoulder. 'You look like Clark Kent.'

'Who's he?' Bill asked.

'Not sure. I've heard the name somewhere.' Jack topped up their glasses with the remains of the beer cans. 'As long as he's alive and not gay I'm happy.'

'She does seem particularly attracted to queens, doesn't she? I think it's that her favourite uncle when she was a child was a very camp actor. You remember him, surely?' Bill asked.

'Ah, yes, Uncle George'. Jack smiled. 'Katie adored him, followed him everywhere apparently. You'd know. Not that I've anything against gays, one of my best buddies is as bent as a boomerang . . . She loves that they take care of themselves, which is why I always worry that I've overdone it when she says I look well.'

'Don't worry, old chap, she was saying the other night that she's going to bring you shopping soon. Claims you're wearing the same clothes day in, day out. I'd say she's happy once you don't smell.' Bill wrinkled his nose.

'That's another bloody thing about women. Nora bleached some of my shirts and stuff the other day, then wanted to buy me new underwear. What is this preoccupation with doing things for us? I've been buying my own jocks and socks since I was twelve, yet most women I've met don't think I'm capable of making my own bed. Nora keeps leaving clean sheets outside my door, as if trying to encourage me.'

'Kate was sniffing all my socks in the drawer yesterday,' Bill remarked without a trace of annoyance. 'Said I was putting dirty ones back in. Better to just let them have their way. Much less stress.'

* * *

Eventually, they all put on another layer of clothes and sat down to steaks and salad and baked potatoes. The girls were finished in minutes and went indoors to watch a DVD. The conversation flowed and it was light and easy and fun, thanks to a gorgeous bottle of Rioja Jack had brought.

'So, Nora, what do you do when you're not keeping these three on the straight and narrow?' Bill wanted to know as they tucked in. 'Do your family live locally?'

'My mum and dad live in Terenure, but I have an apartment in Ringsend.'

'Do you have brothers and sisters?' Kate knew they'd talked about her family at the interview, but she couldn't remember.

'I have two older sisters, Orla has two children and lives in Portmarnock and Claire is single and works for a bank in London.'

'Any boyfriends we should know about?'

'Bill!' Jack and Kate got in together, both with mouths full.

'Sorry, I guess that's not politically correct or something,' he apologized.

'No, it's OK. No boyfriend at the minute — come to think of it, it's been a while. Actually,' drink had loosened Ellie's tongue, 'I was engaged a couple of years ago but it didn't work out, so it sort of . . . came to a natural ending.'

The other three looked sober. Ellie had the distinct impression they were feeling sorry for her. 'It's fine, honestly, it was . . . basically . . . my decision. No spark,' she added for good measure and decided to change the subject. 'But, I've got three great friends and we're all single — well more or less — and having a ball.' Before she knew what she was doing, Ellie was telling them all about the club and their spectacularly unsuccessful attempts to lose weight.

'So, let me get this straight, you meet once a week to try and encourage each other and so far have ended up ordering takeaway and drinking copious amounts of alcohol?' Jack was intrigued. 'How exactly does that make you slim?'

'It doesn't.' Ellie grinned. 'Of course, that's never the plan. We have a weigh-in and usually have some exercise planned . . . '

'Like what?' Kate immediately wanted to join. It was a woman thing.

'Toni is great at yoga, or Maggie might suggest aerobics, or we might just put on some music and dance, well, jostle about really.' Ellie was conveniently forgetting that they'd got more exercise from opening bottles than they had from dancing so far, but it sounded impressive. 'And we don't always end up drunk eating Chinese,' she felt compelled to add, 'we do occasionally share tips and things.' She couldn't remember a single one. 'Although if Pam had her way we'd be fat as fools.'

'Which one's she again?'

'The one with the two boys.'

'Right, so who's the healthiest, then?'

'Toni, I suppose, although Maggie is too. I'm not great and Pam is worse. Toni does cook sometimes, though, so we can be quite healthy the odd time.'

'What does she cook? I could do with a few less calories myself.' Bill patted his waist.

'Tofu, lentil soup and em . . . ' Ellie was having to stretch her imagination at this point. 'Oh, she had a great recipe for aduki beans one week.'

'What the hell are aduki beans?' Jack wrinkled his nose at the sound of them.

'No idea. We never got to try them. Maggie was depressed so we had spiceburgers and batter sausages and things instead.'

'And what about these tips you mentioned?' Kate was all ears.

Ellie had to think fast. 'Oh, Toni's a genius. All stuff about chewing your food properly — '

'Until it's liquid,' Jack chipped in.

'Please, too much information.' Bill swallowed a whole baby potato in fear of what was coming.

'Listen, you two have no idea what this woman

has done to me.' Jack was warming to this. 'She even has me inspecting my . . . what did you call it? Oh yes — '

'Stop right there,' Kate pushed her plate away but Bill was hooked.

'Go on, Nora, you can tell us.'

'Well, if you've finished eating . . . ' She glanced around the table and then wondered if she'd regret this in the morning.

'We have now.' Jack took the four plates and put them on the buffet table.

'Actually, on second thoughts no. It's not an after-dinner story.'

'Spoilsport.' Bill wanted some fun.

'Trust me, mate, you don't want to know,' Jack offered.

'I agree, I think we should discuss this between ourselves, Nora.' Kate's face was a picture. 'Anyone for some dessert?'

'Nora, you and I must have a chat sometime, you're a very interesting young lady.' Bill refilled their glasses and gathered up their dishes.

'Sorry.' Ellie realized she'd gone too far. 'I'll help you clear up.' She grabbed some plates and headed for the kitchen.

'Happy now?' Jack laughed at his sister's face. 'You know how paranoid I am about my privacy and there is nothing sacred as far as Nora is concerned. Give it another month and she'll be watching me have colonic irrigation.'

'I'd love to try that, it's supposed to — '

'Enough, woman, we men need some element of mystery about the female sex.' Bill returned and slapped his wife's bottom and turned to

Jack. 'I had no idea about all this, dear boy. It's quite fascinating the things women talk about amongst themselves.'

'Oh and your tongue tells you lots, too, according to a new book just out.' Ellie was back. 'It's too dark now but I could check all of yours in daylight sometime, after I've read up on what we're supposed to be looking for.'

'I love a good tonguing.' Bill's smile was reminiscent of Tommy Cooper.

'I can hardly wait.' Jack winked at his sister. 'Roll on Monday morning.'

23

Toni was feeling a bit tipsy, sitting in the Tea Rooms in the Clarence Hotel, quaffing bubbly with her married date and nibbling at the most fabulous wild mushroom risotto. The place was buzzing, but then it always was, mostly with visitors hoping to meet Bono or some of the other members of U2, who'd been involved in the purchase of the hotel. A couple of B-list celebrities were at the next table, and some members of the cast of *EastEnders* had been at the bar earlier.

'So, what made you change your mind?'

'I hadn't had a decent meal all week.'

'It's not doing your figure any harm.' Gordon looked at her with pleasure. 'You are one gorgeous woman.'

'Are you always so forward?'

'What's wrong with that? I meant it as a compliment. You must be well used to men admiring you.'

She didn't tell him he was ogling. 'So, what about your life, now that you know all about mine?'

'Businessman, travel a lot, too much on, stressed out, not enough hours in the day. You know the story I'm sure.'

'Children?'

'Two. Boy ten and girl eight. One cat named Tigger.'

'Wife?'

'You know that too.'

'What does she do?'

'Runs the home, plays tennis, ferries the kids around.'

'Where is she tonight?'

'Out at some charity do, I expect.'

'Aren't you supposed to be with her?'

'We don't live in each other's pockets. Besides, those sort of things are boring. I'd much rather be here.' He was cool, she'd give him that.

'Dessert?' He signalled a waiter. 'Or would you rather have brandy and coffee somewhere quieter?'

'I'd love a black coffee, actually.' He ordered a pot and excused himself. She realized the champagne was going to her head and felt she might need to stay sober if she was to keep up with him.

★　★　★

Much later, they headed back to his car where the driver was waiting patiently. 'Would you like a nightcap? I have an apartment near here.'

'Why not?' Toni was dying to see his bachelor pad. They didn't have far to go. It was overlooking Leeson Street bridge, two minutes from Grafton Street. They pulled into a private, electronically controlled garage away from the rest of the parking. The lights went on inside as soon as the door started to open. It was very plush for a car port, Toni thought. They went directly to his apartment in a lift located inside the garage, ensuring he didn't have to meet any of the other residents.

When they got into the place she had to admit she was impressed.

'The view is amazing.' She smiled at him and raised an eyebrow. 'Is this where you bring all the girls?'

'I hardly use it, to tell you the truth.' He pulled open the curtains via a remote control, and the canal and practically the whole of the city unveiled itself. 'I have a smaller place in my office building. I crash there quite often. It's easier to get to work in the morning.' He smiled as he put on some music and poured them two brandies. 'No traffic.'

They chatted and he asked her about herself, which was unusual. Most men never bothered. 'You're not a typical nurse,' he told her.

'What do you mean?'

'Those nails, for a start. Much too perfect.' He picked up her hand and held it, stroking her arm and making her shiver.

Just when she was about to take it away, he placed her hand gently back on her lap. 'You're also much too . . . exotic. I can't see you being happy looking after old people.'

'I always wanted to be a nurse, actually. I had enough 'exotic' during my childhood to last me a lifetime. My father was an ambassador and I was always paraded round at posh parties. I'd lived in ten different countries by the time I was seventeen and knew hotels better than any of our homes.'

'Sounds exciting.'

'It was lonely, actually. I was an only child. I could do anything socially but couldn't play snakes and ladders or complete a jigsaw.'

'Poor little rich girl.' He pulled her close and stroked her hair. 'I know that feeling. My family gave me everything but never stayed with me long enough to share any of it with me. I grew up calling my nanny Mummy.'

'Had you brothers or sisters?'

'Two brothers, but they're much older. I think I was . . . unplanned. At that stage my parents were both into their careers, she was a top litigation lawyer and he was a judge. I'd say I was quite a surprise.'

They sat for a while, her head on his shoulder, sipping their drinks and watching night-time Dublin unfold before their eyes. She liked the feel of him near her. They were very similar, in many ways. And his manner was not unlike her father's.

'You're almost asleep.' He kissed the top of her head. 'I'll have Tom drop you home. Let him know what time you need him in the morning and he'll bring you to collect your car.'

She smiled and stretched. 'Thanks.' There was something about him. He was brash and over the top and not really her type, yet she was definitely attracted to him. He seemed so alive. And she liked his smile.

Toni yawned. The brandy was definitely going to her head, she was beginning to think of reasons to stay. 'I am tired. It's been a long week.' She stood up quickly and saw him watching and knew he wanted her. She was used to it with men, but oddly enough, for the first time in ages she wanted someone back.

★ ★ ★

He walked her to the lift, pressed the button and as the doors opened he waved her in.

'Off you go and get some beauty sleep.'

'I had a good time.'

'Me too. You off tomorrow?'

'Yep. And Sunday. Unusual, two weekends in a row, but I've a few swaps owing to me and I've decided to call them in. I must be getting old, because I'm wrecked all the time at the moment.'

'You don't look it. You look beautiful.'

'Thank you.'

'Goodnight.' He leant in and took her hands in his and kissed her gently on both cheeks.

He was treating her like a china doll and it made her feel oddly vulnerable. He had nice manners. 'Goodnight then.'

He stepped back and grinned at her. 'No going clubbing now. Tom is too old.'

She laughed and he let the doors close and she didn't want him to.

★ ★ ★

Maggie was wide awake. She listened to Doug snoring beside her and felt the tiniest bit detached. The evening had been lovely, though — he'd insisted on collecting her after all and when she'd arrived at his apartment it was

193

homely and comfortable in a 'boy making an effort' sort of way. Dinner was tasty even if it was helped along by St Michael, the patron saint of would-be gourmets everywhere. Afterwards they'd had strawberries and cream in front of the fire and watched *The Late Late Show*. When it was over he'd kissed her gently on the lips and asked, 'Ready for bed?'

It wasn't what she'd envisaged happening, but she knew he was nervous and trying to make it easy for her, so she nodded.

He took her hand and led her towards the bedroom. There were candles flickering and the stereo was playing something easy. 'There's an en suite through there,' he gestured, 'and I left your bag here.' He picked it up and passed it to her. 'Take your time. I'll use the other one.'

When she came out in her nightdress, with her underwear underneath, he was already in bed. She'd agonized over what to wear, even bought a silky slip thing. But it looked like she was trying too hard so she settled on her new fleecy, comfortable one and she left her underwear on because she wanted him to see it. Anyway, she didn't want to appear too brazen, she had a feeling Doug wouldn't like that.

He pulled back the duvet and she slipped in beside him. It felt like they'd been married for twenty years, she almost expected him to hand her a cup of cocoa and a Rich Tea biscuit. Instead he leant over and took her in his arms and kissed her very gently. Usually first sexual encounters with a new partner were all about rough and tumble, both carried away with the moment. This was a new experience for her and she wasn't sure how to handle it. But she loved that he wanted to make it special. It took a while but they got there in the end.

Their lovemaking was warm and tender but not red hot and passionate. She told herself now that she'd been expecting too much. She really liked Doug, but she'd envisaged being carried away on a tide of desire the way Mills and Boon had promised all those years ago. Instead it felt more like putting on a comfortable cardigan.

Maggie lay there thinking about the last guy she'd had sex with. That had been red hot all right, but Martin Downes had been a shit. She had known he was trouble the first day he'd started work in her firm. It lasted six weeks and she only found out it was over when one of the girls in Accounts told her she'd seen him in the Montrose Hotel, looking very smoochy with an actress from *Fair City*. She still couldn't look him in the eye without feeling like a twit, but she'd learnt a lesson: great sex means nothing if the guy is an asshole.

Doug was a dote and the sex had been good. He'd been very patient and loving and overall it had been a great night. So what if there were no fireworks? They'd come later. She curled up to him and he pulled her arm around to his chest and held it there and she kissed his back and was content.

24

'Are we on for brunch?'

'As long as it's healthy.'

'There's a new place open in Temple Bar. Italian. It's supposed to be fab. Great salads,' Pam added as an afterthought.

'Count me in.' Maggie was unusually cheerful. 'Have you spoken to the others?'

'They're both on answering machines. I'll text them now. See you there about twelve?' Pam gave directions and hung up. She was glad they were meeting. She needed to talk.

★ ★ ★

Tom the driver had told Toni he'd be waiting outside any time she wanted him. 'But I've no plans, really, don't worry. I can grab a cab.'

'I have my orders. I'll be waiting from nine thirty. Is that early enough?'

'I won't even open my eyes till ten. See you at eleven.'

'Fine, Miss Toni.' He decided not even to try to pronounce her surname. 'Here's my mobile number. Call me any time if your plans change.'

'Tom, it's two a.m. My plans are not going to change. And don't call me Miss Toni, please,' she begged. 'It makes me feel like I'm in the deep southern states of America. It's just Toni, OK?'

'Yes, ma'am.' He grinned at her and she

thanked him again and went inside.

It took her ages to get to sleep and now it was ten thirty and she still felt tired. As soon as she switched on her mobile she got Pam's message. Damn, she'd have to hurry if she was to collect her car first.

She came outside at eleven fifteen and Tom was in the same spot, as if he'd been there all night. A huge bouquet of roses was resting on the passenger seat. He hopped out, opened the back door and handed them to her with a note.

Please keep Tom all day, you seemed tired last night. Just come over for a drink at some stage this evening. Don't worry if it's late. I'll be working there from about four.

'He says I'm to keep you all day. That's ridiculous.'

'I'm all yours, Miss . . . eh, Toni. Might as well enjoy it.'

'But I can't just . . . swan around in his car all day.' She could very easily, actually, and they both knew it.

'Where to first?'

'Well, I'm meeting people for lunch, but not until twelve.'

'Anyone you'd like to pick up en route?'

'What a great idea.'

She rang Ellie, who'd just been woken by the phone and was not a happy camper.

'Are you ready for lunch?'

'No.' Ellie's mouth was furry.

'I'll collect you. Be there in ten. Get into the shower now.'

She hung up and tried Maggie.

'Where are you?'

'I'm in Doug's house, why?'

'Aren't you coming to lunch?'

'Yes, he's dropping me in, we're leaving now.'

'I'll collect you in five. Give me the address. Ellie's still in bed, so it'll be half an hour at least before she comes to.'

'There's no need, really, I — '

'I've a car and a driver at my disposal, so shout.' Maggie did and Toni clicked off.

'Right, we have a plan,' she told Tom.

* * *

Maggie was excited to be picked up by a car and driver, although Doug said he was looking forward to dropping her into town. Ellie wasn't quite so keen, afraid she'd throw up all over the leather seats.

'Have a good day, ladies.' Tom tipped an imaginary hat as they all trooped into the restaurant.

Pam was waiting for them impatiently. 'Hurry up, I'm starving.' It was her usual Saturday greeting. 'What took you so long and how come you all arrived together?'

'I tried ringing you but you'd just left. I have a car and a driver so I'm on driving duty.' Toni smiled and Pam's mouth dropped open.

Only Toni, she thought, feeling slightly miffed. 'OK, now that Tom's stopped grovelling, tell

198

us all. What exactly are you doing in a silver Jag with a driver?' Ellie had kept her head out the window for the journey into town and was feeling slightly more human. She filled her water glass and buttered some bread, anything to take the taste off her mouth and help her swallow two painkillers.

Toni talked and they all listened, wondering why it only ever happened to her.

'So, you decided to go for it, then?' Pam asked.

Toni nodded. 'I like him,' she said simply. 'He's great fun.'

'He's still married, though.' Maggie was suddenly feeling jealous, it looked like Toni's night had been way more exciting than any of the others' and she'd been looking forward to being the centre of things for once.

'So? Since when did you join the Legion of Mary?' Pam was pouring wine despite Ellie's protestations. Her glass was filled through her fingers before she could argue and soon they were all toasting Tom the driver and Gordon the millionaire and anyone else they could think of, and that was before they'd heard Maggie's news or Ellie's adventures.

'What does he do, anyway?' Ellie was interested.

'Property developer. He told me they're developing that huge site near Tallaght Hospital. I remember reading somewhere a couple of months ago that it had been bought for seventy million by an Irish company.'

Pam whistled. 'That's big.'

The waiter came to take their order and the discussion turned to why Ellie was feeling so fragile.

'I think it was nice of them to include you, shame you had to make a show of yourself,' Toni teased when Ellie explained the reason for her hangover.

'I didn't, honestly. I was fine when I left. I felt quite happy, actually, it's ages since I've done any sort of family things. My lot are not exactly renowned for tea parties, as you all know. And I went home about ten, and left them to it. I swear I only had two glasses of champers and a couple of glasses of wine. It must have been something I ate.'

'So, what are they like when they relax?'

'Good fun. Kate's husband is a hoot. They all seemed really interested in our club.'

'You told them we meet once a week in someone's house to guzzle tap water and nibble rice cakes and swap tips and flail around on the floor?' Toni was mortified.

'Guzzle Merlot and nibble prawn crackers and swap sex lives would be a slightly more accurate description of us so far, don't you think?' Ellie raised her eyebrows. 'Anyway, stop looking as if you take no part in any of the debauchery and tell us exactly how you've become Driving Miss Daisy overnight.'

'There's nothing to tell, really. I just decided to have dinner with him last night. I quite fancy him, to be honest.'

'You slept with him?'

'Absolutely not, what do you think I am, a

slut?' Toni grinned. 'But I wanted to.' She winked.

They lost interest, slightly, and Maggie decided to take advantage.

'Well, some of us got some action last night.' Her face was pink.

Brilliant, something juicy at last. 'Tell all.' Pam slurped her wine. 'Sorry, Toni, we do want to hear how you didn't have sex, but only after we hear how she did.'

Maggie gave them the edited highlights, enjoying being the centre of attention.

'So, how was it?' Ellie cut to the chase.

'It was fine, you know what first times can be like sometimes. Actually it was good, great even.' Maggie wasn't sure she could keep embroidering.

'They're words to describe your mammy's Victoria sponge, darling.' Pam was all ears. 'What we want to know is, was it sensational? Is he a monster in the sack? Has he a ten-inch todger? That sort of thing.' They fell about. Typical Pam to say it like it was.

'Leave her alone, at least she has a sex life, which is more than the rest of us,' Ellie said eventually, seeing Maggie look slightly uncomfortable.

'Speak for yourself. I can have one any time I like at the moment.' Toni twirled her pasta around and managed to look like she was performing a striptease. 'I'm just trying to decide if it's what I want, that's all.' It was and they all knew it. The loan of his driver for the day had just swung it for Mr G & T.

'Well, be careful.' Ellie was still playing with her food. The smells were beginning to make her nauseous again.

'Listen, girls, can you think of anyone who needs our advice less than Toni the torturer?' Pam couldn't. 'Remember the last guy she toyed with for a while? What was his name again?'

'Moustache.' Maggie tried to think of his name.

'Oh yeah, Ronnie. I remember. Dr Ronald Bergin. What was our code name for him again?' Nobody could remember. He'd been short-lived.

'Anyway, he was like a lap dog. Followed you around for weeks after you dumped him.'

'I didn't dump him. We were never an item, really. It was just a quick shag, to be honest.'

'Yeah, well, you forgot to tell him that. The poor bastard kept half the florists in Dublin busy for months.'

'Don't mind her, Toni, she's just jealous. He was gorgeous. And Doug is great too,' Maggie said. She wanted to get the subject back round to her and Doug, just so she could convince them that the sex had indeed been mind-blowing.

'Was CJH's column in today?' Toni asked just as Maggie was telling them how cute it had been when Doug had pulled back the duvet for her. 'Sorry, Maggie, I am interested, I promise.'

'Nope, he's still away.' Ellie filled her in. 'Go on, Mags, was he wearing socks?'

'No.' It was indignant.

'Were his Y-fronts bulging?' They all burst out laughing.

The four girls were supposed to be going shopping for the afternoon and then on to an early movie, followed by supper if anyone felt like it, then home by midnight, although the chances of them ending up in some club in Temple Bar was a distinct possibility.

Toni sent Tom off and arranged for him to pick her up at the Fitzwilliam at six thirty. The girls weren't in the least surprised to hear she had no interest in *Mr. & Mrs. Smith*, despite the gorgeous Brad. She was starring in her very own *Mr. & Mrs.*, they reckoned.

After slipping home to change and have a soak, Toni asked Tom to drop her back to the apartment.

'Hi there. How was your day?' Gordon was waiting at the lift and kissed her demurely on both cheeks, just as he had twenty-four hours before. They both knew what was going to happen.

'Great, I was out all day. Thanks for the loan of Tom, it was terrific not having to carry all those BT bags.'

'Pleasure, I'm sure all that flimsy stuff you wear weighs a ton.' He smiled at her. 'You look sensational by the way, that's quite a change from the nurses' uniform.' Last night she'd dressed demurely. Tonight she'd gone for it big time. She was wearing a long silk-and-chiffon skirt in deep-pink with a fitted, strapless bustier hand-embroidered with roses. It was very glamorous. To dress it down she wore a soft cashmere shrug and pale pink, very expensive flip-flops. Even her toenails matched.

He handed her a slender, ice-cold flute.

'How was your day?' She walked over to admire the view, giving him a chance to admire her.

'Busy. I worked, mostly. Got a lot done.' He came to stand close to her and she only knew he'd arrived because she could feel his breath on her neck. 'I'm glad you came over.'

She didn't turn around. 'You're marginally more interesting than Maggie's boyfriend, who was angling for an invitation to our soirée this evening when I collected her earlier.' She smiled and turned to face him. 'Still, I might join the girls later if they hit a club, so you're not safe yet. I'm making no promises.'

'I'd say I'm never going to be safe where you're concerned.'

He sipped his drink and kept his eyes on her face. 'Shall I order dinner? Are you feeling peckish at all?'

'Oh, I'm ravenous.' It was the most overused cliché in the book and she was aware that she'd made the first move, but what the heck, he was attractive, fit and very rich and she fancied him rotten. She also knew the sex would be mind-blowing. It was.

25

'So, you stayed over, then? What time did you get home?' Maggie was sleepy and it was barely ten thirty on Sunday night. Toni had rung her to exchange sex stories, seeing as they were both getting some.

'About four this afternoon. I read the papers and had a bath and I'm ready for some sleep, I can tell you.'

'Didn't get much last night, then?'

'Not really, no.' For some reason she suddenly wanted to keep it to herself, so she changed the subject quickly. 'How about you, did you see Doug?'

'Yep, we went for a walk on the seafront, then he cooked me steak and kidney pie and we watched some TV. I'm only just home.'

'Sounds great.' It sounded worse than an evening playing Scrabble with an elderly aunt, actually. 'When are you seeing him again?'

'Wednesday, he's training for the next two nights.' Maggie waffled on about his rowing and Toni thought how quickly she and Doug had settled into a routine. She knew she'd never have that with Gordon.

'How about you?' Maggie asked eventually.

'He'll call.' She knew he would. The sex had been that good.

★ ★ ★

'Did I make a show of myself on Friday night?' Ellie asked Jack on Monday morning as soon as the kids were out of earshot.

'Not at all.' He seemed surprised. 'You were hilarious. Kate wants to join your club. Does it have a name, by the way?'

'I don't know if I'm ready to share any more of my personal obsessions with you just yet.' Ellie was teasing. 'I didn't take this job to become the main source of entertainment for your entire family.'

'Shame. Bill has lots more questions for you. He was looking for your number the next morning.'

'Actually, I felt awful on Saturday morning, not like me at all.' She tried to sound sophisticated but had the distinct impression he was thinking that it was exactly like her. 'Although, I have to admit I did have a last glass of wine and watched a double episode of *Will and Grace* till one thirty after I got home.'

He nodded knowingly. 'You'd have to.'

'Well, that's it, so. Ballygowan for me from now on. My ab-fab days are over.'

'Now that I think of it, Sam wasn't well on Saturday morning either. Could it have been something you ate?'

'I'd like to believe it, but no.' She thought for a moment. 'Unless those hamburgers I defrosted for lunch on Friday . . . ? Sam was rooting in the freezer and found them and said they were her favourite. Jess didn't eat them, she wanted home-made fish fingers.'

'Oh God, I'm sorry, that could easily have

been it. Everything in the freezer has been there for years.'

'Now you tell me.' She was just relieved it hadn't been down to the hard stuff. 'I'll throw everything out today, except the food I put in myself.'

He made her a coffee and they chatted a bit more. He seemed interested in the club, which surprised her. Most men's eyes glazed over the minute you mentioned a diet. They were all afraid you were going to have them eating iceberg lettuce and drinking spritzers for the rest of their lives.

★ ★ ★

That night the club was on a definite upturn. Now that Toni was having sex she decided the rest of them needed to get in shape with her. It took them all of three minutes to figure it out.

They were in her apartment — it looked like a bomb had exploded, which wasn't unusual. Toni herself looked radiant, which wasn't unusual either. It was just the way she moved around, sort of lording it over them a bit, that did it.

'You shifted him, didn't you?' Pam spotted it first.

'None of your business.'

'Come on, out with it, you know you want to.' What Maggie meant was that she really wanted to as well. 'Tell them what you nearly told me last night.'

'How many marks out of ten?' Ellie cut to the chase.

'Nine and a half.'

That did it. They weighed themselves in double-quick time. Toni was the only one to have lost anything. 'Christ, he must have been good, you'd want to be leaping off wardrobes to have lost two pounds after all you ate on Saturday.' Pam was miffed. 'Let's have a drink and you can tell all.'

'No, that's it, I've had enough of you slouches.'

Bit hard, Ellie thought, they were all making an effort, really.

'We are not ordering in and we are not having wine. I'm juicing a couple of heads of lettuce, some green peppers and Granny Smith apples.' Pam could feel her bowels beginning to move at the mere mention of the thing. 'Look at us, it's starting to show on our faces. We all look tired and haggard.' What she really meant was, you all look tired and haggard; I look, and feel, fabulous. 'Now, after the juice we're doing a yoga class, so get changed and I'll put on the music. Then, I've made us an aduki bean and tofu casserole and we're having peppermint tea to aid our digestion.' She looked at their faces and burst out laughing. 'OK, maybe the peppermint tea is going a bit too far.'

'A cold beer, perhaps?' Pam asked hopefully. 'We'll be sweating after all the exercise.'

'Absolutely not, it'll ruin our sleep. By the way, speaking of sleep, there are sticks of celery there for everyone to take home. Seemingly it's brilliant to eat one at bedtime.'

'Says who?'

'The Internet, I've been doing some research. Now, let's get started and if you're very good,' she beamed at them, 'I just might let you have a treat later.' The way she said it, they knew there was no arguing, all they could hope was that Donald Trump flittered out soon, then she'd be back to comfort eating like the rest of them.

'Remind me again why we like her?' Pam joked as Toni went off to get organized.

'Because she's very kind underneath it all and great in a crisis and, let's face it, she keeps us focused,' Ellie answered immediately. 'We'd never have gone to Italy last year if she hadn't booked it all *and* paid the deposit when you were broke, Maggie.'

'Listen, I'm fine; it's Pam you need to convince.'

'Of course I like her, idiot, she's my friend and she has a heart of gold.' Pam sighed. 'It's just that sometimes she irritates the hell out of me.'

'You're just not in good form at the moment, Pammy.' Ellie rubbed her back. 'Anyway, shush, here she comes.'

'Listen, sorry if I sound bossy, it's just that I really want us all to do well.' Toni came in carrying a lurid green jug of something vile. 'So, if we have another good week I'll make something really tasty at the weekend and we can have wine as well next week. My treat. OK?'

'I thought we were having a drink as a treat later.'

'I didn't say it was an alcoholic treat,' Toni teased. 'It could be chocolate.'

'OK.' Harmony was restored.

Pam had almost persuaded Ellie to take an hour out and meet her for lunch on Thursday. 'Pleeeeease, I need a sounding board.'

'I never take a break, lunch hour doesn't go with the territory.'

'Just this once, please.'

'OK. But I'll have to check if it's all right with Jack and it'll have to be an early one. I collect Jess at one thirty.'

'No problem, I'm off all day. And I can come to somewhere nearby. Thanks, Ellie, I really need to talk and you're never free in the evening.'

'I know. Olga wants me round tomorrow night and if I don't call to see Mum and Dad this evening there'll be hell to pay.'

'And then it'll be Saturday again and all the talk will be of sex,' Pam grumbled. 'And we're still no nearer getting any.'

'Maggie's not saying very much, though. Do you think it's all going OK?'

'Yeah, I do. I was talking to her yesterday and she sounded really happy. Anyway, I wonder how Marla what's-her-name's doing?'

'Stop it, you.' Ellie laughed. 'Anyway, it's not Marla any more. Donald Trump recently married again. And Toni is nothing like any of them.'

'I know, I'm just a grumpy old woman.'

'Well, she's keeping us on the straight and narrow, that's for sure. She dropped me round a soya and lentil loaf the other morning.'

'Me too. The girls on the desk were

complaining about the smell all morning.'

'Did you not put it in the fridge?' Ellie was horrified.

'I put it in the bin.' Pam was amazed she had to ask.

'It wasn't that bad. I brought some in and left it for Jack and when I came in yesterday it was all gone.'

'I don't think neglected separated men count. They're right up there with tramps and dustbins.'

'Oi, you, enough. I look after him very well.'

'I'm sure you do, darling, but let's face it, after a couple of weeks of your cooking, soya and what's-it loaf could be very tasty. Remember that bean curd thingy? Ugh, I can still taste it.'

'Bitch. Gotta go. Here he comes. I'll ring you.'

'Don't forget. I need you.'

Ellie hung up just as Jack came in.

'Everything OK?'

'Yes fine.'

'It's just, you look like you're going to burst into tears.'

Ellie hated asking favours. 'No, it's just, that was my friend Pam on the phone.' She decided to cut to the chase. 'Would it be OK if I took an hour off tomorrow? It won't interfere with anything, I promise. I'll make up the time and everything and I'll collect the girls and all that, it's just — '

'Nora.' He came closer and put his hand on her arm. 'Stop it, will you? Of course you can take time off. Christ, am I that much of an ogre? You look positively in pain.'

'Oh.' She was taken aback. 'Thanks, I normally wouldn't ask, it's just she's in trouble.'

'Man or money or meringues?'

She grinned, knowing what he meant. 'Food is the least of her problems at the moment.' She told him about Stephen wanting to have the boys in New York for Christmas and his eyes darkened immediately and she was sorry she'd said it.

'Christ, I can't think of anything worse.' He had a far-away look and didn't speak for a moment or two. 'Although in my case it's not likely.'

'Has she ever been in contact?' Ellie wasn't sure why she wanted to know.

'Yes, she does send them packages on their birthdays and at Christmas. But it only confuses them.'

'I'm sorry.'

'Don't be. I think she did love them, really. She just couldn't cope with what they represented. She always wanted to be free.' He shook himself out of it. 'Anyway, it suits me just fine now. She doesn't know what she's missing. They're the best thing that ever happened to me.' He seemed to be talking to himself. 'Take as much time as you need,' he told Ellie after a moment. 'Bring your friend here, whatever.' He turned towards the door.

'And Nora.'

'Yes?'

'Take time when you need it. To go to the bank or the chemist or the aduki bean shop or wherever.' He smiled absently. 'You spoil us, and I'm grateful, just in case I forget to say it.'

Now she definitely felt like bursting into tears. She never could cope when people were nice to her.

26

'Christ, this is some house.'

'I know.' Ellie felt a tad uneasy. 'Now, remember, if he comes into the kitchen, make your excuses and skedaddle.'

Pam nodded, although she couldn't resist having a good look round as Ellie made two cups of tea. 'So, what's the story?'

'They're going.'

'When?'

'December twentieth, for two whole weeks.' Pam ran her fingers through her hair. 'I don't know what I'm going to do without them.'

'We'll be around. You did the right thing, Pam.' Ellie rubbed her arm.

'Well, Toni's headed for Trump Towers at least, I'd say, and Maggie's already told me that Doug's been invited to Galway to meet the hobos that masquerade as her family for Christmas. Looks like it's you and me, babe.'

'Christ, don't talk about it, it's ages away.' Ellie hated Christmas, always had done. It was a family thing, although when she thought about it, it was more her particular family thing.

'It's November in a few days. The crackers have been out in Tesco since the copybooks came down. Any day now the lights will go up in Grafton Street and the buskers will start doing fifteen different versions of that Shane McGowan song.'

'OK, Grumpy, Dozy here will keep you sane.' Ellie laughed and Pam felt better. 'It'll be fine, I promise. I'll make mince pies, although on second thoughts . . . '

Pam nearly spluttered out her tea. 'Oh God, yes, I'd almost forgotten, you thought they were made of real mince.'

'Stop it immediately, I was only about five at the time. I'm sorry I told you.' Ellie laughed at the memory.

'Didn't you put onion in them when your mother wasn't looking?'

'No, you made that up. Every time Christmas is mentioned you add another layer to that story.'

They chatted for a while and the conversation came back to the boys.

'I bet they're pleased, though?' Ellie wanted to know.

'Delirious. Andrew's never off the Internet checking up on things to do and Paul has his case full — shorts, snorkel and Tayto crisps.'

'Shorts? For New York? In December?'

'Wouldn't you bloody well know it?' Pam was bitter again in a flash. 'He's taking them to Florida for New Year. As if I hadn't enough to compete with.'

'Wow. He must have money.'

'Oh, he has. Never had a bean when I was married to him but now, it's like a cross between a lotto millionaire and John Carey. They're going to Disney World as well.'

'I think you're fantastic to let them.'

'I never had any choice really, did I?' She wasn't looking for an answer. 'If you love someone set them free, and all that shite.'

'I'll be here for you. Don't worry. Keep thinking about lovely lie-ins, being able to find the remote and the lack of smelly socks in the kitchen.'

'In the fridge, you mean.' Pam nodded at Ellie's puzzled look. 'Seriously, that's what Andrew did last week. One of his mates told him to chill his dirty clothes. Supposedly it takes the smell away.'

'Not great for the left-over roast beef, though, I'd say.'

'Anyway, thanks, you're a real pal.'

'And so will the others. Be there, I mean.'

'I know that too, I was only joking earlier. I just needed to talk, that's all — make sense of it in my head. I've been going round in circles for days and the girls at work are no help.'

'Speaking of no help, how's your mother?'

'Acting like the separation was all my fault and if I'd played my cards right her present this year could have been coming straight from Barneys.'

'As opposed to Dunnes Stores?'

'Yeah.' Pam's eyes were watery. 'Actually, I'm being unfair. She's fine most of the time. I just get the feeling she wishes I'd stayed married to him.'

'He left you, remember?'

Pam nodded. She was so relieved to get it all off her chest that she suddenly burst into tears and Ellie was torn between wanting to cry with her and being mortified in case Jack caught them. He thought she was crazy enough as it was.

216

Life was one long round of bubbles and bonking and baubles for Toni, who now belonged to the BBB Club as well.

On Monday morning a package from Appleby's had arrived at the nursing home addressed to her. Inside she found a diamond bracelet and even she knew enough to know they weren't CZs. She had to shield her eyes from the sparkle. On Tuesday evening he called in to see his father and was waiting for her when she came off duty.

'How did you know what time I finish? I could have been on till midnight.' She laughed as she got into the car.

'If I can make half a million euros in one day, I think I can find out your schedule. Like it?' He noticed the bracelet.

'I love it. Was that why I got it?'

'Hmm?'

'A share of the profit?'

'Nope. You'd have got it even if I'd lost that amount.' He leant over and kissed her nose. 'You deserve it.'

'How come you're driving yourself?'

'I'm not completely helpless, you know. There are some things I do very well.'

'Like to show me one?' She put her hand on his thigh. They were driving along the coast road in towards town.

'Here? Now?'

She moved her thumb up and down.

'Are you mad?'

'Pull in, I know a little place. It's dark.'

She knew he wouldn't be able to resist it. Men never were.

Afterwards, he nibbled her ear and murmured. 'God that was great.' He tweaked her hair. 'Totally unexpected. I hadn't realized how much I needed it. It's been a bitch of a day.'

'Like you collected me just for a chat.' Toni smiled at him innocently.

'I did actually.' But it was one of the things he liked about her. She knew the score.

'Fancy a bite to eat? I'm starving.'

'Me too.'

They pulled in at the 40 Foot, a trendy eating place with great views. He ordered champagne cocktails without asking. He drank a lot, Toni noticed. She'd been planning a night of water and salad but what the heck, there'd be plenty of time for that once the novelty wore off.

★　★　★

Maggie and Doug were becoming a proper couple. He picked her up from work most evenings. She liked the way he rang her if it was raining, or cold, to see how she was getting home, even if they weren't having a proper date. He thought nothing of driving in from Dalkey or Killiney, or wherever he was working, to pick her up if she was tired and couldn't face the bus. When they did meet they usually went for a walk or coffee or sometimes the movies.

'I know, let's go to The Orchid Sichuan for duck.' She was all smiles when he picked her up on Thursday. She'd spent the whole afternoon

218

daydreaming about him.

'Sure, only their prices are madly expensive.' He laughed. 'It works out at about twelve euros a pancake, and that's mostly cucumber and spring onions, or whatever they give you to fill the things up.'

'Well, they do serve seaweed with their duck. Mind you, it is deep fried.'

'What has that got to do with anything?'

'Ellie's been doing some research and apparently it's full of iron or minerals — everything, in fact. She's determined to get us eating the stuff; she's cooking it for us next week. I think she may have even tried it out on that family she minds. You know, slipping seaweed in their cereal, that sort of thing.'

'How could anyone not notice seaweed in their cereal?' Doug was puzzled.

'I'm joking, silly. She didn't actually put it in the muesli, at least I hope she didn't. Anyway, tonight is a good excuse to try some. My treat, I got paid today.'

'Oh well, in that case, come on, I'll buy you a drink first, you look like you're parched.'

'No, if I'm having real food, I can't have alcohol as well, club rules.' Maggie screwed her face up. 'Or, at least, my version of them. Toni has us on a strict regime, even flavoured water is suspect. She left some foul baked-nut and seed thingy round last night. I meant to throw it out. It's stinking up the fridge.'

'I'll take it if you don't want it. I love nuts and seeds, especially when I'm training.'

'Consider it yours.' She linked arms with him

and they headed off to enjoy themselves. 'Maybe I could have a white wine spritzer? I won't tell if you don't.'

'Traitor.' He slapped her bottom. 'I think you look super as you are. You don't need to diet.'

She kissed him playfully. 'That's why I love you.' It slipped out.

'Whoa, steady on. We hardly know each other.' His laugh was a bit too hearty. But then he kissed her back and Maggie should have felt awkward but somehow she didn't.

* * *

'So, how's lover boy?' her sister Karen asked when she arrived home around ten, having dashed in first to get the nut thingy for Doug. Karen was twenty-three, good-looking in a sulky way and knew it all.

'Great, we had dinner in The Orchid and he gave me a present when he dropped me off just now.' Maggie held up a cute little see-through plastic purse with a tiny felt teddy on the front.

'I'd rather have Prada.' Karen was big into labels.

'Well, I wouldn't. It's the thought that counts. He noticed the zip was stuck in mine the other day. Anyway, what are you watching?'

'*Desperate Housewives*.'

'Any good?'

'Yeah, they're wild. Mind you, it only makes me more determined never to get married.' She sat up. 'How about you? Is Douglas the one?'

'Could be; he's good-looking, kind — '

Karen made a face. 'Yeah, right. Dream on. He's small and sort of — '

'He is not, he's the same height as me.'

'Yeah, and you're barely five foot tall.'

Maggie threw a cushion at her. 'That's not true and you know it. Just because you're a lanky skinnymalink.'

'Seriously, Mags, what do you see in him?'

'He takes care of me . . . '

'So does Dad.'

'Look, when you've dated as many shits as I have, you really appreciate a nice guy. And Doug is really nice, very considerate, and he makes me laugh.'

'God, you're sad.' Karen turned up the volume and went back to her fantasy world.

★ ★ ★

Ellie pulled up outside her parents' neat, semi-detached house on Thursday evening and hoped it wouldn't be too much like hard work. She loved her folks — it was one of the reasons she'd never lived abroad — but they were old-fashioned and set in their ways and everything had to be just right. Her mother made Hyacinth Bucket look laid back. Now, even though it was just after 7.30, the kitchen table was set for breakfast and the cereal was already in the bowls, covered in cling film to keep it from going soft overnight. Ellie looked around. It was straight out of a fifties dirndl-skirt TV commercial for kitchens. It still had the original 'kitchen cabinet' and the table was

Formica and the presses were red and shiny. Oh, and it had wallpaper with cucumbers and tomatoes on.

'Hi, Mum.' Ellie had let herself in and now her mother appeared in from the back door. 'Where's Dad?'

'Out in the shed, fixing something, no doubt planning to leave half of whatever it is all over my kitchen floor. I've told him it's too cold but when did he ever listen to me? How are you, love? Cup of tea?'

'Yes, please. What are you up to?'

'Just about to watch *EastEnders*. It's already started. Go in and sit down, the kettle's just boiled.'

'OK, thanks.' She never could keep up with her mother's appetite for soaps, but it was usually easy to catch up, although she sometimes got mixed up with *Emmerdale* and *Corrie*, which her mother told her was ridiculous, given that one had cows and sheep all over it and the other had lamb's liver and bacon butties that had never come from a pig. Still, seen one barmaid's tits and you'd seen them all, she reckoned.

'Ham sandwich, love?'

'No thanks, Mum, I'm on a diet.'

'Ridiculous.' She put a plate of Chocolate Goldgrain down in front of them. Ellie's mother was not one to agree with you easily. Not unless you were making your will in her favour, she guessed, and even that was pushing it. 'Your father was just saying how tired you look this last while, Eleanora. It's not eating properly. Why don't you come home for the weekend and let me look after you?'

'I'm fine Mum, thanks anyway.' Ellie would've sooner had laser surgery on both eyes without an anaesthetic. Her parents were just so . . . so careful, really. Everything was thought out, like the one time they nearly took the family to Butlins, in Mosney, County Meath, and then decided there was a risk of mosquito bites. Small, admittedly, but after they'd consulted their GP, the local health centre and the Department of Tropical Medicine or something, they decided not to take the risk. They weren't short of money at all, yet they measured out everything, even the small sherry they allowed themselves at weekends. They rarely went out, at least not since that one case of food poisoning in Dublin in about 1958, unless one of the girls dragged them out for dinner or Sunday lunch as a treat, and that was usually Ellie. Her sister Orla was about as frivolous as her mother, except when it came to herself, and Claire had been away too long. All that, and their house was worth three-quarters of a million, according to spotty Sam, their next-door neighbour but one, and they were rattling around in it.

'How's Orla?'

'Fine, she was asking about you. You should call in and see her new kitchen.'

'I will, maybe next week.' The problem was that it was easier to get away from the Taliban. Visiting Orla required a week's leave and a visa.

'Mrs Mooney's sister died.'

There was always someone. Her parents had a

morbid fascination with death. 'Which one?' Ellie could barely remember Mrs Mooney and had no idea if she'd one or twenty-one sisters.

'The eldest, Maura. The big C. I couldn't bring myself to go round there, even. You know me. Dad called, though. I made them soda bread.'

'Nice.' Ellie was nibbling on a biscuit before she realized and stuffed it quickly into her pocket. Her mum was terrified of hospitals, doctors, death, the VHI and BUPA even and her father was only marginally better, so Ellie could never understand how she was the type who'd sign herself into a clinic at the first feel of a spot on her ankle, never mind her lungs.

Her father came in at nine o'clock to the second, and as always pretended to be surprised that the news was on.

'Oh, is it that time? Glad I made the headlines, so. What's happening, El?'

'Hi, Dad.' Ellie rose to kiss him just as her mother passed him his nightly half ham sandwich, again covered in cling film and probably made at about three o'clock yesterday. The edges sprang up nicely as soon as he stuck his finger in the cellophane and the smell of sweating pig hit her nostrils.

'Want some, El?'

She'd sooner have Whiskas. 'No thanks, Dad.'

'She's on a diet. Again.' Her mother poured him a cup of stewed, lukewarm treacle and milked and sugared it for him as she had been doing for yonks.

'No need, you're grand as you are, just big-boned.'

There was only one phrase Ellie hated more than big-boned and that was 'fine girl y'are', which was what horrible Uncle Jim said every time he met her.

'So, what's the story?'

'Nothing much, Dad, working away as — '

'Shush, love, just till I hear what's happening.' He reached for the remote and turned the news up to glass-shattering levels and that was the end of that.

★ ★ ★

It was after eleven by the time Ellie finally turned in, having watched *Crime Scene Investigation* and TV3 news, exactly the same as the nine o'clock on RTE down to the newsreader — shorter bob, slightly different shade of luminous pink jacket, no Newbridge silverware — and resisted all offers of lemon sherbet, clove rock and bull's eyes.

Her phone rang just as she turned off the light.

'Have you had your celery stick?' It was Maggie, giggling.

'No, but I'd say you've had a bloody mary with yours, by the sound of you.'

'Nope, I had crispy duck though, with all the trimmings. I asked for celery peelings with the veggies but they gave me carrot instead. The waiter was very cute but hadn't a word of the lingo. He thought celery was sherry and kept bringing me little glasses of Harveys Bristol Cream.' Maggie was on a roll. 'The place was gorgeous though, very posh. I kept looking round, expecting Toni to jump out of the jungle of greenery or swing from the nappy of one of the gold baby Buddhas.'

'I'd say she was most likely swinging from a chandelier tonight, darling. G & T was bringing her for dinner in his private plane.'

'Oh my God, where?'

'No idea. She's saving that for Saturday. I'll tell you something, I'm beginning to feel as if I'd do anything for a bit of lovin' myself, Mags.'

'Romance or a ride?'

'Sweetie, I'd settle for a shish kebab and a shag, thank you. He wouldn't even have to brush his teeth.'

'That bad, huh?'

'Spent the evening with my folks.'

'Not a bundle of laughs, I'd say.' Maggie knew them well. They were as different from hers as George and Laura Bush were from Bill and Hill.

'Give Pammy a call, by the way, she's a bit down.'

'I will, I promise, first thing tomorrow. Sorry, I know I've been a bit scarce lately, but, I think I'm in luuurve.'

'Good for you. I'm jealous. Lusty love or real love?'

'A bit of both.'

'The 'I want to ride you senseless' kind or the 'I want to have your babies' kind.'

'Wooh there, babies, that's serious. He's just so nice, so good to me. Makes me feel special.

Mind you, Karen more or less said she'd sooner date Willie O'Dea.'

'Which one's he?'

'Minister for Defence, I think. Small, at least he looks it on TV. Big moustache.'

'Oh yeah.' There wasn't really any reply to that one. 'Well, eh, don't mind her. As long as you like him.'

'I do, El. I really do. He makes me feel like a princess.'

'Princess is good.'

27

Jack loved Saturday mornings. He read all the papers at leisure, although some of the articles were questionable, especially in the magazines. Anything to fill a supplement, he reckoned, as he skipped past a full two pages on what to do with leftover kangaroo steaks, with step-by-step instructions in glorious colour. He couldn't begin to imagine what the adult population of Bohola, Co. Mayo, or some other small Irish village, would make of that one. Come to think of it, kangaroo was on the menu in a place in Mullingar he'd passed through last year, so maybe he was just out of touch.

The girls were playing with cut-out cardboard dolls with real hair, dressing and undressing them faster than Naomi Campbell at London Fashion Week. They were like a three-dimensional version of what his sister did with the back page of *Bunty* when they were kids, except miles more sophisticated. Sam's doll was black and called Chloe and had four different afro arrangements for hair. She was currently dressed in fishnet tights, over-the-knee shiny boots and a skirt that made Britney look overdressed — all of this in paper, although not nearly as flimsy or as hand blackening as they used to be. These were all wet-look and garishly bright. They even had real bits of jewellery and Sam had spent an hour sobbing because

Rashers had got one of Chloe's earrings and it was now languishing somewhere in his colon and would probably require an operation that would cost an arm and a leg to remove. And their vet, Mr Costigan, had already nearly reported them to the ISPCA a few months back when Jess had stuck a blue felt pen up Rashers' bum and tried to teach him to write by wriggling, just because she'd seen him trailing his bottom along the floor at some point earlier in the day. Still, with any luck the earring and its minuscule back fastener — essential, according to Sam — would be excreted in due course, and, as he would shortly be inspecting his own pooh if Nora had anything to do with it, it wasn't really a hassle to keep an eye on Rashers'.

He poured another cup of coffee and marvelled at how clean the place was. And it smelt good, too. The fridge was well stocked because the shopping had been done yesterday and there was a — what had she called it again? — oh yes, medallions of pork in white wine and saffron sitting looking very tasty — suspiciously so — on the top shelf. It was her only flaw, and it wasn't even a major one, because she nearly always almost got it right. A bit of a garlicky flavour in the trifle, a sliver of anchovy or something similar in the bread and butter pudding, but hell, they were all eating way better than they ever had, even when Lorna was around, and that loaf thing the other day was actually very tasty.

No, life was good for all of them right now. He

must remember to give her a bonus, or buy her something nice — Jane Malone seemed to be the new big thing, according to Sarah, who suddenly knew everything about women's cosmetics and had asked him to bring her back fruitti de la mare or something equally poserish-sounding from his next trip abroad, because she claimed her skin was dry. Sam had been patting her own face with something every morning since Sarah had told them about her spots. It was amazing what having an older cousin was doing for Sam's development. Most of her friends were still into *Jungle Book*. Kate was probably still laughing about his phone call last night — he had asked her to pick up a tube of the cream for him to give Sarah. It's Jo Malone, idiot, and the cream is Crème de la Mer. And it costs about two hundred euros for a week's supply,' Kate had said, exaggerating only slightly. 'And if Sarah's been using mine I'll beat her senseless. It was a present from Bill's boss.'

★ ★ ★

'Dad, I really love Nora.'

'Me too, darling.' He flicked through the *Star*, wondering again how it was possible he knew absolutely nothing about *Big Brother*, given the twenty-eight pages of colour devoted entirely to a transvestite, a Brad Pitt in *Thelma & Louise* lookalike and a bleached-blond bodybuilder wearing leopard-skin underwear who looked like a carry-over from the A Team. He'd better keep up, he was slipping badly, next thing he'd be wearing a paisley dressing gown and whinging every time he missed *The Archers*.

'Do you really?' His youngest daughter was poking him in the ribs.

'What?'

'Love Nora?'

'Yes. No. Not exactly, no.'

'Why not? She loves us. She told me so yesterday and that includes you.'

'Yes, well, I do love her in the same way you do, of course . . . ' He cleared his throat and swivelled round in his seat. God, was this what telling them about sex was going to be like in years to come? He hoped not. Still, Bill had told him he'd tried to explain to Sarah how intercourse was best saved for that special someone and preferably after he'd bought two rings so heavy you could barely reach for your glass of Bolly with your left hand and all she'd said was, 'Yes, Dad, I know all that, but is a hand job OK?' He shrugged the horrible thought away and turned with a bright smile to his baby. 'I'm very fond of Nora, darling, she's a lovely girl, woman, eh, I mean nanny.'

'Yes, but — '

'No buts, off you go and get dressed. We're going to see Rembrandt at the National Gallery.'

'Is he like Gandalf?'

'No, not exactly. Now run along and I'll tell you all about it in the car.'

'What she means,' Georgia — who had been for a sleep-over and was now playing with the girls — sidled up to him just as Jessie headed off, 'is would you have sex with Nora?' Oh God, here it comes.

'Georgia, that's not appropriate. I'm Nora's employer and of course I — '

'Do you fancy her, then? You know, the way you fancy that teacher in Jessie's playschool.'

'I do no such thing, young lady, I — '

'Do too. I heard Dad asking you would you give her one and you said yes.'

He had absolutely no recollection of ever having mentioned her to Bill, he didn't even know her name, for Christsakes. Mind you, there was that drunken conversation about barmaids the last night Kate had cooked dinner for all of them here. He didn't remember much about that, either. That's it, he was going to have to cut down on the booze.

'If I did say something like that, and I'm sure I did not, well, I probably meant I'd give her . . . one . . . of . . . my . . . books. She mentioned she was a fan and — '

'Yeah, right, well that's not what Rocky O'Toole meant at school the other day when he said — '

'Young lady,' he reached up to his full height and prepared to cut this shorter than a hooker's foreplay, 'I have no interest whatsoever in what Rocky or 50 Cent or whoever else in your class said and neither should you, so please — '

'Uncle Jack, 50 Cent is a rapper.' She nudged him and giggled and looked mortified for him.

'Well, you know who I mean, the one with all the freckles. You pointed him out when we were all in Eddie Rocket's last week.'

'William Goldsmith?'

'Who?'

'Dollar Bill, that's what his dad is called at work. Herman White told us. Anyway, he's the fat kid with — '

Jack was getting very confused. 'That's it, Dollar Bill, what did I call him?'

'50 Cent.'

'Same thing. And don't ever let me hear you calling him a fat kid again, he might be very sensitive.' He was relieved the conversation appeared to have taken a more straightforward turn.

'Nora calls herself a fat-bottomed girl and slaps her butt when she sings that Queen song to Jessie and Sam sometimes.' She gyrated like a noughties version of Uma Thurman in *Pulp Fiction* and she had all the actions. He nearly corpsed.

'Yes, well, ehmm . . . ' He pretended a coughing fit. 'I'm sure she wasn't being derogatory.'

'What does that mean?'

But he'd had enough. He was exhausted and the day had barely started. 'Never mind, what I mean is, it's OK to tease yourself, but not other people.'

'You tease me and Sarah and Sam and Jess all the time.'

'Yes, but I love you and you know I don't mean it. Dollar Bill might not.'

'OK, that's fine.' She flicked her horse's mane in his direction and was gone. It always amazed him the way they took you right to the edge and then something clicked and they were satisfied.

Jack abandoned plans to see Rembrandt once he realized it was a fabulously mild winter's day. They dropped Georgia off at a party as Kate had asked, then headed out of the city. First up, a long walk for Rashers and then a big lunch for them in a country house that welcomed children, quite a rarity in post-Celtic tiger Ireland. 'Too many antiques, they'll all be fingering them,' one Princess Anne wannabe had informed himself and Bill a couple of weeks ago when they'd tried to give her bundles of dosh for an unexciting lunch menu, just because Jess was desperate to go to the loo.

'I wouldn't finger her if I was told I had twenty minutes to live and she was the only one with the injection,' Bill had whispered and they'd taken themselves off to Kitty's in Arklow instead. No such adult comedy today, though. Bill and Kate had gone to visit a sick relative so Jack and the kids had a terrific lunch — smoked salmon salad with nutty brown bread for him and goujons of *poulet avec patatas frittes* for the girls. The café was a cross between a trendy chic French sidewalk café and a bustling-with-tattoos kiosk in Majorca, he decided, having spent ten minutes trying to decipher the menu. They tucked into decent portions of crispy chicken nuggets, though, and the slightly pompous waiter brought a very snazzy-looking bowl of lurid red tom kat — as Jessie called it — without being asked, which was a definite plus. The girls dunked their chips in immediately and were happy.

There was a painting class all set up in the garden — retired folk by the look of them — just about to break for lunch, so easels and pallets were abandoned in favour of straw hats and canes as they made their way slowly into the conservatory, where huge pots of tea and cucumber sandwiches minus the crusts awaited them. It was all very relaxing.

Jack paid the bill then took a pot of coffee and the remains of his cheeseboard on a tray outside and the girls ran happily about while he finished the last of the *Telegraph* mag.

'I like this place,' Jess announced about ten minutes later, coming to sit on his lap.

'Me too.'

'Can I bring my own paints next time?'

'Sure, darling.'

'Cause I had to stretch really high to paint my dinosaur and now my arms are hurting.' She held one out for a kiss and he absent-mindedly obliged.

'Fibber, you weren't painting dinosaurs, there aren't any around here.' He tickled her under the arm as she knew he would.

'It was one from my magic nation, like the long red one from George and the Dragon.'

'Ah yes, we never have to worry about you, do we, your imagination will always keep you going. So,' he stood up and stretched lazily, 'want to show me where this magic, invisible dinosaur is then? Or is it a dragon, maybe?'

'No, it's not. Look, it's over there, see.'

'Where?'

'On the big board, right there. Can you see it?

235

It's purple, cause I couldn't find any red.'

'Jess, don't tell fibs, darling.' His eyes were drawn to a huge purple squiggle diagonally across a gentle landscape in the near distance. He looked at his daughter, then back at the almost-finished painting. No, they were wild foxgloves, definitely. There was only one problem, they looked slightly more amateurish then the rest of the work, even at this distance. His heartbeat quickened.

'You didn't?'

'She did.' Sam appeared from nowhere. 'I tried to stop her and then I shouted for you but you weren't listening, so then I started to run over to you but it was too far, so then I ran back to pull her away but she'd already finished.' She was breathless, he knew it was anxiety. She always felt responsible for her little sister.

He took a deep breath. 'It's OK, Sam. It's not your fault.' He bent down. 'Jessie . . . ' but she was backing away faster than a cow in an abattoir. He grabbed her hand and pulled her towards him. 'Jess, look at me.' She lowered her eyes until they were burning holes in her patent-leather pumps. 'I said, look at me.' Her 'it wasn't me, really, I was only joking' eyes barely met his desperately anxious ones before she resumed her navel gazing. He tilted her head up and kept it there.

'That is not a good thing to do. Some nice man or woman has spent all morning' — hell, all weekend, probably — 'drawing a very pretty picture of the garden and you've ruined it.' Her big conker eyes went all glassy and her lower lip wobbled.

'I thought it was a sad picture and you said I should try and make people happy. Remember that song you used to sing to us in bed when Mummy went away?'

'Yes.' He almost choked. Sam started singing it, just in case he wasn't feeling guilty enough to slit his wrists wide open, twenty miles from the nearest casualty ward.

'Yes, I know the one, Sam, thank you.' He took a deep breath. 'Look,' he glanced around at the group of innocent old dears, who looked as if they were about to make tracks back to the task in hand, 'we'll talk about this in the car.' He gathered up their stuff in the time it would take some poor oulwan or oulfella to cry 'jeepers creepers', or something less charitable, and led the girls at what his old games mistress would have described as 'a rollicking pace' in the direction of the car.

'I want to say sorry,' Jess was screaming at an octave he never knew she could reach. Takes after her mother there, he thought grimly.

'Yes, well, you can put your next five years' pocket money in the poor box. That should just about cover it.'

28

'You did what?'

'I legged it.'

'But . . . but, what does that say to the children? What kind of example does it set for the future?' Without realizing it, Ellie was doing her best Orla impersonation. Her sister would lecture Jesus on the right way to preach, if he appeared on earth again.

'I know, but I only thought of that afterwards.' Jack ran his fingers through his already greasy hair. 'Anyway, Miss Self-righteous, haven't you ever done anything like that yourself?'

'Only once, when my westie, Mungo Jerry, tried to have Lauren McKenzie from next door's rabbit, Snauser, for his tea and I thought about it long and hard for almost three seconds then I simply smoothed it out flat with the bloody side hidden and combed it nicely and scarpered to clean Mungo's beard.'

'It was dead then, I take it?'

'As a dodo.'

'Well, now you know how I felt.' Jack and Ellie were speaking for the first time since the 'incident'. He hadn't been about to admit it to anybody, except that Jess had burst into tears as soon as Ellie had arrived this morning. He'd disappeared into his office and left them to it. It was only the worst pangs of hunger that had made him re-appear at four thirty. No tasty morsels had come his way today, that's for sure. She had clearly taken sides.

'Jack, you're going to have to talk to her about it,' Ellie said now. 'The poor baby is traumatized.'

'I did, all the way home from Wicklow and again over a Knickerbocker Glory in the Embassy Grill, her favourite. I explained carefully how she couldn't tell anyone what Daddy had done, until the woman in the next booth started giving me funny looks. I swear she was trying to find the number of the child protection agency as we hot footed it out of there as well.'

'Well, talk to her again. Keep trying.'

'Look, it was a terrible day from the start. Jess asked me if I loved you and then Georgia was here and she asked me if I'd give some teacher one like I apparently told Bill I would.'

'You are a baaaaad papa.'

'Actually, it was definitely all your fault.' He was remembering. 'You've been singing to them about fat-bottomed girls. So, who's a bad example then?'

She slapped her ass and repeated the line, looking only marginally older than Sam. 'That's innocent, compared to giving her teacher one.'

He decided to ignore that. 'Would you help? We could bring them for a pizza tonight and — '

'Sorry, no can do. It's club night, and it's my turn to cook. Actually, would you mind if I left a bit early? I am seriously dreading tonight. Your dinner's in the oven and the lunches and all are done. I'm supposed to be making millet and spinach mash with lightly steamed vitality veggies, and I've no idea what millet looks like, never mind where to get it.'

'Tomorrow evening, then?'

'Fine. I'm just going to hang out this wash and then I'll be off. Good luck, captain. May the Force be with you.'

★ ★ ★

The millet mash tasted slightly of banana. There was a perfectly simple explanation for this: Ellie couldn't find millet anywhere, so she added mashed banana because a knowing shop assistant told her millet was yellowy beige, smooth and tasteless. A bit of salt and no one was any the wiser. They were all way too interested in Maggie's declaration of love, Ellie's boss's suicide mission, Pam's near-hysterical conversation with the whinger about tuxedos for the boys for Christmas dinner at the Plaza and, most importantly, Toni's private plane to dinner in Ashford Castle. Apparently, she found diamond earrings in her crème brûlée and would have swallowed them except the tin foil they were wrapped in had hit off one of her fillings. Her shriek could be heard in nearby Castlebar, according to Maggie. Millet mash didn't even make it on to the agenda.

They'd had to skip brunch the previous Saturday so there was lots to catch up on, although Toni had insisted on a 'Bend it like a Loos Beckham' stretch class, so named because apparently after a couple of sessions you were so supple that you could have phone sex by texting with your toe.

'Did anyone see the column on Saturday, by the way?' Pam asked as soon as they drew breath, after about three hours.

'No, is he back?'

'Yep, and raring to go, by the sounds of it. It was all about one-night stands.'

'Here it is, I kept it for you.' Maggie pulled a dog-eared page from her bag. 'Like my purse by the way?'

They did. 'Present from Doug. Anyway, listen to this. He's talking about the difference between men and women.' She found the bit she was looking for.

'The consensus among the women I know is that men who only want a one-night stand are shits. It happens a lot, apparently. They meet a guy, arrange to see them again and then spend hours getting dolled up to the nines for the first real date. This involves several trips to the gym (if there's time) or Andrews liver salts if they're really up against it. Then they spend a week's wages at the hairdresser's, raid their friends' wardrobes and have their teeth cleaned (bad breath being one of the worst first-date turn-offs, apparently). They meet the guy, offer to split the bill for dinner and invite them back home. This may appear to be a casual invitation but it involves taking bed linen to the laundry, having mini-maids in for two days and several trips to gourmet

shops for some fabulous new muesli and the latest venison sausages. It all goes swimmingly, they spend the next day doodling, checking how their joint names might look on the wedding invites and he never calls. When they tell it like that, you can understand that they might be just a little bit miffed. 'Why can't they just be up front?' my pal Julia screamed last week. She didn't believe it when I said simply, 'Because we are the biggest cowards on the planet.' A few of my rugby mates were even more forthcoming. 'Why ruin a perfectly good shag when you can just give her your mobile number with one wrong digit?' Martin said over a pint. 'I'd rather chew some of that stuff that Jordan had in the jungle, then get into a 'I'm not ready for commitment' type chat."

'Doesn't it just sum up everything we know already?' They all agreed it did.

'I'm dying to read it.' Ellie grabbed the cutting. 'Anyone fancy a seaweed bath, by the way? They have them in Sligo, apparently.'

'Well, off you go. Have one after you've had your colonic.' Toni smiled sweetly.

'She's right, you're on your own there, sister.' Maggie wrinkled her nose.

'This peppermint tea tastes like toothpaste.' Toni grimaced. 'Any chance of a cup of Nescafé?'

'Even better, I'll make some of that nice Italian stuff in the plunger.' Ellie was up in a jif.

By eleven they were all talked out and one or two of them thought about visiting the chipper on the way home, so yawns began in earnest after Pam slipped Ellie a note asking if she wanted to meet her at Caffolas in ten minutes for a batter sausage and curry chips.

★   ★   ★

Next day Jessie was beating her dolls to death with a hairbrush and saying 'bold Daddy' as she lashed out. Ellie had them ready at five o'clock when she tapped on his office door.

'Still on for the 'don't do as I do, do as I say' lecture?'

'What? Oh yes, thanks, Nora.' He looked seriously distracted. 'Actually no, I'm trying to answer this fucking Q & A thing for America. I hate these things. You're supposed to be witty and I never am. They want to know if I played with hatchets as a child. Seemed quite surprised that I didn't. The best I could offer was that I made blood potions out of Tabasco sauce. Pretty dull, eh?' She had no idea what he was on about. 'You know, inspiration for becoming a crime writer?'

'Oh I see.' She hadn't a clue.

★   ★   ★

It was funny the four of them being out together, all muffled up against the shuddering winter blast that had hit the east coast of Ireland — and most of Europe — in the last day or so. There

243

was a Christmassy feeling already and Ellie did her best to ignore it, although Sam was humming 'Jingle Bells' in the car.

The chat went on for a lot longer than either of them had expected and Jack, to his credit, grovelled and admitted that yes, they should have stayed and owned up and 'taken their penance' as Sam suggested.

After humungous pizzas the girls wandered off to inspect the first Christmas tree of the festive season being erected by Antonio and Tomasso, and Jack ordered two glasses of wine and visibly relaxed for the first time all evening.

'Thanks, Nora.' He raised his glass and tried to ignore her smirk. 'Christ, I need this drink.'

'It was all going fine until you tried to involve me in your wrongdoing. It was a rabbit my dog bloodied, not a group of pensioners.'

'You still tried to cover it up.' He wagged his finger at her.

'One more smart remark out of you and I'll insert an anonymous notice in *Artists' Weekly*.'

'Hello, you two. This is a nice surprise. The girls just told us you were here.' Kate and Bill arrived at their table clutching two glasses and a bottle of Chianti, Kate doing her best to hide her delight at seeing them so cosy. It wasn't lost on either of them, Ellie suspected, judging by Jack's leap into the air and rush to sit his sister down beside her. He practically joined the couple at the next table in his efforts to appear casual.

'Jolly cosy you look too.' Bill wasn't nearly as cute as his wife. 'So, what great mysteries of life were you unravelling, then?'

He topped up their glasses without asking and Kate had to shimmy hers under his nose. 'Sorry, darling.'

'Oh, the usual.' Jack winked at Ellie. 'Great art fiascos of our generation, you know the sort of thing.' Ellie smiled and kept mum. It was a light-hearted extension to what had turned into a very enjoyable evening.

★ ★ ★

Toni, meanwhile, was not a happy bunny. Gordon had cancelled their date, twice. The first time he'd called from London, very apologetic and promised to make it up to her later in the week. Then, less than an hour before they were due to meet, his very snotty secretary rang to let her know that Mr Thornton had been unavoidably delayed and no, she didn't know anything further. Her simpering 'I'm sure he'll be in touch later in the week' sounded very much like 'don't hold your breath' to an already frustrated, La Perla-clad nurse. She took her frustration out on the WWW Club, renaming it the Wimpy, Whingin' Wagons in a ferocious email, targeted specifically at the other three, as if she didn't belong. They were to meet for a swim at eleven on Saturday, itself a shock to the system.

'Maybe all she got this week was a Prada handbag?' Pam rang Ellie on Friday evening to see what was going on.

'No, she told me they were planning a weekend in Paris when I spoke to her on Wednesday.'

245

'Well then, either her father has reduced her allowance or some old codger at the home has clapped it and not named her in his will.' Pam laughed. 'You know how she expects her special sugar daddys to deliver.'

'Poor Toni.' Ellie understood her friend. 'She equates money with love, cause her parents showered her with gifts every time they uprooted her from her friends and dragged her off to another new school in another new country.'

'I know, I know. Anyway, I'm just moaning about having to go for a swim. I'll be fine once I get there.'

* * *

After a gruelling aqua-aerobics class that saw Ellie's right leg shoved over her left shoulder and Pam's bum a bit too close for comfort, it was on to the latest health café, cheeringly named in neon as No Fatties Here. Pam was outraged and immediately rang the *Sunday World* and the Director of Consumer Affairs and they had to practically pull her off Toni.

'Remind us again why we're not telling her that she's really pissing us off,' Maggie whispered to Ellie. 'Oh yes, I forgot, she had too many toys as a kid.'

'Relax, it's a wind-up.' Maggie had read a review of the place. 'It's called the Slim for Life Café really, that other thing's just a joke.' Pam was still muttering.

'Chill, babe, you're wired.' Maggie smiled and nearly landed herself a black eye.

They eventually settled on Vegan Heaven and only tucked in with gusto to quinoa porridge because they had no idea what it was, and besides the alternative was mung bean hotpot with sweet potato soufflé, which they all agreed was not to be trusted.

29

The dreaded season of goodwill was upon them and none of them had much of it themselves, although Ellie had bought eleven lime-green satin hot-water bottle covers in M&S as 'oh fuck' pressies. She'd ended up using that phrase quite a lot last year, like when her mother's next-door neighbour but three gave her an aphid sprayer. She'd no idea what aphids were and when she found out she didn't have the heart to tell Mrs Bonnington that she didn't even own a window box — and anyway, wouldn't know an aphid from a wasabi-flavoured dried pea — her latest addiction from the health food store. Still, she managed to get rid of that to the long-forgotten person who gave her a screwdriver that lit up when you hit a live wire — a bit late she would have thought — but that's what it said on the box. Still, she had nothing to give in exchange for the passion-fruit peeler or the water wings or the grouting-made-easy manual. Well, problem solved this year.

She was spending a lot of time with Olga and Rudi, and still feeling as helpless as ever. She arrived early one Sunday evening to find her friend in bed watching TV in the company of a giant bag of nachos and a velvety green dip that looked like snot.

'Want some?'

'Ugh, no thanks. God, how can you eat that stuff?'

'Try that other dip over there.' The thing she pointed to looked like sticky orange marmalade and had the consistency of congealed vindaloo. It was delicious.

'How's my baby?' Rudi held out his arms to her and she picked him up and swung him about. He was still in the same dirty pyjamas, which meant that he hadn't seen daylight today and it was too late now to bring him for a jaunt in his buggy. He demolished the yoghurt she fed him and cried when it was gone, which normally never happened. He was such a good-humoured, placid baby — the type who smiled all day at everyone.

Olga yelled at him in Russian but the child continued to howl. Ellie quickly made a bottle and sat with him in her arms as he drank.

'Olga, are you sure he's OK? He seems a bit clammy.'

'Yes, yes, don't fuss. Come and talk to me.'

'How are you feeling?'

'Tired. The tablets make me drowsy.'

'Well, why don't you have forty winks and I'll give the baby a bath in the sink?'

'No, no. Pour me a glass of that nice-looking wine you brought.' Olga gestured at the bottle.

'Are you sure you should be drinking with those tablets?' Ellie was kicking herself for having brought it. 'It'll only make — '

'Please stop fussing, my friend. I will be fine. Now, come and tell me about your plans for

Christmas and let us eat and drink and be merry, for tomorrow we die.'

Ellie laughed and finished feeding Rudi, then lay him down on the rug away from the gas fire. She poured them both a glass of wine and they chatted and Olga seemed to relax for the first time.

'So, what about Christmas for you?' Ellie knew she'd have nothing planned but realized she'd been waffling on about the girls and Jack and her sister. 'You know you're invited to Orla's with me? Although to be honest, I'm trying to come up with an alternative.'

'Yes, thank you. Your family are very kind to include me.'

'Well, the kids would be charmed with the baby and even if we do all end up in Orla's, we can stay over if you like. I'll keep Rudi in my room and that way you could relax and get some sleep. The kids will all bunk in together, I'm told, so you'll have a room to yourself, plenty of peace and quiet.'

'We'll see.'

'You will come though, won't you? Wherever we are? Even if it's just you and me and the baby . . . and Pam?' Ellie didn't want them on their own.

'Can I let you know later? There are a few things still undecided.'

'Of course.'

'Good. Now, show me the photos of Toni and the girls that you were telling me about. I can see them sticking out of your bag.' The subject was closed.

Ellie thought about Christmas again as she drove home later. All she knew was that she and Pam were doing something together and it would not involve her family if she could help it. She'd said as much to Pam the other day.

'Don't be ridiculous, an excuse hasn't yet been invented that would get you out of spending Christmas Day with the family,' Pam had said when she'd told her what she was thinking.

Pam's mum was off to Canada to her brother, and her eldest sister Ros was heading for Cape Town with her husband and a golfing society. All Ellie knew about her own family was that Orla was having her mum and dad and that meant her as well. Single women never actually got invited to Christmas dinner anywhere, Ellie decided, they were just automatically included with their parents — a sort of charity case. It had been arranged on the second of January — Orla's husband didn't like surprises — and Claire was coming home for a day, less if she could manage it. She had a new boyfriend, a heart surgeon, and he already had hers, it seemed. Orla was cooking so it would be a sweet sherry on arrival, prawn cocktail covered in cling film — a hangover from her days at home — and made two days in advance so that the Marie Rose sauce had a nice skin on top, making it only marginally less appealing than it normally would have been. Main course would include Paxo stuffing, lots of lovely, smelly, extra-soggy sprouts and matching peas that managed to be both mushy and

251

bullet-like, although they had probably been soaked for a week. Instant mash was sure to feature — well that was probably a slight exaggeration, to be fair — but definitely it would all be washed down with some warm screwtop Pedrotti. Oh, and Bird's trifle so that the hundreds and thousands got stuck in your teeth. Ellie had decided, on the third of January to be precise, that she wasn't having any of it. This happened to her every year — as soon as it was over she vowed never again, but of course she'd done nothing about it and Orla would get into a right snot if she pulled out now. She'd been sure they wouldn't want Olga and Rudi but that seemingly wasn't the case, given the detailed sleeping arrangements that Orla had outlined to her, via her mother.

She had more or less made up her mind that she would offer to cook for Pam and Olga and Rudi and any other strays she could find, and then break the news casually to her mother. She planned to invite them all over for a drink after dinner, knowing full well they wouldn't come. No one wants to drive on Christmas night, she knew from experience. She'd no idea what Jack and the kids were doing but he'd told her she could have a full week off with pay, which pleased her no end. She imagined their Christmas dinner would be spearheaded by Kate and include succulent roast crown of free-range turkey with organic veggies and lots of bubbly.

★ ★ ★

Less than three weeks to go and Toni called an emergency meeting of the Wicked Wasted Wans. It wasn't even a Monday or a Saturday so no one was expecting it. Although she laughed loudly and tried to jolly them along, Toni was clearly not having it off with G & T.

'OK, let's face it, we are not making much progress here.' She pulled out a large chart full of yellow dots, green rectangles and purple squares. Their names were in black marker on the left-hand side and none had a star beside it. Pam was up to scrutinize it immediately.

'Ellie, according to this you've gained two and three-quarter pounds, actually no, it's really closer to three, in the seven weeks since we started.' Pam looked confused.

'That's right and Pam,' Toni leant over, 'you're up almost . . . well, let's just say your knicker elastic must be tight.' She elbowed her friend jokingly but Pam was in no mood. Ellie got between them, just in case.

'Maggie, you've lost over two pounds, well done, must be all that sexercise.'

Maggie beamed, her only smile of the night. She'd been peculiarly quiet since they'd arrived. 'How about Toni?'

'Me, I've lost almost six pounds. Start looking for those dates, girls.' This was proof, if any was needed, that Gordon preferred spending time with his dentist than with her.

Just as they were digesting this news Maggie had a go at Toni for no reason and Ellie snapped at Pam — she still blamed her for reading that horrible chart — then Toni dropped the wretched thing and burst into tears, another major one for the books. Ellie decided it was her or Pam to sort this one out, and she felt she was marginally less confrontational right now.

'OK, let's all just calm down. We need to talk this through. I'm making coffee, yes, real coffee, Toni, no arguments.'

'I wasn't going to argue.'

'Make mine an Irish.' Pam took full advantage of Toni's weakness.

'Kalua for me.' Maggie was in like a shot.

'Actually, I think I'll just have ginger and lemon tea with Echinacea and black cohosh,' Toni managed in between hiccups.

'Now, first up, let's talk.' Ellie returned with a tray and several bottles. 'Here, make your own.' She handed round all the bits.

'Where's the cream?' Maggie asked and Ellie gave her a look before deciding things were bad enough without any more aggro. She returned with a carton. 'I'm not whipping it.'

'We'll need the back of a spoon then,' Pam suggested.

'You'll get the back of my hand if you don't shut up and get on with it.' Ellie was getting miffed. 'So, listen up, you lot, because you won't like me if I'm forced to get mad.' She grinned at them. 'As I was saying,' she shifted in her chair, 'we're all a bit overwrought, so let's get the weight thing sorted first. Toni is right, we're not taking it seriously, well, seriously enough.' She held out her hand to acknowledge Maggie's goldfish mouth. 'No, let me finish. And, the thing is, we need to.' This new, powerful, in-control

Ellie was an alien but they liked it. 'Look how much time we three spend gawking at our spare tyres and pasty faces and tongues with cuts on them.' That last one was a new one on them but it was Ellie's latest addiction, she just hadn't got round to sharing it yet. 'There's still time to do something before Christmas, so I propose we make a clean sweep. Now, how about a detox weekend, a proper one, algae and spirulina — isn't that what you called it, Toni — and all that rubbish?'

'What the fuck's spirulina when it isn't wriggling around in a tank?'

'No idea,' Ellie said cheerfully. 'So, I propose that . . . ' She looked around for inspiration and it came to her suddenly in a flash of genius. 'Pam, when are your boys leaving?'

'In the morning.' It was said in the smallest voice imaginable for big-hearted Pam. 'He's now taking them for nearly a month.' That explained why she'd been so snappy earlier. It suited Ellie's plans perfectly. 'Well, I propose we all move in with Pam for the weekend — starting tomorrow — no, Maggie, don't say it, you can manage without Dougie woogie for three days.'

'I was just going to say he's off to London for a match.' Perhaps that answered the question as to why Maggie wasn't her usual cheerful self.

'Excellent. At least, not good for you, Maggie, but it means we can all get together and start a proper regime, really get stuck in, and we'll all feel much better, I promise.' Nobody looked even remotely convinced except Toni.

'I was just going to suggest the same thing.'

She sniffled and blew her nose. 'I have the plan all worked out.'

'Right then, it was meant to be.' Ellie was in full nannyish mode. 'But first, we need to clear the air. We haven't had a proper — I mean proper for us — chat in weeks, so, I want you all to tell us . . . ' she glanced at the clock, 'and make it one sentence for now because it's almost eleven and we're getting pissed. Maggie, no more Kalua.' She slapped her friend on the wrist. 'Tell us in one what's really going on for you at the moment.' She sounded just like Anna Nolan in *Ask Anna*. 'We can discuss it in full over the weekend because, let's face it, we're not going to be eating or drinking or anything so we'll have lots of time to kill.' All heads were down. 'It will give us all time to think, OK, so no spiteful comments, ya'all hear me?' She was positively in preacher mode now.

They needed no prompting.

'That cunt Stephen keeps extending the bastarding trip and his fucking mare of a partner is making more and more demands and it's all a load of tuxedo bollocks this and surf-board wank that and I hate them all.' Pam was first out of the trap.

Encouraged, Toni joined in. 'I think Gordon is seeing someone else.'

'Besides his wife? Sorry, Ellie, sorry, Toni, continue, please.'

Maggie was puce.

'One of the physios told me he'd had an affair last year with a Canadian lung specialist and she said it followed exactly the same pattern as mine,

256

even down to the tin foil and crème brûlée.' Ellie almost whistled but managed to turn it into a sort of snorty cough. It was unlike Toni to be so openly vulnerable, and practically unheard of for her to be upset over any man. 'I'm going to cut his balls out with the garden shears and remove his toenails one by one with pliers.' She blew her nose.

Thank God, Maggie thought, she's OK really.

'Poor you.' Pam immediately forgot her own troubles. 'I knew there had to be a reason why you've been such a cow these last few days.' Pam had a way of delivering insults in a kindly, motherly fashion.

'I'm sorry. I know I take it out on you three. It's just, I know if we lose weight you'll all be really happy and like me for pushing you and — '

'OK, this might be another conversation entirely.' Ellie didn't think anyone was going to accept that miserable excuse, not the way they were all feeling at the moment.

'What she means is,' Maggie smiled kindly, 'you might be . . . eh, going the wrong way about it entirely.'

'I know, sometimes I push away the people I care about most.' Toni sniffed.

'Warmer,' Pam said with a grin. 'Listen, lighten up, Toni, we're your friends, we're not going anywhere.'

'Maggie?' Ellie felt it was time to move on.

After all that, Maggie felt she'd absolutely nothing to worry about. 'Well, it isn't anything really, it's just that . . . ' She didn't really know how to put it. 'I think Doug might be a bit tight.' She went red again.

'Tight in his trousers?' Toni had genuinely never heard that expression, she confided in Ellie later.

'Tight in his wallet, idiot . . . sorry,' Pam barely whispered. She and Ellie weren't in the least bit surprised, just amazed that Maggie was only copping on now. They'd known it since the 'I'll pay for myself, I only had coffee and you four all had toast with butter' conversation the first time she'd introduced Doug to them over breakfast in Dirty Nannys. Toni wasn't as sharp obviously, but hey, she had several diamonds in that Prada bag slung over her Gucci coat so the same thing hadn't been a problem for her, that was for sure.

'Ellie?' Pam was getting into this on-the-couch stuff. She almost reached out her hands to them.

'I don't know, really. I've been fed up on and off for weeks now and I'm not sure why. I'm really worried about Olga and Rudi and I'm sort of jealous of Jack and Kate and their happy families, even though I don't begrudge them it after all he and the kids have been through. I guess, just seeing them up close and personal like, it makes me realize that I want a relationship. I have a feeling my biological clock is counting down to explosion.'

No one said anything for a couple of seconds.

'Christ, what's happened to us? We used to tell each other everything,' Maggie was smiling — the only one of the four, but then she was on her third 'coffee'.

'You're right, Maggie, we need some bonding. OK, that's it. I'm wrecked.' Toni was up. 'We start tomorrow. You said the boys leave in the morning, Pam? We'll meet at fourish, so, in your house. Bring an overnight bag, we're there till Monday morning, seven a.m.' She smiled at Ellie. 'And thanks for the chat.'

'Pleasure.' Ellie felt better already.

'But I've to take Doug to the station at — ' Maggie was panicking.

'Say you're sick. Let him get a fucking taxi. No excuses,' Pam said. She wanted the company.

'Actually, I'm not sure I can make it by four either.' Ellie felt she just couldn't ask Jack.

'Tell him you've just got your period. That always shuts them up. He'll give you Monday off as well, wait and see,' Maggie joined in.

Come to think of it, Ellie realized she was supposed to finish early on Fridays anyway, she'd just never managed it yet.

'And over in God's waiting room, they can all empty their own rotten bedpans. I've had it with men.' Nobody reminded Toni that they were mostly women in the home. It seemed silly to bother.

30

'Nora, want to help us buy our tree after school?' Jess asked as soon as they'd picked up Sam.

She did. They'd been talking about the tree for weeks and she couldn't wait to see their faces when they were decorating it. 'I'd love to, really, but I don't think I can, hon, I've got to leave early today.'

'My mum always made us mince pies while Dad put up the tree,' Sam told her in an 'I don't want you around anyway' voice. Ellie racked her cells to think of a way to cheer up the older girl. From what Kate had told her, Lorna couldn't cook, wouldn't cook and was barely around to watch the caterers deliver Christmas dinner, so it was clearly a case of very rose-tinted spectacles today.

'Well, last time I made mince pies I put onions in them.'

'Ugh, that's gross.'

'I know, I'd never actually tasted them and I thought mince meant real mince, as in moo cow.' That gave them a giggle, anyway.

'I have an idea, why don't we make doughnuts, and deep fry them and coat them in sugar? Much nicer.' Her brain was already trying to store up some fat for the torture ahead. Toni had warned them to have only fruit for breakfast and salad for lunch, and to ignore the headaches and lethargy and nausea. She *had* nibbled an apple on the way to work but it was half rotten inside and she didn't notice until she tasted it. Served her right for doing a full make-up job and having breakfast while driving and singing along with Rick and Ruth on 2FM all at the same time. Then Jack was buttering hot toast when she arrived and she'd added marmalade and gobbled up two slices before he could shout, 'Oi, make your own,' from the utility room.

'Can we make cookies too? You know, trees and angels and things, and sew them with thread and stick them on the tree like they do in the movies?' Jess was daydreaming again.

'They don't sew them, stupid, they stick them on with glue, don't they, Nora?'

Ellie ruffled Jessie's hair and hoped she would be able to find such a thing as doughnut mix in the shopping centre, not to mention cookie cutters in Christmas shapes for that matter. Christ, it'd be midnight before she got to boot camp, but then again ... She turned off her mobile with a nasty cackle.

* * *

'Look, Dad, we've made cookies to glue on the tree.' Jess held up a big one that looked like a submarine on its last legs.

'Fabulous, what is it?'

'An angel, silly. There's her nose.'

'And a cute button one it is too.' He tried to grab a bite. 'Can you eat them? I've had strawberry ones and vanilla ones but never glue flavoured. What an inspiration you are you to us,

261

Nora, always introducing our taste buds to new delights.'

'At least they don't know about the pleasures to be had from sniffing the stuff yet, so chill,' Ellie whispered. 'Anyway, Jess wanted to sew them on so it's that or a lump of blue cotton stuck in your gullet. And there ain't no high to be had from thread either.'

He produced a bottle of red wine. 'I think we might need some sustenance. How about I make some mulled wine with blackcurrant juice for them and add something stronger for us?' He waved the bottle under her nose.

'Yes, please, although I'm driving, so I have to be careful. And you shouldn't be thwarting me, you know what I'm facing later. But one glass should just about keep me from throwing up once I hit Fort Knox.'

'Oh yeah, you'd just started to tell me when my agent rang. Sorry.' He popped the cork. 'Listen, why don't you come with us to pick the tree and tell me all about it in the car?'

'No, you go on your own with just the kids.' She didn't want him to feel he had to include her in everything.

'The girls will have none of it. Anyway, it'll be two against one and we'll end up with a yoke so big that I'll have to put in a mezzanine floor to accommodate it. I need you.'

'OK, so, just let me wash my hands.' She was pleased she'd held out for so long.

'Right, kids, time to take that poor oulfella in the fruit and veg shop for every cent we can, as usual,' he shouted in their general direction. 'He starts off asking a hundred and fifty euros for a bonsai tree every year,' he told Ellie. 'I swear he decides the price by the sort of car you drive.'

'We'd better go in mine, so. That should nab us one for a fiver.'

★　★　★

On the way she filled him in on their plans for the weekend, although not the emotional stuff, of course.

'So what do you eat, then?'

'I think it's all liquid, actually, lots of juices and water and herbal tea.' She tried to sound cheerful. 'But there is some sort of barley broth with wild yam allowed on Sunday. Oh, and sauerkraut.'

'Yum yum.'

'I think the reward if you're not in casualty at the end of the day is a warm bath with rosemary and lemon oil, although in my case I'll probably have drunk it, so it'll just be Epsom salts.'

'Aren't they for when you're bloated? How the hell can anyone be bloated on herbs?'

'No idea. My granny used to soak her feet in Epsom salts and then drink it afterwards. Not the same water, I hasten to add. Or maybe that was bicarbonate of soda.'

'Perhaps we'd better pick up some Chinese on the way home,' he said to no one. 'We could make you a tuck box, couldn't we, girls?'

'Toni would smell it. She has a nose like Monica Sheridan.'

'Who?'

'My mother's favourite, years ago. The Irish equivalent of Delia, I think, although custard powder was as exotic as she got, as far as I can tell. I've inherited all her recipes.'

'I want tuck too.'

'The only tuck you're getting is in bed this evening, madam.' He smiled at Ellie. 'This Toni sounds like fun. What's she like?'

He was being sarcastic, she suspected, or at least she hoped he was. She'd made her friend appear as much fun as Martha Stewart's prison chef.

'Actually, she is. And she's gorgeous looking, thinner than any of us, her family are loaded, men fall all over her and she doesn't even see them. Even her pet budgie's got class.'

'You'll have to introduce us.' He looked intrigued.

'And she's great in bed too apparently,' she was able to say because the girls were on their fourth verse of 'Santa Claus is Coming to Town', and weren't paying attention. 'She's so good that her last fella put diamonds in her crème brûlée and damaged two fillings and . . . ' She just realized she was talking to her employer so she changed the subject faster than she normally switched off *Morning Ireland*.

'Go on.'

'Sorry,' she mumbled in a low voice. 'Anyway, she has this new book. It's called *You Don't Have to Be a Block of Lard or a Lump of Meat — If Nuts and Seeds are All You Eat*. Something like that, it rhymes, anyway.'

'Who's the author?' He was settling into a very

convenient parking spot.

'Some American, wouldn't you know it? The same one who wrote *Ten Easy Steps to Better Bowels and Cleaner Colons*, subtitled *How clean is your internal kitchen sink?* I believe.'

'How about I make you a present of a case of wine, in case it all goes pear-shaped by ten tonight.' He could be very generous sometimes, she was beginning to notice.

'She'd confiscate it, I'm afraid. Hard to hide in a weekend case.'

'Well, the offer's there. My American agent sent me a couple of crates this morning. *Storm Clouds Gathering* went into the top ten apparently.' He never talked about his work and Ellie was intrigued.

'Wow, is that your latest?'

'Nope, ten years old. I don't know where they dug it up.' He was preparing to change the subject, she could tell by his uncomfortable shift, but the girls saved him the bother.

'Come on, Nora.' They were already out of their safety belts and clamouring at the doors to be let out.

'Hello, you lot. What ya doing?' Kate was all smiles.

'Buying a tree,' Jack said with a grin. 'Want to help?'

'Sure, Sarah and I are just here to collect ours, too. We picked it out yesterday on the way to the dentist. Bill was supposed to get it, so he spent two hours putting the roof rack on and then came home with a holly wreath and a cylinder of gas.'

'On the roof?'

'No, silly, in the boot.'

No one had the energy to ask how come, so they spent an enjoyable half-hour bickering over non-shed and spotless-clean house or filthy mess with needles everywhere and nice pine, toilet smell. Ellie was glad the bog won out, although not in Kate's case.

★　★　★

Within an hour the house was bedlam, with boxes — supposedly of decorations but no one was quite sure because they weren't labelled — obscuring the floor. Jess was covering the tree with photos simply because they were in one of the boxes and Ellie caught a glimpse of a very good-looking blonde with big boobs and a small waist before Jack's eyes darkened and he took them gently away.

'I want photos of Mummy on the tree,' Jess was howling but there were no actual tears.

'We have one, look. Remember the one of us all taken with Santa that Aunty Kate gave us a hanging frame for?' Sam was being Mum again and Ellie tried to distract Jess.

'Let's put the cookies on.' She handed the little girl a plate as Jack went to warm some of the mulled wine, to escape with his thoughts, she suspected. Ten minutes later they were eating jam-filled, million-calorie doughnuts that were surprisingly tasty, and it took them another fifteen to realize why they couldn't find any of the cookies that Jessie insisted she'd glued to the tree. The answer came in an almost human belch from under the table and a tail that was wagging so hard it nearly gave Ellie whiplash — not bad for a boxer who only had a stump. He must have been feeling mighty pleased with himself, they all reckoned.

31

'The important thing is not that you succeed, it's that you die trying.' Toni was reading inspirational sayings from a book entitled *Your Soul is God's Greatest Garden*. It was meant to encourage them and keep their mind off food.

'Die being the key word there, I'd say,' Ellie mumbled.

They'd all settled in, stretched out, puckered up and were currently at the grin-and-bear-it stage — it was still only nine thirty.

'Yeah, well the last book I read says, *Be positive, if you're going after Moby Dick take along the tartar sauce*. So there.' No one had a clue what Pam was getting at and they were too tired to ask.

Ellie was actually not feeling too bad, although the three doughnuts she'd scoffed in the car on the way over made some of the yoga movements rather difficult to do. Still, at least she'd managed, Pam had tried to balance on one foot, keeled over and announced. 'That's it, I'm having a fucking Long Island Iced Tea, and before you ask, Toni, no, it is not made by Twinings, it's made by Gilbey's.'

'Calm down, breathe in, remember the piece of thread pulling your pelvic floor up and your tummy in and stretching all the way to your chin.' Luckily, Toni's eyes were closed and she didn't see Maggie grabbing Pam's fist.

'Your chin will have teeth marks in it if I don't get some food fast.' In fairness, Pam was the worst off. She'd been too upset to eat before the boys left and had been in floods of tears when Toni arrived early with the yoga mats and mini trampoline, but now she was calmer and the hunger pangs were beginning to kick in. Also, Ellie suspected she was the only one not to have cheated — besides Toni of course — simply because she'd been too busy blubbering for Ireland. They'd all forgotten what a drama queen she was. Maggie's tummy had a nice little bulge and Ellie was afraid she'd throw up and a whole doughnut would come rolling out.

'Oh why haven't they rung or texted? Anything could have happened.'

'Look, you delivered them safely into the hands of an Aer Lingus cabin crew member, they had name badges, colouring books, three credit cards between them and two mobile phones. The way you're acting you'd think they'd been spirited away by Saddam's second-in-command.' Toni was getting slightly peeved.

'You didn't give them your credit cards?' Maggie was horrified.

'Of course not, she's exaggerating as usual. But you hear of terrible things on aircraft nowadays — old ladies ripping off their burkas to reveal beards and machine guns and stabbing the pilot to death with their tweezers. I am so scared.'

'Well, it hasn't been on Sky News yet today,' Ellie reminded her gently. They'd sat through every news bulletin on all the British channels since they'd arrived, just in case they got the story before RTE. If she had to look at the arse end of one of the royal corgis just once more . . . Thank God for Camilla, she was supposed to detest them.

The phone rang, Pam scarpered away none too gently, leaving Maggie prostrate on the floor with her foot in her ear and Ellie clutching her left shoulder, which had gone into spasm when she'd taken a sudden wrong turn and hit the coffee table.

'Hello, hello. Andrew, is that you? Darling, are you OK? Did anyone have tweezers or a . . . a chopstick or any other lethal weapon on the flight?'

The others grimaced.

'Oh, you're in Bloomingdale's all-you-can-eat-for-fifty-dollars rooftop snack bar?' I think you must have the name wrong. Oh. Right. Yes, I see.'

'I'd murder a snack myself right now.' Maggie looked fed up.

'OK, love. Put Paul on to me. What? What do you mean his mouth is full of pancakes with maple syrup, blueberries and hickory bacon on a bed of parsley purée? He won't even eat parsley sprinkled on his Heinz tomato soup for me.'

She arrived back at the by now defunct class, looking sadder than ever. 'They're having a great time.' Hic. 'He collected them in a limo.' Swallow of contents of nose. 'I hate him and I want a drink.'

'Do you want to try some of this fenugreek and garlic juice with broccoli?' Maggie offered. 'It might help.'

'Take your fucking fenugreek and shove it up your — '

'OK, OK.' Ellie grabbed the cup just in the nick of time and glared at Maggie. 'Girls, I think we should let her have a small brandy. Now I know it's not listed in the book but, really, we've all had a tr . . . what I mean is she's had a more . . . trying day than the rest of us.'

Maggie, feeling guilty for upsetting Pam further, had poured her friend a large brandy and was spooning it into her with a ladle.

'Actually, I'm going to bed if no one minds,' Toni said. 'My shift started at six this morning and I'm wrecked.' She did look bushed. 'And don't anyone even think about getting pissed, I've marked all the bottles.' She grinned at them as she headed off.

'Not this one she hasn't.' Ellie produced a very posh-looking, gold-threaded bottle.

'She'll kill us.' The brandy had made Pam giggly. 'Where did you get it?'

'Jack sent it just in case we were desperate.'

'Well, we'd better dispose of the evidence and chew gum all night, in case Toni gets up at four a.m. to smell our snores.'

'No, let's leave her a note and tell her what she missed.' Ellie laughed. 'It's not like Toni to go off to bed, though. Hope she's OK.'

Five minutes later Toni was back. 'I heard the cork popping. I'll just have a small glass.'

They all relaxed for an hour or so and resolved, with the moral support of some vintage Rioja, to give it a serious go for the next two days.

'You never know, it might not be so bad,' was the last thing Ellie heard before she drifted off to sleep. That and Pam's alcohol-filled zzzs.

★   ★   ★

Actually, it was hell at first. There was no other way of putting it. Ellie was so hungry on Saturday evening that she gave serious consideration to eating a rotten apple she'd found in the garden while plucking some dandelions for soup, and Maggie was wondering about trying to sneakily barbecue a few snails. Even their cosy chats weren't cosy at all, because someone — mostly Pam — bit the head off someone else — anyone actually — so they had to abandon their plan to help Maggie encourage Doug to make with the loot after Pam said he probably wouldn't part with the steam off his piss and Maggie was in floods for hours. But Toni turned out to be great and she kept them all going and by Sunday lunchtime they were agreeing that yes, garlic and beansprout masala with chillies and coriander was much tastier without all that cream and yoghurt and no, you hardly missed the chicken or fillet of beef at all, really.

And strangely enough, at about four o'clock on Sunday Ellie realized she'd hit the wall, as in a marathon, and come through it, literally almost, because she fell over a step on their five-mile hike. After a long soak and another cup of herbal something or other she slept better than she'd done in a long time.

'You look great, how did it go?' Jack was in like a shot when she arrived on Monday. 'Here, grab a cup, I've just made a fresh pot.'

'No thanks, I'm off caffeine.' She squeezed some lemon into a tall glass and added hot water.

'I'm impressed.'

'Actually, I hate to admit it but I feel great. The hunger pangs have nearly gone and I swear my stomach has shrunk.' She pulled up her blouse and then decided her grey, doughy tummy — flat and all as it was — was not the least bit attractive so she sat down quickly.

'So what did you eat?'

'Lots of things.'

'Such as?'

'Millet, quinoa, amaranth — '

'That last one's a new one on me and I won't be requesting they put in on the menu in Thornton's by the sound of it. So, give me an idea of what lunch was like.'

'Yesterday it was a choice between cold raw cucumber soup with parsley flakes and a dash of Tabasco, blanched chicory with cracked black pepper or polenta with shaved Brussels sprouts.'

'You're trying very hard with the flakes of this and sprinklings of that but when I think of shavings I think of parmesan, lots of it.'

'Oh, we had parsnip crisps as a special treat while watching *The Clinic*.' She beamed at him. 'No, I feel full of energy and Toni was great.'

'No alcohol at all, then?'

Damn, there was no point in lying. 'We did open that one bottle you smuggled into my case, yes, I'll admit it.'

'Toni as well?'

'Yep, although she was in bed to start with. But that was our only moment of weakness and obviously I'd no hangover because every time you left your glass out of your hand someone else was gulping it and then swearing they thought it was theirs. That was mainly Pam, though, and she was suicidal, so that's different.'

Jessie interrupted his laugh, screaming for her feely.

'I forgot to tell you, we lost her blanket somewhere yesterday. She didn't sleep a wink at all last night and neither did I.'

Ellie felt like screaming herself. 'But . . . but, this is a disaster,' she whispered as she tried in vain to pick the little girl up. 'It's not just her blanket, it's her feely.'

'You think I don't know that?'

'The pink, furry one with the blue thread and the rabbits and . . . ?' She had to clarify it once more. 'God, the poor child. I'd have died if I'd lost mine. It was a pink candlewick, I used to eat the little bits of thread, pull them out with my teeth.'

He frowned. 'So, what do we do? I tried everything pink in the house, tea towels, scrunchies, brillo pads. How long do they keep these? Sam never bothered with one. When did you give yours up?'

'Just before my twenty-first and then only because my father accidentally set it alight when he was doing the candles on the chocolate biscuit cake.' She grinned and tried to rescue Jess from under the table, where she was flattening poor Rashers and probably deafening him too. 'I'll get her dressed. You make a list of every place you visited yesterday and I'll start phone-bashing as soon as I've dropped them off. This is an emergency, we may have to call in the FBI.'

32

Pam called in sick, she just could not face another 'do you not have any of the Sicilian artichokes, the ones in Bollinger champagne vinegar like they have in Morton's?' day. She went back to bed as soon as the others had left and pulled the duvet so far up that she nearly suffocated. The only good thing was that she didn't feel like eating, not even the Superquinn sausage sandwich that her friend Annie next door had tried to slip through the letter box, thinking Herr Toni was still in residence. She got up for the second time at 2 p.m. and drank black coffee and watched *Judge Judy* till ten to five, when the monsters rang. They were in F & A Schwartz.

'Gee, Mom, it's like so cool, I'm having a neat time,' Paul told her in his best Raheny meets Manhattan accent. Andrew tried hard to be chilled but only managed it until he got to telling her about the Empire State Building. She kept it together until they told her they had to fly cause they were having 'eggs over easy' for brunch in a real New York diner on the corner of 52nd and then going to see *Superman 12* or something, just like they would at home really. She bawled her eyes out, went back to bed and slept for fourteen hours.

★ ★ ★

Maggie was having a lovely day. She'd met Doug for lunch — his treat — and he'd offered to pick her up from late-night shopping in Swords to save her two bus rides later. He'd also asked for her keys so that he could fix her leaky radiator and put a new plug on her bedside lamp. She felt loved and secure and best of all he had wanted hints on what she'd like for Christmas, and also what he should bring to her mother's, which was more than generous. She was thrilled and planned to splash out on a designer jacket for him, all unsettling thoughts forgotten.

★   ★   ★

Toni got a text from Gordon the grotesque.

Champagne cocktail in the Merrion followed by oysters in Guilbaud's then dessert in my apartment?

It was almost covered in spits before it was erased. Four dozen blood-red roses had their heads cut off next, a bottle of Cristal was used to celebrate batty Myrtle's ninety-ninth birthday, but a full-length, baby-wipe-soft leather coat did the trick. It was just that she missed him, although she wouldn't have admitted it in a fit. They had sex in a doorway in the arch near the halfpenny bridge while the busker in residence had dinner with U2 or some other celebrity in the nearby Clarence Hotel, courtesy of G & T's donation. Toni decided she'd been a little bit

277

hasty in writing him off just because of what someone had said.

* * *

Ellie, meanwhile, had lost about three pounds, she reckoned, re-tracing Jack's steps around Dublin, enquiring about a filthy, half-eaten rag and offering several hundred thousand euros of Jack's royalties as a reward. By the time she returned at five, he was ready to tear his hair out because she'd left him with the kids, and she had a blister the size of a gobstopper on her shin, so she wasn't much better.

'Any luck?'

She shook her head in despair. He ran his fingers through his hair and it made him a dead ringer for Shakin' Stevens. Sam had taken to gelling his locks every morning this week and he kept forgetting. Now he looked like he'd been plugged in.

'How is she?'

'Not great. Kate came round with Sarah's little teddy that she's been trying to steal for years, but I caught her trying to blitz it in that food chopper thing, which luckily you'd disassembled.'

Ellie made all Jess's favourite bits for tea but nothing worked. She stayed late and gave the child a warm bath and then spent half an hour trying every other thing she could find to use as a security blanket. She was just making her way downstairs when she met Jack, on his way up because the crying had stopped and he couldn't concentrate in the silence.

'How did you get her to nod off?'

'The only thing that worked was the belt of your dressing gown. She felt it for ages and then something clicked.'

'The blue striped one?' She nodded absently. 'You gave her the belt off my three-hundred-euro Christian Dior dressing gown?'

'Serves you right for owning such a ridiculous luxury.'

'Kate gave it to me for my birthday.'

'So how do you know it cost three ton?'

'She gave me the receipt because she thinks nothing she buys me is ever right.' They trooped downstairs together.

'Thanks, Nora.' It wasn't sarcastic.

'Pleasure.'

'Tea, coffee, glass of wine?'

'Detox, remember?'

'Ah.' He walked her towards the door. 'Any chance I'll get the thing back, do you think?'

'Not while you're still trim enough to fit into it, I'd say.'

'Well, I'm going to try, but not tonight. Besides, I've just remembered she puts her feely in her ear at night, doesn't she?' He made a face.

'Not any more.' She smiled like an angel. 'This one's up her nose. Nite nite.'

★ ★ ★

The rest of the week was slower than a turtle race for Pam. She snapped the head off an old woman simply because she tried to use a 'fifty

279

cent off when you spend five euros on fruit and veg' coupon and her bill was only four euros ninety-eight, then ran after her, mortified, and tried to shove free carrots and lettuce in her bag. She spent hours on the Internet every evening, looking up facts and figures about New York, so she'd have something to talk to the boys about when they next rang, and she cleaned the house to within an inch of its life and prayed for a ring around the spotless bath again soon. The others minded her and called round for chats and for once none of them wanted to eat rubbish or drink alcohol — Pam had no appetite whatsoever, Toni was getting so much sex that she was too exhausted to eat, Maggie was desperately trying to fit into the new black catsuit she'd bought for Christmas day to impress Doug and Ellie was run off her feet, with work, her mother's endless Christmas lists and most of all with Olga Blake.

'You're going round there again tonight?' Pam was amazed. 'What's up with her?'

'I don't know. She just wants to talk, but it's all a bit odd, to be honest. She keeps asking me if I'll have any children, or if I'm going to marry Jack, or — '

'Jack? Surly Jack?'

'He's not that bad, actually — '

'You're thinking of marrying him? Ellie, listen to me, this is not a good basis for a — '

'No, I'm not thinking of marrying him, I'd give G & T one first and you know how I hate bouffant hairstyles.' They had no proof that Gordon had even a blade of hair on his head, it was all in their imagination, but they spent hours fantasizing about him. Impossible not to really when Toni described their love life in such detail.

'He's athletic, anyway, I'll say that for him.' Pam was thinking of the time they'd had sex on the Luas line two minutes before the last tram was due in from Sandyford. Toni did a mean impersonation of him hitching up his Calvin Kleins and legging it as some driver shouted, 'Hey you, ye dirty wanker' at him. Still Toni loved it, apparently.

'Last time Olga asked me if I thought children should be circumcized.'

'And do you?'

'Listen, I barely know how to spell the word.' She shook her head. 'She just seems to want me around at the moment — lots of deep bonding going on, on her part anyway. I'm fine about it, it's just, I could do without it in the run-up to Christmas. Mum wants to go shopping all the time and Orla is trying to get me to make a pudding for her. She says I'm not taking part enough.'

'You still haven't told her we're not going?'

'She never knew you were in in the first place.'

'We'll end up there, I can tell. Anyway, I'll do the pudding for you.'

'You will? You angel.' Ellie hugged her. 'It's just, I'm so tired all the time, trying to lose weight. I can't be bothered juicing and slicing any more so I've simply resorted to eating practically nothing, and Jack isn't really around much, some deadline or other, so it's full-on with the girls all day, every day, now they've broken up for Christmas.'

'Stop taking on everyone else's problems, Ellie, you do it all the time.'

'I know, I know. Actually, I am going to talk to him about it. The kids aren't even dressed when I arrive in the morning and I have to knock to tell him I'm leaving and could he please supervise Sam's homework.'

'Go for it.'

'I intend to, on Friday. Anyway, I'm off. Ring you tomorrow. Love you, want you, need you.'

'Missing you already.'

★ ★ ★

Luckily, when Ellie saw Olga that night she was tired and not in the humour for long chats, so Ellie played with Rudi for an hour and escaped, felling glad to be free of the cheap flat with its chip-shop smell. She had a long soak as a reward for getting off so lightly. Usually, she'd have had a single of chips on the way home, with lots of salt and vinegar, so she figured her habits were changing slowly.

★ ★ ★

On Wednesday Olga sent her a text, then phoned her, twice, asking her to call round on her way home from work.

'It's important.'

'OK, but I can't stay past — '

'I won't delay you, but promise you'll come.'

'Fine.'

'Promise.'

'I promise. Olga, what's this about?'

'Nothing, but I need to know you won't let me down.'

'I've already said — '

'Fine, so what time?'

'About six thirty, seven at the latest.'

'No later than seven.' She must be cooking dinner, Ellie thought.

'I'll leave my key under the mat, in case I'm dozing.' That put paid to that theory; it must be Christmas presents, although she hadn't a bean. Christ, Ellie hadn't got her anything, nor Rudi, although she had bought his Christmas outfit the week before, but Olga had let him wear it and he'd grabbed a pen and drawn a clown, well a squiggle really, on his sleeve. Olga's casual attitude really pissed Ellie off sometimes.

'OK, look, I gotta go, I'm in work.'

'Seven then.'

'Yes, or earlier.'

'Don't forget. It's very important.'

'I won't.' No chance of calling it off later, Ellie realized. She was exhausted and Sam was coming down with a cold and was more precocious than Bart Simpson.

* * *

It was ten to seven when Ellie let herself in with Olga's key, two bags of groceries threatening to topple her over. The TV was blaring — not unusual — but Rudi had obviously been crying, and for quite a while too, his face was streaked and swollen and he was secured in his cot, which had been pulled over in front of the TV. It meant he could stand up and move around but not attempt to climb out, which he'd started to do recently. It was something Olga did sometimes when she wanted to sleep and it really annoyed Ellie, because the child could easily get caught up in the strap. It made her nervous and she quickly unhooked him and called out, 'Olga, I'm here.'

No answer, again not unusual. She opened a carton of juice and gave it to Rudi but he started screaming and she knew from the smell that his nappy needed changing. He was hot, too, even though the flat was permanently cold, so she picked him up and took him with her. 'There there, it's OK, let's go wake Mummy up.' She hopped over the toys, most of which she'd bought for him herself, and wrinkled her nose at the combination of stale urine and sick as he clung to her, crying and sweating. She was getting fed up of this.

'Olga.' She pushed open the door of the tiny bedroom. The curtains were drawn and it was stuffy and damp at the same time. She reached over to gently tease her awake and even before she saw the empty vodka bottle she knew.

33

Afterwards, Ellie didn't remember touching her but she knew she must have done. It was part of the first-aid training, nanny style. She'd never forget those mask-like, waxy features. And the blue-tinged lips and the feeling of cold in the air. She did remember getting Rudi away fast, just in case he sensed something. Later, they told her she had dialled 999. All she really knew was that she had flopped, like a giddy drunk, into the only chair in the place and held the baby very close, his earlier nauseating smell comforting her, reassuring her that nothing awful had happened to him, which probably would have finished her off.

That's how they found her, anyway. She'd even left the front door conveniently open, and within seconds of the screeching blue light arriving a crowd had gathered. They were mostly bored adolescents, Ellie knew from the brief encounters and furtive whistles that had often made her smile and even flattered her on a really bad day. The gang — mostly teenage boys — waited, asking questions, trying to get closer to the door. For them, it was a major happening, what with police and medics involved. Besides, anything that eased the boredom of living in a run-down council estate was welcome — and the more bizarre or grotesque the distraction the better.

The cop car and ambulance had arrived almost simultaneously, although she hadn't notified the former. She hadn't needed to feel Olga's pulse and didn't even notice the empty bottle of pills, nor had she picked up either of the two notes propped up beside her on the cheap, melamine locker. She could still see the awkwardly positioned body, lying as if all the bones were broken in a loose, rag doll sort of way. They shooed the kids off and closed the door and a nice young ban garda sat with her and asked all sorts of questions and she heard muffled snatches of post-mortem and state-pathologist type conversations and she had to keep repeating, over and over again because they didn't seem to believe her, 'no, no family, no one, just her and the baby'.

Later she was able to say, 'Oh yes, there were relatives — in Russia — but they disowned her' and 'Blake' was all she could come up with in response to constant requests for a surname. When they prompted that Blake was hardly Russian, the only thing she could think of was Dostoevsky.

It was much later that they asked her if there was anyone they could call and she tried hard to think of someone, but her mother would panic and her sister would be horrified and Pam had enough on her plate and Maggie would be too upset. She eventually rang Toni, thinking that her medical background might be useful, and simply said, 'Please could you come round to Olga's and help me?' There must have been something in her voice, because Toni responded immediately. 'Yes, give me ten minutes.'

'Thanks.'

'Ellie, is everything OK?'

'No, not really.'

'All right, listen, stay where you are, I'm on my way.' And she left Gordon in the very posh French restaurant near the Troc, with no more than a quick 'I have to go, something's wrong with Ellie'. She refused his slightly bewildered offer of a lift, half explaining as she gathered her stuff that it was quicker to grab a taxi outside the door. She was greeted by uniforms and silence and noise and that instantly recognizable smell she knew well from the nursing home.

Thinking back, it was the best call Ellie could possibly have made, because Toni was well used to taking control and the uniforms were blown away by her aura of sex and power and cool intelligence.

'What happened, darling?' she asked in a calm voice. And eventually she was the only one able to persuade Ellie to loosen her grip on Rudi, who was clutching her back with almost the same degree of ferocity.

'She's been really odd, lately, did I tell you that? No, it was Pammy I was telling. Anyway, this morning she rang me a few times and texted me as well, insisting I call round, making me promise and silly things like that. I always come when I say I will, you know that.' Toni nodded and kept rubbing her hand and the policewoman listened and made notes. It was the most they'd got out of her so far.

'How did you get in? Have you got a key?'

'I have, actually, but she seemed to have forgotten, cause she told me hers would be under the mat at the front door. She's sometimes sleeping, you see. She's been very depressed lately — taking tranquillizers and anti-depressants and sleeping tablets.' Ellie swallowed and tried not to cry. 'Same as most of the people you see in a lot of working-class surgeries in Dublin most mornings, eh?' Toni didn't know, neither did Ellie really, but she'd heard enough, on the local buses and in the tiny post office and barricaded chemist where she sometimes went for Olga.

'Tell me what happened then?'

'Rudi was screaming and the TV was blaring, nothing new there. He looked a bit more . . . neglected than usual and he smelt.' She sniffed his bottom, wondering if she'd changed him and forgotten. 'He was fastened in, which Olga sometimes does if she wants to sleep, and it irritated me, although she means no harm.' She kissed the top of his head and he never budged. 'I picked him up and he kept howling until he saw her and then he just stopped.' She looked at Toni in a puzzled way. 'He knew, I know he did.' Toni nodded. This was all much worse than she'd imagined.

'I knew, too. Suddenly it all made sense.'

'What did?'

'All her odd questions lately. She was checking me out.' Her eyes were glazed. 'She planned this, Toni.'

'How do you know?'

Ellie didn't seem to hear. 'I wonder if she was planning it when she asked me to be his godmother. Do you think?'

'I don't know. Oh, Ellie, you poor, poor thing.' And Toni, gorgeous Toni with the five-thousand-euro leather coat and the diamonds and the gloss, pulled the smelly baby and the equally pathetic nanny into her arms and held them close.

They let her go, after they'd checked her address and knew where the baby was being kept. They told her that a social worker would need to see her, and the baby.

'Not tonight,' she insisted. 'He needs to rest and so do I.' They persisted, talked about taking the baby into temporary foster care, but she replied quietly, 'I'm his godmother, he's my responsibility,' in a tone that brokered no argument, and besides, they'd already found Olga's notes and knew a lot more than she did.

'I'm a nurse, I'll stay with them tonight.' Toni offered her accreditation for inspection and they seemed happy.

★   ★   ★

Nevertheless, they were barely in the door of Ellie's apartment when a social worker arrived, a slip of a thing who looked about fourteen. It was after ten o'clock by then and Rudi had eventually fallen asleep in Ellie's arms in the back seat of the taxi. The ban garda promised to deliver Ellie's motor later because nobody was overconfident of its chances of surviving in the

289

neighbourhood, once everyone knew it had been abandoned for the night. The young civil servant asked the minimum of questions, ensured they had everything needed for a young baby and promised to call the following morning. Toni saw her to the door.

'Ellie, go get into your dressing gown, you're shaking.' She gently prised the baby out of her arms. 'It's OK, darling, you need to get out of those clothes.'

'Actually, I do need to go to the loo.'

'I have his bag here. Go get organized and I'll change him and get him ready for bed and put the kettle on and then we'll make a plan, OK?'

'OK. I'll just set up the travel cot. Lucky I bought it last year, eh?' She thought for a second. 'I bought it to cheer Olga up when she was pining for Russia. Told her she'd need it for their first visit home.'

'You were a great friend.' Toni wanted to say more but Ellie swung around sharply.

'No, Toni, that's where you're wrong. I wasn't. I was annoyed and pissed off and everything, especially today. I should have realized what was going on.'

'You were the only light in her life, I'd say.' Toni kissed the top of her head, just as Ellie had done with Rudi. 'She chose very wisely when she picked you as her friend.' She smiled sadly. 'As we all did.' But Ellie was shaking uncontrollably and eventually Toni had to ring Pam, because she needed to mind them both and couldn't. Ellie was upstairs changing when a totally stunned Pam arrived half an hour later, followed by a bewildered Maggie as soon as she got Pam's slightly hysterical message. They hugged and kissed Ellie, and Pam took off her make-up and helped her undress and Toni changed the baby and frowned at his soaked, blotchy bottom and putrid nappy and Maggie made them all strong, sweet tea and wondered what Ellie would do now.

They lit the fire and made a bottle for Rudi, but he showed no interest, just stared at them all with those saucer eyes and Maggie had to keep turning away and eventually she made an excuse and escaped to the kitchen, where she cried her eyes out. Pam felt very guilty when she thought of her own two gorgeous boys and she prayed for them and for their safe, speedy return, something she hadn't done in years.

Ellie thought of ringing her mother but decided it was too late and, anyway, she was afraid they'd all descend on her.

'I need to ring Jack. He'll be expecting me in the morning.'

'Want me to do it?'

'No, it's OK.' She smiled vaguely at Toni. 'Actually, yes please. I don't think I can face anybody right now.'

★   ★   ★

'Hello.'

'Hello, could I speak to Jack please?'

'He's not here right now. Can I take a message? This is Kate, his sister.'

'Oh, hello Kate, this is Toni Francescone, I'm a friend of Ellie's.'

'Yes, hi, Toni.'

'I'm sorry, but Ellie won't be in tomorrow.'

'Is everything OK?'

'No, I'm afraid not.'

Kate was stunned when Toni explained, as briefly as she could.

'Oh my God, she never mentioned this friend, at least not to me.'

They chatted for a while and Kate promised to tell Jack and took all their numbers and gave them hers, and when she hung up Kate too said a prayer for her kids, and for Jack's and for the little boy left orphaned that night.

34

Pam was loitering outside Ellie's room next morning and brought her a cup of tea as soon as she heard her stirring. Ellie looked at her vacantly for a split second, then jumped up with a frightened look. 'The baby?'

'Still fast asleep, don't worry. Here, drink this.'

'I have to get up,' she protested, but when she tried her bones hurt, probably because she'd slept all hunched up like a baby herself.

'I had terrible dreams.'

'Me too. Are you all right?'

'I don't know, I feel very strange.'

Pam sat on the edge of the bed and handed Ellie the cup.

'Here, drink this, it'll give you a boost.'

'It'd take more than tea to give me a lift this morning, I'm afraid.'

Pam smiled weakly and rubbed her arm and the baby stirred and startled them both.

Ellie reached over and picked him up and he looked surprised to see her, she thought, which was stupid. He was too young. It was only a flicker, before his face assumed that same accusing stare he'd given her last night. Oh God, this is a nightmare, Ellie thought.

Pam sensed her fear and lifted the baby gently out of her arms. 'I'll feed him, the girls have a bottle made downstairs. You just stay there for a second.'

'No, I need to get up, there'll be people calling and things to organize and — '

'It's not even seven o'clock.'

'Oh, right.' She lay back for a second. 'God, the funeral. Pam, I don't even know if she had any insurance.'

'Let's not worry about that right now. We'll see what they say later.' 'They' being the police.

'Do they bury them, anyway, you know, make the state pay for it?'

'I've no idea, but I can find out pretty quickly.'

'I have to give her a proper burial. She was proud, you know.'

'I know.' It was a whisper.

They stayed together, each lost in their own thoughts, until the baby mooched once more and Pam went off to feed him and Ellie hoisted her dead weight out of the bed and into the bathroom.

★　★　★

By eight thirty they were all washed and dressed and by nine the phone started, then the doorbell. Pam had to go in to work 'because of my stupid self-pitying episode earlier in the week,' she told the other two, ashamed of herself now. Toni and Maggie stayed and filled the kettle a million times as Ellie prepared to tell her family.

Her folks were stunned and Ellie could feel the unasked questions lingering like static between them. She had to get off the line. 'There's someone at the door, I have to go, I'll ring you later, Mum. Will you tell the others?'

'Yes, and Orla and I will be straight over.'

'No, Mum, please.' She was risking a major offence, but she hadn't the energy for them. 'What I mean is,' she tried to soften the rejection, 'there are things to do, legal stuff, the police, that sort of — '

'The police, what do they want with you?'

Ellie tried to be patient. 'Mum, she killed herself. I was the one who found her, of course they need to see me.' And then there's the baby, she didn't say it but she could feel it was what her mother was thinking.

'I suppose the baby will be taken into care?'

'I don't know. Listen, I'll talk to you later, once I've spoken to the social worker.'

'Are you sure?'

'Certain. Maggie's here with me, minding the baby.' Her mum liked Maggie the most, so that helped. She didn't mention Toni. This was all on a need-to-know basis.

★ ★ ★

The next few hours were a bit of a blur, when she thought back later. Jack phoned, she heard Toni talking to someone in a low voice for ages and then she asked if Ellie wanted to speak to him.

'Hello.'

'Nora, I don't really know what to say except how sorry I am.'

'I know, thanks. I . . . hardly know what to think myself.'

'It must have been an enormous shock for

you, I can't even begin to imagine.'

'Yeah, it was.'

'Were you very close?'

'No, that's the funny thing. I never really knew her, not like my friendship with the girls, you know. We sort of became mates by accident, really. But in the last few weeks, she was saying funny things, asking strange questions. Looking back I don't know how I didn't put two and two together.'

'It's not something you could ever have guessed, from what I've heard. Don't be too hard on yourself.' He was gentle.

'I suppose.'

'Is there anything I can do?'

'No, thank you.' She felt oddly formal with him. 'I don't know when I'll be back to work, that's the only thing, I — '

'Forget it. Ring me when you've had time to think. And you can take as much time as you need, you know that?'

'Thank you.'

'And Nora . . . '

'Yes?'

'If there's anything, anything at all — I mean that. I hope you know.'

'Thanks.'

'Mind yourself.'

'I will. Thank you again.' Her voice sounded odd.

'Talk to you soon and please, do ring, even if only for a chat.'

'OK.'

'Promise?'

'I will. Bye.'

'Bye.' He had the strongest urge to add 'God bless', very strange. He was turning into his father. But then it was always God or your parents in these kinds of situations.

★ ★ ★

When he hung up he was hardly any the wiser. Oh, he knew the details, Toni had filled him in. And Nora had sounded so . . . normal, he realized afterwards. Not a bit like the usual bubbly girl he'd come to know.

He rang Kate.

'Well?'

'I don't have any more news. You know as much as I do, really. No obvious reason why she'd top herself. Nora's friend Toni said she'd always been a bit odd, whatever that means.'

'Christ, I'd say she was more than a bit odd. To do that to a child. I couldn't sleep all night, thinking about it.'

'Mmm, makes a great story, though.'

'Always the journalist, eh?'

'Yeah, I suppose.'

'Still, it won't be a major story. She was a foreign national, remember?'

'Yeah and we all know our tolerance level in that regard.' It was one of his pet topics. He thought for a second. 'No, I was thinking more of a book.'

'God, you're callous.'

'I don't mean to be.' He sounded genuine. 'Writers are always looking for storylines, you should know that by now.'

'I do. Poor Nora, though. She doesn't deserve this. And what on earth is going to happen to that helpless baby?'

'No idea. Adoption or long-term foster care, I presume. I mean, Nora's no relation, is she?'

'No, I don't think so. The woman must have family somewhere, though. I'm sure they'll be able to trace them.'

'They disowned her, according to Toni. She used her ex-husband's name. He disappeared as well, as soon as he found out she was pregnant.'

'That's a lot to deal with.' Kate felt like crying — for the unknown woman, for Nora, but most of all for the pathetic-sounding bundle of a child.

'Is there anything we can do, money or anything, d'you think? I didn't feel I should offer directly to Nora, you'd be better at that sort of thing.'

'Should I call round?' Kate asked him.

'Yes, she might talk to you easier. Just let her know, if you can, that we can help.'

'You're a good man, bro, you know that?'

'Hey, I'm just another selfish bastard. Don't want to lose a good nanny.'

'You mean the one you didn't want in the first place? The one I forced on you?'

'Gotta go, my mobile's ringing. Can't hear you, sorry.' He hung up with a sad smile.

* * *

It was after six by the time Ellie realized that she hadn't eaten a thing, despite the trays of ham sandwiches and stuff that the girls had magicked. She wasn't hungry, just all talked out.

Pam arrived with at least one of everything Tesco sold, it seemed, and they were just drawing breath when Ellie saw her sister's car pull up outside with her mother's perm clearly visible in the front seat.

She panicked and Maggie sensed it instantly. 'OK, upstairs. Now. Pam, run a bath. Toni, you're on junior duty. I'll get rid of them after a decent chat. Don't worry, I won't be rude.' She saw Ellie's face. 'I'll just say you're lying down.'

'Don't tell them too much, I just can't handle the barrage that will follow. Not yet, anyway.'

'Sure. Go on, they're coming.'

'Don't offer them a drink. They'll be here all night.'

'Right so.'

* * *

Pam added every smelly oil she could lay her hands on to the piping-hot water and Ellie soaked for Ireland. Now that the shock had worn off a bit she had no idea how she was going to handle it. She was responsible for a baby, another life — and one she was not even related to. Or wanted. God, that made her feel guilty. Oh, they'd talked about foster parents and adoption and relations in Russia, but the family or the husband weren't a runner, Ellie was fairly sure from what Olga had told her. And as for care, she couldn't do it to Rudi, she'd known that the minute she found Olga. He'd never had

299

a chance, not a snowball's in hell, right from the start, but she could give him one. Maybe so could a new set of parents, but she was tied to him, if not by blood then certainly by holy water. What about a father? she wondered — not his real one, obviously, but the fact that she didn't have a man in her life to provide a father figure. Would that make a difference to him in years to come? She thought of her own father, but abandoned the fantasy. He could barely deal with people from this country, never mind from another one.

'They've gone.'

'How come? They've only just got here.' As she spoke she realized the bath water was much cooler.

'No, it's nearly eight. We made them tea, told them just enough and persuaded them that we were doing a good job of minding you both.'

'You are.' Ellie heaved herself up and let her friend towel her dry. They'd even washed her dressing gown because Rudi had puked on it twice this morning.

'Jesus, your sis is something else. You're not a bit like any of them, d'ya know that?'

'Thank God. Why, what was she saying?'

'Oh, nothing really.' Maggie felt guilty already. 'She's just so . . . so . . . '

'Irritating?'

'No . . . '

'Smug?'

'Yes, that too, but that's not the word I was looking for.' Maggie grinned. 'Miserable, that's it. Everything's a problem.'

'A trial,' Ellie agreed. 'Mother of sorrows, we used to call her when we were little.'

Her own childhood was playing on her mind a lot today — not surprising really. 'God, Olga, what the fuck were you thinking of when you chose me?' she asked for the tenth time.

35

The fog never lifted, really, even though it had been days. Little kindnesses astounded Ellie. Neighbours she didn't even know left sponges still warm in cake tins, kids called with toys, and flowers arrived by the bucketful.

Kate stopped by with a huge bag of clothes that had belonged to Sam and Jess but would easily transfer — hooded jackets and jeans and blankets and bits. The girls themselves drew pictures — of Rashers and Dalmatians, their other obsession at the moment — even of their dad with his hair standing on end. Kate didn't stay long, sensing Ellie's weariness, but urged her to call if she needed anything at all.

Her sister Claire came home too and that was easier, they'd always been close enough. Having her around mattered. Suddenly family had taken on a whole new meaning.

Eventually, they were allowed to proceed with the funeral and Ellie added another worry to her endless list. Would anyone come? There was no family, just a handful of Ellie's friends. Even Olga's neighbours had said they never knew she had a child, except one who said she heard him crying a lot, which sent a fresh wound straight to Ellie's heart. She longed more than ever for a relationship. Actually, just someone to hold her close in the dark would do.

* * *

Ellie decided to keep the ceremony simple. Even if funds hadn't been a problem, she sensed Olga wouldn't have wanted fuss. She rejected all the caskets inlaid with apostles and saints, as she did the ones with shiny gold handles, opting instead for a simple blond wooden coffin. She placed one white rose gently on top.

She didn't know any priests but Pam did and so a lovely, compassionate man received the remains and spoke about Olga and Rudi as if he'd known them for years.

Ellie and the baby were the chief mourners — the only ones, in fact — and sat in the front row, with the girls taking up the row behind, along with Ellie's family. The church was almost empty, despite Olga's neighbours turning out in force, as well as most of Ellie's friends, some of whom she hadn't seen in years. The people who came surprised her almost as much as those who didn't show. Bill and Kate and Sarah and Georgia were first up at the end. They each gave her a huge hug and almost made her cry. The queue that formed to shake hands was no longer than that seen in any supermarket on a slow weekday afternoon. Ellie waited, just in case anyone arrived late, but eventually Toni wrapped Ellie's scarf around her neck and Pam rubbed her arm and suggested it was time to go.

'Nora, Nora.' Ellie heard the echoey little voice and she turned to see Jess flying up the aisle, all legs and teddies and pom-poms, followed much more sedately by Sam and Jack.

'Nora, I miss you, please come home soon,' she yelled as she ran straight into Ellie's already full arms.

Maggie took Rudi and Ellie dropped to her knees in the aisle and hugged the small child. Jack looked worried as he walked as quickly as was decent in a church to where they stood huddled together in a small group.

'Hello.'

'Hello.'

Ellie felt as if she was seeing him for the first time. She gathered the little girl to her and stood up. He looked different. Cleaner. Taller. Less troubled. He was wearing his glasses again and looked very intense. It made her want to giggle, which was ridiculous, given that she'd never felt less like laughing in her life. Those and a long black soft woollen coat with a thick polo neck sweater underneath made him much less approachable than the dishevelled artistic type she was used to. Standing there in the harsh winter light that added nothing to an already icy church and with his youngest child trying to strangle her, Ellie felt as if she'd never really noticed him before.

'Who the fuck is that?' Pam whispered through tightly pressed lips.

'Whoever he is he's mine, even if there's a wife loitering at the back of the church, which there's bound to be.' Toni prepared to dazzle him with her smile, trying it out first on Pam, who had to don her shades immediately.

'It's Jack Bryant,' Maggie offered.

'Fuck.'

'No.'

'Has to be. Kids called her Nora. Remember that story?'

'But, but she said he was . . . ' Pam was dumbfounded, which was most unusual.

'I know. She's a lying bitch, obviously.' Toni winked at the others, threw back her gleaming mane and adjusted her bra, ready to pounce.

Nearby, Jack stood back until the kids had hugged Ellie to bits. Even Sam wanted some of her loving. Eventually, they looked towards their father.

'I'm so sorry, Nora.' Jack reached out for her too.

Seeing them reminded Ellie of a former, much more carefree life and she burst into tears on his shoulder. He didn't seem to mind, just held her and rubbed her back. He smelt clean and sort of citrusy.

'I feel so . . . Ssss . . . ad,' Ellie sobbed.

'I know.'

The kids, unusually, said nothing. They were used to her being in control, smiling, cajoling, even scolding. Tears were not part of the parcel where she was concerned but they adjusted rapidly, as kids do.

'Here's my hanky. I only used it once.' Sam handed her a little embroidered cotton square with a pink rose.

'Thank you,' Ellie glugged.

'You can keep it. Aunt Martha gives me boxes of them every year. I've hundreds.' Sam smiled. 'Besides, they're useless. They're all hard and they hurt your nose.'

'Not today they're not.' Ellie wiped her eyes and Jack kept his gaze firmly on her.

'You all right?'

She nodded unconvincingly.

'I brought my teddy for Trudy.' Jessie held out one of her favourites.

'Rudi,' Sam hissed, poking her in the back.

'That's what I said.' The younger girl shrugged her off.

'But that's Howard,' Ellie said. 'He's one of your favourites.'

'I know.' The little girl looked slightly forlorn.

'Dad said it had to hurt, else it doesn't really count when you give something away.' Sam sounded just like Ellie's mother.

'I don't think I said that exactly . . . never mind.' Jack decided it wasn't what she needed right now. 'Is there anything I can do?'

Ellie shook her head and bit her lip. Her eyes were red and her nose was running.

'So, which one of you is Jessie?' Pam stepped in and whisked the girls out of earshot, in case they needed a moment. She could only remember one of their names.

'You're so kind to come. Kate and Bill and the girls were here earlier.'

'Yes, I spoke with them. We were here for the service, we just stayed in the background. I was afraid the girls would take over, so we were waiting for you to finish here. Until Jess escaped.' He grinned. 'She misses you.' He looked at her sadly. 'We all do.'

It was too much for Ellie and she was off again and he didn't look in the least bit mortified, simply put his arms around her again until the sobs lessened.

'We should go.' Maggie appeared eventually. 'I think they're waiting to close up.'

They all trooped down the aisle, kids skipping, friends and family hesitant, Ellie shuffling like an old woman. Jack stood back to let the girls go in front. He guessed who they were and they all nodded politely to each other.

Outside it was too cold and wet to stand around.

'I'll see you at mass in the morning.' Jack smiled at the group as the kids pulled him towards the waiting car and the promised meeting with Mr Eddie Rocket and his famous sundaes.

'You don't have to, honestly.' Ellie was surprised.

'I know that, but I want to. Kate and I'll come without the gang.' He looked at her. 'Ring if you need things done, lifts or anything . . . '

'Here.' Jess held out her teddy in Rudi's general direction and he looked terrified.

'Are you sure, love?' Ellie asked, holding the little boy tighter in her arms. Every time she saw that scared look on his face she blamed herself.

Jess nodded fiercely. 'I have loads and loads of teddies.'

'Well, thank you. I'll give it to him when he's going to sleep.'

'Bye, Nora. We love you.' By now she was skipping away.

Sam ran back and hugged her and Ellie was touched.

Next morning the mass seemed to take for ever and each hymn brought new tears. Local pensioners attending morning mass wiped their eyes and stared at the child, clucking and shaking their head when the circumstances were explained in hushed tones.

By the time they came to lower the coffin Ellie was numb. She clutched Rudi and closed her eyes and prayed that Olga was finally at peace. She also asked God to help her cope. Her grief was multi-layered. It was a complicated peel of sadness, worry and guilt.

Pam had organized lunch in her own house, which was reasonably close to the cemetery and empty of the boys, who would have scoffed all of the goodies if they'd been home. Ellie was surprised to find Jack and Kate among a small handful of people who came.

'Anything I can do?' Kate was pulling off her coat and rolling up her sleeves.

'No, I don't think so, maybe just check with Pam?'

'Sure.'

'Can I get you a drink?' Ellie was suddenly self-conscious with Jack hovering.

'No, someone's already doing the honours.' He pointed to one of Pam's neighbours who was mingling with a tray of coffee and hot ports and whiskies to ward off the chill.

'Is it my magic nation, as Jessie would say, or are graveyards always freezing, even in summer?' Ellie asked him. 'I was so cold that I still can't feel my toes or fingers.'

'Here, try this.' He reached over to the offered tray.

'Ugh, no, way too early.'

'It'll warm you up, go on.' He placed the tall glass in her hand and took one himself. Even wrapping her fingers around it helped and the smell always reminded her of Christmas and today that thought calmed her.

'I never introduced you to the girls last night.' Ellie led him over to where they were standing, watching. For some reason she was anxious to be rid of him.

'This is Jack Bryant.' She smiled too brightly at the three, who already knew everything they could about him, courtesy of a few racked brains.

'Hi.'

'This is Maggie, that's Pam over there and this — '

'Hi, I'm Toni Francescone.' She held out her hand and exaggerated the Italian pronunciation and he liked her firm grasp.

'We spoke on the phone the other night,' he greeted her warmly. 'I, eh, feel I know you lot rather well, actually.' He looked around to include them all.

'Oh God, what's she been telling you?' Pam was in like a shot.

'Nothing, really, I promise. It's more what she's been doing to me. One or other of you is responsible, I gather.'

'Depends.' Toni was giving him the 'I'm a celebrity and I wish you'd get me out of here' treatment, all pouty lips and big eyes and hair. It was clear she wanted his vote.

'What exactly has she been doing?' Maggie grinned.

'Well, she hasn't quite followed me into the loo yet, but my tongue has been very closely examined.'

Toni was looking at his mouth as if she'd like to examine his tongue very closely herself. If this wasn't a funeral and he wasn't Ellie's supposedly crotchety employer she'd have been in like Flynn.

'Oh God, I'll bet he knows everything.' Pam was mortified.

'It's her fault, mostly,' Maggie gestured in Toni's direction, 'although Ellie started it, really.'

One of the neighbours came to talk to Ellie so she excused herself and left them talking. Much later when she glanced over he was still there, laughing with the girls and looking completely at ease.

36

Things settled down remarkably quickly over the next day or two. Pam insisted that Ellie and Rudi stay with her, so they could all get used to each other. Another more senior social worker visited and talked at length with Ellie, who'd gone from being fiercely protective of the baby to praying they'd insist on taking him into care, so enormous was the weight of responsibility she felt when she looked at him. The chronic shortage of foster parents in the Dublin area meant there was little chance of that, unless they had serious concerns for his well-being. Before the social worker left she dropped another bombshell.

'You know that Olga left a note.'

'Yes, I think there were two, actually.' Ellie suddenly remembered.

The lady nodded. 'One for us and the other for the gardai.'

'What did they say?'

'She just made it clear to us that she wanted Rudi to be brought up by you. She said you loved him and that you'd been her best friend.' Ellie could feel the tears welling. 'And the other?'

'She asked the gardai not to try and trace her family. In fact, I believe she destroyed all her personal papers — passport, that sort of thing. Was the split with her family very bad?'

'Yes, I think so. They threw her out, literally, after she announced that she was seeing an American. She ran away to London to live with him . . . she called him her husband but I don't think they ever actually married, although she used his name. Her story was a bit confusing. All I know is he left as soon as she told him she was pregnant.'

'Did her family know about the baby, do you know?'

'Yes, I remember she told me she contacted them for help, after he left. They told her never to appear back home with a child out of wedlock. Her father cut her out of his will, although I don't think they were very wealthy or anything.'

'And do you know anything about the American?'

Ellie shook her head. 'I don't even know his first name, she always just referred to him as the American, or Rudi's father.'

'Any idea where he went to when he left?'

'No, they were living in London, somewhere around Islington, I think. He went back to America as far as I know. He didn't want anything to do with her. I remember she said something about Rudi not being his first child.'

'Anything else?'

'No, she wasn't very talkative on the subject, sorry,' Ellie apologized. 'Usually, she got fed up after a bit and simply refused to say any more. I know that she had two sisters who also left home. One went to Canada, I think, and the other to Australia.'

'Do you know whereabouts in Russia her parents lived?'

'No. Maybe she mentioned it, but I don't remember.'

The lady smiled and thanked her and left.

'Ellie, you need to think this thing through very carefully.' Pam was cautious as they sat sipping tea after the visit.

'I know.' She was much less sure now.

'It's a huge undertaking.'

'Yes.'

'And you don't automatically have to do it . . . ' She wanted to point out again that Ellie was not a blood relative, but decided not to. Neither did she mention that her mother was practically camping out on Maggie's doorstep, looking for information on when the child was being 'taken by the authorities'.

'What are you thinking?' Pam was treating her like a baby herself.

'One minute I'm determined to care for him as if he was my own, the next I'm . . . terrified he'll ruin my life.' Ellie was crying again. 'I feel so bloody selfish . . . and afraid . . . and . . . lonely.' It was by far the greatest of all the emotions that swamped her, mostly late at night.

'That's all perfectly normal. Oh, darling, come here.' Pam held her tight and Rudi slept soundly in his travel cot beside them, unaware of his precarious future.

★ ★ ★

313

Ellie moved home the following day, determined at least to try it out. Toni volunteered to keep her company for the next few days as she was working nights. Maggie was there every evening and stayed over a lot. When they weren't around Ellie watched TV and washed Rudi's few borrowed bits and pieces and tried to play with him, although he didn't really respond.

Kate phoned the following weekend.

'How are you managing?'

'OK, thanks, as long as I don't have to meet anyone.' She smiled into the phone, looking down at her filthy jeans and crumpled sweater.

'Is there something I can do? Take him for an afternoon, maybe . . . anything?'

'Oh no, thank you, you're very kind.' Ellie felt she didn't really know her well at all. Her previous life had shrunk dramatically in her mind. 'The three girls are fantastic,' she assured Kate. 'They seem to have a rota going. I'm rarely alone.' It was true.

'You're lucky, but then I think we make our own luck.' Kate had always known Ellie was a decent person and she firmly believed in what goes around comes around. 'Tell me, what about Christmas?'

'My mum is cooking.' Ellie was dreading it so much she didn't even want to think about it, although it was only a few days away. 'Orla, my sister, was supposed to do it, but she's not feeling very well, apparently. I haven't a clue, to be honest. If all this hadn't happened I wouldn't have been going. I was determined to break loose this year. It's a bit complicated . . . ' She trailed

314

off, wondering why she was going on about all this.

'Who else will be there?'

'My two sisters — Orla is married so her gang will be along, and my other sister has a new boyfriend and he's coming. I haven't met him . . . oh, and Pam, too. Her sons are with their father in New York this year.' She realized she'd barely spoken about it to Pam, so wrapped up had she become in her own narrow little world.

'Yes, she was telling me all about it the day of the funeral,' Kate said. 'I liked her enormously. Great fun. I'd say she's a brilliant mother.'

Ellie was glad she'd said that. 'She is.' She smiled just thinking about Pam. 'She's a hoot as well. As long as you don't mind her very colourful language.'

'I've used a few choice words myself over the years, I can tell you.' Kate laughed. 'Actually, Jack and I were wondering, would you come round and spend Christmas Eve with us? We always try to make a family day of it; we had a younger brother, he was . . . killed in an accident on Christmas Eve, so — '

'Oh my God, I'm so sorry, I didn't know.'

'It was many years ago.' Kate spoke almost to herself. 'He was only seven.' She gulped. 'I still miss him, isn't that funny?'

'Not at all.'

'Jack took it the worst. Blames himself, it's a long story. Anyway,' Ellie could feel Kate mentally shaking herself, 'I'm sorry, I don't know where all that came from, you've enough on your plate as it is.' Her tone brightened but it sounded forced. 'Will you come, please? It's Jack's turn this year. We have lunch and exchange presents and sit around. I'd collect you, and the baby too, of course. The young ones miss you, and my two are dying to get their hands on Rudi, especially Georgia.'

'I don't know, I really don't want to intrude, and besides, I usually meet my friends for brunch or something, early in the day, before we all go our separate ways.'

'Bring them along, the more the merrier.'

'Oh no, I really couldn't. They'd drink Jack out of house and home.' She was only half joking. 'I'm only teasing, they're not that bad really,' she felt she should add, just in case Kate felt that her entire circle of friends were foul-mouthed alcos.

'Listen, think about it.' She'd promised Jack she'd ask. The girls were driving him mad about Nora and besides, they'd all grown very fond of her and the baby was a constant topic of conversation in both their houses. 'We don't meet till threeish, anyway, so you could still see your friends for brunch. Your presents are already under the tree, by the way, and the pile for Rudi is taking on gigantic proportions.'

Ellie was touched. 'I will, I promise.'

'Great. I'll call you again anyway.'

★   ★   ★

The truth was, she was absolutely dreading Christmas, especially the day itself.

'I think you should go. Want me to come with

you?' Toni asked later.

'No, I've got to start facing people. I'll give it some thought.'

'Tell me about Jack, by the way.'

'Not much to say, really.' Ellie was surprised at the question. 'I more or less told you everything I know.'

Toni decided not to ask anything more for the moment so she simply shrugged and changed the subject.

★　★　★

The weather suddenly took a turn for the worse and that meant days of sleet showers and icy nights. It was an excuse for Ellie to stay put. The only good thing about what had happened was that no one, her family in particular, put any pressure on her to contribute to the festive season.

Maggie had managed to persuade Ellie's parents, nicely, to back off, and even Orla had, for once, stopped making sarcastic remarks.

Rudi was no trouble, and the girls put all their plans on the back boiler and shopped for Ellie, decorated her apartment and even made a hair appointment for her.

Suddenly it was Christmas Eve. The Club met at eleven for breakfast because Toni was flying to Italy in the afternoon to be with her mother's family and Maggie and Doug were driving west later. Pam had booked Pete's, the latest trendy greasy spoon, where they tucked into huge breakfasts — organic this and free-range that.

Everything was wild or traditional and the juices all had exotic names. It cost a fortune, but the customers felt healthy, even though the fat content was exactly the same as it had been twenty years ago when the place was called the Napoli Café and run by Charlie and Ida from Glasnevin.

Ellie's sister Claire was babysitting Rudi, who showed no emotion whatsoever when a complete stranger took him off. Ellie couldn't believe how free she felt — free and monumentally guilty.

The girls exchanged presents but their banter was subdued and the slagging non existent — everyone was conscious that Pam was lonely and Ellie was numb. All talk of weight was abandoned and even Da's or G & T's ears wouldn't have been burning. They weren't in the mood.

Afterwards, they hugged and kissed and promised to spend New Year's Eve together and Ellie collected the baby and headed for Jack's, where the place resembled feeding time at the zoo.

'Girls, please, Ellie will go home in five seconds if you don't leave her alone.' Jack needn't have bothered. The kids were all over her like a rash, a real baby offered much more scope than even the noisiest Little Miss whatever.

'Jess, remember what I said — be gentle.' He looked worried. 'She asked me earlier if his arms and legs came out,' he explained with a very creased brow. 'She has a baby doll that does all sorts of tricks.' After a couple of anxious minutes Ellie abandoned all concerns for Rudi's safety and sat him on the floor where the girls circled him like vultures.

Kate took her coat and Bill brought her a glass of bubbly, which for the first time in her life she didn't want.

'You look lovely, Ellie. What have you done to your hair?' Kate asked, smiling, glad the younger woman appeared to be making an effort.

'Just a trim and highlights. The girls made me, they even bought me this top and new jeans and boots.'

'You've lost weight.' Kate could have bitten her tongue off. 'What I mean is . . . ' She sounded flustered.

'Don't worry, I know exactly what you mean and you're right. It's one of the very few positives from all this. I've been off my food, although in the last few days I've been comfort eating — Mum's Christmas pudding, especially. I keep stealing slices from the bottom and she can't understand because it still looks exactly the same but she says it's shrinking.' They were laughing together and Jack watched her, relieved.

'You've been seeing a lot of your mum, then?'

'Yeah, I know that underneath it all she's worried, especially since Rudi is still with me. So I've been dropping by for an hour most days, hence the addiction to her pudding, which she never lets us touch till Christmas Day.'

They chatted on and Kate had lots of questions about Rudi, but she decided to tread carefully.

Jack had called in the experts to do the food

and so they ate well — a large smoked ham, lots of salads and a fragrant, lemon-scented chicken dish with rice were on offer and the kids had decent sausages and real chicken bits — not a nugget in sight. Bill was better than Father Ted at making them laugh and the fire and the alcohol made them all drowsy.

The presents cured that. It was bedlam. Ellie had never seen such abandonment — paper everywhere, hugs and kisses offered freely and whoops of delight at barely two-second intervals. It was so different to her own family's controlled gaiety that it made her eyes water, not that it took much for that to happen these days. Rudi sat in the middle of it all and looked terrified. He didn't touch any of his presents but the girls opened them and ran around demonstrating everything. Kate gave Ellie a fluffy dressing gown and the girls bought matching slippers and Jack gave her a gorgeous Lainey sweater. She was mortified because her offerings comprised selection boxes for all the kids, a book for Bill and a CD for Kate and a bottle of single malt for Jack, all bought by Pam in her store at midnight the night before.

'I don't know what to say, this is all way too generous, I'm afraid I — '

'Listen, my wife has nothing else to do but flex my increasingly fragile cards, and we had to stop Jack buying you a Cartier watch to keep you with him,' Bill whispered as he topped up her drink and patted her back nervously. 'Don't get all emotional on me or

I'll force you to sing karaoke on Sarah's new thingy. She's been trying to teach me 'Smells like Teen Spirit' or something equally revolting all day. Whatever happened to 'I Saw Mommy Kissing Santa Claus'? It's quite frightening really. When she opened it just now she uttered the immortal line, 'Oh, deadly buzz, ta Pop.' I shudder to think how much I'm paying for her education this year, so that she can learn English.' Ellie couldn't help laughing, he had that effect on most people.

★ ★ ★

Later, she helped Jack stack the dishwasher while Kate played with the kids and Bill dozed and Rudi just looked on.

'So, tell me about tomorrow, what are the plans?'

'You wouldn't believe it if I said, it'll be as different to today as fish fingers are to sole on the bone.' He raised an eyebrow.

'My family are . . . careful.' She felt disloyal saying even that, but he'd seen her mother's thin lips that turned downwards and her father's permanently anxious smile at the funeral, so he understood.

'I don't know where they got you, so?'

Now it was her turn to arch her brows. 'Is that good or bad?'

'Good, of course.' He realized she was teasing. 'Well, if you must know, since you haven't been here I've realized how good you've been for the girls — in fact for all of us, really. They keep

321

telling me about all the little things you do that make them laugh. I'm afraid I can't compete.'

'Nonsense, you're a great — '

'No, it's true.'

'Thank you.' Neither of them seemed to know what to say.

'Kate told me that today was your brother's anniversary.' Ellie wanted to mention it. He looked caught out for just a split second.

'Yes. It was a long time ago but still, you never forget.'

'Were you very close?'

'Yes, although he was only seven.'

'Younger or older than you?'

'Younger by just over two years. I was supposed to be minding him . . . '

'What happened?' Her voice was gentle.

'We were playing in the garden. He was kicking his ball against a wall. I was digging. The ball rolled away, the gate was open . . . he ran, shouting. I ran after him but a truck was thundering along . . . '

'I'm so sorry . . . '

'He was killed instantly. On Christmas Eve, can you imagine?'

'It must have been awful.'

'Yeah.' He sighed. Neither of them spoke for a second. He had a far-away look in his eyes and she wanted to hug him.

'It took a long time to get over.' He seemed to try and shake off the memory. 'So . . . ' He bent down and started messing with the dishes to avoid looking at her. 'When are you coming back to us?'

Ellie knew she had to tell him sometime. 'I don't think I will be. I can't. I'm really sorry.' She hadn't intended saying it today, hadn't really thought it through fully. It came out all wrong.

37

'When did you decide this?' He hoped he sounded calm.

'It's not that I've really decided, it's just that . . . ' Her eyes filled with the ubiquitous tears. 'I have a child now. Everything's changed.'

'Do you want to stop working here?' His voice was gentle.

'No, but I can't continue . . . ' She wasn't sure of anything.

'Bring him with you.' He wasn't sure either.

'What?'

'I mean it.' Suddenly, he realized he did.

'But I couldn't work properly, it just wouldn't — '

'Well, put him into playschool with Jess, then.'

'I don't know if I could afford it.' There was no point in not being honest, he deserved that much.

'We'll work it out, don't worry.'

'No, I really don't think . . . '

'Well, don't then.' He put his finger to her lips. It felt like an intimate gesture. 'At least, don't make a decision now. You think too much, that's your problem. Live with the idea for a day or two.' Her chin was edging towards the floor. Kindness always did that to her. He caught it just in time, forcing her to look at him. 'You have been very, very good for this family and I — we — don't want to lose you.' He couldn't believe

324

he was saying this when he'd done everything to avoid having her in the first place. Must be the champers, he thought, smiling to himself.

'You two look very cosy.' Kate glanced from one to the other and realized she'd disturbed something. She could have kicked herself for bursting in like that. She tried to rescue the situation. 'Sorry, am I interrupting?' She winced at the way it came out.

'I was just telling Nora that we can't live without her.' He never took his eyes off her face.

'I knew that the moment I set eyes on her.' She decided to add her tuppence worth. 'Anyone for a top-up?' was all she could think of to say.

'Not for me, thanks,' Jack shook his head. 'Just convince her to stay, will you, sis? I'll go and wake up your husband. I can hear his snores from here and they're not pretty. Might frighten the baby.' He strolled off.

★ ★ ★

'Are you OK?' Kate asked and Ellie nodded.

'Here, sit down, I'll put the kettle on.' She turned away to give her a second. 'Actually, I forgot. The caterers made fresh coffee just before they left. Like a cup?'

'Yes, please.' Ellie blew her nose, even though she hadn't been crying. 'I'm sorry, I'm all over the place and I can't seem to make decisions and people being nice to me makes it worse.'

'Well, I can solve that one.' She poured two cups, grabbed milk and sat, forcing Ellie down with her. 'I'm not being nice, honestly — just

325

practical and a bit selfish when I tell you that you're the best thing that's happened to this family in a long time. No, wait,' she held up her hand as Ellie tried to protest. 'The girls love you, the house has become a home and even Jack, who has the manners of a little boy racer sometimes, sees that. He told me the other day you'd changed his life.' Her smile was completely genuine. 'And in turn you've changed my life too because I was really worried about the three of them. So,' she reached over and rubbed Ellie's hand, 'I'm afraid you're not getting away that easily. Why don't you forget about it for the next few days and see how you feel then?' Ellie felt like one of those stuffed dogs you often see in the back of Fiesta cars. She just kept nodding.

'Good, now let's go assemble that giant monster thing. Bill started it earlier, but he always gets in knots. Last year he swallowed two fingers and a sword belonging to one of the robots, because he kept trying to hold all the pieces in his mouth and read the instructions at the same time. Sam had wanted it for months and the bloody thing never got finished. Come on,' she stood up and put her arm around Ellie. 'Don't look so worried, it'll be fine.' But Ellie wasn't so sure.

★ ★ ★

Next day was the big one. It passed off well, or maybe Ellie's expectations were so low that it could only have surpassed them, no matter how much Bird's trifle she had to eat. Pam helped enormously, as did her sister Claire, and the new boyfriend played with Rudi for ages, so after a while Ellie's mum stopped looking terrified that he'd puke on her expensive patterned carpet, which looked like vomit swirls anyway, or smash her completely useless crystal menu holder. Ellie's mum was still the only person alive who typed up a menu for every occasion — on her ancient typewriter — and polished the ridiculous glass thing every year. The dining room was only used for special occasions anyway, so her parents were particularly precious about it. And all that for marrowfat peas and lumpy smash! Jamie's school dinners had nothing on it.

★　★　★

Later, back at Pam's house, the two girls put the baby to bed, opened a bottle of wine and had a good laugh. Pam was relieved, she had been slightly afraid that Ellie hadn't noticed anything about the day at all, and that would have been seriously worrying.

'Even the sherry to start was awful, and I could still taste it in the trifle hours later.' Ellie hadn't yet recovered.

'She did mention that it was last year's bottle, and even I know sherry doesn't keep once you open it.' Pam was glad to see her friend smile.

'Ugh, and those pre-packed turkey and ham portions . . . '

'They weren't?' Even Pam knew she wouldn't go that far.

'I'm sure they were.'

'The stuffing was definitely made by Paxo . . . '

'Not to mention the vol-au-vents . . . '

'Campbell's soup and pastry was all I could taste.' Pam ran her tongue round her mouth and grimaced.

'It was the smell of sprouts stewing that got me.' Ellie wrinkled her nose.

'The Christmas cake was my personal highlight.'

'I think she made it in June. I told her she needed to keep pouring brandy on top to preserve it but she wouldn't listen. I swear I scraped off a bit of mould — '

'Enough, I feel sick.' Pam was wiping her eyes. 'It's no wonder you can't cook, darling. Your mother would put anyone off.'

'Listen, compared to that I'm Darina Allen. And remember, that's her making a huge effort. You should try her tripe and onions every Tuesday. It gives a whole new meaning to the word delicacy. And you know, they could afford to have caterers in every year, or treat us all to a fancy hotel.'

The phone rang and Pam jumped up. It was the boys, they'd rung earlier in the day as well, so they were obviously missing their mum, despite the twenty-four-hour diners and endless supply of Hershey's bars.

★   ★   ★

The next few days passed in a blur of Milk Tray and black-and-white westerns and afternoon tea and *Little House on the Prairie* re-runs. Maggie came back beaming, sporting very pretty silver earrings, and Toni returned to find a gift voucher for Harvey Nics for millions loitering on her mat in the hall. Suddenly it was New Year's Eve and they were excited because Kate had invited all four of them to her annual bash. Ellie said no but the girls insisted, especially when she made the mistake of telling them that Jack said there was always a great crowd there, a smattering of Bill's celebrity clients and a handful of trendy lawyers.

'That'll do nicely,' Pam assured Ellie.

Because she couldn't get a sitter for less than a thousand euros Rudi came too, which slightly tarnished her image as a carefree girl about town, but Kate's Sarah took him out of her arms in the hallway and brought him to the master bedroom that doubled as a crèche and Ellie didn't see him for hours.

'Hello, there.' Jack appeared and Ellie had to fight for floor space as three well-endowed *Sex and the City* lookalikes swung into action. She stood back, a bit self-conscious since he'd said all those nice things to her on Christmas Eve. he shook hands with them and kissed Ellie on the cheek. 'Let me get you all a drink.' He looked around. 'Where's the baby?' Everyone called him that. Rudi was just too like Rover, no matter how many times you said it.

'Sarah's kidnapped him.' Toni was gazing at him and licking her lips. I'd like to kidnap you, was practically tattooed on her forehead.

Lots of people came to chat, mostly because of Toni, Maggie suspected, not really caring, thanks to her gorgeous new boyfriend safely tucked up in bed — in training for the rowing club next morning at seven, she told the girls. If Pam hadn't seen him she'd have suspected he was shagging someone else.

Toni did indeed look stunning. She'd definitely lost weight and she was wearing low jeans, tower-block-high boots and a really sexy silver halter-neck top. Her boobs were still practically up against her chin — Pam hoped there was sticky tape involved, otherwise they were all doomed.

Maggie was dancing about looking like she'd ants in her pants and Ellie and Pam were laughing with a guy who clearly thought he was a younger version of Elton John, judging by the rug and the jacket.

'He reminds me of someone. Who? quick.' Pam asked as soon as his back was turned.

'I was just thinking the same thing. It's Father Dougal.'

'Who?'

'You know, the young fella from *Father Ted*, the one with all the hair. A bit thick.'

'That's it exactly, he even has the accent.' Pam was delighted. Ellie smiled as the guy came back over to them and she looked around and noticed Jack and Toni talking by the window. She was just about to join them when Kate cornered her and asked for her help.

'Yes, sure, anything to get away. Who's yer man?'

'Bill's brother.'

'Oh my God, I'm sorry I — '

'Don't be, we've been mortified by him for years. Cross between Jimmy Saville and Alan Titchmarsh. Serious identity crisis, which wouldn't be a problem except that he thinks he's Bono. Stop laughing, you.' She poked Ellie in the ribs. 'I've had years of it.'

'You married into a right family. I admire your courage,' Ellie said with a grin and followed her into the kitchen. They began to wash and dry some glasses. 'Actually, let me just check on Rudi, first. I haven't seen him since I arrived.'

'Sure, second on the right upstairs. But I should warn you, last time I put my head in the girls were painting his nails violet.'

Ellie was still smiling as she pushed open the door of the bedroom. The girls were watching a movie, gathered in a heap on bean bags on the floor, older ones as engrossed as the tots. In a corner, Rudi was propped up with pillows, sucking his shiny blue thumb. Jack was kneeling in front of him with his back to the door, chatting.

'Hey, buster, how ya doin?' He was right down at the child's level. 'You are one gorgeous fella, d'ya know that? And we are goin' to have great fun together in the New Year. I'm gonna teach you to swim and play football and everything, so make sure you tell your new mum that you want to come back to us, cause we think you're great.' He leant over and ruffled the child's hair, then gently kissed him on the head. It was a funny moment for Ellie, but not funny ha ha. The Jack she didn't know was back again. Something had changed for her that evening at the funeral and her brain was too full of Rudi and Olga to sort it out just now. All she knew was that when he'd held her that night it had felt right. Like coming home. She could still smell the lemony scent of him and she remembered how soft his neck had been when she'd buried her head on his shoulder. It was too difficult for her to figure out what all this meant. For now she only knew it was different. And that, for her, there was no going back to the way it had been before.

38

Ellie backed out of the room, straight into Toni and Maggie.

'But what about G & T?' Maggie sounded puzzled. 'Oh hi, Ellie, your boss has just become the latest geezer to be targeted in her quest for world domination.' She nodded in the direction of Toni, was about to say something else then shut up quickly. 'Oh hi, Jack, we're . . . eh . . . just looking for the loo.'

'Two doors down.' He smiled at the three of them. 'I've just been checking on the kids, the baby is OK, bemused but fine. I think it must be the noise levels or else he's been sniffing the nail polish.' He smiled at Ellie and headed back downstairs.

The girls chatted for a few minutes about a couple of tasty guys they'd spotted and Ellie was relaxed as she headed back to the kitchen and Kate.

When they returned to the main room the party was in full swing. Toni was being chatted up by a Richard Madeley look-alike and Jack was deep in conversation with Jordan's twin sister. Kate's daughter Sarah had noticed. She swept past Ellie and Kate, flicked her hair and glared in Jack's direction. 'That's gross,' she said to her mother.

'It's called flirting, darling. I'll give you another two years.' Kate slapped her daughter playfully. 'God I feel old.' She sipped her drink and smiled at Ellie. 'Five years ago I'd have been right in the middle of this lot.'

'I wouldn't.' Ellie hated to admit it. 'I've never been much good at parties. They scare me.'

'I know what you mean.'

★ ★ ★

Jack and Pam had just arrived at the makeshift bar together when Bill swooped. 'Jack, introduce me to this beautiful creature immediately.' He smiled at Pam, liking her voluptuousness, or as Toni called it, the Barbara Windsor school of sex appeal.

'I'm Pamela.' She grinned at him.

'And how did I get so lucky that you came to my party?'

'I'm Ellie's friend.'

'Ellie who?' He hadn't a clue who half of them were tonight.

'Nora.' Jack filled him in.

'Ah yes, I knew I'd heard it before. That girl has more names than a royal.'

Jack grinned and turned to Pam. 'The girls call Ellie Nora, I'm sure you heard. It's sort of stuck.'

'Nora is not cool, trust me. Try Ellie, it'll grow on you.'

He shook his head. 'I like Nora.'

'I like her too.' Bill's eyes were slightly glazed.

'Yes, well, whatever.' Pam glanced in the direction of her friends. 'Poor Ellie, she's had a really rough time.'

'I know.' Jack was thoughtful. 'I don't want to lose her, you know. Maybe you'd talk to her?'

'What about?'

'She's thinking of not coming back to work.' Jack hoped he hadn't said too much.

'She never mentioned that to us.' Pam was worried. Toni joined them and Pam quickly filled her in. She was horrified.

'Look, I think she needs this job more than ever. She'll go mad stuck at home all day with a baby.' What Toni really meant was that she'd go mad if it were her. 'Don't worry, we'll work it out. She's just in a bit of a muddle at the moment.'

'I hope you're right.' Jack was preoccupied. Bill meanwhile had totally lost the plot. He was looking around from one to the other, still trying to figure out who they all were.

Toni had had enough of babies and jobs, she'd just spent ten minutes listening to a potentially hot guy talk about his three-year-old twins and earlier she'd been cornered by a tight-faced woman who wanted to know all about nursing homes. Boring didn't even begin to cover it.

'So, what are your resolutions this year?' She smiled up at Jack, and Pam took the hint and made herself scarce. Someone shouted 'thirty seconds to midnight' and they all gathered in a circle. Jack held Toni's hand on one side and Kate's on the other. Ellie was wedged between Pam and a rather attractive guy called Dave.

Suddenly it was 'ten, nine, eight . . . ' and they were all caught up in the usual flurry of hugs and kisses. Ellie got a real smacker on the lips from

Dave and when she looked up Jack and Toni were hugging. Poppers exploded and crackers burst and the children all ran downstairs to join in. Sarah was clutching Rudi, who was wearing his usual 'I've just been bitten' look.

'Dad, I want a kiss too.' Jess was tugging at Jack's leg.

'Oh, you do, do you?' He picked her up and swung her round. 'Well, here's one and here's another and here's another.' He was kissing her all over her face and spinning himself in a circle. She squealed until he stopped.

'Happy New Year, darling.' He finally let her down and turned to Sam. 'Come 'ere, my other baby.' He grabbed her in a bear hug and kissed her head. 'Or are you too big to kiss your daddy, eh?' Ellie held Rudi close and stroked him and said a quick prayer to Olga to watch over them all.

'Happy New Year, you two.' Bill appeared and grabbed Ellie, followed by Kate, then Maggie and Toni joined them for a group hug. It was bedlam.

'Happy New Year, Nora.' Jack stood beside her. He reached out and kissed the top of her head, as if she too were a child. He then wrapped his arms around her and Rudi and held them both close. 'We're going to have a great New Year, I can feel it,' he murmured, then bent down to Rudi. 'Hey, buster, gimme five.' He held up his palm. To everyone's amazement the little boy responded, tentatively smacking Jack on the hand.

'My God, that's the first time he's shown any

sign of recognition.' Ellie was delighted. 'You may have just worked a miracle.' She beamed at Jack.

'See? I told you you can't live without me.' He stuck out his tongue and tugged at her hair. 'So come back to work.' He made a stupid face and left her.

★ ★ ★

Next day they had their last official celebration and it didn't come a moment too soon for any of them.

'I'm completely shattered,' Pam announced as she carried a tray of lasagne and a bowl of salad to the table where the other three were waiting. It was four thirty in the afternoon, already dark and they weren't long up. They'd all stayed overnight at Pam's and one of the great things about Rudi was that if he woke up he simply sat there and amused himself, waiting for anyone to come and get him. Ellie had woken early to find him staring at her. She fed and changed him and took him into bed beside her. When she woke later he was sitting up, playing with the quilt cover.

Now he was drinking juice greedily from a beaker on the floor beside them. Ellie handed him a soft piece of bread and he nearly bit her finger off in his efforts to eat it.

'To the end of being blobby.' Pam raised a glass in their general direction.

'I'll drink to that.' Toni looked at them all. 'Now, I propose we get the WWW Club up and running again tomorrow evening. I've a few new ideas.'

'Well, this time it can be the Weary, Wrinkly, Wobbly Club. I have never felt so out of shape in my life.' Maggie sighed.

'God, why is it all so difficult?'

'Listen, at least you've a fella to want to look good for. What about the rest of us?'

'Speak for yourself, I've had a few offers over Christmas.' Toni was grinning.

'Yeah, but it doesn't count if they're in nappies or not toilet trained any more.' They all laughed, even Toni, who knew they were taking the piss.

'Well, don't forget, first to half a stone gets three dates anyway. I'm feeling pretty confident.'

'So, back to work tomorrow.' Maggie decided she'd better broach the subject. 'How about you, El, what have you decided?'

'I'm going to give it a try — bringing Rudi with me, that is. If that doesn't work then I'll see if I can afford to put him into playschool.'

'Isn't there some sort of grant or something available?' Toni couldn't imagine being in Ellie's position. It was intolerable.

'Yes, at the moment I'm his foster mother, so I will be entitled to a monthly payment to help with his expenses, but if I decide to adopt him then . . . '

'And are you thinking that way?' Maggie was dying to know what was really in her mind, she'd been so uptight since Christmas.

'Maybe.'

'Well, think very carefully.' Pam felt she had to say it and Maggie could see Ellie bristle.

'Taking it one step at a time is good.' Toni had also sensed what was happening. 'Let's see what the next few days bring. I think Jack's idea was an excellent one.' She was so full of 'Jack said this' and 'as I was telling Jack' that only Ellie, it seemed, was oblivious to the fact that she had designs on him.

'Now, should we meet in Ellie's apartment tomorrow night at, say, seven? Straight from work?' She smiled at the other three, but their nods were less than enthusiastic.

39

The first day back wasn't as bad as Ellie had imagined. The girls were thrilled to see her for one thing and Jack greeted her in his bare feet with wet hair and a mouthful of toast.

'Welcome back. I'm in trouble with my American editor. Will you be OK?'

'I think I preferred your 'can't live without you' routine.' Ellie was determined to keep things light between them, until she sorted out her feelings.

'Ah, yes, I only use that when I'm desperate.' He got down on all fours to where Rudi was, sitting in the travel cot that Ellie had quickly assembled. 'Hey, buster, you OK?' He ruffled the baby's hair. 'Gimme five.' But it appeared Rudi didn't like mornings much. He stared straight ahead. 'Jess,' Jack shouted, 'give the baby some of your toys to play with. I think he's making strange. Poor guy, don't worry, it'll be great.' He got to his feet.

'For someone who said they didn't like babies much you pay him a lot of attention.'

'Who said that?'

'Bill told me you used to hate having Sarah and Georgia over when they were small. You said all they did was puke and poo.'

'Ah, that's different. They were monsters.' He grinned to let her know he was joking. 'Rudi's a dote, he sort of reminds me of myself.'

'In what way exactly?'

'Now that is way too deep for this hour. Sure you're OK? You won't do a runner?'

'No.'

'Good. Bye, girls, have a good day.' He kissed them and disappeared and Ellie didn't see him again until she said goodnight, feeling totally pooped. Minding three was definitely harder, even if Rudi was no trouble. It was mostly having to remember he was there. That and carrying him around all the time.

★ ★ ★

The girls arrived bang on time. For Ellie, this meeting was right up there with mumps on her list of must-haves.

'How did you get on with the baby?' Maggie wanted to know as soon as she'd taken off her coat.

'Fine. It's just all a bit strange. Having to think of someone else when you get up in the morning. Trying to get yourself and him ready. I'm bloody well allergic to mornings anyway. I'd rather hear shotgun fire than an alarm clock. My body goes into spasm.'

'Tell me about it. You should see my two in action in the mornings.' Pam was all smiles. 'They give new meaning to the term driven. Still,' she beamed, 'I can't wait to have them back later in the week. The house is so quiet.'

'How was Rudi at work?' Toni wanted to know.

'Hardly knew he was around except that he's

worse than my sister's dog when food comes out. He crawls up to wherever I am. I nearly stood on him twice. And I think I have arthritis from carrying him around on my hip.' She rubbed her lower back. 'He seems to have reverted to being a baby.'

'He is a baby.' Toni smiled at her.

'I know, but I mean a baby baby. Sucks his thumb, doesn't make any sounds like he used to. The social workers think it's the trauma he's been through. They say we have to be patient.'

'Poor kid. Where's he now?' Maggie asked.

'Just gone to bed. He was exhausted. He wouldn't settle for a nap, just sat in the play pen most of the day watching me. Then the girls played with him for hours. Jess was trying to squeeze him into her toy airplane at one stage. She dressed him up as one of the Incredibles — made the costume from a few tea towels and a pair of tights.'

'I used to wear tights on my head, tied up with a ribbon so that it looked like I had a ponytail,' Maggie remembered.

'Didn't you look sort of bald at the front?' Ellie was trying to picture the knicker part on Maggie's head. She wondered how you'd hide the gusset.

'Nope, I arranged my fringe so that it covered the elastic. I put tennis balls in the feet to give it weight. Only problem was that when I pranced around I gave my brothers quite a few bruises. Every time I swung around the balls got one of them.'

'I'm very glad we were more civilized.' Toni

342

pretended not to be impressed, but the truth was she'd have loved brothers to give bruises to. 'Now, back to the delicate subject of our weight.'

'There's nothing delicate about any of us,' Pam said cheerfully. 'I feel like a sumo wrestler.'

'Yes, well, speaking of grown-ups in nappies, I'd like to see you all in your underwear this week for the weigh-in.' She ignored the guffaws.

'You've more chance of seeing Johnny Depp in his boxers than me in my knickers,' Pam told her.

'Don't be a spoilsport, it'll be fun, you'll learn something. Anyway, it's all part of another plan. Now, Maggie, you first.' She decided to tread the path of least resistance.

'Yeah, great idea.' Ellie was trying not to laugh. 'Get your kit off, Maggie.'

'I will not.'

'Oh come on, it's only us,' Toni tried to cajole Maggie. 'I promise you it'll be worth it. Anyway, I have a nice surprise for us afterwards if you all cooperate. Now,' she strolled over to Maggie and simply lifted her sweater over her head and said, 'Arms up, good girl,' as if she was talking to dotty old Miss Trundle in the home. Maggie's jumper was draped over the chair before she could say 'bugger'.

'Next, jeans.' While Maggie was clutching her middle Toni had whisked away her pull-on suede boots, stood her upright and had her jeans around her ankles in a jiffy. Pam's jaw was touching her shoulder blades at this stage.

'Get off. I'm not one of your old dears.' But Maggie was wasting her time.

'It's what Toni does all day, dresses and undresses people. Face it, Mags, you're losing the battle.' Ellie was half enjoying it.

'OK, you can leave your socks on.' Toni laughed at her friend's reaction. This was no help. There was only one thing worse than standing in your underwear with goose pimples and off-white knickers without a shred of lycra left in them — and that was doing it while wearing black pop socks against white, emery-board legs that were an ad for Vaseline Intensive Care lotion.

'OK, now the reason for doing this is simple. I want to talk about shape. It's vital to how we lose weight.' She reached into her Gucci bag and produced a copy of her latest bible *Pears, Doughnuts and Lollipops* — *Are you turning into the food you crave?* The front cover showed a horrendously round woman. Her top half made Jordan look anorexic. The inspiring quote coming out of a bubble next to her mouth was, 'I used to be an egg, now I'm an egg timer.' The caption urged the reader to turn to page 63 for the 'reveal'.

'Let's see, Maggie here is a sort of banana shape.' Nobody was even going to begin to think what that meant. Not to worry, Toni was going to save them the bother. 'That means she's sort of straight down then she curves at her bottom.' She coughed. 'Outwards.'

'Isn't that what you're supposed to do?'

'Well, yes, thank you, Pam.' The sarcasm was dripping like runny honey. 'Except that Maggie curves rather more than she should. A bit like a boomerang.' Her smile said she thought she was being kind. 'That's good. Honestly, Maggie, trust me,' she added quickly, seeing Maggie's lower lip jut out. 'Please don't be upset. It simply means you need to concentrate on your lower half, raising your bottom, tucking in your tummy, that sort of thing. Don't worry, you've practically no work to do.' She was looking at Maggie's waist but decided not to mention it, otherwise the others would never do it. 'Now, I'll go next.' She united her very flattering wrap-around print dress to reveal a gloriously sexy one piece.

'Bitch, you're not even wearing tights.' Pam slapped Toni on her butt and nearly broke her wrist. It was like concrete.

'And get those six-inch high heels off,' Ellie ordered.

'OK, OK, take it easy.' Toni slipped out of the shoes. Now, me, I'm sort of egg shaped.'

'Easter egg.' Ellie laughed.

'Don't be nasty, Ellie, you're next.' Her smile was as cruel as the Minister for Finance on Budget Day. 'I could do with a bit off my waist.' Her one piece was obviously Lycra mixed with cement, Maggie thought, because she was held in everywhere. 'I also need to work on my bingo wings.' She'd heard that expression from one of the ladies in the Tuesday-afternoon games club and thought it was disgusting. But she decided she'd better keep them on side, otherwise she'd be lynched. She held up her arms for inspection. 'Remember, no one over forty should ever wave goodbye.' She tried it and Ellie could see what she meant.

Pam was having none of it. 'Go away out of that, I've seen more fat on a turkey's neck.'

'OK, Ellie, you next.'

Normally, Ellie would have told her where to stuff her book and her egg timer, but she was too exhausted and besides, in some perverse way she wanted to know that she wasn't the worst. As if she'd been wound up, her hands moved haltingly to her zipper.

'That's it, good girl.' Within seconds, ably assisted by Maggie who was shivering and giggling, Ellie's skirt and blouse were on the mat. She was glad she was at least wearing black. Nothing beat pale grey for the horror factor, she'd already decided as soon as she saw Maggie. And hers matched, another big plus. Still, the hair under her arms was down to her navel, her pubic stuff had formed two very neat bushes either side of the lace on her pants and her legs and Immac hadn't met since well before Christmas. She could have auditioned for a part in *Werewolf, the Sequel*.

'Well done. That's the spirit. Now, Ellie as you can all see — '

'Needs a shave.' Pam, the only one still fully clothed, got a serious fit of the giggles. Within seconds tears of laughter were streaming down her face. 'Just look at you three, you make those girls in the Dove ads look like beauty queens.'

'Very funny.' Ellie was laughing at Pam, who was choking at this stage.

'OK, maybe we should get you to join us before we go any further.' Toni winked at Ellie.

'There's more chance of me joining the Sons

346

of Divine Providence,' Pam managed in between clutching her stomach. 'If you three could only see yourselves.' She wiped her eyes.

'Yes, well, you're in this bloody club too.' Maggie gave a whoop and pounced on her. 'C'mon, girls, let's see if she's as brave in her Tesco knickers.'

Ellie decided she quite liked this game when it wasn't her being picked on and so she found herself unzipping Pam's black shift dress while Maggie pulled down her tights. This was not easy. Think of stripping the Incredible Hulk in the middle of one of his turns.

'Oh no you don't.' Toni snatched the dress and sat on it just as Pam tried to pull it back over her head. At the same time Ellie reached the door of the kitchen and locked it in case she tried to escape. She was clutching a tea towel and trying to stretch it round her middle when Toni whipped it away and tossed it over her head like a matador. Poor Pam looked like that bald, baby-faced guy from *Little Britain* — all pink and chubby. She hated that her underwear bits didn't even look like they were related, and worse still both her top and bottom were flesh coloured. Kate Moss couldn't have got away with this set of smalls.

'OK, Ellie, I'll come back to you in a minute.' Toni decided it was safer to do Pam first. 'Pam, come here, I won't bite.' Pam was now behind the sofa firing cushions at them. Ellie ducked and shoved the settee away as easily as if it were a dinky car. 'Now, Pam is what the book calls the Christmas pudding shape, I'd say.' No one could argue with that, Toni decided, it wasn't unkind.

'Well, if you gave her a drop of brandy I'd say she'd flambé quite well, her face is that hot.' Maggie's eyes were wet.

'Stop it, that's cruel, and that is not the purpose of this exercise,' Toni said, wagging her finger. 'What I mean is, she's nicely round, but a bit wider in the middle.' Actually, she'd got it spot on, Toni decided as she glanced at her book. 'So, she needs to . . . ' She leafed through the relevant pages. 'Actually, she just needs to . . . tone up really.' There was no point in wasting time. 'Right, El, back to you.' Toni gazed at Ellie as if she were looking at mouldy cheese. 'If you were a food, I'd say you'd be a . . . waffle.'

Initially, Ellie quite liked the sound of this. 'You mean, sort of smooth and golden?' She enquired hopefully.

'No, I was thinking square, you are rather square shaped, and I mean that in a positive way. Look at her shoulders, girls. She's very . . . eh . . . structured. Yes, you're square and, em . . . dimply.'

'Dimples, as in my cheekbones?' This wasn't too bad at all, Ellie sucked hers in for good measure.

'No, darling, dimples as in cellulite.' Pam corpsed. 'No, wait.' She put her hands over her face as Ellie lunged. 'We're being honest here, girls. It's really the only way we can get to grips with our true selves.' She grabbed a handful of clothes and ducked behind the sofa to avoid the missiles.

'I'll get to grips with your teeth with my pliers

if you don't give me back my clothes,' Ellie warned.

'OK, OK, girls, stop fighting. Just let's have one look at these charts,' Maggie said, trying to restore calm. 'I promise you'll feel better, won't they, Toni?' Maggie decided to become Toni's VBF for the rest of the evening, in order to avoid any more humiliation.

'Absolutely. Then I'll let you have my surprise.' It was the best she could think of.

'Your surprise'd better be at least twenty per cent proof or the food you'll most closely resemble is a hamburger, cause I'll make mince meat out of you.' Pam was still glaring at the offending book. She reluctantly joined the others and within seconds four bums were round the table pouring over diagrams of various fruits and other foodstuffs. Thank God I wasn't a cauliflower, Ellie looked at the unfortunate woman who bore that title on page 130.

'How can anyone possibly look like a lychee?' Pam was trying to look over Ellie's shoulder.

Maggie took one look at her three friends from behind and started choking. Apart from Toni, who obviously knew this was coming, they looked like rejects from *What Not to Wear*.

'Just look at us, apart from you, bitch,' she gestured at Toni. 'Bet you don't wear that every day at work.'

'Haven't you ever heard about being prepared in case you get run over by a bus?' Toni asked innocently. 'I choose my underwear with as much care as I put on my make-up.'

'And I choose mine with as much thought as I

put into separating my waste.' Pam had never been into recycling.

'Actually, Pam, I'd have expected you to be more glamorous. You're very sexy and the bras we normally get a good glimpse of are always gorgeous.'

'Listen, I was wearing a blue and green striped polyester blouse and crimplene trousers today. What do you expect?' They looked confused.

'My very stylish uniform, remember?' They did. 'So, Ellie, what's your excuse?'

'Ellie's actually not bad, considering.' Toni jumped in.

'Considering what?'

'Well, black is sexy.' She turned Ellie round for inspection. 'Hmmm, well maybe not when it has a bright orange mark on the left buttock.'

'Where?' Ellie looked like a dog with fleas as she tried to inspect her own bottom. 'Oh, I remember, I spilt bleach on that pair.'

'How exactly?'

'I was bleaching the tea towels.'

'You wash your underwear with your filthy dish cloths?' Toni was thinking of her silky smalls that cost a packet.

'Listen, her double gussets are so thick you could use them as floor cloths,' Pam said, getting her own back.

Suddenly, they were rolling about, twanging each other's straps and trying to inspect knicker labels for polyester content.

Toni's surprise turned out to be a huge tray of wheatgrass for juicing, so they stripped her of her one piece and flung it over the lamp shade.

To everyone's consternation her boobs stayed up around her chin, even without support, and to round it all off she'd even had a Brazilian.

'Did it hurt?' Pam was practically down on her knees inspecting the damage.

'No, well hardly.'

'You look like you've been plucked.' Ellie couldn't bear the idea.

'Well, darling, far be it for me to criticize but you could do with a trim yourself.' Toni wrinkled her nose.

'Ellie'd need a lawnmower to trim that,' Maggie said and they were off again.

★ ★ ★

After they'd calmed down Toni forced them up on the scales, one by one.

'God, those old people must be terrified of you, you're a bloody bully.' Pam couldn't believe she was agreeing to this.

'Shut up, Pamela, you're down four pounds since the last time.'

'What?' Suddenly it wasn't so bad.

'Still, don't get carried away, your clothes probably account for two of those.'

'But . . . I can't believe it. How much have I lost overall?'

'Eh, let me check.' Toni consulted her multi-coloured wall chart.

'Four plus . . . em, let's see, four and a half in total.'

'Kilos?'

'Pounds, I still can't get to grips with those

ghastly metric things. But well done, that's a lot.'

Pam was beaming.

'OK, Ellie, hop up.'

She did, but only because she knew she'd lost weight, all her clothes were hanging off her.

'My God, you're down six pounds. That's fabulous.'

'That's nearly half a stone.' Maggie did a little dance. 'Oh, well done, Ellie, that's brilliant.'

'Well, I would not recommend doing it my way to anyone.' Ellie's smile was barely there.

'That gives a grand total of . . . six pounds. Brilliant. Only one pound to go before you get three dates.' Toni's wink and broad smile said she had no intention of letting anyone else win that one.

'Maggie?'

'OK, you win.' She hopped up. 'Break it to me gently. I've been demolishing Christmas pudding and custard all week.'

'You're down two pounds, plus one from the last time. Good, now me . . . ' Toni wasn't wasting any more time.

Pam jumped up, hoping to catch her out. She should have known better.

'Ooh, I'm down four and a half pounds. Excellent.' Toni didn't wait for Pam. 'Added to the, let's see, two and a half pounds in total I'd lost at the last meeting . . . and . . . that makes me . . . seven pounds. Yes.' She threw a punch in the air.

'Well done, Toni. You deserve it, even if you are a complete cow for putting us through torture tonight.' Maggie smiled and the other two added their encouragement.

'OK, let's get dressed and talk about the dates you're getting me.' She had only one on her mind. 'Ellie?'

'I told you before, I don't know anyone.'

'What about Jack?'

'Jack?'

'You know, your employer, the hunky one you've been keeping to yourself for months now.'

'Jack wouldn't go.'

'Oh, I don't know, he was pretty chatty on New Year's Eve. Anyway, why don't you ask him, it's a start?'

'I couldn't.'

'Why not?'

'I just . . . he wouldn't . . . no way, it would be mortifying.'

'Try it. We had a deal, remember? Now, Pamela, how about you?'

'I'm thinking.' Pam had just remembered a Ricky Gervais type who'd joined Wines and Spirits as Assistant Manager. Jane Gray had told her he was single. His suits were nice and shiny and he wore white socks.

'Remember, no nerds, anoraks, spots, glasses or lazy eyes. And don't even think about that butcher person you mentioned before. I am not going out with someone who smells of liver and has bits of chop between their teeth.' She wiped her hands as if ridding herself of the smell of kidneys.

'Maggie?'

'There's a guy in our Cork office who — '

'No.'

'What do you mean, no?'

'No culchies. I cannot stand their accents or their jumpers.'

'You've a cheek, considering some of the thugs you've gone out with. Besides, Doug is from Leitrim originally.'

'Exactly.' Toni raised one eyebrow. Maggie belted her.

'Jack's actually from Donegal . . . ' Ellie was desperate.

'I'll risk it, he sounds educated.'

'Look, why don't we all have coffee and talk about it later. That OK with you, El? I'll make it.'

'Fine, there's bisc — '

'No refined sugar, how many times do I have to tell you?' Toni was feeling fantastic. 'You can have some grapes or kiwi, I see some over there in the bowl.'

'Coffee and kiwi. Yum yum.'

'Listen, Maggie, you've lost the least amount of any of us, and you have a man to keep, so I'd skip even the fruit if I were you.' Toni teased her. 'Pam, black coffee only, please. Now, I propose we take a completely new approach and get down to this seriously.'

Ellie could feel a headache coming on.

40

The first days of January saw the girls adopt a varied approach to life, love and the pursuit of a flat stomach. Pam was very happy to have her babies home, even if all they talked about was going back to the States for another 'vacation' with their dad. Andrew called her 'Mom' and Paul called the two of them 'you guys' and wanted to take a 'cab' everywhere and buy things for 'a few bucks'. Still, the most amazing thing was that they tidied their rooms without being asked.

'What are you looking for now?' Pam asked Andrew the first afternoon she came home to find the dishes done.

'Nothing, why?'

'You're not going back to the States for Easter, so don't even think about it.'

'No, I know. That's OK.'

'So what's with the dishes.'

'Dad said we were to help you around the house.'

'Why?' She was even more suspicious now.

'He said we did nothing while we were there, so he gave us chores each day.'

'I've been giving you chores each day for years and you still haven't done the first lot.'

'I tidied my room this morning and made my bed.' Paul had joined them to see what was for dinner.

'You, first cousin of Dennis the Menace, tidied your room without being asked?' Pam felt his forehead.

'Yeah, Rhonda made us.'

It was enough to make her almost like the whinger.

'OK, well then, seeing as how you're reformed characters, I'm going to draw up a list of chores and you don't get any pocket money until you've done them.'

'Fine.'

'Cool.'

And that, it seemed, was that. Suddenly Pam had more energy, a bit of space for herself and time to actually prepare some food instead of opening packets all the time. It was nothing short of a miracle. She was dying to ask Stephen how he'd done it but wasn't sure she wanted to give him the satisfaction. She still wasn't entirely convinced they weren't planning to move her children out of the country.

*　*　*

Maggie and Doug had become a regular couple — with a routine. They saw each other on Wednesdays, Doug liked Mondays and Tuesdays to himself, to 'get the week started'. In fact, he didn't like being out after midnight during the week, but if Maggie managed to persuade him, they usually went to a movie, otherwise they sat in and watched the soaps and she made popcorn. On Fridays they splashed out and went for a drink and a meal, Saturdays were their own, Doug had lots of chores to do and Sunday afternoons they usually went for a walk, although lately he'd started to bring her around new housing schemes — 'just out of interest'. Then they had an early night, separately, and got ready to 'grab the week by the balls' — her term, not his, although she only said it to see his reaction. He didn't like women being 'vulgar' he'd told her last week and it had irritated her no end.

'Are you happy?' Ellie asked her one night as they sat having coffee after a spot of late-night shopping, with Rudi asleep in his buggy beside them. 'Only, it seems very early in the relationship to be in such a rut.' She hoped she hadn't gone too far. 'Not that I can talk. There isn't a rut big enough to fit my life into at the moment.'

'Do you know something? I think I am. Although he really bugged me last week.' She told Ellie about the 'vulgar' episode and Ellie agreed that yes, that sort of talk had to be resisted.

'Maybe it's like playing at being married or something, I don't really know. But I like that he's caring and reliable and honest and . . . that there are no surprises.' She shrugged.

'But aren't surprises what make a relationship?'

'I've had too many bad ones, then. Remember George, who turned out to have a fiancée in Waterford? Or Patrick, who kept 'borrowing' money from me all the time?'

'But you were just unlucky.'

'El, I've a string of those kind of stories. Doug

treats me well and we have a good time together and that's all I want, for the moment.'

'Fair enough so.'

★ ★ ★

Toni had finally ditched Gordon, after he messed her around another couple of times. She consoled herself by spending the Harvey Nics vouchers he gave her as a Christmas present. 'I deserve better,' she shouted each morning as she jumped out of bed on her way to some class or other. She felt empowered at the prospect of the year ahead and everyone said she looked like a model. All the good clothes and jewellery certainly helped. And she had three dates to look forward to, she reminded herself as she texted her friends to jolly them along on a daily basis.

Maggie knew that she'd really liked Gordon, though, Toni had admitted it one night as they shared a taxi home after the four of them had gone bowling.

Ellie was too tired even to be depressed at the short, grey days of January that normally dampened her spirits and put a dent in her annual resolution to visit the sick. She was up and out early, baby in tow, and worked hard to make sure the girls weren't neglected and Jack had no cause for complaint. By the time she got home, tidied her own place, changed and fed Rudi and put on a wash or two it was bedtime for both of them. Dieting was no problem: she rarely thought about food and she hadn't had a drink in weeks.

'Coffee?' Jack asked one morning when she returned from dropping the girls off.

'Yes, please.' She sighed as she deposited Rudi in the playpen Jack had bought for him. Everything seemed like such an effort today.

'Are you OK?' He handed her a cup.

'Yeah, just tired.' She saw him looking at her closely and wished she'd had time to put on make-up. What had happened to the well-groomed nanny in crisp white blouse and smooth hair? she wondered as she rubbed a spot of dried sick from her bally blue jumper.

'Actually, you do look tired. Here, sit down for a minute and talk to me.' He'd been so busy and she was so efficient that he hadn't really been paying her any attention since she'd come back, he realized now. 'I probably haven't been much help,' he apologized. 'Deadlines always consume me and you've been rushing off every evening, so I guess our routine's been knocked for six.' He saw she was quite pale. 'You're not dieting again, are you?'

'I wish. No, but the weight is falling off me.' She pulled out the waistband of her trousers to show him. 'I can't remember the last time I had any interest in food.'

'What's up?'

'I'm just exhausted all the time and I'm worried about Rudi.' She looked down at him, staring as usual. 'He's so quiet. In fact, I can't even blame him for my lack of energy. He makes no demands whatsoever.' The truth was she'd been wondering what her future held — single parent, not a lot of money, no prospects as her mother would say. Suddenly, everyone around her seemed to be getting on with life. Maggie was in a solid, cosy relationship; Pam had joined a complementary therapy class and was wafting around smelling of jasmine and extolling the virtues of agnus castus for heavy periods, even though no one had any problems whatsoever in that direction. Toni was so busy practising her asanas or something that two of her patients had to be taken to hospital — one because he'd ducked to avoid her outstretched arm and broken his hip and another because she'd had a minor heart attack thinking Toni was going to clock her when she was only trying to touch her right ear with her left toe. All their energy made Ellie feel even more exhausted.

'Mentally, I'm a hundred and four.' She looked about five as she said it, but Jack could tell she was close to tears. He was slow where women were concerned sometimes, but now he got the message.

'Look, Nora, some of this is my fault. I should have been more understanding, it's just — '

'It's not you. It's just that there's no fun in my life any more.' As she said it she realized that she was feeling mighty sorry for herself. 'Actually, I did have a bit of fun with the girls the other night.' She grinned up at him, realizing that she'd missed their chats. 'Toni made us all strip off at the club. It's part of her new 'learn to love your love handles' regime. Another bestseller, bought from Amazon, I suspect.'

The mere thought of the four of them taking their clothes off aroused him. 'Tell me all.'

'Only if you take that leering look off your face.' He blushed and then she realized what he might have been thinking and blushed too.

'I was just thinking that men would never, ever, take off their clothes for an inspection with their mates.'

'Really?'

'I'd say they'd rather eat rat droppings.' He gave her a cheeky grin. 'But then, the thought of you four peeling off your — '

'Hold that thought right there, mister. It was about as sexy as a glamorous granny contest.'

'Go on, I'm so sexually deprived that it's probably worth hearing anyway. Tell me all.'

She did and he fell about laughing, all raunchy thoughts forgotten. He wanted all the details. She liked that, it was unusual in a man.

'By the way,' she decided it was now or never, 'remember the deal about whoever lost half a stone first?' He didn't, probably because she'd been too mortified to tell him.

'So who won?' he asked after she'd explained, wondering if she was about to ask him out.

'Toni.'

'Toni?' He was confused.

'So now we each have to find her a date.'

'Shouldn't be too difficult.' He was remembering how well she'd looked on New Year's Eve.

'You're the only single person I know,' she offered by way of apology in advance.

'Me?' He never thought of himself as single.

'Would you do it?'

'Hang on, let me get this straight. Toni's won a

date off each of you, and you want me to be your offering?'

'Would you?'

'Yeah, why not?' Toni wasn't really his type but it might be fun and besides, he could practise his charms again, he decided, warming to the idea.

'You will?' She didn't know whether to laugh or cry.

'Who pays?'

'I don't know but I can check it — '

'J-O-K-E.' He pulled a face and she laughed in spite of herself. 'Listen, Nora,' he leant over in his chair and tilted her chin up, 'I haven't seen you smile in ages, so it's already worth it and yeah, it might be fun, although I'm a bit rusty. You'd better warn her. Oh, and it might be best not to mention any of this to the girls. Girlfriends for Daddy were popular once for about five seconds, when they reckoned that anyone on the scene would spoil them senseless. Then someone at school told Georgia, who told Sam — stick with it — that her new stepmother made her eat shepherd's pie and wear patent shoes with bows on the front. Now anyone new is right up there with parsnips in terms of things they do not want to face.'

'Of course I know that. I already overheard Georgia telling Sam that if you ever marry again she and Jess should consider moving to Jamaica.'

'Why Jamaica?' He looked puzzled.

'She's just discovered Bob Marley.'

'Nora, she's twelve, if even that.'

'Thirteen,' Ellie corrected him. 'Thirteen going on thirty. Did you see that movie?'

He hadn't.

'Anyway, I think it's just dreadlocks in general. And dark skins. One of Georgia's teachers is seriously cool. Sam pointed him out to me the other day. Wooh,' she pretended to fan herself. 'Very sexy.'

'In my day teachers wore tweed caps and cycled to work with their lunch in a box. Think Mr Chips.'

'Well, for this guy think Eminem dipped in chocolate. And I think he keeps his lunch down the front of his trousers.' She forgot who she was talking to for a split second.

'Nora!' He was pretending to look shocked but she was having none of it.

'Well, men look at women's breasts and we're not supposed to notice things at all. Anyway, with Mr Johnson you couldn't help yourself. His lunch was very tightly packed and I'd say he had a few Scotch eggs in there.' They both started laughing again and it cheered Ellie up.

'I'll text Toni now,' she said when they'd calmed down after trading a few more teacher stories. She didn't know what else to say so she got on with it.

'By the way, there's one condition.'

'What?' She didn't look up.

'You babysit.'

She wasn't sure she wanted to be this close to his date, but felt she couldn't refuse.

'OK.'

'Right then, suggest Friday night, that way you could stay over.' He was putting this together as he spoke. 'Then, on Saturday, I'm going to

363

arrange a day out for all of us.' Ellie looked surprised. 'My treat.'

'But what about Rudi?'

'Oh, I thought we'd just leave him here for the day.'

'Seriously.'

'What do you think? He comes with us, of course. We all go, even Rashers.' She looked sceptical.

'We'll have a picnic.'

'Jack, it's January.'

'We'll have a picnic in a fun factory. I dunno. I've only just thought of it.' Her eyebrows were up around her hairline. 'Leave it to me. I have a plan.' He didn't, but women liked that sort of thing, or so he thought.

★   ★   ★

Her phone bleeped about twenty seconds later.

'Toni says great and will she pick you up?'

'No, the girls, remember? I'll have to tell them a story.' He thought for a second. 'Tell her I'll pick her up in a cab about eight.' She relayed the message.

'Where does she live?'

'In a very cool apartment in the IFSC building.'

'In town, great. Where should I bring her?'

'Dinner?'

'Even I figured that one out. But where? I'm kinda out of touch, you know.'

'Let her choose, then. She knows every trendy bar and restaurant in Dublin and the neighbouring counties.' Ellie was trying very hard not to be bitter.

'Good idea. Will you tell her to book somewhere?'

'Fine.' She started to text. 'Actually, take down her number, otherwise I'll be a go-between for the week. You can text each other senseless.'

'I don't have a mobile.'

'Seriously?'

'Have you ever seen me with one?'

Come to think of it, she hadn't.

'OK, she's to book.' She sent the message. 'Now, here's her address and phone number.' He jotted it down.

'Hang on, another one.' She hit the button. 'She says she'll meet you in, eh, I've no idea. She's spelt it wrong. Anyway, she'll meet you there.'

'How will I know where?'

'You'll cope. You're on your own now.' Ellie had had enough, she'd done her bit.

41

Toni was delighted. It had all gone much more smoothly than she'd imagined. One down, two to go. And that meant she'd be able to keep Jack Bryant on his toes, which was nice. The Over-90s Ladies Cinema Group were watching *Grease* that afternoon, so she went around humming 'You're The One That I Want' for the rest of the day.

'I know that song.' Mr Collins started singing something she'd never heard of. Mind you, his teeth were loose, which didn't help. 'It's one of Bobby Darin's songs.'

'*Grease*, actually.' She rubbed his back.

'Something to do with the sea, I think.'

'Travolta,' she shouted as she shuffled across the room.

'It's not revolting at all.' He looked quite put out.

Toni just smiled. She even let him dunk the ginger nut biscuits without wearing his yellow plastic bib with the drip tray.

She planned Friday night with the same enthusiasm as Maura Ferguson — a young, pretty nurse she hated — was planning her four-day, 350-guest wedding with the twelve-tier — different filling in every one — cake and the hand-sewn, twenty-two-thousand bead dress. Suddenly, she detested new money, a hangover from Gordon perhaps.

Maura's husband-to-be was a jockey and Toni reminded her sweetly that he'd have to be lifted up to cut the cake if she wasn't careful. That shut her up.

She booked Cruzzo's in Malahide, close to where Jack lived, she wanted him to see she could be quite provincial if needed. She also told him — via Ellie — that she'd meet him there at eight. Toni liked to make an entrance.

★ ★ ★

Jack was slightly uneasy as the day drew near. He'd no idea how to behave on a date, not a clue how to dress — jeans or a suit? He was equally unsure if he'd be expected to snog her or shag her at the end of the night. Where had all his confidence gone? he wondered.

'Down the sink with most of your hair,' Kate teased him when he plucked up the courage to tell her. She was delighted, although she worried slightly that Toni might get her claws into him. That one was on the lookout for a husband, preferably a rich one, and Jack could easily fit the bill.

'Jeans or a suit?'

'For God's sake, it's dinner in one of our poshest locals. You can't turn up in jeans, they probably wouldn't let you in.'

'Good point, sis.'

'Buy yourself some new clothes.'

'Are you mad? I'll never wear a suit again. My cotton sweat pants have a shiny arse, for God's sake. I live in them.'

'I know and they're awful. Ring up Louis Copeland, he'll send you out a load of stuff. You're a famous author, remember?'

'Get outta here.' He poked her playfully, but later in the day he did just that, then panicked in case Ellie saw them arriving and slagged him or, worse, spilt the beans. He rang the shop back and asked them to call him before the delivery van left, so that he could intercept the arrival.

* * *

Kate voiced her concerns to her husband that night and he was still guffawing hours later in bed. She had to elbow him twice in order to get to sleep.

'You're worried that she'll get her claws into him? I'm telling you she'll be lucky if she doesn't have scratch marks on her bum from Jack by the end of the night.'

'You are truly disgusting?'

'And you are truly insane. She's a ride.' He was delighted to be able to quote one of his younger colleagues who'd been eyeing up Toni at the party. 'You wouldn't even be cold in the grave before I'd be giving her one myself, given half a chance,' he joked.

Kate punched him and decided to wait and see what happened.

* * *

Ellie didn't know how she felt about the date. She'd pushed all uncomfortable thoughts about

368

Jack to the back of her mind over Christmas, and apart from New Year's Eve they'd stayed in their box. But when she saw him on the night of the date she realized she'd been wasting her time. They tumbled out as abundantly as Jessie after a nap.

'Nora, I know I'm behaving like a teenager or, worse still, an anorak, but please be honest. Am I overdressed?'

'Eh, no.'

'That's about as convincing as Jess assuring me she wasn't the one who fed aspirin to Rashers, after I caught him chewing the remains of the foil wrapper under the table with her sitting beside him.'

'When?'

'Last night.'

'Was he sick?'

'He was, although he managed to contain it, which is something. He aimed for, and filled, my new shoes, the left one to be precise. Then Jess put it in the bath. Gives new meaning to the term cushion sole. Anyway, tell me. I can take it.'

'No, you look good.' It was the understatement of the year.

'Glasses or lenses?'

She couldn't help herself. She knew Toni wasn't mad about men with glasses. 'Glasses, definitely. Intelligent.'

'OK, at least you'll hear it all back anyway, so I suppose a slagging is inevitable no matter what I do.'

'No way, I am not being a go-between for you two any longer. You're on your own.' The truth was she couldn't bear it. She had too many emotions bursting to get out. Since she'd fixed up the date she'd felt sick with jealousy and she was struggling to be happy for Toni.

'It's just that, I realized last night that I've never really been on a date in my life. I met Lorna when we were kids and we just sort of ended up together. Anyway, I was younger then, bursting with confidence and self-importance. Now, I'm ancient, separated, got two kids, haven't interacted properly with people for years and write ridiculously far-fetched, axe-murderer stories for a living.' He grinned at her and looked about sixteen again. 'I guess that puts me right up there in the top one hundred guys you'd most like to date, eh?'

'You'll be fine.' To her horror she found herself brushing a speck off his jacket. What was she, his granny? 'Besides, Toni is great fun. You'll have a ball.'

'Yeah, that's true and at least it's not a real blind date. That would be truly horrendous. Never know what you'll end up with. Bill calls them bow wows.' She didn't understand.

'Dog rough. Instead of saying hello you just yelp and lick them. Bill almost forced me into one a few months ago. Some friend of a girl in his office. But then he saw her. Said she was so ugly that even the tide wouldn't take her out.'

'That's not remotely funny. And I wouldn't tell that story to Toni, either.'

'Speaking of stories, did you read about the dog who fell into a hole in Grafton Street yesterday and had to be put down?' he asked.

'No, don't tell me.' She shuddered. 'I hate those kind of stories.'

'He just slipped down a hole. They had to shoot him.'

'Oh my God, just like that? They actually shot him in the hole?'

'No, actually, they shot him in the head.' It took her a second. 'Bill suggested I tell it to get the evening off to a good start. Think it's good?'

'No.'

'That's what I thought. It's also about a hundred years old, which might date me slightly.' The doorbell rang. 'God, there's the taxi and I haven't even finished my make-up.' He winked and she wished he were doing all this for her.

★ ★ ★

Jack was sitting in the restaurant wondering if he should order a stiff drink when she arrived. In terms of entrances it was right out there. He spotted her immediately, long before she saw him. She was wearing a floaty see-through thing and lots of jewellery. As she followed the waiter to their table quite a few heads turned and people seemed to want to know who she was meeting. He was glad he'd invested the price of a small plane in a new suit and very glad he hadn't worn a tie. Too old. She looked young and alive. It was the hair and the legs that did it, he decided as he stood up to greet her.

'Hi.' He kissed her only once, deciding not to even try to be smooth by air-kissing her seventeen times the way most Irish people did

371

these days. He hoped his breath smelt OK, he'd been eating garlic last night. He should have asked Nora to check it.

'Hello. It's nice to see you again.' She was even sexier than he'd remembered, all bee-stung lips and tousled hair. 'Thanks for agreeing to come.'

'Pleasure, you've got to have some reward for all that dieting.' That sounded wrong. 'Not that you need to diet, I should add quickly before you smack me.' He grinned playfully. He hoped it was adult playful as opposed to the tickle-you-under-the-armpits stuff he did with the kids.

'I thought I'd leave the smacking till another night. I was afraid my whip might put you off.' It was the same kind of thing Nora would say, he could immediately see why they got on so well. The difference was that with Nora, it just came out, whereas he had the impression that Toni knew exactly what she was saying. Anyway, it worked.

'Like a drink?'

'Love one.'

'Wine OK? Or would you prefer an aperitif?' Wrong thing to say, made him seem like he should be wearing a cravat.

'Wine is perfect.'

'Red or white?'

'White, ABC.'

He looked away nonchalantly, wondering if that was a trendy new drink, sort of like a spritzer. Fuck, he hadn't a clue. Two minutes in and he was already showing how out of touch he was. Rip Van Winkle was only trailing after him.

'Hope you don't mind, it's just I hate

Chardonnay.' She sipped her water and he tried not to look relieved.

'Oh, no, no problem, I'm not a fan myself.' He went for one of the most expensive French wines and hoped it'd come quick.

42

It was at least an hour later before he realized he was enjoying himself. She was a curious mix. One minute it was all bling bling and the next it was bedpans and incontinence pads. Still, he liked the idea of her in a nurse's uniform, wouldn't mind getting up close to that sometime.

Toni was trying hard to be casual. And funny. And sexy but not too slutty. Men liked it when you talked dirty, she knew. The secret was not too much too soon. A lick of the lips here and there and a bit of fingering her jewellery near her cleavage worked and she touched him once or twice too, always in jest, of course. Actually, now that she'd had a chance to get to know him he was a much better catch than she'd imagined. He was very funny and she liked his self-deprecating manner. Even the glasses didn't put her off, he had gorgeous eyes and she loved his smile. And best of all he was successful. She'd no idea his books sold all over the world until he laughingly told her about his first book tour of America, and how his driver had tried to sneak him in the back door of all the bookshops, in case he got mobbed. Jack had been afraid to tell him that his biggest worry was no one would turn up at the stores. He'd emailed everybody he knew in America, including a guy from Amazon.com whom he'd met only once — and who could have been a serial killer for all Jack knew — and a cab driver who'd taken him to the airport twice, all in a last-ditch attempt to try and rent a crowd. Toni quickly decided that he was educated too — had to be if he could write. And he had nice hands. As he laughed again at something she said Toni realized that this could possibly be a 'should I give him a blow job tonight' moment. The girls would kill her if she did, not that she'd be discussing it with them; Maggie and Pam were still a bit protective of Ellie and seemed to regard Jack as out of bounds.

★　★　★

Jack wondered later if he should order another bottle of wine, but she declined and he was happy — afraid he'd get drunk and dribble. Toni was afraid she'd get drunk and throw her leg over, so they settled for coffee and brandy and he told her all about his daughters. Normally, this was a real turn-off for Toni but now she found herself dreamily wondering if they'd call her Mummy or just Toni. It was all going swimmingly. Much later, and after a second round of brandies, they ordered a cab and Jack insisted he'd drop her home, despite her vaguely protesting that they should order two cabs because he lived so much closer.

He asked the driver to wait and walked her right to the front door of her apartment.

'Nice place.' He looked around at the ultra-modern décor. He'd always wanted to try apartment living, it seemed like fun.

'Yes, I love it, come in for a sec and look at the view. I don't want your cab driver to think you've absconded.'

He followed her in and was impressed. It was all light and glass and pale wood, and the views across Dublin from the enormous roof garden were stunning.

'Well, I'd better go.' He smiled at her. 'I really enjoyed myself. It's been too long.'

'You should have let me pay. After all, I invited you, or at least Ellie did.'

'My pleasure, you get the next one.' He thought he slipped that one in nicely.

'I will, definitely.'

'Great. I'll call you.'

'I'd like that.'

'Goodnight, then.' He leant over to kiss her on the cheek but as she came towards him his glasses or their noses or something got in the way and he ended up kissing her on the lips. He was secretly relieved because he wasn't sure he'd know how it was done these days. He needn't have worried, Toni was an expert. It was warm and inviting and promised much more. No tongues, Bill had warned. Actually, what he'd said was 'sew your dick to your leg and glue your tongue to your teeth. Girls don't like the feel of either on the first date.'

'Goodnight, then,' he said again when they eventually broke apart, her first.

'Goodnight, Jack,' she whispered and stayed where she was, perfectly silhouetted in the darkness while he let himself out.

The taxi driver was definitely relieved to see him.

* * *

Ellie was wide awake. It had been a funny night. The girls were over the moon that she was staying and even Rudi had seemed more interested in what was going on. They had a 'midnight feast' at eight o'clock on the rug in front of the fire, with jelly snakes and raspberry and custard creams, Sam's favourite. They made cocktails — in real glasses — from cranberry and orange juice, although Jess insisted on adding milk to hers, which was a bit off-putting. Ellie made popcorn and they watched *Shrek 2* — again. By ten thirty all three were in bed and Ellie was in her pyjamas watching the end of *The Late Late Show* and trying to fish out bits of corn from between her teeth. At midnight she gave up on Jack returning to cosily tell her all about it, made cocoa and went to bed.

She heard him come in at about one thirty. He was humming softly, a bad sign — for her anyway. His room was next to hers and she thought she heard him yawning and groaning with pleasure as he stretched out in bed. It added to her loneliness.

* * *

Toni was delighted. It had all gone well and she really fancied him. She slapped on masses of anti-everything cream and curled up in bed to plan her next move.

★ ★ ★

For Jack it had been like being a schoolboy behind the bike shed — packed with anticipation and promise. He was suddenly dying for sex and this was his big chance.

★ ★ ★

Next morning chaos ruled. The girls descended on Nora and the baby at about seven. She came to rather quickly once Jess started walking a Barbie across her forehead. Sam had plucked a still-sleeping Rudi out of his cot and he was rubbing his eyes and looking like he might cry for the first time in weeks.

'Here, give me the baby and climb in beside me.' She patted the bed and took Rudi in under the covers.

'It's OK, little fella.' She felt protective and the feeling surprised her. He'd been hard to love recently, she thought guiltily. She snuggled him in against her and caressed his head and he seemed to actively try to get closer to her, pushing his skinny arms against her ribs and causing her to wince. It was all too much too early. She yawned.

'Can we watch a video, Nora?'

'No, it'll wake your dad. Hop in and we'll tell stories.'

'Dad snores. Nothing wakes him, even when we want to.'

'I do not.' Jack strode in, knocking as an afterthought and tying his dressing gown as he walked. He smiled at the four of them, Rudi barely visible beneath the mound of females.

'Girls, I thought we agreed that Nora would be allowed to sleep on? And how exactly did that mutt get in here?'

'She was awake.' Jess got in fast.

'And tell me how you discovered that?'

'She opened her eye when I screamed cause Sam stood on my toe.'

'That'd do it all right.'

'I was only playing with my Barbie.'

'On my head.' Ellie tickled her.

Jack sat on the bed. 'Cup of tea?'

'Yes please.' She was conscious of her slept-in hair and morning breath.

'Coming up.'

'Now can we watch a video?'

'Yes, go get your favourite and we'll watch it under the covers.'

Jess ran off and came back almost immediately, and by the time Jack returned they were all engrossed.

'How was your night?' she asked as she sipped the strong tea. The girls had climbed out after a while to sit on the floor right up beside the small combi unit.

'Great.' He ran his hands through his hair and looked enthusiastic. 'She's fun. We got on well, I think. Brilliant apartment she's got.'

So he'd been back at her place. Toni wasn't

playing it cool, obviously. It shouldn't have hurt as much as it did.

'Eh, I was just there for a minute when I dropped her off.'

She tried not to look relieved. 'Will you see her again?'

Would he hell as like? 'Probably.' He grinned. 'Is that OK with you?'

'Nothing to do with me.'

'You're frowning at me, Nora, and I don't like it.' He got up, smiling. 'How about pancakes for everyone with maple syrup?' he asked the troops.

'Yeeeees,' two voices roared in unison, although they hadn't obviously been listening.

'All right, let's get this day started. Downstairs in five minutes everyone. Rashers, come on, there's a good boy.' No reaction so he was forced to haul the dog off Ellie's legs, just as they were heading towards paralysis. He turned to give her an apologetic grin. 'You can stay on for a bit. I'll feed and dress them and call you in an hour if you like.'

'Nah, I'm awake. I'll be down in a minute. I think Rudi will snooze on, though. He fell asleep as soon as I took him into the bed.'

'OK.' He disappeared and Ellie brushed her hair and teeth and they all trooped down for breakfast.

Jack made fresh orange juice and a mound of pancakes and then took the girls upstairs to get washed and dressed for their outing, leaving Ellie to relax and flick through the papers, which had been delivered at about eight.

She tidied up because it was what she always

did in this kitchen and then made fresh coffee and enjoyed the silence.

After skimming the headlines she turned eagerly to her favourite column. She hadn't read it in months, partly because he'd been on hols and then because of all that had happened to her. She was smiling when Jack came back into the room.

'What's so funny?'

'This, I love it, it's my favourite every Saturday.' He glanced over her shoulder as he poured himself fresh coffee.

'Ever read it?'

'Sorry, Nora, that's Jess crying. Back in a mo.'

'Well, it should be compulsory for men. This guy really understands women. This week it's about binge drinking,' she called after him. 'It's so funny.'

He was back in a minute with Jess on his shoulders. 'Anyway, here's the plan.'

'Hmmm?'

'Listen up.' He tugged at the paper.

'Stop it, I'm enjoying that.' She gave him what she hoped was an annoyed glance.

'Well, hurry up, I want to talk to you.'

'Who stole your rattle?' She finished reading and put the paper away.

'NOW, what's the plan?'

'Well, I thought we'd go to Wicklow, have a big long walk on the beach and then go somewhere nice for lunch. There's a new place opened and they really welcome kids. They have a play area with bean bags and sand and toys, right in the middle of the restaurant. Well actually, not quite in the middle, a bit off to one side so that it's not deafening but you can still keep an eye on them. They show a different video every day too. Afterwards we could take in a movie, or go to that new Fun Factory place, although that might be too much effort. Then, a stop-off for afternoon tea in Avoca on the way home. How does that sound?'

'Great.'

'And, Nora?'

'What?'

'You're not working so let me look after them, OK?'

'Cheers.'

★   ★   ★

It was barely ten thirty by the time they all climbed into Jack's Volvo estate, Rashers deliriously happy even though he was screened off in the boot. It was a perfect winter's day, all crisp air and soft light and the beach was deserted. They put Rudi in his push chair but he looked agitated and it was impossible to push anyway, so Jack put him up on his shoulders and he smiled, so they had to take photos. The girls and the dog ran like caged animals, a tumbling mass of ribbons and dribbles. Jack whistled and sang. Ellie was amused to hear he had no talent in either direction.

'You're in good form.'

'Yeah, I am. Come 'ere.' He pulled her towards him and zipped up her jacket. 'You'll catch cold.' She liked his concern.

'You know, Nora, I think I have been hiding away.' He took a deep breath. 'Been licking my wounds for too long. Last night was fun. I felt alive. And do you know something?'

'What?'

'I think she liked me.' He seemed surprised.

43

Ellie put all thoughts of Jack and Toni out of her head and concentrated on having a good time. It was so much easier having two adults — she suddenly understood what single mothers meant. The kids acted up less for a start and it was nice having a man to do all the lugging and carrying that went with kids.

Lunch was controlled mayhem. The restaurant was bright and spacious and the girls disappeared immediately and were soon swanning around with two reluctant playmates. After a while Rudi climbed down off her lap and crawled over to see what all the fuss was about. He pulled himself up to his feet when he reached the girls.

'He hasn't really tried to stand much at all,' Ellie was delighted. 'Although he was starting to before Olga . . . died. And he never seems to want to be out of my sight unless he's asleep.'

'Poor little kid. He must be traumatized.' Jack had ordered Ellie a glass of wine and was drinking water himself because he was driving. She sipped the chilled white and relaxed.

'Are you still OK about having him?' He was watching her closely, the way he did every now and then.

She shrugged. 'Sometimes. It's hard, though.'

'Kids are hard work, and very trying most of the time,' he said, smiling over at Jess who was sitting on somebody's lap. He made to get her but the woman waved him away. He sat back down. 'Anyone who tells you different is lying.'

Ellie nodded.

'Will you keep him?'

She'd been wondering that herself for a long time. 'Yes,' she said, realizing she'd made a decision. It felt easier now that she'd said it out loud.

'Well, lean on me as much as you like. I'm an old hand at it.' He sat back as huge plates full of gigantic prawns on skewers arrived, with wedges of lemon and a green salad.

'Thanks. I really appreciate that.' She squeezed the lemon. 'This looks great, I'm starving.' She had a prawn in her mouth before she realized she was dribbling. 'Must be all that sea air,' she apologized.

'I like it that you enjoy your food. Toni picked at hers last night, I noticed.' Ellie realized this Toni thing could get very tiresome. 'She's not fond of meat, she told me.'

'Yeah, that's why she purrs like a very sleek Cheshire cat and I oink and roll about like an overfed sow.' Ellie patted her middle.

'Happy as a pig in . . . ' He saw her face. 'Only joking, I swear. I'll go get the troops.' He stood up as real chicken pieces and home-made chips arrived, with freshly squeezed orange juice instead of fizz. 'What are we like, eh?' he ruffled Ellie's hair. 'We're like an old married couple.'

I wish we were, she thought, and the idea scared her. 'Don't flatter yourself,' was what came out of her mouth full of prawns, as he disappeared to rescue the elderly couple who'd now been adopted by Jessie.

'Mama.' The voice jolted her back to reality and she looked down to see Rudi sort of swinging towards her with one arm out and the other clutching the table.

'He just spoke.' Jack was hot on his heels with the girls. 'Did you hear that? And he's definitely trying to walk.'

She nodded, afraid to speak in case she cried and her nose ran.

'You're not his mama,' Sam said quickly.

'I think I am now, darling.' Ellie picked Rudi up and held him close, then went to make a fuss of Sam in case she felt left out.

'Does that mean you'll be going away?' Sam asked as Nora settled her napkin.

'No, love, don't worry.'

'Do you promise?'

'I promise.' Ellie kissed the top of her head. Jack watched them.

'Good,' he said, wiping a dribble of garlic butter off her chin.

★   ★   ★

They managed the Fun Factory for about an hour, then everyone started to get tired. Hot chocolate with marshmallows and a cream tea in Avoca revived them all and Jack and the girls slipped away and bought a gorgeous piece of pottery for Ellie.

'What's this? It's not my birthday for ages.'

'It's to say . . . thank you.' Sam handed her the package.

'It's cause we love you, Nora,' Jess said it like it was.

'I love you both too,' Ellie looked at Jack. 'Thank you.'

'Pleasure. Now, what say we load up and hit the road? Poor old Rashers will need a wee soon.'

'I need a wee now.' Jess hopped about.

'I'll bring her. Here, you hold Rudi, he's unconscious.'

'And he smells.' He wrinkled his nose.

'I've changed him twice today and now I've run out of supplies.'

'He'll survive till we get home.' The way he said it made them seem like a proper family.

★ ★ ★

It was almost seven thirty by the time they arrived back in Howth and everyone, adults included, was wrecked.

'I'll change him.' Jack lifted Rudi out of the baby seat.

'Thanks.' Ellie was touched. 'Right, girls, who's for a bath?'

'Nora, stop. You're on a day off.'

'I'm so tired now that another half-hour is not going to make any difference. Then I'd better head home.'

'Why not stay? Your place will be freezing and the baby is knackered. He'll be asleep in minutes. You could go in the morning. Mind you,' he grinned, 'all I can promise is a take-away and a cold beer. But I will light the fire and you can put your feet up. I'll even get a DVD out.'

'Are you sure?'

'Absolutely. So, you run the bath and I'll hand this little guy in to you. He's really ponging. Then I'll organize the rest.'

'OK, thanks.'

Rudi had a great time splashing about. He roared laughing. Ellie realized he'd probably never had a proper bath. She didn't have one and Olga had barely wiped his nose most of the time. The suds and ducks made him cackle and the girls loved having him. They played with him as if he were a real live toy. Jack wanted to join in with them, but he realized that might be pushing it just a bit too far with the children's nanny.

An hour later the children were washed and ready for bed, after milk and biscuits and a final round of showing teeth. Jack carried Rudi up the stairs on his shoulders and the girls climbed into bed without a struggle.

'Go kiss your offspring,' Ellie said when she found him talking to the baby, who was gazing, mesmerized, at him.

'I already have, twice. C'mon, Mrs.' He put his arm around her. 'Feet up, cold beer on the way. Fire is lighting and I'll be back in twenty with food and a movie. Sound good?'

'Sounds like heaven.'

'God, you're a cheap date.'

'Always have been.'

★ ★ ★

Fifteen minutes into the movie, the phone rang. Ellie had been half watching and half daydreaming. The fire was blazing, empty food containers were strewn about, along with a couple of bottles of beer, and they were tucked up on the couch. At least Ellie had been curled up like a baby when Jack dropped in beside her and stretched out, feet up on the coffee table. He groaned now at the interruption.

'Bet it's Kate, she's always checking up on me. Here, you answer, give her something to think about.'

'Hello.'

'I hope you're looking after him for me.' She recognized the voice instantly.

'Toni, hi.' She looked at Jack and he winked.

'You're working late.' Toni sounded pleased she was there.

'Yep, we only just got back and the kids were bushed.'

They chatted for a couple of minutes and then Toni asked to speak to Jack.

'Hi there.'

'Jack, hi. Sorry to disturb you. I just wanted to say thanks for dinner last night. I had a lovely time.' Toni sounded breathless.

'My pleasure. It was fun. How was your day?'

'Great, busy. I'm just off out now for a drink,' she lied.

'Shame, I was going to invite you round for breakfast in the morning. I made Nora perfect pancakes this morning. I suppose you'll be too tired if you're up half the night gallivanting?'

'Not at all, I'd love to come.'

'Well, it would break the ice with the kids.' His way of thinking was not lost on Ellie, or Toni for that matter. 'I could introduce you as Nora's friend. Do you know where we live?'

She did, but she said no and he gave her directions.

'See you about ten, so. Nora is under lock and key in the morning. The girls woke her at seven today.'

'Yuk.'

'My sentiments exactly.' He hung up, still smiling.

'Hope that's OK with you?'

'Of course. I won't be hanging around for long, anyway. I've a lot to do at home and it's almost Monday again.' She sounded deflated.

'I don't want to see you on Monday.' She protested but he insisted. 'You've worked all day today and last night as well, which I'll pay you for, by the way.' He slapped her arm when she tried to disagree. 'I'd have had to pay a sitter anyway. I'll be fine and we'll see you Tuesday at lunchtime, OK?'

'I can't it's — '

'You can and you will. And I've moved the cot into my room. You're sleeping in, that's an order.'

An hour later she was yawning and fidgeting — Toni's call had sort of broken the spell. 'I'm off to bed,' she announced as she stretched and tried to loosen her shoulders.

'But it's the best part.'

'Tell me what happens. Goodnight.'

'Women.' He paused the DVD and smiled up

at her. 'Thanks for today, it was fun.'

'I had a great time.'

'You OK?' he asked her.

'Yes, fine, just tired.'

'Sleep well.'

'You too.' She felt sore with tiredness as she climbed the stairs.

★ ★ ★

Next morning, to her astonishment, she slept till almost ten. The baby, she thought immediately, and then remembered where she was. She dragged herself out of bed and into the shower, then pulled on the same jeans as yesterday. Luckily, she'd brought an extra T-shirt and a pretty, pale grey cardigan in case Rudi puked all over her. She caught her hair back and left her face bare. She couldn't face make-up until she'd had something to drink.

Toni arrived almost as soon as she'd poured coffee. The kids were playing chasing and Jack was fixing breakfast for a football team if the mess was anything to go by. He went to answer the door. When he returned he was clutching flowers and a bag of croissants and Toni was almost clutching him.

'Hello,' she said, holding out her hand to the girls. She kissed Rudi and hugged Ellie.

'Did you drive?' Jack was gazing at her like a man who hasn't yet had sex but knows he's going to.

'No. Taxi. I wasn't sure where I was going and didn't want to get you up too early.' There was as

391

much energy between them as there was in an average t'ai chi class.

God she looks great, Ellie thought. Toni's hair and make-up were immaculate although her outfit was more Hawaii than Howth.

The girls were fascinated by 'Nora's best friend' and kept bringing things to show her, in between games of chasing. She handled it well, Ellie thought, and was delighted when she picked up Rudi and kept him on her knee for ages.

Toni and Jack were showing all the signs of new lust — lots of eye contact and silly one-liners and laughing at stupid jokes. Ellie watched it with interest, secretly hoping to pick up a few tips and then eventually she couldn't take it any more.

'Well, I'm off, got a lot to do.' She began to gather up her stuff.

'I'll come with you.' Toni was up in a flash.

'No, honestly, it's OK I — '

'I was going to call in to you anyway, later. We haven't had a proper chat in ages.' She gave Ellie the look, the one that said 'I need to know everything about him so please don't argue or I'll force feed you yams for a month.'

'OK, fine.'

Ten minutes later they were in her car with Jack and Rashers waving them off and the girls continuing their chasing game in the shrubbery.

'Thanks for breakfast, those pancakes were bad for my waistline,' Toni said through the open car window.

'Thanks for the flowers. That's a first for me.'

'Well, at your age there can't be many firsts left.'

'Ouch.'

'Bye.' She waved at him like she was three years old.

Oh, go on, ride each other senseless and let the rest of us stop vomiting. Ellie kept a smile pasted on her face.

'Bye bye, Ellie. Remember, Tuesday lunchtime.'

'Are you sure?'

'Positive. Take care. Bye, buster.' Jack reached in to touch Rudi's hair.

'Speak soon.' Toni couldn't help herself.

'Sure.'

They drove off at last. 'Oh my God, I want to know everything about him. Start when he was born and take it slowly.'

'I don't know — '

'I think I'm seriously in lust.' Toni beamed.

And I think I'm in love, Ellie finally admitted to herself. She immediately wondered what Pam and Maggie would think. Not that she had any intention of telling them, really, but God she could do with talking to someone. This was all much harder, seeing him with someone else. She sighed heavily.

'You OK?' Toni wanted to know.

'Yeah, just a bit tired.'

'Tell me the truth, would you say he's into me?'

'Truthfully?' Ellie looked at her friend. 'I would, yes.'

44

Toni would have still been there the next morning, Ellie decided, if Rudi's dirty nappies and the sight of reconstituted Liga, which he then tried to eat, had not driven her into the arms of the nearest taxi driver two hours later.

Ellie flopped in the comfiest armchair and opened the button on her jeans. The phone rang.

'Rudi, tell them I've gone to Tibet with a monk,' she begged the little boy. He smiled, itself a minor miracle. She wondered if one day he'd be big and strong and able to protect her.

'Hello.' Her voice sounded weary.

'Hi, how's it going? Haven't talked to you in ages.'

'Oh, Maggie, how are you?'

'Fine. Can I call around? I bought a gorgeous Aran sweater for the baby in Kilkenny Design today.'

'Only if you promise not to mention the name of my employer — even in a throwaway comment — or I'll throw you away somewhere and it will hurt, I promise.'

'Toni?'

'Two hours.'

'I take it the date was a success?'

'Tom Hanks and Meg Ryan have nothing on them.'

'Which movie?'

'Take your pick. Although she's shaping up for

a classic — a modern-day *Romeo and Juliet*, I'd say.'

'That was a tragedy, darling.'

'So is this. It's tragic listening to her.' Ellie laughed to hide the pain. If she didn't keep it light she knew she'd bawl.

'Oh dear, that means she'll be in great form tomorrow night at the meeting.' Maggie sounded happy for Toni. 'Sure, what would we do without her? Life would be very dull.'

There was no arguing with that.

'Anyway, put the kettle on. I'm on the way.'

'I've no food in the house.'

'There are a few Madeira cakes here. Pam bought me six which all have to be eaten by yesterday. Hardly a calorie though. And only a small bit of mould on one end.'

'That'll do.'

* * *

After half an hour they were laughing and it didn't seem as bad any more. Or maybe it just seemed even more surreal talking about it like this. Ellie felt tense and she was trying hard to relax. 'So, how's Doug?'

'Oh, you know, fine.'

'But?'

'No but.'

'I sense a but.'

'I dunno, maybe all this domesticity is getting to me a bit.'

'How d'ya mean?'

'He's quite . . . eh . . . sensible, y'know?'

395

'Yeees.' She was treading carefully.

'Also, he says the silliest things and thinks he's being outrageous.'

'Example, please?'

'Last night he went all giggly on me and then announced, 'Oops, sorry, I'm afraid I've done a bum yodel.''

'What's that?'

'An SBD.'

'Hmmm?' Ellie was puzzled.

'Silent but deadly.'

Ellie burst out laughing. 'Mags, that's Samantha-speak.' She shook her head. 'God, but it's juvenile.'

'Actually, there are loads of those and they were very cute at first . . . '

'No, trust me, they were never cute. You were just going through your 'ooh, you play snooker, I've always wanted to learn' phase.'

'You think?'

'I know. It happens to us all. You never hear a man saying 'I'd love to learn how to knit', though. Anyway, how are things on the money front?'

'Great . . . well better. Oh, I dunno. He thinks we should open a joint savings account.'

'For what, exactly?'

'A rainy day.'

'Tell him that's why credit cards were invented.'

'I do like him, Ellie. Really.'

'Well, don't let him take over, Mags. You know how you are, a bit over the top in wanting everyone to like you. I hear you've joined a baking group with his mother.'

'But she's lonely.'

'She's also in her seventies and you can't tell sultanas from bird droppings.'

'Point taken.'

'So, what are you going to do?'

'Nothing. I'm just a period-head at the moment, don't mind me.'

'Well, take it slowly and don't get swallowed up.'

★ ★ ★

Later that evening Pam phoned. 'I've just had Lady Antonia on the phone. Your boss is in for one hell of a ride, literally I mean.'

'You too?'

'Yeah, she's very funny.'

'Let's change the subject, please.' Ellie had laughed with Maggie until her jaws ached. She couldn't keep on pretending.

'What's up?'

'Nothing. What do you mean?'

'Something's wrong, I know you.'

'No, I'm fine. Just the usual.'

'I'm sensing something more, so you might as well tell me. You always do in the end.'

Ellie said nothing.

'Come on, out with it.'

'Honestly, it's — '

'El, either you tell me or I come round.'

'It's just that . . . I . . . sort of fancy him myself.'

'Who?'

'Eh . . . Jack.'

'Jack?'

'Yes,' Ellie croaked.

'Jack Jack?'

'Yeah.'

'Oh God.'

'I know.'

'I knew it. At least I didn't but . . . I said to Maggie that I didn't like the idea of Jack and Toni. I just sort of had a feeling that you and he might sort of . . . get it together eventually.'

Ellie yawned. 'Anyway, Pam, I'm just too tired to talk about it right now. But don't worry, it'll pass. And don't mention it either. I don't want to spoil Toni's moment.'

'Want me to come round and not talk about it?'

'No, thanks for the offer, but I'm fine, I promise. Nothing broken,' she lied. 'Now, tell me how you are.'

Pam knew when to stop. 'I'm great, I've been reading self-help books in an effort to deal rationally with my ex-husband and his psycho girlfriend.'

'That's not like you.'

'What, to read books?'

'No, to be rational.'

'Yes, well, there's this really nice man who comes into the store. Always changing dog food and scouring pads. He can't seem to make a decision on his shopping, yet he keeps talking to me about books. I'd say he's a bit of a disaster really. He's a scheduler at RTE Television.'

'That explains the TV this Christmas, so.'

'He's big into these self-help books, see.'

'Sounds like he needs them. So, is there a vibe?'

'Sort of. Ah, he's probably married. Although he does keep returning a lot of ready meals for one.'

'He's giving you the hint.'

'Well, he'd better go in there with a sledgehammer, so. You know me for subtlety. Oops, gotta go. There's a strange noise coming from the bedroom and Paul's been in there for ages. Sounds like he might be drilling the wall.'

'Not good, he's ten, you'll be arrested for letting him have a weapon.'

'I know. Sure you're OK?'

'Yeah.'

'Don't worry about it.'

'I won't.'

'And ring me if you need to chat. Promise?'

'I promise.' Ellie hung up and sighed.

★ ★ ★

The Monday meeting was put off till Tuesday because Jack and Toni were circling each other like dogs on heat, apparently — Maggie's description — and Toni was exhausted from all the phone sex. Ellie was relieved. She and Rudi went to the park and then she shopped and tidied the apartment and he followed her around, on all fours mostly, and tried to help. He was uttering the odd unrecognizable syllable every now and then and she was chatting to him as if he were Einstein. By Tuesday lunchtime she felt rejuvenated.

'Nora, what type of thing does Toni like to eat?' Jack greeted her with, as she staggered in with three kids and a truckload of shopping after the school run.

'Girls, upstairs and change.' She shooed them away and put Rudi into the playpen.

'Em, what did you have in mind?'

'No idea, it's just a joke. She sent me a box of shortbread biscuits by courier this morning. They're all shaped like penises. They're called not-so-short bread. Isn't she a gas?'

'Hilarious. Well, they've got some giant-sized marshmallowy things with cherries in them in Tesco. They're called Wibbly-wobbly Wandas. They might do.'

'Brilliant, could you pick me up a pack tomorrow?'

'Jack, that's a joke. I think you need to go to Ann Summers for the sort of thing you want.'

'I like girls who are out there, you know, not afraid to give it back to you.'

'The only thing Toni gives back is the bill,' Ellie mumbled to herself in an uncharitable moment as she started tea for the kids. 'So,' she tried to keep it light, 'when are you two meeting again?' She needed to torture herself.

'We're going to see a movie tomorrow evening. Don't suppose you're free to sit with the girls?'

'No, sorry, I've a date.'

'What? Who?'

'Oh, just a guy I met at a party over the

Christmas. Don't say anything, I haven't told the girls.'

'Eh, great, yeah, sure. So, tell me about him.'

'No, it's bad luck.'

'Oh, I see, OK.' He went off scratching his head.

Shit, Ellie thought, now I'm going to have to keep it going.

★ ★ ★

That night the club assembled promptly at eight at Maggie's place. Ellie needed a break from her flat and her mum had agreed to babysit. There was no weight loss but no one had gained anything either. They were hoping for a bit of a ticking off and then a pizza.

'Not good enough, we are bone lazy, all of us,' Toni announced. 'It's just as well I had another plan up my sleeve. I saw this January slump coming.'

'What's the latest, then?' Pam glanced at the others. 'I can't wait for the next adventure.' She smiled, her tongue so far in her cheek it was threatening to permanently deform her.

'We're going on TV.'

45

'If Toni had said 'we're having a foursome, don't forget your double-ended dildo', her words could not have achieved any more of the desired effect.

Maggie turned purple, Ellie squirmed like a maggot and Pam said it for all of them, in her usual eloquent terms.

'What the fuck do you mean — TV?' It was little more than a squeak.

'That's what I said.' Toni beamed at them. 'Come on, it'll be fun.'

'Explain?' Ellie was the first to recover.

'*The Afternoon Show* are looking for groups of people who've made firm New Year resolutions and are already some way towards achieving — '

'Yes?' Maggie waved her arms around, like an over-enthusiastic woman at an aerobics class. She simply wanted Toni to cut the bullshit.

'They want . . . US.'

'But . . . but, we're a disaster.'

'No, we're an inspiration. Look at us.' Toni fixed her gaze on Ellie. 'Now, we need to focus.' She was doing her best Uri Geller imperson- ation. 'Look. At. Us,' she emphasized and held out her arms and glowed like Maggie imagined the Virgin Mary must have done after discover- ing she was pregnant.

'Yes. Look at us.' Pam jumped up. 'We're

walking disasters.' She sat down again. 'Tell me, how exactly do you intend to fool the nation?' She sounded just like Oprah.

'Nonsense, we've achieved so much. We're an inspiration to women all over the country. They'll be clamouring to buy the book — '

'What shagging book?'

'The one that Jack is going to ghost write for us.'

'Whaaaat?'

'Now, he doesn't actually know anything about it yet but leave it to me and Ellie.' She smiled encouragingly in her general direction. 'Now, not a word, OK?' She put her finger to her lips, a definite Jack mannerism. Ellie wanted to puke.

'Excuse me, let me get this straight.' Pam stood up again. 'We are going on national TV as an inspiration to women in Ireland . . . sort of role models for the new millennium? What a load of wank.'

'Darling, the year 2000 is long gone. Get a life. No, we're forging a new road, paving the way for women who will not be controlled by men telling them how they should look, teaching them a new way forward, inspiring their souls towards — '

'Bollocks, who's been reading the fucking self-help books — me or her?' Pam was almost short of words, which was very worrying.

'Listen, Toni, we've lost — what? — maybe a stone between us?' Ellie said. She was nothing if not practical. 'Let's be honest here, we're no

403

self-help gurus.' Her voice had taken on a slightly pleading tone.

'Much more than a stone, more like two. I've lost half a stone, probably more. And you're fading away, Ellie.'

'But in how long? It's taken us months . . . ' It felt like a decade. 'We'll be a laughing stock.' Maggie was thinking of the women in the baking group.

'Where are my charts?' Toni was rummaging. 'Damn, my nail. I can't go on TV with a broken nail.'

'You'll have a broken jaw to match, I'd say, when they find out we're fakes. Marty Whelan looks as if he has a good left hook.'

'It's not *Open House*, that's finished. It's presented by three women, they'll be on our side.' Toni smiled pleadingly. 'Girls, come on, it's the spirit of the thing. Let's just feel the force.' She was doing her best to be empowering. It wasn't working.

'I really think I'm going to be sick.' Maggie did look pale. 'It's totally mortifying.'

'Now, let's just be calm. There must be a middle ground.' Pam was thinking of the three zillion Tesco customers she'd have to face. 'Toni, there has to be a compromise. Give us a chance to prepare.'

Toni's ultra-cool Motorola V3 bleeped. 'Excuse me, a text message, I wonder if it's from Jack?'

'He doesn't have a mo . . . ' Ellie began, then decided it was a waste of breath.

'Oooooh, it's an RTE number.' Her voice resembled George Clooney's pot-bellied piglet,

Pam imagined. Very, very squeaky.

'OK, let's just work out what to say in reply, we can always thank them and offer . . . ' Ellie was determined that common sense would prevail.

'Too late, we're on tomorrow week. Four o'clock. Book your time off immediately.' Her smile was a disgustingly cheap ad for whitening toothpaste.

★ ★ ★

The other three women woke up the next morning in different circumstances, each convinced it had all been a bad dream.

Ellie was woken violently at about six thirty when Rudi let out a wail. She leapt out of bed, grabbed him and only realized she was in danger of suffocating him when he burped helplessly very close to her chest.

'There, there, it's OK,' she crooned, half asleep. Seconds later they were both dozing and she realized they had well and truly bonded. Five minutes into a very pleasant knight-in-shining-armour daydream reality dawned on her. What the fuck was Toni thinking of? she asked herself as she drifted off again. I must get Jack to talk some sense into her. The only good thing about this very nasty situation was that it had taken her mind off the fact that the man she loved was about to have mind-blowing sex with her thinner, younger friend and there wasn't a thing she could do to stop it happening.

* * *

Pam was eased into reality by Andrew bringing her a cup of tea.

'Mum, are you OK? We heard you shouting in the middle of the night.'

'What about?' She wiped her eyes.

'Something about not really liking to eat six doughnuts in one sitting.'

She remembered. She was being savaged by Pat Kenny and trying desperately to defend herself. 'No, love, I'm fine, it was just a nightmare.'

* * *

Maggie's first vision of the day, seen through one half-open eye, was the ever-achieving Doug — Doug's crotch actually — jogging on the spot at the foot of the bed. It was pitch dark. He'd surprised her by being there when she got home — her fault, she realized now. She'd forced a key on him during a drunken Christmas pledge of undying love. Her head ached.

'Coming for a run?'

'Eh, no thanks, I've a pain in my stomach. Time of the month, I think.' It was the only thing she could think of that was guaranteed to send him packing.

'Oh, right, see you later. Eh, want anything before I go?'

'Actually, a cup of tea and a glass of water and, eh, two aspirin . . . for my tummy . . . would be good. Thanks.' She had a sudden memory of the end of the night before. They'd been so traumatized that they'd dragged a laughing Toni off to the nearest pub as soon as they could. Unfortunately, Pam had ordered Baileys shots in an effort to calm them all quickly — not good for their cells or their cellulite. Toni kept trying to jolly them along, promising it would be great fun. An hour later they were all in fits of laughter and agreeing that yes, it would be an adventure.

* * *

'Oh fuck.' Ellie.

'Fuck, fuck, fuck.' Pam.

'Fuck me, this is a nightmare.' Maggie.

Their hungover first thoughts were astonishingly similar.

* * *

'You're on what?' Jack was smiling.

'*The Afternoon Show*. Stop shouting.'

'Jesus, she's fantastic.' That was the moment Ellie realized he was truly a lost cause. It should have helped her go off him — but it didn't make the slightest difference.

* * *

'Have you read *The Road Less Travelled*?' Pam's RTE weirdo friend was back with a Healthy Options Chow Mein, wanting a Tesco Finest Champ with real butter instead.

'I built it.' She glared at him, her head thumping a perfect beat on the refunds till.

'Yes, well, perhaps I'll look up my collection.'

'See if you have one entitled *Lose a Stone in Seconds and Don't Look a Twit on TV*,' Pam said with a half smile. She had a very muddled, half-arsed thought. 'Actually, is there any way you could get me off TV?'

'Normally, it's the other way round.' He looked confused. 'However, I can recommend a very good book called *Feel the Fear and Do It Anyway*.'

'Listen, I'm feeling so much fear that the only thing I'll do is throw up on their posh sofa. Fancy a drink after work? I need to talk this through with someone who understands.'

'I'd be delighted.'

★   ★   ★

'No, Mrs Pearson . . . oh yes, sorry . . . Vera. No actually, it would not help if I came to the meeting and baked Eccles cakes.' The dehydration was getting to Maggie. 'Yes, I know what Doug told you but, actually, I need to eat less this coming week if I'm appearing on national TV.' Maggie had always been the realistic one of the group.

★   ★   ★

The rest of the week saw different approaches emerge.

Toni decided the best way to look fabulous was to fuck, fuck, fuck, so she tormented Jack relentlessly.

'So, how's the great romance?' Kate asked Jack on Thursday afternoon as Ellie ironed near by.

'Good, yeah, great actually. Listen, do you fancy having the girls on Saturday night?'

'Sure, no problem. What's on?'

'I'm cooking dinner for Toni. She loves chilli, apparently, can you believe it? It's my favourite too.' He beamed. 'Just as well really, it's the only thing I can cook with confidence.'

If Toni loves chilli then I'm very fond of Pedigree Chum, Ellie thought.

'Oh . . . eh, good.' Kate glanced at Ellie.

'And, em, could they sleep over, by any chance?'

'Yeah.' She tried to look modern, but only managed uncomfortable.

'Great, thanks.' He disappeared.

'So, what do you make of all this, then?'

'Actually, Kate, I'm too tired to care.'

Kate thought she'd never seen the younger woman look so truly miserable before. She always put on a brave face and cracked a joke.

'Well, I know my brother. This is all a novelty for him.' She smiled weakly. 'I hope your friend isn't expecting . . . anything long term . . .'

'It sounds to me like Jack's the one who's in this for the long haul.'

'Really? No, you've got it all wrong. Jack needs . . . a soulmate. And I don't think Toni quite fits the bill, do you? Sorry, Nora, I know she's your friend and all that.'

'No, you're fine,' she said, thinking, you've no idea how much that cheers me up actually. For a split second, Ellie wanted to tell her. She started to say something then stopped. That was all she needed. Kate would say something and she'd lose her job.

Kate looked at her for a long moment. 'Don't worry, he'll find the right person, eventually. It takes him a while, sometimes, but he always gets there in the end.' She gave Ellie a little smile and headed off.

★　★　★

'Eh, Doug, I'd like us to go running every morning and, eh, every evening as well for the next week,' Maggie said, trying to look healthy.

'I thought you had your . . . eh . . . you know.' His coyness irritated her.

'False alarm.' Her smile was Persil white. 'And no alcohol or takeaways or . . . chocolate.' She felt virtuous just saying it.

'Can we have popcorn with the movie on Saturday?'

'Yes, but no butter.'

★　★　★

Pam was convinced it was all a question of mind over matter. Luckily, so was Quentin, her new VBF. They spent hours pouring over *How to Make Love to the Same Man for the Rest of Your Life* — his suggestion — which taught her lots but nothing that offered immediate benefit.

She stuck with it because she was convinced he could have the programme taken off the air at the last minute, even though he told her he worked in an annex miles away from the studios and had never even seen Gerry Ryan.

46

If they had to have sex, Ellie realized much later, it couldn't have happened at a better time. The reason was simple. From the moment Toni had announced her world-domination plan for the WWW Club, Ellie had been galvanized into action. There was simply no time to brood.

A phonecall to her sister Claire, now stationed at a branch of her bank in Wisconsin, had started it.

'What'll I do?' Ellie had wailed, after filling her in.

'Jeez, stop sounding like a banshee, for a start,' Claire retorted in a weird American accent. She'd only been there ten days or so. 'Now, have you got a pen and paper?'

'Sure.' Ellie was getting the American vibe going.

'OK, let's see, you need a personal trainer . . . '

'P — e — r — '

'A dietician . . . '

's — o — n — '

'A masseuse . . . '

'a — l — '

'Make-up artist.'

'Eh? Slow down.'

'Hairdresser.'

'What was that second one again?'

'And life coach.'

'Right, eh, yeah, that's just what I was thinking.'

And so it transpired that Ellie was pinched, pummelled, perfumed and petrified at various stages over the coming week.

'How long have we got?' said Jeff, the personal trainer.

'About five days.'

'And you'll be on national TV?'

'That's the plan.'

'Right, so, we . . . eh . . . need to get going.' He was all smiles. 'Now,' his tone was slightly sharper, 'on the mat.' He sounded stressed, Ellie thought, but she was too out of breath to ask him, and they'd only done the warm-up. 'Now, arms straight, tummy in, head back and one, lift it,' he yelled. 'Two three four.' Very sharp indeed — cut-glass, to be precise.

'Five days, OK, we can do that.' The dietician's smile was that of Liam Lawlor at the tribunal. Forced.

'Five, hey, that long?' The life coach was ecstatic. 'It's a lifetime.' Ellie had always suspected they were fake.

By the time she'd jogged four miles, juiced half an allotment, been to the gym, had her spine adjusted, her follicles conditioned and her eyelashes tinted, the only thing Ellie was capable of was lying comatose on the bed. Her mother, a diehard fan of *The Afternoon Show*, was so thrilled that she'd immediately offered to have Rudi for the week. Ellie felt guilty but desperate as she packed him off and cancelled her appointment with yet another social worker.

How Clean is Your House?, once her favourite TV programme, was recorded and never watched.

'How clean is your temple,' was the mantra her life coach suggested she adopt.

Full of dirty thoughts about what my friend is doing with the man I think I've fallen in love with, she was tempted to reply, but felt he mightn't be qualified to deal with the emotion she knew that would unleash.

★ ★ ★

In three other homes around Dublin, panic had also set in.

Pam had adopted the 'fuck them, I'm OK as I am' approach and was eating for Ireland in an attempt to pretend it didn't matter.

Toni, meanwhile, was more thinking, Fuck me, I'm fabulous. The truth was, she did look great, and having sex, and plenty of it, with Jack Bryant was the nicest way she knew to lose calories.

Poor Maggie, meanwhile, was saying to everyone who'd listen, 'Fuck it, I'm useless.'

'No, you're not.' She and Doug were having a cosy chat on the phone one lunchtime and he had never heard her sound like this. 'You'll be fine. You always look nice.' It was not what she wanted to hear. Nice was what you called your mother's new headscarf. Nice was a five-euro Penneys blouse, or a day-old scone or an emerald toffee watching the news with your gran. Doug scurried off and rang his mother about it.

'OK,' he said when he called round that evening after work, 'Mum says you're to drink lots of water and sprinkle a mild laxative on your cereal every morning.'

It was the Mummy thing that did it. Maggie knew she was being unreasonable even before something snapped in her head. 'And spend the entire programme with a potty strapped to my ass? No thank you.'

'There's no need to be so crude.' He'd never seen her with that wild look before and he was nervous and therefore made the final, fatal mistake of suggesting that maybe his mother would be more equipped to deal with this one herself, and would Maggie like him to get her to call around later that evening? There was total silence. Doug was anxious, so he rattled on. 'By the way, Mum says she's enrolled you in the prayer group and she has your medal. Eh, you owe her one euro twenty-three. Well, me actually cause I paid her already.' He smiled innocently, thinking the prayer group might calm her down.

Maggie suddenly saw white in front of her eyes. 'No, I would not like to discuss this with your mother, or the baking group or the Legion of Mary or any other lousy do-gooders. I am fed up being treated like an old-age pensioner. I am sick of you suggesting we take it easy and go to bed early and save money by eating takeaways from that crap Chinese down the road that was closed down last year for having rats in the kitchen.' She drew breath and tried to calm herself. 'And I will not be opening a savings account with you for a rainy day, or any other type of day. I'm young. I want to travel and party and make a show of myself and I hate fucking baking. It makes my hands all chapped and the margarine gets under my nails. I'm sorry, Doug, but I don't really think we're suited after all and as soon as this show is over I'm going out to get pissed on the dearest champagne I can find in this godforsaken town and then I might just have mind-blowing sex with the first man who tells me I look foxy or ravishing or tarty or voluptuous. Anything, in fact, as long as he doesn't say I look fucking nice.'

★ ★ ★

The big day finally arrived and they met at the studio hours before they were due.

'Hey, are you the WWW Club?' asked a researcher who looked about twelve.

'Yes, I'm Toni and — '

'Great, follow me.' And they were off.

They were interviewed by all three presenters, so it was quick-fire questions all the way.

'So, why did you call yourselves the World Wide Web Club?' (Sheana, blonde presenter.)

'Oh, is that what it actually stands for?' No one got the joke. 'We always thought it stood for Women Watching Weight.' (Maggie.)

'She's joking, no it's just we're, you know, twenty-first-century women and we're always surfing the chat rooms, I mean shopping sites, so we thought, Why not?' (Toni.)

'And your club is different from the usual groups, say WeightWatchers, Unislim and the like, *nach bhfuil sé?*' (Blathnaid, red-headed Irish speaker.)

'Yes. Ours is free.' (Ellie.)

'Actually, ours is based more on the principle of friendship and, eh, rewarding yourself and a belief that weight loss can sometimes be as much in the brain as the, eh, belly. Also, we don't have a points system or anything, it's very simple really. And finally, you must know two people in the group before you can join.' (Toni again, beaming.)

'Now, we've had several callers on the line — this is generating quite a bit of interest, actually. Mary from Dooradoyle wants to know if each of you were a food, what would you be? Unusual question, Mary, but we love to hear from you anyway.' (Anna, gorgeous dark-haired lesbian.)

'Well, I think I'd be toad-in-the-hole.' (Toni.) 'I just love those big juicy bangers.' A bit subtle for everyone except Jack, who's probably wanking as we speak, Ellie thought, nerves making her cattier than usual.

'I'd be fish and chips. Firm white flesh with a lot of greasy bits.' Maggie was still having self-image issues, it seemed.

'For me, it would have to be plum pudding.' Pam was obviously hung up on Toni's earlier comparison. 'Like me, it's dark and mysterious with a bit of a kick.' Pam fingered her cleavage and a few farmers in the West got hot under the collar, the producer suspected.

'And you, Ellie?'

'Well, I'd cheat slightly and be a pina colada:

sweet and very refreshing, and I look better under an umbrella.' Cue lots of laughter and 'fuck you' smiles from the other three.

'So, how do people join your club?'

'Well, we do have a phone number that people can call.' (Toni.)

Strange looks were much in evidence from the other three.

'Yes, and it should be on screen any second now.' Sheana was beaming.

'Also our website, called, of course, www.www.com, will be up and running shortly. There is a book coming out in the summer as well, and we have plans to set up 'friendly groups' in all the major cities by Easter.' At which point two of the cameras had to cut away from shots of the other three, because of the look of total disbelief on their faces. Not good for inspiring viewers, the director decided.

'So tell me more about the reward system again?' (Anna.)

'We usually go to the chipper after the meetings.' (Ellie.)

'Now, Ellie, don't be naughty.' Toni turned to Anna. 'Sometimes, we might allow ourselves a tiny little takeaway, that's true, but — '

'We believe in being nice to ourselves, is what I think Toni means.' Pam wanted some of the limelight for herself. 'I remember once going to a slimming class and I'd lost four pounds, and the instructor said well done and beamed at me. So, I asked her if I could have a treat. And she smiled and said yes, maybe a small portion of fresh fruit salad or a low-fat natural yoghurt would be good.'

'Please don't name the organization concerned.' Irish-speaking Blathnaid looked extremely worried.

'No, of course not, but Deirdre from the convent class, you know who you are.' Pam waved her finger at the camera with the red light. 'Anyway, I went off home and had a choc-ice and two Twix bars on the way.' Pam was all smiles. 'Much nicer.'

'No one we know eats low-fat diet yoghurt, anyway,' Maggie said, smiling for the first time.

'Not that we believe that chocolate is all that good, mind you. Our programme is based on a rather unique approach . . . ' Toni was beginning to annoy the others.

'Now another caller, Dennis from Fermoy, says that you're all very sophisticated, a bit like the *Sex and the City* girls, actually — gosh that is posh — and he wonders if any of you are single?'

'I'm in a long-term relationship, actually, and very happy,' Toni smiled coyly.

Ellie kept a smile pasted to her face. Still, that should put paid to Jack's erection, if he was like all the rest of them.

'I'm divorced and lonely.' Pam sucked her finger.

'I was seeing someone until quite recently,' Maggie blurted out and the other three were amazed. Doug was slagged for the rest of the afternoon in work and he didn't like it one bit. His mammy liked it even less.

'And, eh, I'm a single parent.' Ellie thought for a split second that she might not say it, but then realized she was happy.

'So, as you can see we're about as different from those girls as TG4 is from Hugh Hefner's Playboy channel.'

'Well, I have to tell you our phone lines are jammed so I hope you'll consider a tour of the country, maybe franchise out the idea. We'll certainly be following your progress.' Anna was all smiles. Ellie decided she could really fancy her. It would be so much easier. She was daydreaming and almost missed the next question.

'And will you come back and see us later in the series and tell us if you're all multi-millionaires?' she beamed at the four girls.

Now, most seasoned performers will tell you that if asked that question on live TV you should (a) vomit, (b) faint or (c) top yourself in an effort to avoid answering because what it does is commit you, and certainly in this case commitment might mean a mental asylum or jail for the four of them once they were rumbled, Ellie decided.

'Of course, we'd be delighted.' Toni grinned.

47

'How could you do this to us?' All was not sweetness and light in the dressing room afterwards.

'Will you chill? It'll be fine, don't forget we have — '

'Girls, girls, I think we have bigger problems than this. I suggest we go for a drink and decide how to handle this . . . unexpected mushrooming of our empire.' Maggie grinned at Toni, more relaxed than she had been in days.

'You've a lot of explaining to do, Miss Francescone.'

'It's all under control, I keep telling you. Actually, I do need a drink but I can't stay long. Jack and I are going to dinner with his editor later.'

'And I've to collect Rudi.' The contrast wasn't lost on Pam. She'd been watching Ellie a lot lately.

'Come on, let's just get out of here. Maggie, you're up first. What on earth did you mean by seeing someone until quite recently?' Pam was straight in there.

* * *

Jack was still reeling from the show. Kate had called round to watch it with him, after she'd collected the girls. When Ellie had asked for a

421

few days off, she'd organized a replacement from an agency. But 'Mitch' — a German dental nurse — was not a success. She could extract a tooth at twenty paces, Jack suspected.

'What went wrong?' Kate asked after he'd explained that he'd been forced to tell Mitch she was no longer required. 'She seemed efficient.'

'Cold.'

'Cold? I didn't get that.'

'Freeze the snot on the baby Jesus, to be precise.'

'I thought the girls liked her?'

'After Nora, are you insane? Mitch was the nanny from hell. Sam called her bitch and Jess discovered that witch rhymed quite nicely and I couldn't get used to her lazy eye. I kept thinking she was winking at me. No, if Nora was trying to convince us we couldn't live without her, she gets top marks.' He looked at Kate with a frown. 'Did Nora look different on TV, d'ya think?'

'Different? No. How?'

'I dunno, sort of younger, softer, more girly.'

'No, she seemed the very same Nora to me. She did look fab, though. I loved her hairstyle and the weight loss really suits her.' Kate paused, as if considering it for a moment. 'No, I think it was just the clothes. She dresses, eh, conservatively when she's working. All those pastels and the funky jewellery made her look really cute. I want that top she was wearing too. Very sexy.'

'She's changed her hair.'

'Yep, definitely warmer. Bouncier too. But I think it's just she keeps it tied back most of the time when she's working.'

Jack nodded and finished making the coffee. Kate watched him quietly for a moment.

'So, how did you feel when Toni said she was in a 'long-term' relationship?'

'Three weeks is hardly a commitment.'

'Well, now that you've slept together, she probably thinks . . . Anyway, is it good to be 'back in the saddle', as my subtle husband would say?'

'I don't really want to — ' He stopped as her mobile went, and kept his back to her, annoyed that she was so . . . he didn't know what but he knew he didn't like it.

'Gotta go, kids are locked out of the kitchen and they're starving. Bill has gone mental about security. He's now locking all the internal doors and hiding the keys. It's driving me insane.'

'How come?'

'He thinks he rumbled a burglar the other night when he was out chasing the cat.'

'How did he know it was a burglar?'

'Clothes had arrows on them, swag bag, mask, that sort of thing, I'd imagine. You know Bill. Terrible for jumping to conclusions.'

Jack laughed in spite for himself. 'Tell Sarah I'll need her about seven thirty, OK?'

'Where are you off to?'

'People's. Robert is over. He wants to meet Toni.'

'How does he know about her?' She was intrigued.

'She was here when he rang the other night. Actually, she answered the phone and they chatted for ages. He's another one who's obsessed with me dating again, so he's dying to get to know her.'

'Well, enjoy. See you later. If you're talking to Nora tell her well done from me, will you?'

'Good idea, I'll ring her right now.'

★　★　★

'Nora, hi, it's Jack.'

'Hi. How are you? Nothing wrong?' He never rang her.

'No, no. I just wanted to say well done. You looked different.'

'Good different or bad different?'

'Oh, good. Great actually. Kate said the same. The girls were just wondering when you're coming back?'

'Is Mitch staying till tomorrow?'

'I'm afraid she didn't stay at all, really. Long story. No, we're nannyless.'

'Well, in that case I'll come in in the morning. Mum is keeping Rudi till tomorrow evening anyway, so it'll be easier. I'm wrecked, to be honest.'

'Well, listen, you sleep on in the morning and I'll take the girls to school. Come in at lunch-time, just to be here when Jess gets back, Kate will collect her. Then go off early and collect your own little monster. How does that sound?'

'Great, thanks. Do you want to speak to Toni?'

'Eh, no. I'll see her later. Must go, got a col — eh, call to make.'

★　★　★

'Was that Jack?'

'Yeah. He said he'd see you later.'

'Well, I hope he thought we were fabulous?'

'I'm sure he did.'

★ ★ ★

Jack was uneasy and not sure why. Dinner with Robert went smoothly. Toni charmed the pants off him, as he knew she would. Her mobile rang constantly through dinner, though — it seemed the world and its mother wanted to join their club. Bob started advising her on how to maximize the aftermath of the show and ended up offering to introduce her to a good editor in his own company. 'I like the idea. You're a very clever girl. This could be big. Women are obsessed with new ways to lose weight.'

'Yes, but they haven't actually lost any.' Jack was teasing.

'Jack, that is unfair and untrue.' She rubbed his crotch with her toe under the table. 'Do you have any complaints about my shape?'

'No, but I've only known — '

'Well then.' She winked at Bob. 'Anyway, I think it's improved even since Christmas. Must be all that exercise I'm getting.'

Robert was enjoying the banter and he nudged Jack as they left the restaurant. 'You two must come and see me soon. I owe you a long weekend in the country.'

'Oh we will, won't we, Jack?'

'Well, it's kinda difficult with the girls . . . we'll see.'

425

'Bring them with you.' The older man was enthusiastic. 'My wife would keep them busy and give you two lovebirds time to yourselves.' Toni was practically cooing.

'Sure Ellie will mind them. Jack needs a break and I'm just the woman to pamper him to death.'

'He's a lucky guy. Will you wear your nurse's uniform for him?' His editor was more than tipsy.

'With nothing underneath, if he's lucky.'

'OK, you two, enough. I don't know which of you is the worse. Bob, you take the first taxi.'

'Can I drop either of you? I'm staying in town.'

Jack hesitated for a second. 'You could drop Toni, actually, if you don't mind? That way I can go directly home. I'm a bit worried about leaving Sarah too long.' He turned to Toni. 'She has school tomorrow and I'm already pushing my luck.'

'Right, that's settled then. It'll be a pleasure to have a bit more of your charming company.'

'But, darling, I wanted to — '

'I'll call you during the week.'

'Come on, I'll fill you in on all his bad habits on the way. I know more about him than his mother.'

Toni wasn't pleased. 'OK, then. Goodnight.' Her kiss was cool but lingering.

48

Ellie's phone was hopping by eight thirty and it had been the same yesterday evening. So much for a lie-in. Pam phoned at ten.

'This is madness. The whole country knows I'm on a diet. I tried to buy an éclair for my break a few minutes ago. The girl on the cash desk refused to serve me. Suggested I have an apple instead. Then a little old lady behind me in the queue smacked my backside with her umbrella and said knowingly, 'Remember, a minute on the lips, a lifetime on the hips.''

'I can guess what you said.'

'Told her her own hips would be very close to her lips if she molested me again. People keep slipping me their numbers and saying they want to join. Tesco have offered to set up an in-store club. There's a bigger queue for me than for the Lotto machine.'

'Oh dear. Have you spoken to Toni?'

'Yes, she's in a foul mood. Apparently some old codger called Dingo or Ringo or something hooked her round the neck with his walking stick when he caught her with her hand in the last of the Christmas Quality Street.'

'Right, I suggest we meet tonight. Yesterday we were all too hyper.'

'I suggested the same thing. Toni says she's seeing Jack.'

'Again?'

'Lust is an incurable disease, darling, didn't you know?' It was out before she realized what she was saying. She could have bitten her tongue off. 'Oh Ellie, I'm sorry, I — '

'Forget it. Listen, I have to run, I'll call you later.'

★   ★   ★

She rang Maggie to keep from thinking. 'How's it going?'

'I've just had my photo taken for the firm's website. They want me to sit in on all meetings with clients connected to the food industry. What do I know about the food industry?'

'You've contributed well towards its profits over the years.'

'Everyone is looking at me. A woman on the bus this morning burst into tears and told me her husband had called her a fat cow and walked out on her last night. She wants to become a WWW 'leader'. It's scary.'

'OK, Toni's busy tonight but let's meet anyway at eight. Come here.'

'Right, if I'm not mobbed at the sushi bar during lunch, that is.'

'Stay calm.'

'Yeah. Wait till you go outside.'

★   ★   ★

Ellie abandoned her navy skirt and white blouse in favour of black fitted trousers and a tight-fitting black stretchy shirt. If Mitch in her

428

pristine white uniform hadn't impressed Jack, she felt she was safe enough.

'Hi there, welcome back. Am I glad to see you.'

'Hello. My God, Maggie was right. The whole country is watching us. One of your neighbours just stopped me and asked if we'd consider starting up in London. Her sister heard something about us while listening to Pat Kenny on the net this morning.'

'Well, give me your autograph, so, and be done with it.' He looked hassled.

'Is everything OK?'

'Huh? Yes, fine. I'm just a bit wrecked.'

'Yes, well, Toni tends to have that effect on men.' It was out before she could stop it. 'Sorry, forget I said that. It was childish.' She looked at him sheepishly. 'How's it going, anyway?'

'You're as bad as Kate. I've seen her less than ten times, it's hardly the romance of the century.'

Wow, that was a change of heart. She tried not to think of what it might mean. 'Sorry, I shouldn't have asked.'

'The girls are my number-one priority, OK? Nothing gets in the way of that.'

Ellie had no idea where all this was coming from.

'Fine. God, you're touchy today. Anyway, I'd better make a start. I'd say there's a lot to catch up on.'

'No, actually, Mitch was Miss Efficiency. The place is spotless and she washed and ironed their clothes before they'd taken them off, I suspect. She practically put Mrs O'Sullivan out of a job.'

He grimaced. 'Sorry, Nora. I'm a bit of a grouch. Didn't mean to take it out on you.'

'That's allowed. Just don't make a habit of it.'

'So, what's the next step?'

'For what?'

'World domination, isn't that what Toni has planned?'

'I dunno, if you'd leave her alone for a night we might get to talk. Still, the rest of us are getting together this evening, to try and see what happens next.'

'I have no arrangement to see Toni this evening.' He sounded puzzled.

Ellie shrugged. 'All I know is that's what she said to Pam.'

'I'd better ring her. Excuse me.'

'Sure. It's nearly time to collect Jess, anyway. See you later.'

★ ★ ★

Jessie had hugged her to death and now even Sam threw her arms around her.

'Nora, we missed you. I was fraid.'

'Why, darling? I told you I was taking a few days off.'

'She thought you'd gone for ever, like Mummy.'

'Girls, come here.' She knelt down in the middle of the school yard. 'I'll never leave you without explaining what's happening, OK? If I have to go away, we'll all sit down, your dad included, and talk about it.'

'Are you going?' Sam was quiet.

430

'Not as long as you want me around.'

'Is Dad going to marry Toni?' Jess asked. Ellie sucked in her breath.

'I don't know, love. You'll have to talk to him about that.'

'Georgia told us Dad and Toni were very very good friends,' Sam explained. 'I hate her. She kicked Rashers out of the way. She didn't think anybody seen it but I did.'

'Saw it. No, I'm sure she didn't. Are you exaggerating, by any chance, Sam?'

'What's that?' Jessie wanted to know.

'Never mind, don't worry about it for now. Let's all go and get an ice-cream.' Three very downbeat bodies headed for the car.

★ ★ ★

'Hey, are we happy to have Nora back?' Jack asked as they tumbled in, humour restored, half an hour later.

'We luv Nora.' Jessie was beaming.

'Indeed we do, don't we, Sam?'

'Dad, don't get married.'

Jack drew in his breath. 'I'm not planning to marry anyone, darling. Where on earth did you get that idea?'

Sam shrugged.

'We hate her, she kicked Rashers.'

'Now, Jess, we talked about this already. Toni wouldn't do that. She loves animals.' More than kids, Ellie thought, but it was none of her business. 'I think they're just a bit overwrought. All the comings and goings. Mitch, Toni, me.'

431

She smiled down at them. 'I've told them I'm back to stay and that you'd always talk to them first.'

'There is nothing to talk about. OK, you two?' They nodded soberly.

'Upstairs, then, and get changed.' Ellie shooed them away, 'How about homemade pizza for dinner? You get to choose your own toppings.' They were gone.

'Nora, you don't have to go to that trouble. You head off.'

'I've some frozen bases and there's a bit of tomato sauce in the fridge. It's no problem. Then I'll go.' She smiled at him, although she felt a bit down now herself. 'Don't worry, they're fine. I think it just all came out when they saw me. Spend a bit of time with them this evening. They'll tell you more than anyone.'

'I have to go out for a bit. Kate's coming round.' He moved away.

Why am I worrying? It's his life, Ellie decided, trying to be rational. She'd just have to leave them to it and keep out of it as much as she could. Otherwise she'd end up a basket case.

★ ★ ★

When she collected Rudi he held out his arms to her and it made all her worries disappear for the moment.

'Where's my boy?' She grabbed him and gave him a big kiss and a hug.

'He's been looking for his mama all week. He's a lovely little boy.' Ellie's mother wasn't usually so soft-spoken.

'Yes, he is, isn't he?'

'Eleanora, are you sure about what you're doing? Keeping him, I mean?'

'Yes I am, and, Mum, please don't start asking — '

'I was only going to say that your father and I will help, if we can at all.'

If she'd said she was on the game Ellie couldn't have been more surprised.

'OK, thanks. I'd, eh, better go, the girls are coming round shortly.' Ellie was afraid she'd cry, it was one of those days. 'Thanks, Mum, that means a lot.' She hugged her mother as she left.

★ ★ ★

'Hey, luv, you should be jogging. Slouching along like that won't help you lose anything except time,' a guy on a bike offered as she walked towards her apartment. Given that she had a baby in one arm and two bags of groceries in the other it seemed a waste of time and energy telling him to go fuck himself, which was what she felt like doing. By the time she got to her own hall door three people had asked her for a 'brochure'.

The girls were exhausted too.

'I've been moved off the customer services desk.' Pam fell in the door not long after Ellie. 'Up to this, all they could see was my cleavage. Now I'm on show all day.' She plonked herself on the couch. 'Here, open this. We deserve a glass.'

'So, what are you doing now?'

'Wait for it, cause it took me two minutes to stop laughing in the manager's gob. I'm the new Healthy Eating Adviser. They want me out front. I have to wear a sash.' By the time Maggie arrived Ellie had cheered up considerably as Pam recounted the traumatic effects of the day.

'How are you today, chicken?' Pam asked Maggie. They were all still surprised by what she'd said to Doug. And delighted. She deserved much more.

They were just settling down to 'business' when the doorbell rang.

'It's Toni.'

Pam made a 'don't ask' face as Toni breezed in and announced, 'He's dumped me.'

No one said anything. Ellie's heart started beating faster. Pam kept darting sly looks at her. She'd heard it but was afraid to think Toni might actually mean what she said.

'Said it had gotten too serious and that all he'd wanted was a bit of fun. Bastard. Anyway, I've too much to do to brood. So, let's make a plan.'

'No, listen, Toni, that's terrible. He can't just do that, maybe Ellie could talk to him.' Maggie couldn't understand Pam's filthy look.

'I really don't — '

'Don't be ridiculous. I've never gone grovelling yet to a man.' She bit her lip. 'Although, oh God, I really liked him. I thought we had a future.' With that she burst into tears.

49

The next few weeks were hectic as the WWW Club spiralled out of control. Being on the top-rated daytime TV show had turned the friends into minor celebrities. There were newspaper articles, features, local radio, even the cover of one of the country's leading magazines.

They'd come up with a 'manifesto' and really it was no different to what they'd known all along, yet everyone thought it was brand new. There were no gimmicks, they'd tried every one themselves and found they didn't work — although their system of reward seemed in itself encouraging to many. They incorporated some of the fun elements, such as chewing your food until it's liquid and the old 'eight glasses of water a day' line. To their amazement it all took off. People seemed to like their insistence that only people who knew each other could be in a group. This was based on the idea that friends could be brutal and encouraging in a way that no team leader ever could. 'Also they know your weaknesses,' Pam added with a cackle.

'And, they're the very best when things go wrong.' Toni was very subdued the day she said that, but the interviewer didn't pick up on it, thankfully, Ellie thought.

* * *

Life in the Bryant household got back to normal. Jack never again spoke about Toni and even Kate didn't know anything.

'I never thought it would work.'

'Why?' Ellie was interested.

'Nora, look, I know she's your friend, but she's, well, pushy. I'm sorry if that sounds offensive.'

'No, I do understand what you mean but she has good qualities too. And remember, he pursued her after the initial date.'

'I know that, I'm not laying blame, simply trying to work out what went wrong. Nora . . . I also noticed something else.' She looked at Ellie closely. 'I don't think she really likes children. Even on New Year's Eve, when they were all mingling, there was no warmth on her part. My girls noticed it.'

Ellie couldn't argue with that.

'Let's just say a prayer that the next one is good for him.' She gave Ellie a lingering look. 'He's worth fighting for,' she mumbled and made some excuse and left. Bill would kill her, he'd warned her to leave them alone.

⋆ ⋆ ⋆

The weeks went by like lightning. Toni and Maggie — and Pam to a lesser extent — were travelling the length of the country setting up clubs. The book was in first draft. There was a website and a TV commercial in pre-production. Toni was the brains behind it all. Ellie had taken a back seat, largely because of Rudi, who had become an absolute joy. She had begun the adoption process and he was blooming, almost as if he knew. And Ellie felt calmer, more relaxed. And she was eating healthily. She was determined to look her best, no matter what. Mind you, now that the threat of Toni had gone away she'd begun to daydream, fantasize even. It helped that she'd told Maggie as well the other night.

'You what? I'm coming over,' had been her reaction.

'No, don't, honestly. I'm just off to bed.'

'You fancy him?'

'Yep. Maybe even more than that.'

'But, El, has anything ever happened?'

'No, nothing. I just . . . have grown very fond of him. Oh fuck it, Maggie, I think . . . I love him.'

'Oh God.'

'I know. I'm a fool. Hey, but at least if he meets someone else I won't have to go through it step by step like I did with Toni.'

'You poor thing. That must have been hell.'

'Actually, having the baby and then the show to worry about helped . . . a lot. And in the end it was all over rather quickly, really. Promise you won't say a word to Toni? Pam knows. And I will tell Toni, but not yet. I'd hate to hurt her, you know that. Even if I wanted to bash her head in a few times, but that was me being a jealous cow.'

'I promise. But, El, please go easy. He's a good-looking guy and a great catch, as Toni told us more than once. He might not . . . well, you know.'

'I know. And I'm OK, honestly.' They both knew it was a lie.

* * *

Ellie was hoovering when the phone in Jack's office rang the next day. She ignored it. The answering machine didn't appear to click on, and when it rang again twice in the next couple of minutes she poked her head around the door. It was chaos as usual. He'd gone to meet his accountant that morning and he was in a foul mood. The phone rang again. She sneaked in and answered it. It was some European publisher looking to speak to him urgently. Ellie grabbed a piece of paper and jotted down the details. When she hung up she turned the page over, hoping she hadn't written on the back of something important. It was some sort of spoof story about blind dates, and different ways of meeting people. It seemed like an odd page of his writing — although she'd never read anything he'd written so she was hardly in a position to judge. She transferred the name and number to a yellow Post-it, scribbled out what she'd taken down and replaced the page on his chair where she'd found it.

'Oh, Jack, there was a telephone call for you, in the office.' He immediately looked guarded. 'It kept ringing and I was afraid it was some sort of emergency.'

'There is an answering machine.'

'It didn't click on, honestly.' Why was she being so defensive? 'Anyway, I answered it. The message is on a yellow sticky on the phone. They said it was urgent.'

'Fine. And Nora . . . '

'Yes?' She knew what was coming.

'Please keep out of my study. I don't care what happens. They'll always call back.'

'OK. Sorry.' Where had all their easy slagging gone? she wondered. He was doing her head in.

He sighed. 'No, actually, I'm sorry, Nora, I've been like a bear. I've got a lot on my mind . . . '

She thought of the note she'd read earlier. 'Maybe you need a date, something to relax you, you know.' She was thinking of herself.

He laughed. 'Yeah, I was thinking of a blind date actually.' Her heart sank. So that's what it was about. She needed to know.

'Are you thinking of anyone in particular?'

'No, it's blind, remember. I wouldn't know the person.' He pulled out a chair. 'How would the WWW Club girls go about it, if they were trying?'

'Well, Pam would go to a dating agency, she'd like doing the video, I think. And she looks great on camera. Sure, half the farmers in the West of Ireland were hot for her after the show.'

He nodded. 'Go on . . . '

'Maggie would go to a singles night, I'd say. And they'd all fancy her like mad; she looks great with her red hair and big smile.'

'And Toni?'

'Toni, let me see, Toni would try speed dating, I think. She makes up her mind pretty quickly and if she didn't instantly hit it off, she wouldn't want to waste time and . . . ' God, was he trying to get back with her? Was this what all this was about? she wondered.

'And you?'

'Me, oh, I dunno.' She wanted to tell him how she felt so badly. 'I'd probably go for the good, old-fashioned small ad. You know: 'Nice, reliable, easy-going girl seeks soulmate. Must be kind to animals and children and enjoy walks on the beach and nights in by the fire and . . . '' She coughed. This was getting out of hand. 'Anyway, I'd better get moving. I'm way behind.' He watched her intently as she left. She was mortified in case he'd copped on.

★ ★ ★

Nothing more was mentioned, but he seemed on much better form and Ellie prayed that he hadn't found himself a new date. She finished early on Friday because she had a big meeting with the social workers. Afterwards she put Rudi to bed and climbed in herself, even though it was only eight thirty. Maggie rang soon after, trying to persuade her out for a drink. Her sister had even offered to sit with the baby.

'Honestly, Mags, I'm bushed. Are you OK?'

'Yeah. It's just, since Doug and I split . . . I'm . . . sort of lonely, I suppose.'

'Oh no. You're not thinking of — '

'God no. Ah, I'm OK really. I was just talking to Pam earlier and she has a date tonight with RTE man. It brought it all back. Relationships are nice, you know . . . Listen, don't mind me, I'm useless — '

'Give me half an hour, I'll get up.'

'No, stay where you are, I'm fine, honestly. Pam said to drop by her house later so I'll probably do that. Her man has to go into work so it's just a drink for an hour, but she's really excited. So I'll swing by and hear all the details later. Toni's in Cork but she'll be back mid-morning if we want to meet for a late lunch.'

'Sounds good, we haven't had a good gossip in ages.'

'Fat chance of that, these days. It's all business. Anyway, call you late morning. Sleep well.'

'Nite nite.' She was dreaming in minutes.

★　★　★

Next morning she felt much better and was up and showered by ten, so she and Rudi went for a stroll in the park and bought the papers and some bagels on the way home.

She opened the newspaper, buttered some of the doughy bread and sat down to enjoy her coffee and the column.

As she read it, a sense of having seen it before crept in and she mentally shook her head clear, until she reached a very funny bit about blind dates. 'Who'd go on a blind date,' she read,

> when women have you well sussed before they even meet you? My friend Noel saw a video of the sexiest woman, all cleavage and pouting lips. When he met her she was

gorgeous, but definitely under age. So, the camera does lie, it seems. Then there are the women who look you up and down for ten seconds on a speed-dating night out, and write you off before you've even asked the first question. So, the safest way, it seems to this inexperienced guy, would be a small ad. So, what would you say to try and land your ideal woman? Mine would go something like this: Stupid, blinkered guy, seeks soulmate . . .

It took her a minute or two, but then something just clicked: his interest in everything they did; not wanting her in his study. It seemed unbelievable, but it had to be him. She felt cheated. No, make that stupid. She hesitated, wondering if maybe he'd been sussing her out to help someone else, or editing it even. But it was all too much of a coincidence. She picked up Rudi and grabbed her car keys.

50

'When were you going to tell me?' She thrust the paper at him as soon as he opened the door. 'When were you going to let me in on your little secret?' He stared at her. He was in lazy Saturday mode — bare feet and tousled hair.

'Nora,' Jessie screamed from behind his back. 'Are you taking us to the park?'

Sam appeared down the stairs in her dressing gown. 'Sarah's here as well. We're going to a movie later. You can come too if you like.'

'Not today, darling, I just came by to talk to your dad. Sarah, would you and Sam mind Rudi for me for a few minutes?'

'OK. Can he watch a DVD with us?'

'Yes, sure.' She handed Rudi to Sarah and he went off quite happily with the girls.

'Well?' She felt angry, bemused.

'Nora, look, I can explain.'

'I'm waiting.'

'Well, come in, then.' He headed for the kitchen.

'How could you?'

'Look, it's something I've been doing for ages. It was based on Lorna, originally. When she left I tried to give it up but they wouldn't let me. It had taken off at that stage.'

'But you used me, you used us. No wonder you were so interested in our pathetic attempts at dieting and meeting men and all that stuff.'

443

She smirked. 'How could I not have guessed? Now when I think of it there were so many similarities to things we discussed, silly little things. Sometimes when I read it I thought, Gosh, that's so like us.'

'Look, yes, you did provide me with material, but no more than anyone else I met.'

She kept remembering things that made her even more pissed off. 'I was reading it here that Saturday we went out for the day . . .'

He looked guilty.

'God, what an idiot.'

'Nora, I really am sorry. I wasn't ready to say something then. Nobody knew it was me.'

She changed tack. 'So why did you do it in the first place? That's what I can't understand. You're a serious crime writer, you certainly don't need the money — '

'I suppose I did it to keep in touch. Initially, I liked the buzz — I was in and out of the paper, got invited to all the parties, stupid stuff. But Lorna and I were on the rocks even then and I suppose I used it . . . it got me away from her, sometimes. Does that sound terrible?'

She shrugged.

'And then, later, I just needed an outlet, I suppose. Being stuck in the house, writing about death all the time . . . The column sort of kept me in touch with real life. Because of it I had to get out occasionally, keep up with what was happening, read all the women's magazines, that sort of thing. Also, it was a regular income. They paid me well . . .'

'Don't insult me, please. You don't need a

regular income . . . '

'No, I don't. But old instincts die hard. I didn't always have money like this. And there's always the feeling that it might stop, nobody might buy your books any more. But you're right, it wasn't really about money, I'd planned to give it up a long time ago.'

'And then I came along and provided you with a ready-made story each week. God, you must have laughed.' She was raging, as much at her own naivety as anything. 'I could sue you, you know.'

'Do you want to?'

'No, but I don't know if I can work for you any more.'

'Nora, don't.'

'I mean it.' She didn't really, he was the best employer she'd ever had, but the last while had been different, they'd somehow lost their earlier closeness. He hadn't pulled her hair in ages.

'I don't want to lose you. Please.' He ran his hands through his own hair.

She was tired of hiding her feelings, she wanted to put all this behind her and get on with her life, but he'd become part of it. So had the girls. And even though she knew it would all end, eventually, when he spread his wings again and found someone who mattered more than Toni, she couldn't be the one to walk away. God, it was pathetic. And Toni had fallen for it too. Suddenly, Ellie felt protective of her friend.

'And what about Toni? Was she just to research your article on one-night stands? Mind you, she lasted for a couple of weeks I suppose. Longer

…an your average, I'd say. Why exactly did you …ump her?'

He squirmed. 'I suppose I realized very quickly that I didn't have any real feelings for her.'

'You used her.' He didn't flinch.

'Yes, in a way I did. I wondered if I could cut the mustard on the dating scene, and she was fun. But remember, it was her idea initially. She asked me out. And yes, the sex was great, before you ask.' He glanced over to make sure the kids were out of earshot. He didn't even notice her expression.

The sex bit hurt more than it should have. She didn't understand it. She'd known — hell the whole world had known — they'd been at it like rabbits.

He was staring at her. 'She was . . . I don't know what the word is, and I don't want to hurt you. I know she's your friend.'

She waited.

'She was too, I dunno, too much, I suppose. She wanted it all to move way too fast, and on her terms. The novelty wore off quite quickly, if I'm honest.' He scratched his head. 'We didn't suit each other at all, really, and I finally understood it that night when we had dinner with my editor. He and Toni had much more in common than Toni and I had. Anyway, there was another factor.' He paused. 'I wasn't sure she really liked the girls.' He was watching her face for a reaction. 'And ultimately, that would have prevented it going anywhere, no matter what my feelings were.'

'You hurt her, and she's a good person.'

'I didn't know that, she sort of led me to believe that it was just a fling for her too. Anyway, Nora, it would all have ended sooner or later, that's for sure. And it had nothing to do with us.' He ran his fingers through his hair again. 'Oh God, I've made a complete mess of this whole thing.'

'Us?'

'You and me.'

'There is no you and me.'

'No.' He handed her a cup and poured coffee for them both. 'Nora, I'm sorry. I swear I never meant to hurt you . . .'

'But, this week, how could you be so blatant? At least up to this you were reasonably subtle . . . although, the more I think about it now the more I realize how much material I provided.' She shook her head. 'Anyway, why this week? You must have known I'd cop it?'

'It was my last one. I resigned a few weeks ago.'

She was confused. 'It doesn't make sense. You could have gotten away with it. I'd never have put two and two together . . . if it wasn't for that stupid conversation we had the other day.'

'I wanted to ask you . . .'

'Ask me what?'

'Did you read it?'

'Yes, of course I bloody read it.'

'So, what's your answer?'

'My answer to what?'

He looked at her. He was more nervous than

he'd ever been in his life. 'Did you really read it . . . ?'

'I did.'

'All of it?'

'No, not quite.'

'I thought as much. Well, you may as well know it all, I'm sure your friends will tell you anyway. Here . . . ' He thrust the paper back at her and turned away.

She skimmed the bit she'd already read, and continued:

Stupid, blinkered guy, seeks soulmate. Must love children and animals, especially little girls who can be cranky sometimes and dopey dogs likely to slobber all over her and upset her first day in a new job. Should be able to cook — and must know how to bake butterfly buns with jam and cream. Good bedtime-reading skills essential. Ability to formulate a plan when vital items, such as feelys, go missing would be an advantage. Must look gorgeous in the morning and also on TV and not mind having her hair pulled or dribble wiped off her chin occasionally. In return all I can promise is a GSOH and a real affinity with little boys who might need a loving father. Suitable applicants know where to apply.

She didn't look up for ages.

'I told you it was my last one. I could afford to indulge myself.' He sounded uncomfortable and unsure.

'So, what does this mean?' She still didn'
meet his eyes.

'It means I'd like you to be my . . . I'd like us
to . . . to . . . I'd like to see you sometime,' he
said finally.

'You see me every day.'

'I mean take you out . . . properly . . . just the
two of us.'

'A date, you mean?' She was still way too
thrown by what she'd just read.

'Yes.'

'You want to practise on me the way you did
on Toni?'

'That's not fair.'

'Well, I wouldn't bother. You'll only be
disappointed.'

'I wasn't talking about sex.'

'Yeah, right. It's all been about sex with you,
hasn't it?'

'I suppose it was important, yes. I thought I
was past it.'

'And were you?'

'No.'

'Bully for you. So, what do you want with me,
then?'

'I don't want to have sex with you.'

'Gee, thanks.'

'I want to get to know you . . . as a woman.
Not just as our nanny. Without all this stuff
getting in the way.'

'There'll always be three kids getting between
you and me.' It was what she wanted more than
anything, so why was she hesitating?

'We could try?'

'Where has the closeness gone? Tell me that. It's all changed these last few weeks. I liked it better when you liked me.' She sounded like a child herself. 'What happened, Jack?' She smiled sadly. 'We used to laugh, have fun. We were friends.'

'A few weeks ago, I discovered I had . . . certain feelings for you. I wanted to be more than friends.'

'When?'

'The day I saw you on TV.'

Ellie laughed.

'What's so funny?'

'I had feelings for you long before then.' His eyes narrowed. It was the first indication she'd given him.

'When?'

'The evening you came to the funeral.'

'What sort of feelings?' She didn't answer. 'Nora, please, tell me.'

'Funny feelings.'

'Good funny?' She nodded. 'Why didn't you say something?'

'Are you mad? You were my boss. I liked my job. And when Rudi came along, I needed that job badly.'

He came a bit closer. 'Nora, can we start again? Please?'

'I dunno.'

'I want to.' He tipped her chin up like he'd done before. 'I need you.'

She swallowed hard. It was all she wanted, but she was still afraid. 'How can we keep things going, me working here and all?'

'We're already kind of a family. Look.' He steered her over to where Rudi was sitting between the girls on the sofa. Jess was feeding him from her bottle. 'We just need to spend some time on our own.' He turned her to face him. 'Get to know each other.'

'I won't sleep with you.' It was a downright lie.

'I'm not asking you to.'

'Oh.'

'At least not until we're married.'

'Married?'

'Yes.'

'You and me?'

'Yes.'

'We haven't even kissed and you want to marry me?'

'Yes, Nora, I do.'

She grinned at him for the first time. 'You know, I never thought it would be like this. I thought it would be all bells and whistles. Fireworks and poetry.'

'Thought what would be like this?'

She hesitated for only a second. 'Love . . . '

'Do you love me, Nora?' He came very close to her.

She nodded.

His eyes twinkled. 'I think it just crept up on us, but make no mistake, it can be just as powerful. And I promise there *will* be fireworks. Now the poetry I'm not so sure of . . . '

She still couldn't hack it. 'What about Rudi?' She was determined to know everything before she said one more word.

'Oh, he'll have to go back to where he came from.'

'Seriously?'

'I want to marry him, too. And I've kissed him loads of times. And . . . if you'd come upstairs with me while I clean my teeth, I would be more than happy to kiss you, provided the gang are out of sight.'

'You don't want to tell them, then?'

'Yes, Nora, I want to tell them, but not right this minute.'

She stepped to one side and really smiled at him for the first time in ages. She finally relaxed. 'I need to make sure Toni's OK with all this, I wouldn't want to hurt her.'

'OK. That's fine.'

'Anyway, I'm not going anywhere with you until I've sampled what's on offer. I'll risk the bad breath.'

He reached over and pulled her towards him and stroked her neck, then gently lifted up her face and kissed her very softly on the mouth. 'That's all you're getting,' he smiled, 'until you say yes.'

'Rudi comes as well?' She needed to double-check.

'What do you think?'

'Will you love him as your own?'

'I already do, sort of, but yes, I promise.'

'Then yes.'

'Yes?'

'Yes.'

'Sure?'

'Certain.'

'Thank you.'

'It's a pleasure.' She grinned at him. 'We have a lot to work out. Your divorce, the adoption process for Rudi, the girls . . . '

'Later. Come here.'

He kissed her properly then and they stayed like that for ages. She wanted to touch him and smell him and revel in the closeness and would have done until something told them that they weren't alone any more.

Rudi and Jess were holding hands and staring. Sam's smile was a mile wide. Sarah looked disgusted.

'That's gross.' She flicked back her hair and tried to look grown up as she picked up Rudi and sauntered past. She looked towards the other two. 'Come on, Jess, Sam, let's go get you dressed.' They all trooped off, Rashers tagging along in case there was any food going.

At the foot of the stairs she delivered her parting shot. 'Hey, you two,' she looked over her shoulder disdainfully, 'get a room.'

We do hope that you have enjoyed reading
this large print book.

Did you know that all of our titles
are available for purchase?

We publish a wide range of high quality
large print books including:
**Romances, Mysteries, Classics
General Fiction
Non Fiction and Westerns**

Special interest titles available in
large print are:
**The Little Oxford Dictionary
Music Book
Song Book
Hymn Book
Service Book**

Also available from us courtesy of Oxford
University Press:
**Young Readers' Dictionary
(large print edition)
Young Readers' Thesaurus
(large print edition)**

For further information or a free
brochure, please contact us at:
**Ulverscroft Large Print Books Ltd.,
The Green, Bradgate Road, Anstey,
Leicester, LE7 7FU, England.
Tel:** (00 44) 0116 236 4325
Fax: (00 44) 0116 234 0205